BUSINESS CASUAL

BOOKS BY B.K. BORISON

Lovelight Farms
In the Weeds
Mixed Signals
Business Casual

BUSINESS CASUAL

B.K. BORISON

Berkley Romance
New York

BERKLEY ROMANCE
Published by Berkley
An imprint of Penguin Random House LLC
penguinrandomhouse.com

Copyright © 2024 by B.K. Borison
Excerpt from *Lovelight Farms* copyright © 2021 by B.K. Borison
Penguin Random House supports copyright. Copyright fuels creativity, encourages
diverse voices, promotes free speech, and creates a vibrant culture. Thank you
for buying an authorized edition of this book and for complying with copyright laws
by not reproducing, scanning, or distributing any part of it in any form without
permission. You are supporting writers and allowing Penguin Random House
to continue to publish books for every reader.

BERKLEY and the BERKLEY & B colophon are registered trademarks of
Penguin Random House LLC.

Library of Congress Cataloging-in-Publication Data

Names: Borison, B. K., author.
Title: Business casual / B.K. Borison.
Description: First Edition. | New York : Berkley Romance, 2024. | Series: Lovelight; 4
Identifiers: LCCN 2023037707 (print) | LCCN 2023037708 (ebook) |
ISBN 9780593641170 (trade paperback) | ISBN 9780593641187 (ebook)
Subjects: LCGFT: Romance fiction. | Novels.
Classification: LCC PS3602.O7545 B87 2024 (print) |
LCC PS3602.O7545 (ebook) | DDC 813.6—dc23/eng/20231012
LC record available at https://lccn.loc.gov/2023037707
LC ebook record available at https://lccn.loc.gov/2023037708

First Edition: July 2024

Printed in the United States of America
1st Printing

Book design by Alison Cnockaert

For the ones who haven't found their place yet.
There's a little tree farm waiting for you.

And for Annie.
None of this happens without you.

1

NOVA

THE TREE FIELDS are glowing.

I don't know who was in charge of wrapping the pine trees with strands of twinkling lights, but whoever it was, they did their job with enthusiasm. Every tree in the south field looks like a star plucked straight from the night sky above, a warm, golden glow reaching its fingers across the dusky fields.

There's a dance floor in the middle of the trees pieced together with old rugs pulled from storerooms across the farm, a patchwork of color and patterns littered with pine needles. Tables cluster around the edges, tidy bonfires contained in shallow metal drums to chase the early autumn chill away. The big red barn has its doors thrown open wide, and wedding guests spill out into the fields with laughter and music and light, their hands curled around mugs of wine and cider.

Woodsmoke curls between the blooms that are twined in garland from tree to tree—sunflowers, chrysanthemums, daisies—an unbroken chain of flowers circling the entire wedding. Baby's breath peeks from in between the branches of the trees, nestled so it looks like snow has settled on the thick green branches. Jimmy Durante rasps over the speakers about making someone happy and beneath the canopy of flowers and lights and branches of pine, the groom dances with his bride.

Luka spins Stella out and her pale pink dress flares around her legs. He tugs her back, and she folds herself into him with a smile that rivals the twinkling lights around them. They slip between the trees, and I lose sight of them, nothing but the fabric of her skirt and the edge of his jacket as they spin around and around.

"They look happy, don't they?"

My sister appears at my side, cake plate in hand. She sighs wistfully as the happy couple appears again on the far side of a misshapen Douglas fir, eyes locked on each other. Luka says something, and Stella tips her head back with another laugh, long hair tumbling over her shoulders. Luka's smile softens into something tender and private. It feels like I shouldn't be watching them at all.

"They should be." I reach for the half-empty bottle of wine in the middle of our table and top off my drink until the red is even with the lip of my glass. I lean forward and take a noisy sip, raising my eyebrows at my sister. "It's their wedding."

A wedding that is a decade in the making. Luka and Stella spent a majority of their relationship pretending they didn't want to be more. It took Stella buying a Christmas tree farm and inexplicably deciding she needed a fake boyfriend to nudge that in the right direction.

Harper narrows her eyes and pinches her lips in a look so reminiscent of our mother that I get a shiver down my spine. She takes the seat next to mine and balances her dessert plate on her lap, hunching over it slightly. I think she's afraid I'll swipe it right out of her hands.

"Is that your third slice of cake?"

Harper looks at me with her fork sticking out of her mouth. "You've been counting?"

"Yes, Harper. I've been sitting here in the shadows, counting how many slices of cake you've decided to eat tonight."

I'm surprised there's any left. Layla, the bride's best friend and the owner of the tiny bakehouse in the middle of the tree farm, made quite the statement with her confection. Three tiers of delicious sponge cake. Buttercream icing. Cannoli filling piped between the layers. Tiny daisies iced around the edges and pine branches lovingly hand-painted over every inch. The cake looks like it belongs in a museum, not in the middle of a field with a bunch of inebriated townspeople.

There was almost a fistfight when they brought it out.

I reach out and swipe my finger through the icing on my sister's plate, ignoring her scowl,

Harper pinches the skin right above my elbow in retaliation. "Be nice," she says.

"You be nice." I rub at the spot she twisted. "What? You can't share your cake?"

"You can get up and get your own." She gracefully crosses her legs and tilts her plate farther away from me, gold stilettos glinting in the lantern light. I wiggle my bare toes in the grass. I have no idea where my shoes are.

"I meant be nice about the happy couple." She shoves another forkful of cake directly in her mouth. "Doesn't it make you feel even the slightest bit romantic?"

"The cake?"

She waves her fork in the air, then stabs it in the direction of Stella and Luka. They're barely swaying between the trees, their arms wrapped tight around each other as the world moves around them.

Harper sighs dreamily. I take another loud slurp of my wine.

"Don't you want something like that?"

I don't bother thinking about it. "No."

This day has been lovely, but . . . I don't know. Romance isn't exactly a priority for me right now. Of course I'm happy for Stella and Luka. After an almost decade-long game of "Will they? Won't they?" it's nice to see them happy.

But do I want that for myself?

Not particularly.

I'm comfortable in my solitude. I like the quiet. I like eating dinner by myself and picking what to watch on TV. I like starfishing in the middle of my bed and setting my thermostat to the perfect temperature. I like rolling myself like an overstuffed burrito in all my blankets. I like having my space to myself, and I like not having to compromise. I don't need to share my every day with someone to suddenly feel fulfilled.

My favorite person to be with is myself, and my relationship of choice is brief, consensual, and satisfying. If I have an itch that needs to be scratched, I can always find a casual hookup easily enough.

Though that hasn't happened in quite a while.

Maybe that's what's got me twisted up. I've been so focused on the studio, I haven't had a casual hookup in ages. Maybe the lack of physical release is starting to turn me into a goblin. A gremlin. One of those stone creatures my mom keeps buying me for my garden. Maybe a hookup will soothe some of my anxieties. Maybe it'll help me turn my brain off for a bit.

Harper arches an eyebrow, blissfully unaware of where my thoughts have tumbled to. "You can't marry a tattoo shop, you know."

"Because that's what all women should aspire to, right? Marriage?"

She pokes me hard in the ribs. "No. You know I don't think that." It's true. Harper is just as committed to her design business as I am to the tattoo studio I'm trying to lift off the ground. But she's always had a soft, romantic heart. And I've watched douchebags take advantage of it for years.

I'd rather not lose myself in a relationship, thank you very much.

Harper frowns at me around another forkful of cake. "I don't want you to be lonely."

"Who says I'm lonely?"

Her frown deepens. "You've been sitting over here by yourself slurping wine."

"That doesn't mean I'm lonely," I grumble. I prefer the quiet, and my feet hurt from dancing. "I'm not lonely. I don't have time to be lonely."

I've been running in a sprint for the last six months. If I'm not thinking about the logistics of the new studio, I'm working on some sort of permit or tax form or expense report. And if I'm not working on one of my endless forms, I'm tweaking marketing items and ordering chairs and eyeing my budget with thinly veiled panic. When I crawl into my bed at night, I don't think or feel a single thing beyond bone-deep exhaustion and a lingering sense of imposter syndrome.

But even with all the new, substantial weight on my shoulders, I love owning my own business. I love being one of the only female-owned and female-operated tattoo shops on the East Coast. And I love that I'm getting ready to open up a new location in the place I grew up. My first studio that's fully mine, not just a space I rent with other artists in a co-op. It's a risk opening in a town as small as Inglewild. Foot traffic won't be as strong as it is down on the coast, but I've always wanted a place here. In the town where I grew up. Where all my favorite people are.

I just have to hope that the reputation I've built for myself is strong enough to bring clients over.

But that's a worry for another day.

Harper boops me gently on the nose with her fork. "You just went spiraling again, didn't you?"

I tuck my hair behind my ears. "Possibly."

She clicks her tongue. "You need to relax. Cut loose." She eyeballs my overfull wine glass and the bottle I've claimed as my own from behind the makeshift bar. "If you keep going like this, you're going to burn out."

"Who is burning out?"

My older brother Beckett claims the other chair next to me, tie missing and sleeves rolled. I'm shocked he stayed in a full suit for as long as he did. He'd spent the duration of the ceremony tugging at his collar as he stood next to Luka.

He's at ease now though. A bottle of beer held loosely in his hand, his forearm braced over his knee. His dark blond hair looks strange without a backward baseball cap, his blue-green eyes uncharacteristically bright tonight. I grin at him and he grins back. Beckett and I, we've always been a mirror reflection of one another. More comfortable on the edges of things. Shoes off. Tie missing.

I poke one of the vibrant tattoos painted along his forearm. My first and very favorite client. His arms are completely covered in my work from wrist to shoulder. When I landed my first apprenticeship, I had trouble establishing a client base. But Beckett let me tattoo him when no one else would. He walked right into the studio I begged for space at and plopped down in the chair. Stuck his arm in my direction and gave me a blank, expectant look.

Beckett has always believed in me. Even when I haven't necessarily deserved it.

I tilt his forearm so I can get a look at his latest. A simple collection of meteors drawn in thin black lines.

"It's healing well," I tell him.

"Of course it is." He tilts his arm and peers at it. "You did it."

My smile slips into something that wobbles at the edges. Sometimes it's difficult to live up to the rose-colored glasses my brother wears for me. He thinks I can do no wrong, and I'm afraid the day I finally do something to disappoint him, it'll break both of our hearts.

I drain the rest of my wine glass without comment. Harper and Beckett exchange a significant glance above my head that they don't think I can see.

I ignore them both.

That's the trouble with growing up the youngest of four. I know they mean well, but my siblings tend to treat me like an unruly toddler in need of constant supervision. I know that's why Harper came over here. Beckett too. I think they've got a version of me stuck in their heads where I'm four years old and struggling to keep up, mud on my cheeks and gummy worms hanging out of my mouth. Beckett still puts his big hand on the top of my head when we're in parking lots like he's afraid I'm going to run directly into traffic. I'm twenty-six years old.

I cut my eyes toward him.

"Has Layla forgiven you yet?"

"Ah." Beckett rubs the back of his neck and glances around the field. I spot Layla by the cake table in a pretty maroon dress, her back against her fiancé's chest and . . . glaring daggers at Beckett.

Beckett sighs, low and slow. "I don't think so, no."

"That must make work difficult."

Beckett is one-third of the trio that runs this farm. Stella oversees the marketing and business, Layla runs the bakery, and Beckett is head of farm operations. Things have always been smooth sailing between the three of them, though this certainly seems like a hiccup.

"It hasn't made it easy," he sighs.

"Clearly."

"I think the wedding brought up some feelings."

"Well, she and Mom will have something to commiserate about, then."

Beckett drags his hand over his face. "Is she still mad too?"

Harper and I snort in unison. "Beckett, you're her only son, and you eloped on a Tuesday afternoon. She didn't even get to make a slideshow of your baby pictures. Or do any of those creepy mashup things of you and Evie that predict what her future grandkids might look like."

Beckett's cheeks flush a furious shade of red. Last month he showed up to family dinner with a shit-eating grin, a new gold ring on his finger, and his *wife* on his arm.

"Layla's just mad she didn't get to make the cake."

"Of course she's mad she didn't get to make the cake. I'm surprised she didn't write it in the fine print of her contract."

"She probably did," he grumbles. He glances up, winces, and then finds something interesting in the grass by his feet to study. "She's probably going to take me to court for breach of contract."

"You'd deserve it."

Across the dance floor, Layla's eyes narrow like she can hear exactly what we're saying. Caleb curls his arm around her without looking away from the person he's talking to, his palm at the base of her throat. His thumb rubs up and down the long line of her neck, and she relaxes in increments, head tipped back against his shoulder.

I don't know what the hell is in the water in Inglewild, but the last five years have been a domino effect of couples . . . coupling. It started with Stella and Luka and cascaded all the way down. My brother and Evie. Layla and Caleb. Matty, the pizza shop owner, and Dane, the sheriff. Mabel from the greenery and Gus, the town paramedic. I'm pretty sure the two stray dogs that circle around the fountain in the middle of town are even going steady now.

"It's also entirely possible that she wanted to be there for you on one of the biggest days of your life."

"I wanted something small," he explains with a sigh.

"It doesn't get smaller than you, the bride, and the courthouse official."

He takes a healthy swig from his beer. "The hot dog guy too."

"What?"

"The guy who sells hot dogs in front of the courthouse was the witness."

Of course he was. "That's great, Beck."

Beckett shifts in his chair, leaning back and slinging his arm over the back of it. His gaze jumps around the reception and then his whole face brightens like someone just flicked a Bic lighter behind his eyes. I follow his line of sight to where Evie is weaving through the tables toward him, still in her flower crown from the ceremony. Her eyes find my brother and hold, a soft smile blooming on her pretty face.

For a long time, I thought Beckett was as uninterested in relationships as I am. But then Evelyn showed up and my brother fell fast and hard.

They move together seamlessly, like they've choreographed this dance. Beckett tips his leg slightly to the left as Evie closes the space between them. She perches herself on his lap with an arm around his neck, and he lifts her hand from his shoulder, mouth brushing briefly over the inside of her wrist and the dainty little lime wedge I inked there.

I never thought I'd see him like this. Soft. Content.

Happy.

Evelyn grins down at my brother and combs her fingers through his hair. He hums and tips his forehead against her jaw.

"Do you need your headphones?" she asks in a low whisper. He shakes his head and tightens his grip on her.

"Told you," he mutters as I try not to listen. "S'quiet when I'm around you."

Something in my chest pulls tight. Beckett has always struggled with sound and people. I'm glad he's found someone who loves that bit of him as much as the rest. Someone who makes it easier for him to be exactly who he is.

"Layla's still mad about the cake," Evie tells him, voice louder. "She spent all morning while we were getting our hair done talking about how we need to have a real wedding with a real cake."

"We did have a real wedding," Beckett grumbles. Evelyn drops a kiss to the crown of his head and hums her agreement. "Plus, I don't think the fields can withstand another party." He leans back in his chair to stare critically at one of his branch babies. "Charlie almost took out three spruce trees trying to start a conga line."

He nods toward the dance floor. The music is something heavy and quick now that Luka and Stella have left the dance floor for the carnage of the cake table. There's a small crowd forming at the very center of the layered rugs and in the middle, of course, is Charlie Milford.

Stella's half brother. Party boy. Serial charmer. I don't think there's a good time that Charlie hasn't organized, signed up for, or crashed without explanation. The last time I saw him was at the summer solstice festival, where he was bare-chested for the peach pie eating contest, letting the little old biddies in town put dollar bills in his waistband. Before that, it was Layla and Caleb's housewarming. He brought strawberry shortcake Jell-O shots. I think he consumed the entire tray himself.

"It's funny you think he needs a wedding for that sort of behavior."

I watch as Charlie swings one of Luka's aunts around the dance floor. His broad frame towers over everyone else, the sleeves of his white dress shirt rolled to his forearms. His normally perfectly styled hair is slightly mussed in the back, likely from his attempt at some early nineties dance moves. He points at Dane and demands he join them. He is either trying to organize a complicated line dance or a revolt against the DJ. It's not clear.

"He really took his duties seriously today," Evie adds conversationally, leaning across Beckett for Harper's abandoned cake. I notice that Harper doesn't smack her hand away. "He brought Stella something old, something new, something borrowed, and something blue. All four. I think they both cried for forty-five minutes."

Charlie walked Stella down the aisle during the ceremony, then slapped a flower crown on his head and stood as her maid of honor. He kept wiping his thumb beneath his left eye, pretending he wasn't crying during the vows.

And now he's doing the macarena in the middle of the dance floor, flower crown crooked on his dark head of hair, his jacket abandoned in one of the pine trees. He is . . . very fluid with his hips.

Midnight blue eyes travel the edges of the dance floor as he spins and bobs and weaves, likely looking for his next victim. I reach for the wine bottle just as his eyes lock on mine. His smile dive-bombs into a grin, laugh lines digging deep into his cheeks.

"NOVAAA," he bellows across the field. "COME DANCE WITH ME."

I bite my bottom lip. Charlie Milford is the biggest goddamn flirt on the planet. He is made up of equal parts charm, charisma, and misplaced confidence. The first couple of times I talked to him, I couldn't figure him out.

But now I know that's just how he is. He's happiest when he's making the people around him happy too. Or, in my case, blushing furiously and scowling at his big dumb face.

I have no idea why. He is not my type. He's probably the furthest thing from my type. He works for some sort of wealth investment firm in New York and has an affinity for three-piece suits. Wristwatches that cost the same as the rent for my tiny studio. Color coded spreadsheets and terms like *ideal fiscal environment*. He buys truffle oil. He has pocket squares.

If there was ever a man to be more my opposite, it would be him.

But we're friends. Sort of. We float in and out of each other's lives at barbecues, parties, and trivia nights. My friends are his family and my family are his friends. It's hard to separate the two in a town as tiny as ours, and he visits Stella at least twice a month. More and more often, now that I think about it. For someone that doesn't actually live in Inglewild, he does seem to be here a lot.

He's been helpful with my business stuff too. He walked me through the ten thousand pieces of licensing paperwork. He is the creator and originator of all the spreadsheets I'm using for my expenses. He answers every single text question I lob at him in the middle of the night, and then sends me a string of flirty, innuendo-laced messages in return.

He says he wants a tattoo in payment for all his consulting. A scorpion on his ass or a Pikachu on his bicep. He says he's torn.

I spent way too long thinking about his ass after that. Specifically, his ass in those perfectly tailored Burberry pants he always seems to be wearing.

Beckett's mouth tugs down in a fierce frown. "Why is Charlie screaming at you?"

Because he's a ridiculous human being who would flirt with a wall if he could. Because he loves trying to get a reaction out of me. Because that's what he does.

I watch as he knocks into someone while trying to throw an imaginary lasso in my direction. He ducks immediately to make sure they're okay, distracted when a little girl in a bright pink dress tears through the dance floor. She bounces at his feet, and he drops his flower crown on her head, those damn lines by his eyes deepening with his smile when she squeals in glee and runs back to her parents.

His eyes flick up and hold mine. He lifts his hand and crooks two fingers, beckoning me forward.

"I think he wants to dance with me."

"You're not going, are you?"

I stand and rub my palms over the silky material of my dress. The wine has left me feeling warm and loose. Untethered and unconcerned. I could use a dance with a handsome man.

I could use more than a dance. I stare at the man in the middle of the dance floor, shimmying in place, thumbs hooked beneath his suspenders. Would Charlie be down for some meaningless stress relief in the form of bedroom shenanigans? He certainly seems like he would be.

Either way, Harper is right. I have been focusing almost exclusively on work. I deserve to cut loose. I deserve to have some fun.

I gather my skirt in my hand and begin making my way to the dance floor.

Charlie looks like a whole lot of fun.

2

CHARLIE

NOVA PORTER IS walking toward me like she can't decide if she wants to dance with me or tear me limb from limb.

Storm cloud eyes. Dark blond hair twisted in a low messy bun. A dress that was either made in my dreams or my nightmares. It shimmers as she walks, a soft gray material that looks like it would slip through my fingers like water. Plunging neckline and a skirt that flares out around her ankles. Bare feet. Pink cheeks. Tattoos all along her arms and down her shoulders.

She looks like she could eat me alive.

I fucking love it.

She stops six inches away from me and tips her chin up, a queen on her throne from half a foot below my chin. I grin, she scowls, and everything is as it's always been between Nova and me.

I had my doubts that she'd actually come out on the dance floor. She hasn't taken an ounce of my shit since I met her.

"Hey" is what slips out of my mouth as I stare down at her, like I haven't spent the past seventeen minutes trying to coerce her out here with my entire arsenal of ridiculous behavior. I reach out and curl my hand around her hip, tugging her closer. "How's it going?"

She falls into me with a huff, both of her hands flat against my chest. I get half of an eye roll and a quirk of her lips. "It's going."

"Oh yeah?"

"Better if this giant buffoon of a man would stop yelling across a tree field."

"Hmm." I pick up one of her hands and fold it in mine, taking care to trace my thumb over the delicate bouquet of flowers inked from her wrist to her knuckles. I arrange her into a proper dancing stance. "That sounds embarrassing."

She gives me a droll look, unimpressed as ever.

"You've been bellowing my name across the dance floor, Charlie."

"Wouldn't have to bellow if you joined me sooner." Closer like this, I can see the deep navy-blue halo that rings her irises. The one, single freckle under her left eye. "But let's let bygones be bygones. The end result remains the same."

"And what is that?"

"You, dancing with me. I didn't even have to bring out the big guns."

One eyebrow pops up. "I'm afraid to ask."

"It involves a string of lights, the bottle of moonshine Clint spiked the apple cider with, and a very elaborate choreography routine." I tip my head closer to hers. "Maybe if you're good, I'll show you later."

She snickers under her breath. I grin and spin us around.

Flirting has always been easy for me, but flirting with Nova is a goddamn delight. Her whole body comes alive under the attention, like a flower tilting toward the sun. I'm greedy for her reactions. For the way pink lights up her cheeks.

The song switches from a Spice Girls remix to something smooth and sultry, Duke Ellington's horn echoing out the long notes to "Stardust." It's a deep swelling beat, slow and romantic.

Her entire face collapses in dismay.

I laugh, grip her hand, and spin her once, watching the material of her dress flare around her legs. I get a tease of ink on the smooth line of her calf before I tug her back to me and set us across the dance floor.

"This isn't what I signed up for," she grumbles up at me.

"What did you sign up for?"

"A perfectly respectable top hits pop song and four feet of distance between us."

I tug her closer. My nose nudges her ear. "Liar," I whisper.

She tilts her face until her nose brushes against mine, wide gray eyes blinking up at me. I think it's the closest I've ever been to her. I like it a lot.

"Yeah," she smiles, slow and teasing. "You're right."

A deep, rumbling groan rushes out of me. Only half of it is for show. "Say that again, but lick your lips a little when you do."

She laughs. "Maybe later."

"That sounds promising." I adjust my grip on her and ease our steps into something slower. Something she can follow with her bare feet against the rugs. Her shoes are still probably sitting kicked to the side in the big red barn. I think she waited all of six minutes into the reception to slip them off.

She hesitates slightly behind the beat, attention focused almost entirely on her steps. I squeeze her hip and then her hand. I thought she was sitting on the side of the dance floor because of her moral opposition to fun. Not because she didn't know how.

"Follow my feet with yours," I tell her. "I won't let you fall."

"I know you won't," she mumbles with her eyes cast down. It's the bare minimum of compliments, but it's enough to have me tugging her the slightest bit closer, every puff of her breath warm against the hollow of my throat. I like the way she feels beneath my hands. I like the way I feel with her against me. Like one of those flickering light bulbs I twisted around the trees last night at two in the morning, trying to make this day as special as Stella deserves.

A smile hooks the corner of her mouth as she falls into the rhythm I set, her face watching mine in consideration. I always get the feeling Nova wants to crack open my head and take a look around.

I'd probably let her and thank her for the pleasure.

"Did you bribe the DJ?"

"For what?"

"The song."

"What about the song?"

"It switched to a slow song as soon as I came over here."

I did bribe the DJ. Best twenty bucks I've ever spent. I would have given him my Rolex if he had the sense to barter. I clear my throat. "A gentleman never tells."

She gives me a look.

"What?"

"You. A gentleman." Her fingertips inch under one of my suspender straps. She toys with it and then snaps it against my chest.

All the blood in my body surges in one direction, and I have to force myself to keep moving around the dance floor. This is a development. Nova doesn't typically flirt back. She entertains it, sure, then moves our conversation along to something mundane.

This is a first.

My eyes narrow. I'm suspicious. "I'll have you know I can be very gentlemanly."

"I'm sure you can."

"I'd be happy to demonstrate."

She tucks herself closer to me and I get a hint of honeysuckle. Paper and fresh-spilled ink. "I'm sure you would."

I don't know what to do with her easy agreement. Conversations with Nova usually feel like a battlefield where she's armed with the infinity stones and I'm wearing a bunny suit. Curious, I take a chance and inch my thumb up higher to where her dress dips in the back. I trace bare skin, and a hum catches in the back of her throat, her body lightly pressing into my touch.

I am bewildered.

Also, a little turned on.

Okay, a lot turned on.

"What's going on with you?" I ask.

"What do you mean?"

I glance pointedly at where her hand is still toying with my suspender strap. She smiles at me, all predator, and slips her hand from my chest. I should probably be afraid, but I'm too entranced by her fingers playing along the neckline of her dress. It's like silver ink poured over her skin, clinging to her curves. The cut of it frames the tattoo between her breasts almost perfectly.

She traces it with one manicured finger. "A gentleman would probably tell me he likes my tattoo."

I clear my throat and stare at it. I can't seem to drag my eyes away. "I like all your tattoos."

"But especially this one," she encourages.

She leans back in the hold of my arms and glances at herself. She has a deep red rose between her breasts, the long stem dipping down her sternum.

I can't stop looking at it.

I'd like to bite it. Very much.

I drag my attention back to her eyes. It takes me a full minute to figure out where we are in the conversation. Luckily for me, Nova is focused on our footwork and not the length it takes me to reply. "All right," I snap. Explain yourself."

She blinks up at me innocently. "Explain what?"

"Why are you flirting with me?"

A faint blush rises on her cheeks. I think I like that more than the rose between her pretty tits.

"You always flirt with me," she points out.

"And you usually tell me to get lost," I say with a laugh. "Take, for instance, about three minutes ago. When I had to yell across the dance floor for you."

She huffs, puffs, and averts her eyes over my shoulder. I laugh again, delighted, the material of her skirt brushing against my suit pants with every shift of our feet. The music feels far away, nothing but me and Nova and the twinkling lights overhead. A flower petal in her hair and her hand in mine.

"Okay, so I was thinking—"

"Whoa."

"Shut up. Let me finish."

A thrum of heat pounds once, right at the base of my spine. I love an authoritative woman. My hands flex and release. "Okay."

She takes a deep breath. "Well. You know I've been busy with the tattoo studio. It's been brought to my attention that I could"—she scratches once at the back of her neck—"relax a little bit."

She stares at me meaningfully. I stare back. If she wants me to infer something from that, she's going to need to elaborate.

"Relaxation is great," I try.

She gets a little line right between her eyebrows. A frown on her pretty lips.

"Do you need a referral for my acupuncturist?" I offer. "Because he's really . . . great." I swear I know more words than *great*.

She blinks at me. "No, Charlie. I'm not asking for your acupuncturist."

"Massage therapy?"

"No."

"Goat yoga?"

She sighs. "Shockingly, I am not asking about goat yoga."

I swear to god I need a road map with this woman. I never have any idea what she's thinking. "What are you asking about then?"

"I'm asking—" She exhales sharply and looks up at me with her bottom lip between her teeth. She lets it go and I barely track the indents left there before she releases in a rush. "I'm asking if you'll come home with me."

My face twists in confusion. "Sure, Nova. I can walk you home."

"No, you idiot. I want you to *come home* with me."

I stare at her blankly. "For snacks?"

She drops her head back and looks up at the night sky, pleading for help. I'm distracted by the line of her throat and the little black stars inked behind her ear. They slowly twist into flowers as the ink moves down her neck, delicate petals falling across the slope of her shoulder.

"Not for snacks," she says, still gazing unseeingly at the sky. She tilts her head back and levels me with a look. I am being weighed and measured. Probably found wanting. "You know what? Forget I said anything."

"I don't even know what you said."

"Good. Let's leave it that way."

"Nova."

"Charlie."

"Nova," I laugh. "It's hysterical you think I'm capable of letting this go. Tell me what you meant."

The color on her cheeks burns darker. Her eyes flick over my shoulder and back. I tighten my grip on her hip, unwilling to have her run off through the trees. I can tell she's considering it.

"I don't know, Charlie," she bites out. "What in the hell do you think it means when a woman asks you to *come home* with her?"

It takes me a second, but the words finally slot themselves together in my brain. My chest pinches, my mouth goes dry, and I stumble over my own feet. I almost send us head over ass into a Douglas fir. I try to correct us and almost dislocate her shoulder.

"Shit. Sorry. Shit."

I catch us at the last moment and swing Nova around me, arm outstretched. I tug her back into my chest and try not to freak the fuck out.

I'm wheezing. Am I wheezing? What is that ringing noise? Am I having a stroke? I might be having a stroke. Maybe I fell over one of the twenty thousand boxes my sister keeps stacked haphazardly outside of her office and I'm in a hospital bed somewhere, hooked up to some really stellar drugs. I don't know.

The pinch is a punch now, a faint ringing in my ears. The constant chatter in my brain has gone silent. Everything around us has too. I don't know what to do with the quiet. I don't think I've ever been so caught off guard in my life.

Nova is watching me with a faintly amused expression. "You doing okay over there?"

My mouth opens and nothing comes out. I close it, then open it again. "I, ah—I don't think so."

For all my flirting with Nova, she has never shown an ounce of interest in return. Not once. Most of my text messages get a vaguely apathetic smiley face back. I have categorized her under the unattainable category. Unavailable and uninterested.

Not that I've let that deter me, but . . . she wants me to take her home? Tonight? I'm no stranger to a fleeting romance with a woman, but Nova—I see her every time I'm down here. I know how she likes her tea and the kind of car she drives. I know the names of her sisters and her least favorite categories at trivia night.

It's Nova.

I'm having trouble untangling my thoughts.

I'm also unreasonably, incredibly turned on. Half of my brain is trying to make sense of her request while the other half is running wild with the possibilities. I am the Dr. Jekyll and Mr. Hyde of one-night-stand requests.

The longer I'm quiet, the more her expression slips. She drops my gaze to look back at our feet, her mouth set in a firm line. Her hand tightens against the back of my neck, and she puts two inches of space between us. I'd wince if I were capable of feeling a single thing above my belt.

"Stop making that face," she seethes from between clenched teeth.

"What face?"

"The one you're making."

"I have no idea what my face looks like, Nova. It's my face."

She huffs, leans back, and presses her fingertip to the corner of my lips. "You look like someone just shoved an entire lemon into your mouth. Fix it."

"Sorry." I try to school my features into something neutral, but everything feels numb. Like I'm underwater. I'm not entirely convinced I'm *not* having a medical event. "Is it better? Did I fix it?"

She shakes her head, sighs, and looks at the trees around her, her chin to her chest.

I've embarrassed her.

Worse, I think I've hurt her feelings.

"Nova."

"Forget I said anything."

I don't mean to laugh, but I feel slightly hysterical. "It is burned into my brain."

I'll be hearing her murmur *come home with me* in her husky, sweet voice for the rest of my life.

She frowns. "I don't want to talk about it anymore."

"That makes one of us."

She makes a frustrated noise under her breath. Finally, she meets my eyes again. "Charlie. Please. I don't know what I was thinking. Let's just . . . let's just talk about expense reports instead."

A faintly pained noise leaves the back of my throat. "I don't know how you expect me to talk dirty to you on top of everything else."

Amusement flickers across her face. "You're ridiculous."

I am ridiculous. I'm also confused.

"Nova," I say gently. "Last week I told you that your hair looked nice and you told me to get a grip. I'm trying to figure out how we got from there to here."

She gives me a long, considering look. Her eyes look darker tonight, like a dense fog in the middle of the woods. Lazy mornings beneath the sheets, rain pelting at the windows. Tea on the kettle and nothing but socks and bare skin.

"You know how we got here," she says quietly. The start of a confession, I think.

"Humor me."

She catches her bottom lip between her teeth again. Before I can even think about it, I reach up and curl my fingers around her jaw, my thumb popping it free. It feels imperative, a need burning through my blood. I rub once. Her mouth feels like silk. Her tongue barely touches the pad of my thumb and I almost send us back into that tree.

"That's how we got here," she explains, her voice still a low hush. "You've been flirting with me forever, Charlie. You're surprised I want to flirt back?"

"I'm surprised you want me to take you home," I murmur.

I return my hand to the small of her back, fingertips splayed wide, and then clear my throat three times in a row for absolutely no reason. She looks up at me from beneath golden-tipped lashes, a smile flirting with the corner of her pale pink lips.

I move us across the dance floor, painfully aware of every place our bodies touch. Thighs, hips, chest.

This dance I begged her for is now my personal hell.

I blow out a slow breath. "How much have you had to drink tonight?"

"Enough to make me feel warm and fuzzy, but not enough to have me asking for things I don't want." She pats my chest once, a resigned look on her face. "It's okay, Charlie. We're going to finish this dance. I'm going to go find something else to drink. And we will never discuss this again."

My hands tighten against her. I do not like that plan.

"Nova—"

"Please," she whispers, eyes still carefully averted from mine. "Please, can we not?"

I give her a jerky nod, but my mind is still racing. My thoughts slip through like tiny grains of sand, slowly piling up until I feel overwhelmed. My brain is excellent at catastrophizing. I spin us around, one thought screaming louder than the rest.

"Are you going to find someone else?"

"Hmm?"

The song plays out its final slow notes, a lone trumpet echoing out over the field. I panic. I'm not ready to let her go yet.

I nudge us farther into the trees until shadows are clinging to our ankles.

"Are you going to find someone else?" I ask again.

She loosens her hold on me but stays in my grip. "For what? A drink?"

Now I'm the exasperated one. "To go home with you."

"Ah." Understanding lights her eyes and her lips twist to the side. "Maybe—"

"Don't." I cut her off. If I see her talking to Jimmy from the bar or Alex from the bookshop, I will lose my actual shit. I scratch my hand over the back of my head roughly and try to organize the scattered pieces of myself. I have no right to ask anything of her, I know, but the idea of her asking someone else what she just asked me has me borderline murderous.

God.

She broke my damn brain.

She crosses her arms over her chest and arches a single, imperious eyebrow. "Any particular reason why I should let you dictate what I do and don't do?"

"I'm not trying to dictate anything. I'm just—" I drag one hand over my face and curl my hand around my jaw. I won't be able to stand it if she sidles up to goddamn anyone else at this wedding. "You wouldn't want to miss the cake," I point out half-heartedly.

"The cake," she repeats.

"Yes, the cake."

"The cake that has been out for almost an hour now."

"It's going quick." I wince. I sound like an asshole. An idiot asshole.

She scoffs and steps into my space. I try to back up, but I'm standing right in front of an evergreen. The needles scratch roughly at the backs of my arms. One rogue branch slaps me across the back of the head. It feels like immediate karmic retribution.

Nova digs one finger right into the center of my chest. "You don't get to tell me what to do."

Color blazes in her cheeks. Anger this time, instead of embarrassment. She pokes me again. I am a bizarre combination of scared and turned on. I hold up both hands, palms up. "I know."

"Especially after you said no."

"What? I didn't say no."

"You said no."

"I did not. You didn't even let me answer the question." I curl my hand around the finger digging into my chest and pull our hands to the side. "If you'd like an answer, ask me again."

Her eyes flash in the fairy lights twinkling over our heads. She has a faint dusting of something sparkly on her cheeks. She looks like she's glowing.

And glowering. She's definitely glowering.

"Excuse me?"

"If you want me to take you home, I'm going to need you to ask me again."

I'm not opposed to the idea of a hot and heavy night with Nova Porter. It sounds like something out of my dreams, actually. She's gorgeous. Funny as hell. Sarcastic and sharp as a whip. I've thought about tumbling into bed with her more times than I can count. I've been flirting with her for months, for god's sake.

But her request is out of left field. I had no idea Nova was even . . . looking at me like that. I'm used to being a good time. A fun deviation from normal patterns and behaviors. But with Nova, I want to be a choice. Not a whim. Not a regret.

So, yeah. I need her to ask me again.

She scoffs and wraps her arms around herself. "I'm already halfway to pretending this never happened."

I step into her space, closer than when we were dancing. Her head tips back as she watches me with heavy eyes. She acts like she's unaffected by me, but I'm on to her now. She's been hiding a big ol' secret beneath all that indifference. Little Miss Grump put all her cards on the table when she asked me to take her home.

"You're not going to pretend it didn't happen." I take a chance and drag my knuckles down her arm, delighting in the goose bumps that rise in response. "You're going to ask me again."

"Oh yeah?"

I nod. "Yeah. I can be patient." I let my hand drop to my side. "You don't need to ask me tonight. You can think on it."

A disbelieving laugh bursts out of her. "Oh, thank you very much."

I smile because she's not moving out of my space. She's shifting closer, one of her hands curling beneath my suspender strap. She tugs on it, testing, and my hand finds her hip above the silky material of her dress.

"The only thing I'll be thinking on—" She tips her face toward mine, her breath ghosting over the hollow of my throat. Fuck. She smells incredible. Something wild and dark and just out of reach. "Is the look on your face when you almost dragged us both into a spruce tree."

"It was a Douglas fir," I mutter back. I slip my hand up her side until I can curl my palm around the back of her neck. I've just unlocked a new level of flirtation with Nova Porter, and it's my favorite yet. "And at least you'll be thinking of me."

"In your dreams," she breathes.

"With alarming frequency and incredible detail," I answer back.

She tries to hide her smile by ducking her chin, but I see the edges of it. Her eyes cast over my shoulder to the dance floor. Muted music drifts around us. The branches rustle in a slow-moving breeze. She shivers, and I'd offer her my jacket if I had it.

She'd probably light it on fire.

"I'm gonna—" She pulls herself out of my grip and nods toward the barn. Her smile is soft, her cheeks are pink, and I want to taste the edges of that quiet, rare amusement. "I'll be seeing you, Charlie."

I dig my hands into my pockets. "You sure will."

"Okay."

"Fine."

"Great."

A ghost of a laugh slips from between her lips, "unbelievable" whispered under her breath. She gives me one last look and then wanders in the opposite direction, shoulders back, chin up.

"Pretend this never happened," she yells over her shoulder, a parting shot. Her hands grip the fabric of her skirt, her bare feet hopping along the path.

I grin at the smooth line of her shoulders, the slip of silver material over the curve of her ass.

"Highly unlikely," I yell back.

3

CHARLIE

NOVA LEAVES ME standing in front of a Douglas fir with a semi and a whole lot to think about. I have to drag both hands over my face and do some deep breathing exercises to make it out from behind that tree without embarrassing myself.

Not that it helps much. My brain feels like it's full of wool and whatever perfume Nova was wearing.

I stroll my way over to Luka and Stella's table and try not to look like I'm having an existential crisis. It was a bold move, telling her she needs to ask me again. But I stand by it. I'm not going to take Nova Porter home and hope for the best. This town is too important to me. I'm not going to risk my place in it because I decided to think with my downstairs brain.

By the time I make it to the table, Stella is smirking at me. "What?"

She flicks me in the shoulder. "You know what."

I cast a quick glance at Beckett at the other side of the table, but he's busy with his wife in his lap, his chin on her shoulder and both of his arms wrapped around her waist. They're probably talking about pet adoption or the best soil for planting carrots.

Not that I have anything to be worried about. Nova and I were just dancing. It doesn't matter that she's one of my best friend's sisters.

His youngest sister. His favorite sister. The one he is still kind of scarily protective over.

The one who asked me to take her home for a night of no-strings sex.

I force my gaze back to Stella. "I have no idea what you're talking about."

I grab the bottle of champagne sitting in the middle of the table and take three long pulls. It's too sweet and the bubbles almost give me a heart attack, but it's a good distraction from what I really want to do. Which is scan the fields for Nova.

You know how we got here.

I need a cold shower and a stiff drink. Another cold shower after that.

I blow out a deep breath and ignore the faintly amused look on my sister's face. What I need is a distraction and I have the perfect one. I reach into my back pocket and pull out a carefully folded envelope. "For you."

She stares at it, face twisted in confusion. "What is it?"

"An envelope."

She rolls her eyes.

"A wedding present," I laugh.

She gives me a look. "You've given me a wedding present. You've given me like . . . six wedding presents."

She lightly touches the small sapphires in her ears, one of the gifts I gave her before I walked her down the aisle. I did sort of go overboard, but I couldn't help myself. Stella is my only sister—a sister I didn't even know I had until well into adulthood. I grew up a lonely kid bursting with energy and no one to share it with. I asked my mother for a sibling relentlessly until I was old enough to realize what that wounded look in her eyes meant and I stopped asking.

And then, one day in my twenties, Stella appeared on our doorstep with a bunch of letters in her hand and the same exact eyes as me.

Turns out our dad was less than loyal to my mom. The first in a very long line of transgressions.

Thankfully Stella was receptive to the idea of a relationship, and we became fast friends. I like to think we're both trying to make up for the missed years between us. She's the sister I always wanted. Part of the family I never thought I'd have.

Six presents for her wedding doesn't feel like enough, frankly. I want her to know how much it means to me to spend this day with her. To have a place on her Christmas tree farm and in the community she's made for herself.

Luka appears behind her with a dopey-ass grin on his face and rests his chin on top of her head. He curls both arms around her shoulders and rocks them back and forth while simultaneously thrusting his left hand in my face. He wiggles his fingers, the glint of his new shiny gold ring reflecting in the lights overhead.

"Charlie," he singsongs. "Do you know what this means?"

Stella pulls his arm back around her, their wedding bands clicking when she threads their fingers together.

I grin. "I think it means you two are married."

"Yeah, we're married." His entire face lights up with the word, a grin tugging at his mouth. Either he's been hitting the homemade moonshine that Gus snuck in, or he's drunk on love. Luka is exactly the type of man I would have chosen for my sister, if I'd had any sort of say in that decision. Luke presses a kiss to the tip of Stella's ear. "It also means you're my brother now. Officially."

My throat tightens. Maybe I'm an idiot, but the thought never crossed my mind in all the lead-up to today. I've been entirely focused on Stella, on being exactly what she needed.

"Oh my god," I breathe out. Stella's eyes grow wide with faint panic as my arms fall limply at my sides. A ragged exhale bursts out of me. I sound like a balloon that's slowly losing air. A submarine going under. "Oh my god," I say again.

Stella touches my arm. "Are you okay? Are you going to pass ou— *oomph.*"

She can't talk when she's squished between me and Luka, my

arms wrapped around his shoulders. Stella got a husband, but I got a brother. A *brother*.

Luka pats me on the back, his laugh low. Stella wheezes somewhere in between us.

"This is the best," I mumble into his jacket. "I take back what I said when you told me you weren't moving back to the city."

I called him a defector. Some other rude shit too. When he lived in New York, we'd have lunch together twice a week at a deli halfway between our offices. Luka was one of the few people in the city I actually enjoyed hanging out with. I've been sitting at that stupid counter by myself for the last couple of years like a sad sack.

"Yeah, well." He leans back and claps me on the shoulder. Stella sucks in air and tries to untangle some of her hair that's stuck in my suspender strap. "Maybe we can convince you to come down here more often."

Like I need an excuse to spend more time in Inglewild. I like how I feel when I'm here. I like who I get to be. I already visit every other weekend, content to force everyone to deal with me on a regular basis. I'm pretty sure that's why Stella built that guesthouse at the edge of the property line. She said it was for an Airbnb, but I know it's for me.

"Thank you, that reminds me." I hold up the envelope again and wave it between us. "Your wedding present."

Luka's face twists in confusion. "Didn't you get us like six wedding presents?"

Stella tips her head back. "Thank you."

I ignore them and force the envelope in Stella's hands. I might have gotten them six wedding presents, but this is the one I'm most excited about. This is the one I've been plotting and planning over the last couple of months.

Stella tears open the envelope and peers at the piece of paper in her hand. "Are these plane tickets?" She brings the paper to her nose. "For tomorrow?"

"Mm-hmm."

"To Italy?"

"Yes, that is what the ticket says."

She drops the paper with a frown. Behind her, Luka mirrors it. It is . . . not the reaction I was expecting.

"I can't go to Italy tomorrow."

"Why not?"

She gestures around her at the farm. She's making a point, but I'm distracted by Gus from the firehouse standing on a table, whipping his shirt over his head to a Backstreet Boys song. Mabel, his girlfriend, is sitting at one of the seats below him like absolutely nothing is amiss, calmly sipping a mug of cider. I guess she's used to that sort of behavior from him.

Stella snaps in my face. "Because it's September and I have to oversee the farm. It's pumpkin season."

"Ah, yes." I roll my lips against my smile and shove my hands in my pockets. "Whatever will the pumpkins do without you?"

Her frown deepens. She looks like an angry cupcake in her pretty pink dress. I can't take her seriously at all. "Charlie."

I lower my chin and give her the same look she's giving me. "Stella. You really weren't planning for a honeymoon?"

"We were planning on Annapolis for the weekend," Luka offers, taking the ticket out of Stella's hand and studying it. "Why is the return date on these tickets a month from now?"

Stella gasps like I've just pulled a raccoon out of my pants and plopped it on top of her head. "A month? Charlie!"

"What?" I laugh.

"We can't go to Italy for a month! That's practically the start of the Christmas season! How much is this costing you?" She rips the ticket out of Luka's hand and tosses it at me, pressing it into my chest. "Take it back. We do not accept."

Luka straightens behind her, trying to grab the ticket. But she's like an angry little spider monkey, trying to shove it down the front of my shirt. "Hold on a second, La La."

"Yeah, *La La*. Listen to your husband," I tell her. When her glare intensifies, I hold up both of my hands. "Don't worry about how much it costs. Don't worry about the farm. We have a plan."

Her eyes narrow. "Who is we?"

"Beckett, Layla, and I talked."

She crosses her arms. "So, there was collusion?"

"In the name of your honeymoon? Yes. Yes, there was collusion." I make no move to take the ticket that she is dangling limply between us. Thank god it's just a printout and the tickets are digital. That thing looks like it's been to hell and back. "Layla packed both of your bags, and they're waiting in the living room of your house. There's a car coming to pick you up at the end of the night to take you to a hotel by the airport. Your flight leaves in the morning and everything has been taken care of. You just need to go where you're told."

Stella shakes her head back and forth, dark hair flying around her shoulders. "It's too much."

"It's really not."

I make a boatload of money. This is a drop in a very large bucket.

"It is. It's way too much." Her eyes fill with tears. "Charlie, I can never pay you back for any of this."

I grab both of her hands with mine, plane tickets crumpled between us. "I don't want you to pay me back. It's a gift, Stella. You don't repay those." My throat tightens again and I have to clear it. My voice drops and I rub my thumbs over her knuckles. "Do you remember that day you came to the house? All those years ago?"

Her mom had just died and she wanted to know her birth father. So she looked him up and found our address, brought all the letters her mother wrote over the years but never sent. She didn't know about me, didn't know about my mom, and didn't know our dad was a giant disappointment with a track record of horrendous decision-making.

"When you were walking out the door, you told me, 'We can be family, if you want.' Well, this is what family does. I know we're both on a bit of a learning curve, but I have around twenty birthdays and Easter holidays and Christmases to make up for. Just . . . bundle it up together, okay? Let me do this for you."

She sniffles. "You don't give presents for Easter."

"There are baskets, I'm told."

"Easter baskets don't have plane tickets in them."

"Stella."

She grips me harder. "You don't have anything to make up for," she whispers.

I shrug. She deserves to have a family member who's not a disappointment. I want to be that for her. "Agree to disagree."

"Charlie."

"Stella, just say yes." I exaggerate a head nod, my eyes wide. "Come on. It's easy. Just say, 'Yes, Charlie. I will go on this very nice vacation that I deserve with my husband.'"

She looks at Luka over her shoulder. He wipes a streak of eyeliner off her cheek. They have a silent conversation and then her body curves into his. She turns back to me with a wobbly smile. "Okay."

"Let's hear it."

She blows out a noisy breath. "Yes, Charlie. I will go on this very nice vacation with my husband."

"Ah." Luka grins behind her. "I love that word."

"What? Vacation?"

"No." His smile melts into something satisfied. "Husband."

She smiles at him, and I get that feeling I usually get when I spend too much time in their orbit. Like I'm intruding on something private. Like they've completely forgotten I'm two feet away from them. I avert my eyes to the dance floor. Gus is now trying to scale one of the trees. I can't imagine that will end well.

Silver catches the corner of my eye and I see Nova, her back to me. I trace the strong column of her spine, the tease of dimples at the small of her back. The swell of her ass beneath the silver of her dress and the curve of her legs. She sways back and forth absentmindedly to the music, another strand of hair spinning loose from her bun and falling between her shoulder blades.

"I still have a question though."

I jerk my eyes away from Nova. I guess Stella has emerged from her impromptu make-out session with her husband.

"What's that?"

"Who is going to run the farm while I'm gone?" Her forehead scrunches up until she has that narrow line between her brows. The same one I get when I stare at my computer screen too long. "There's the pumpkin patch and the bonfire and hayrides start up soon and—"

"Relax. Everything will be fine, okay? It will be taken care of."

"How? Who is going to take over for me while I'm out of town for the month?"

"Isn't it obvious?" I slip my thumbs under my suspender straps and pull them away from my chest. I'm about to enter my farmer era. Cowboy Charlie, unlocked. "I am."

4

NOVA

I WATCH CHARLIE from the other side of the reception. He's been talking to Stella and Luka since we left the dance floor, an easy smile on his face. He certainly doesn't look like a man who just rejected my clumsy attempt at a one-night stand.

It was impulsive. I felt his hand against the small of my back, saw the way his eyes kept drifting to my mouth, felt the thrill of tension between us, and just . . . asked.

And he laughed at me.

Then he told me to ask him again. Probably so he could laugh some more.

It's not going to happen. I am not going to ask him again. I don't think I'm ever going to look at him again. He reacted like the possibility never even crossed his mind. Like he hasn't been flirting with me for the last two years and counting. I'm going to be haunted by that look. I'm going to think about it in between the edges of sleep and awake and sink into a horrific state of recollection.

Why the hell did he say no?

I'm embarrassed. And immensely, incredibly grateful that Charlie lives four hours and twenty-three minutes up the coast. The next time I see him, I'll just pretend this never happened. It'll be fine.

I'll overthink it to death and cringe on the inside, but it'll be fine. I've endured worse. And I have plenty of other things to focus on that have nothing to do with men over six-feet tall with laugh lines by their eyes.

"What are you doing?"

I jump and almost flip the table where only a couple slices of wedding cake remain. My sister Vanessa emerges from between two trees like a movie villain, face cloaked half in shadow.

"What am I doing? What are you doing?" I press my hand to my chest. "Why are you impersonating Michael Myers? How long have you been there?"

"Either three minutes or thirty. It's unclear." Vanessa frowns and leans precariously to one side. Like me, she's also missing her shoes, but I have a feeling that she parted with hers unintentionally. She squints in the glow of the twinkle lights, confused. "Michael Myers. The guy who plays Austin Powers?"

I sigh. She somehow managed to make that sentence one big slur. I eyeball the bottle of wine in her hand, then grab her elbow and help her stand straight. "No. The guy from those slasher movies."

She leans into my grip and buries her face in my neck. "Oh."

I stumble beneath our combined weight and wrap both of my arms around her, trying to hold her steady. "Nessa?"

"Hmm?"

"Were you drinking from the bottle the firemen were handing around?"

She nods. "It was delicious. It tasted like schn-schna-schna—"

I raise both eyebrows. "Schnapps?"

"No. I was gonna say schnozzberries. You know." She tilts back up and grins at me. *"These schnozzberries taste like schnozzberries."*

She collapses in a fit of giggles. Giggles that slowly turn into quiet hiccupping sobs.

Oh boy. The last time I saw Nessa like this was when she sprained her ankle and had to stop dancing for four to six weeks. I smooth my palms over her arms. "Ness. What's going on?"

She rarely drinks. Usually at events like this, she's spinning around and around the dance floor, making the rest of us look bad. She comes alive under the music, her joy contagious. Beckett usually has to drag her off the floor at the end of the night.

But she's hiding in the trees with a bottle of wine and some questionable moonshine.

Her bottom lip trembles. "Nathan broke up with me."

"Who?"

"My dance partner."

My sister is a professional ballroom dancer. She and her partner Nathan have been paired together for almost six years. I didn't know they were dating too.

I rub some of her tears away with my thumb. "When did you two start dating?"

"Who is dating?" She laughs, garbled and thick. "No, we're not—we're not dating. We are not ever dating. He wanted to, but I said no, thank you. No, sir. No, no, no thank you. I was very polite about it."

She swipes at her cheek with the back of her hand. The one still clutching the wine bottle. Some pinot noir goes dribbling down her chest. "He said he couldn't be around me anymore. He said his heart couldn't take it and that I—I owed him. That asshole. He said I owed him, but that's not how love works, and now he's ruined everything. I've worked too hard in my career for that wiry little—that wiry little, tight stealing—oh, oops."

She drops the bottle and it rolls beneath the cake table. I stop her with a hand on her shoulder when she tries to crawl after it. She blinks up at me with big watery eyes.

"Maybe I need to be more like you," she says.

I smooth her hair away from her forehead. When we were kids, she used to do the same for me when I'd get migraines. I'd hear the pad of her feet on the floor between our beds before her slight weight curled behind me. She'd pull my comforter over both of us and drag her fingers through my hair until the pain stopped.

"What's that?"

"I think I need to get claws," she grumbles. She leans her head into my touch. "Not let—not let myself be bullied. I think my heart needs to be tougher."

My hand stills in her hair.

"What?"

Nessa raps her knuckles against my breastbone. "Need to bundle up my heart some more," she slurs. "Bubble wrap it like baby sis."

She says it like it's something I should be proud of, but all I feel is a hollow ache, right in the place she's tapping out an uneven beat. Is that what everyone thinks? That I've sharpened the edges of myself to hold people at arm's length?

Beckett's concern. Harper's sad, knowing eyes. Charlie's surprise. The ache grows sharper. A thumb pressed to a bruise.

Nessa rocks her head against my shoulder, and I tuck away the hurt to consider later. I resume running my fingers through her hair and blow out a deep breath. "I like your heart just the way it is."

"Jell-O heart," she mumbles. "Wiggly and wobbly."

"Yes, I love your wiggly, wobbly Jell-O heart." I look over her shoulder and through the cluster of trees to the reception. The party is still in full swing, the dance floor crowded and music thumping. My parents are at the edge of a burgundy rug, my mom draped across my dad's lap in his wheelchair, her arms around his neck as they sway to the half beat. Beckett and Evie stand together in front of one of the low-burning fires, heads tipped together. Charlie is nowhere to be found, but I don't let myself look too hard for him.

Vanessa can't go back out there. Not like this.

I eyeball the distance between us and the shuttle in the parking lot, waiting with its lights dimmed to ferry people back to the town square.

"How's your stability right now, Ness?"

She looks down at her feet as she considers it, leaning out of my grip to stand straight. She gives me a very serious look, which is hard to take seriously at all when her hair is a mess and she has makeup on her cheeks. She looks like she got in a fight with a rabid animal.

"I can probably jazz square somewhere," she slurs. "If you ask very nicely."

"Nessa." It's a battle to keep myself from laughing at her. "Can you please jazz square your way to the shuttle bus?"

She tips to the side and straightens one leg in front of her, toe perfectly pointed. She then executes a series of movements that are shockingly lucid and controlled. I guess her muscle memory has remained untouched by the pinot noir.

All right. Unexpected, but I can work with it."

We begin a slow, shuffling walk-dance to the shuttle. My phone, purse, and shoes are back at the reception, but that's fine. I'm sure Beckett will grab everything before he leaves for the night. Or I can swing by the farm tomorrow and collect them.

Vanessa mutters the step count beneath her breath. I watch her feet to make sure she's not about to chassé her way over a tree root. I link my arm with hers.

"Hard heart," I mutter. Would someone with a hard heart make sure their drunk sister didn't embarrass herself in front of the whole town? I don't think so.

"What did you say?" Nessa shouts into the darkness.

"Nothing," I sigh. "Don't worry about it."

VANESSA IS PRACTICALLY asleep on her feet by the time we make it home.

I rouse her enough to make her drink an entire glass of water and take two ibuprofen before tucking her in on the couch with the quilt my mom made when I was six years old. All the tassels on the ends are faded and losing strings, but the colors make me happy.

Satisfied she's not going to tumble off the deep cushions to her death on the refurbished wood floors, I shuffle my way into my bedroom. I slip out of my dress and drape it over the back of an overstuffed armchair, pulling on an old crew neck before slipping beneath my collection of blankets and comforters. I left one of my windows cracked before I left tonight, and my room smells like wet leaves and smoke from the fireplace next door. Fresh night air and the hydrangeas I planted right below my window. I close my eyes and will myself to settle, but I feel untethered, unmoored, slipping and sliding my way over my thoughts.

The things I have to do at the tattoo shop before I open. The stack of papers I left on the top left corner of my desk. The chairs I still haven't put together and the floorboards that need painting in the front.

Vanessa and her tear-stained cheeks shining in the moonlight. Her knuckles rapping against my chest and her words, muted but honest.

A bubble-wrapped heart.

I know I'm not soft. I know I'm not gentle. I can be abrupt and to the point. But I don't think I'm unapproachable. I don't think I'm cold.

I lift my arm and twist it beneath the faded yellow light that filters in from the streetlamp on the corner, finding the ink that decorates my skin. One tattoo in particular.

Five strands of ribbon, twisted and braided. Each slightly different than the others, but together something strong and unbreakable.

I rub my thumb over it and frown, hating the unsettled press right beneath my ribs. When sleep finally does claim me, I tumble into restless dreams where I'm dancing through a field of trees beneath an open moonlit sky, a warm hand at the small of my back holding me steady.

I WAKE UP annoyed.

At the universe, mostly, but also at the blankets I'm tangled in, the birds squawking through the crack in my window, and the rumble of a car passing in the distance.

Charlie, for getting in my head.

At myself, for allowing him space there.

I probably wouldn't be this twisted up if he just came home with me like I asked.

I fumble my way out of bed and dig my shoes out from the closet, slipping on an old pair of sweats I stole from Beckett in high school. I tiptoe down the stairs and through the front door, my body still not fully awake, but my head and heart needing the steady thrum of movement and breath to sort myself out.

I run until the ghosts of last night's embarrassments are no longer clinging to my heels. Until I'm not thinking about anything at all.

By the time I circle back to the house, my legs are wobbly and my lungs are burning with the brisk morning air. But my head is clear and everything feels slotted back into place. As much as it can be, anyway.

Nessa is sitting up on the couch when I wander in, my blanket wrapped tight around her shoulders. She frowns at me and digs her knuckles into her left eye.

"Morning." I stretch both arms over my head and collapse forward with a groan, trying to stretch out my back. "How are you feeling?"

She squints at me and mutters something that would definitely make our mother blush. I toe off my shoes and toss my keys on the kitchen table with a clatter.

"Nova," she whines. "Are you trying to kill me?"

"I think you took that upon yourself last night when you drank enough moonshine to serenade my garden gnomes upon our return."

She sat in my front yard and plucked all of my garden fixtures out of the mulch bed, lined them up in a neat row, and sang song after song until Mr. Hale from across the street came out on his front porch and threatened to call the cops. Too bad the only cop on duty last night was Sheriff Dane Jones, and the last I saw of him, he was swinging his husband around the dance floor.

Nessa slumps dramatically over the arm of my couch. "Were you running? What's wrong with you?"

What's wrong with me is I embarrassed myself in front of Charlie Milford last night. I was rejected in front of a spruce tree, and then I had to cart my drunk sister home without our parents seeing.

I feel like I am somehow reliving my high school days, with an extra dose of rejection.

"Nothing is wrong with me," I mutter.

"Then why are you making that face?"

Because I have no idea what Charlie is thinking. Because I tipped the scales of our relationship and asked for something purely physical, and I've unlocked a part of my brain that can't stop thinking about it. Charlie told me last night that I broke him, but I think I broke myself.

I glance at Vanessa. I can only see her eyes overtop the couch, like a grumpy little crocodile sitting in still water.

"I don't know, Ness. Life?"

She nods sagely. "I get it."

I shuffle to the fridge and pull out a bowl of cut strawberries for myself, the egg carton and some bacon for my sister. I'm eager for a subject change. "What's going on with you and Nathan?"

Her eyes narrow to slits. "Nathan," she seethes.

"Yes, him."

"He's an idiot."

"So you've said." Almost eighty-two times, set to the tune of various early nineties sitcom theme songs. "He wants to date you?"

She heaves her body off the couch, graceful as a dancer even in her debauched state. In the early afternoon light, the wine stains on her dress are more noticeable. My blanket drags behind her on the floor. I'm pretty sure there's a drool stain on my upholstery.

She limps her way to the kitchen and slides onto a wooden stool I stole from Beckett's greenhouse. She plucks a strawberry out of the carton and takes a bite. "He told me he loved me."

"I'm guessing you don't return those feelings."

She sighs. "I don't. I'm not convinced *he* has those feelings. I think he's mistaken proximity for intimacy all these years. He told me we pair well together and that's fine with dancing, but—I don't know. I told him I didn't feel the same, and he said—" She rubs two fingers across her forehead and sighs. "He said some shitty things."

"What sort of shitty things?" My hand clenches on the handle of the cast-iron pan I'm using to fry up some bacon. I may be the youngest of four, but I am just as fiercely protective of my siblings as they are of me.

She waves her hand, but I don't miss the wince. "It doesn't matter now."

It matters to me. "Do you want me to key his car?"

Her mouth twitches with a suppressed grin. "No, I don't want you to key his car." She reaches for another strawberry. "But I reserve the right to change my mind."

"Fair." I flip the bacon. Beckett will help me key his car. "What are you going to do about it?"

"Well"—she sighs—"not much to be done. He's not my partner anymore. No coming back from that one. And I don't want to compete solo. Maybe it's time to hang up my dance shoes."

My hands freeze over the pan. Vanessa has been dancing her whole life. My mom likes to joke that she did a samba right out of the womb. I can't imagine her giving it up.

She sneaks a piece of crispy, burnt-edge bacon. "Don't look at me like that. There are plenty of ways to dance without competing. I'll figure it out."

"And I'll key his car."

"Deal."

We settle into the routine of coffee and breakfast with minimal pained groans from Vanessa at the counter. I crack open the window above the sink to let in the crisp autumn air, and she turns on the radio to something that bursts with static. It used to sit in my dad's workshop, and I like keeping it here for company, a thumbprint smudged in paint over the volume dial that I like to fit mine to. Some of the weightless, ambling feeling making my lungs feel tight fades as Nessa chatters away on the other side of the countertop, nimbly chopping fruit and refilling my cup with fresh coffee.

I watch the trees outside my window wave back and forth in a meandering breeze, their leaves just starting to turn a brilliant, sunburnt red.

I wonder what Charlie is up to this morning. If he's on his way back to New York or if he's staying for the pumpkin-cinnamon streusel waffles they serve at the diner during the fall. How late he stayed at the wedding and if he ever figured out he had pine needles stuck in his hair.

I think about his palm against my back. The way his cheerful face settled into something heated the longer we danced together. A heavy considering twist to his lips. I don't think I've ever seen him look so serious. I wonder if that's how he'd look above me. Below me. If he'd be just as demanding with his touch.

I catch myself and scowl.

I should not be thinking anything about Charlie.

"Saw you dancing with Milford last night," Nessa says around a gulp of jet-black coffee. I almost fling my English muffin across the room.

She raises both eyebrows. "I wasn't that drunk," she defends, mistaking the intent of my breakfast projectile.

"You sang 'Greased Lightnin'' to my bird bath."

"Okay, point taken." She drops her chin in her hand. "I do remember you dancing with Charlie though. One of my last coherent memories. What's that about?"

"I'm not allowed to dance with my friends?"

She gives me an assessing look across the counter. "Since when have you been friends with Charlie?"

I frown. "I've always been friends with Charlie."

Nessa tips her chin down. "Hmm."

"What does that mean? That hmm."

She shrugs. "It's just a hmm. I didn't realize you were friends who danced. When was the last time you willingly danced, by the way? You screeched at me when I tried to get you to dance at the solstice festival."

"I didn't screech."

"You screeched."

"There's a difference between dancing at a wedding and dancing in the middle of the town square at two p.m."

"Not much, but okay."

I sigh and press the palm of my hand against the back of my neck. Everything feels too tight from the base of my skill to the spread of my shoulders. Whatever good my run did me this morning has already evaporated. If I'm not careful, I'll tip myself right into a migraine, and I don't have the time.

Vanessa watches me carefully. "Headache starting?"

I shake my head. "Just stressed. The shop opens in about a month. There's a lot to do."

"You need to take care of yourself."

I squeeze the back of my neck and release. Squeeze and release. My family means well, but there's nothing on my to-do list that can simply be dropped. I know what my triggers are. I know when I'm pushing myself too hard. I know my limits and know my body.

"And you need a shower," I counter. "You look like you rolled around in my front yard last night."

"I did roll around in your front yard last night."

"Exactly." I nod toward the stairs. "There's a bunch of stuff in the guest bathroom. Help yourself."

She slips from her stool with her mug of coffee curled in her hands, shoulders hunched to keep my blanket wrapped tight around her. "Oh, hey," I call before she disappears. "Can I borrow your phone?"

"It's probably dead, but sure."

I find it wedged beneath a pillow and swipe open the lock screen. I scroll to Beckett's name and tap out a message.

> NOVA: Please rescue my phone from your tree field.
>
> NOVA: This is Nova, by the way.

It takes him a second, but three dots appear.

> BECKETT: Next time tell me when you're leaving. Dad wanted to send out a search party.

I snort. If anyone wanted to send out a search party, it was likely Beckett.

> NOVA: No search party necessary. Vanessa stayed with me last night.
>
> BECKETT: Figured. Alex said he saw the two of you get on the shuttle.

I'll have to thank Alex, then.

A picture of Beckett's cats appears on my phone in response, Comet and Prancer curled in tiny little balls of fluff on the edge of his couch. Beckett has adopted a fleet of animals in the past couple of years. It started with a family of cats he found in one of the barns. He quickly added two ducklings and a cow. He tried to adopt a raccoon, but Evie put her foot down.

I bring the phone to my nose. It looks like the cats are using my clutch as some sort of sleeping bag.

> NOVA: That is criminally adorable. I don't even
> want my purse back. They need it more than
> I do.

> BECKETT: I was hoping it would soften
> you up.

I frown.

> NOVA: For what?

> NOVA: Is my phone fertilizer?

> BECKETT: Nah. It's with Charlie.

I throw my head back and groan at the ceiling. I'd splay face down on the floor if I had any confidence I could get back up again. Of course Charlie found it.

> NOVA: Can he give it to you?

Immature? Maybe. But I have no intention of seeing Charlie for the next decade.

> BECKETT: He said he'd drop it at Layla's. She'll be
> open tomorrow.

> BECKETT: Or he says he can come drop it off for you if
> you need it today.

Over my dead body is Charlie Milford coming over to my house and standing on my front porch. No, thank you. I would rather pick it up from Layla's bakehouse once he's well on his way to New York. I can do without my phone for one day.

Sighing, I roll my neck.

> **NOVA:** Bakehouse, please. And send me a picture of the ducks.

5

CHARLIE

THE DAY IS off to an excellent start.

The sun is bright in a cornflower blue sky, the birds are singing, and Luka left the good coffee in the kitchen of the guesthouse. Stella is officially out of the country, which means she can stop texting me every seven minutes to ask if I'm sure I want to watch over the farm, and for the first time in years, there's not a single pressing alert on my calendar.

I also have Nova's cellphone in my back pocket. A guarantee that I'll see her today.

Solid tens across the board.

I close the door behind me and step down the porch, dried grass crunching beneath my boots. The weather is just starting to change, summer releasing its grip for a freefall into autumn. The mornings are cooler, the colors brighter. Flocks of geese drift overhead in perfect formation, their calls echoing out across the fields.

I'm not used to this sort of commute. Pine trees in neat little rows instead of skyscrapers. A pumpkin patch instead of a half-naked cowboy strumming a guitar. While my brain usually has trouble with silence, I like it here. I can hear the soundtrack of this place when I listen for it. Wind whistling through the fields and the whisper of the branches as they sway gently back and forth. The rumble of a tractor somewhere in the distance.

My phone rings in my pocket, and I dig it out, balancing my coffee in the crook of my elbow. I almost trip over a pumpkin vine and answer my phone with a bitten-off curse.

A beat of silence greets me. Then a dry, amused voice. "I guess the country is agreeing with you."

I readjust my grip on my coffee and thank god for closed-top travel mugs. I dressed for the day, wearing my best flannel, and I'd prefer it if I didn't walk around with a massive coffee stain. "Good morning, Selene."

She mutters something under her breath that I don't quite catch. My work has been flexible about allowing me to be remote for the month, but my assistant, Selene, can't conceive why I would want to. I don't think she's ever willingly left New York in her life.

"How are the scarecrows, farmer boy?"

I squint into the distance. "I haven't seen any yet."

"I find that difficult to believe."

"Well, believe it." A gust of wind rolls its way through the trees, burrowing in through the collar of my shirt. I should have brought my jacket. "I am walking through a pumpkin patch though. If that fulfills whatever fantasy you have going on about my time down here."

"If by fantasy you mean waking nightmare, then yes. That is exactly what I pictured you doing when you told me you'd be spending a month on the farm." She sighs and I hear the clink of a glass in the background. The clink of a glass and . . . nothing else. None of the ambient sound I usually hear when she's at her desk in the small alcove in front of my office, half hidden behind a wall of plants of her own making.

I frown.

"Where are you right now?"

"I'm at work," she deadpans. "Doing my job."

That's debatable. "Selene. Are you in my office?"

"Of course I'm in your office. You're not using it." There's a pause and I hear a drawer open. "You have more sticky notes than any man your age should."

"They help me stay organized," I murmur. Notes and lists and strategically placed phone alarms are the things that keep my chaotic brain in line. "Whatever. Just don't drink all of my coffee."

"How about I eventually replace whatever I use."

"That's fine too." Sometimes it feels like Selene is running the show and I'm just along for the ride. "Is there a reason for this call or is this a welfare check?"

She makes a sound that tells me she's amused. "When have you ever known me to check in?"

"You called when I was sick last year and asked if I needed soup."

"Because I was afraid you would die, and I'd get saddled with one of the useless fuckboys in the east wing."

My lips twitch with a grin. Selene is right. Those guys are assholes. Most of the people at my firm are assholes.

Still. "We've talked about this. You can't say 'fuckboy' at work."

"I can when I'm in your office and the door is shut. Do you ever take naps in here? It's really quiet. I can't hear anything through the door."

"No, I don't take naps in my office." Though sometimes I want to. Other times I want to throw my desk chair through the window and scream into the void. "Did you need something? Did I forget a meeting?"

I keep everything programmed down to the minute in my phone. If I don't, I lose track of it. I thought I had kept this morning intentionally blank, but it's possible something came up over the weekend while I was focused on Stella's wedding.

And distracted by Nova.

"No, you didn't forget a meeting." I hear the shuffle of papers and the click of her heels across the floor of my office. A drawer opens and closes, and the whir of a machine starts up. I guess she found the Nespresso. "I wanted to give you a heads-up. You had about ten messages from your dad on your office phone. And two from Mr. Billings."

I grind out a curse between clenched teeth and rub my knuckles across my forehead. My dad almost tanked the company completely about three years ago with a boatload of shitty decision-making. Not only was he disregarding client interests and recklessly investing money on their behalf, he'd also been making inappropriate comments to a bunch of our female employees. Needless to say, the board decided to quickly and quietly relieve him of his position.

"How likely is it that Mr. Billings is calling about something my father told him?"

"Uh, safe to say that's highly likely."

My father has had . . . difficulty . . . letting go of his role. He calls me weekly with "advice" on how to do my job. He keeps in touch with most of his old clients too. The ones that didn't care how he was acting or who he hurt in the process. The ones that were assigned to me as "legacy" when my dad was canned.

I sigh and breathe in deep through my nose. A plume of smoke has started to rise from the chimney stack over at Layla's bakehouse, a hint of cinnamon carried by the wind. This place is my priority right now. My dad's bullshit can wait. Mr. Billings can too.

"Can you slot Mr. Billings in for thirty minutes this afternoon? I'll do damage control."

"And your dad?"

I exhale, my breath a puff of white in the chilly morning air. "I'll take care of it."

At some point. Maybe.

THE LITTLE BELL above the door signals my arrival at the bakehouse, the smell of melted butter and crisp apples smacking me in the face. A rumbling groan tears its way out of my chest. This early, there's only a few people in the front of the shop. Clint from the firehouse sits at a booth in the corner, sipping from a mug of coffee. And Cindy Croswell is busy at the takeout counter, collecting white carryout boxes with headphones on.

I love everything about the farm, but the bakehouse might be my favorite. Floor-to-ceiling windows line the front half, pine trees brushing against the glass on every side. Cozy booths with throw pillows and cable-knit blankets sit against the walls. Bistro tables with mosaic tops and mismatched chairs fill in the middle, and a counter runs along the back wall. Display cases with every treat imaginable anchor either side of it, and a little door leads to the back.

It's always cozy, but it feels downright homey during the fall. It's the version of home I always wished for while sitting at the too-big table in my parents' formal dining room, eating a catered meal, and listening to the awkward silence stretch thick. This feels like comfort and belonging. Layla making apple pie in the back with bouquets of dried flowers in vases all over the place. Cinnamon sticks and cardamom and allspice heavy in the air.

Maybe I'll just work from here for the duration of my trip.

Caleb pokes his head out from the swinging half door that leads to the back kitchen, brown eyes searching. They crinkle into a grin as soon as he spots me, the handsome bastard. I feel like he's always either smiling or staring at Layla with heart eyes. I'm glad his unrequited longtime crush worked out for him.

"Hey, man. Wasn't expecting you." He tips his head toward the back. "Layla is working on some pie thing—"

"Apple pie strudels with a caramel filling, Caleb!"

His grin twitches wider. "Layla is working on apple pie strudels with a caramel filling if you want to come back."

Like I'm going to ignore that invitation. I slip back behind the counter and follow Caleb to where Layla is holding a massive mixing bowl in one hand, a spatula-shaped thing in the other. She mixes it around and around in the bowl, offering me a smile.

"Hey. Did you need help with something?"

"Nah, just visiting." I toss my messenger bag beneath the counter where Caleb is leaning. He has a butter croissant in his hand and another one on the plate in front of him, cheek bulging as he chews. As expected, he's staring at Layla with cartoon hearts floating around his head.

I sigh and steal the croissant off his plate. He tries to protest but I shove the entire thing in my mouth.

"I figure if I'm here," I mumble around flaky, buttery pastry dough, "I might as well capitalize on the benefits."

Layla looks amused. Caleb looks irritated.

"That was my croissant," he mumbles.

"I'll give you another one," Layla offers.

He straightens out of his slouch to beam at his fiancée. "Thank you."

I roll my eyes and swallow the rest of the croissant. I don't know how I found myself surrounded by couples desperately in love, but here we are. I love seeing my friends happy, of course, I just wish—

I don't know. I don't know what I wish. I wish it were me? I don't think so. I have no desire for a relationship. That's never been something I've craved for myself. I've seen firsthand how relationships can twist you into something you don't recognize, desperately looking for a way out. No, thank you.

I guess I wish I could hang out with them and not feel like I'm the one that doesn't belong. An aimless, drifting half to a nonexistent whole in a room full of perfectly matched pieces. I don't want to be an imposition. I don't want to be some . . . project or thing they feel like they need to fix.

I roll the sleeves of my flannel. "You need any help while I'm here?"

Layla nods. "You can take over for Caleb. He's been manning the register while I get these strudels in the oven. Nico called in sick and Caleb has to head over to the school."

Caleb is the Spanish teacher at the high school and, judging by the clock, about ten minutes behind schedule. He glances at his watch, curses, and strides across the kitchen. He drops a kiss on top of Layla's head, grabs a croissant off a cooling tray, and then drops another kiss right below her ear. Her entire face scrunches up with her delighted smile and something in my chest plucks, just once. Caleb straightens, shoots me a look that's vaguely accusatory—on account of the croissant, I guess—and disappears through the door without another word.

A pink-cheeked Layla looks at me with a sheepish smile.

"Sorry."

I hold up my hands. "No apology necessary."

She shrugs and continues whipping whatever batter is in that big metal bowl of hers. "I just—I know how it can be."

"What?"

She waves her hand around her head. "All of this. The love at Lovelight. We can be extra and I know it."

I grab a hand towel and fold it into neat squares, just for something to do with my hands. "You deserve extra, Layla. Don't tuck away your happy on my account. I'm doing just fine."

Maybe that's it. It's when they feel the need to walk on eggshells that it bothers me the most. It's like they're all waiting for me to fall apart at my perpetually single lifestyle when the truth is . . . I don't want what they have. I don't want to be held to another person's expectations and fall short. I don't want to build something with someone only to have it sour with time. Casual suits me best, and while I'm certainly no stranger to wanting things I don't deserve and cannot have, a relationship isn't something I yearn for.

Layla arches an eyebrow. I laugh.

"I am! Why does everyone always look at me like that when I say it?"

She clicks her tongue and finally sets down her bowl on the edge of the counter, reaching for a filling bag. She makes the work here look easy when I know it's anything but. "Because you deserve better than fine. You deserve—" She glances around her kitchen, gaze landing on a stack of miniature cakes by the ovens. She points at them. "You deserve the whole cake, Charlie."

I blink at her. "Okay?"

"You deserve the whole cake and I'm worried you're settling for your . . . snacks."

Ah. Okay, there it is. I scrub my hand against my jaw and try to tamp down my smile. "I like snacks, Layla."

"All right."

"Once you pop, you just can't stop."

She makes a face at me. "This analogy got gross."

"You started it."

"Yeah." She scoops some of the caramel from her bowl and carefully folds it into a piping bag. "Yeah, I'd like to be the one to finish it, thank you."

"Would you like to talk about your fight with Beckett instead?"

Her whole face darkens in a scowl. "No, I do not want to talk about that two-faced idiot."

A laugh bursts out of me. "All because he eloped with Evie?"

She takes another heaping spoonful of caramel and shoves it into her bag. "All because he eloped with Evie and didn't invite us. I know he didn't want the whole big thing, but he could have said something." She grumbles under her breath. "I had his cake planned and everything."

"What were you going to make?"

"A sweet zucchini olive oil cake with lemon curd and cream cheese buttercream," she sighs. "It would have been perfect."

Fuck, it sounds perfect. "You could still make it, you know."

Her eyes light up. "I could! I could make it and dump it on his front porch."

Not what I had in mind. "Or . . ."

"Or I could make it and dump it on his head," she finishes. "You're right. That's more satisfying."

I stare at her. For such a tiny woman, she sure has a lot of devious thoughts swimming around in that brain of hers. A bell jingles from the front of the shop and I take that as my cue.

"I'm gonna—" I hitch my thumb over my shoulder in silent explanation.

"Try to sell the chocolate hazelnut cupcakes," she cuts me off. "There's another batch in the oven for later."

"Got it, boss."

Except when I elbow my way through the door, I don't think I'll be selling any cupcakes.

Because Nova Porter is standing on the other side of the counter, one elbow propped up on the display case. Deep red corduroy skirt. Black tights and Converse. A well-loved leather jacket over a faded Ramones T-shirt. She takes one look at me and her whole face turns into a thundercloud.

I smile in the face of her dismay, then slip her phone from my back pocket. "Looking for this?"

6

NOVA

I TURN AROUND and walk out.

I don't need my phone. There's a hookup for a landline at the new studio. I'll get a rotary phone and call it a day. Who needs email access in the palm of their hand? Not me.

Charlie is still here. In Inglewild. Why is Charlie still here? He's supposed to be back in New York, doing whatever it is he does in those fancy suits. And my phone was supposed to be left on the counter next to the register.

Not in his right hand as he fumbles his way out the front door behind me, the bell almost ripping from the little red string Layla keeps it on. I ignore him, storming through the trees that surround the bakehouse.

Maybe I'll get lucky and he'll trip over a root. Land on his face like the big dumb idiot he is.

"Nova, wait a second. Would you just—" He reaches for my arm, but I shrug him off, still walking. I do not want to have this conversation with him. I don't want to have any conversation with him. I asked him to come home with me, he said no, and I'd like to ignore him for the rest of my life. I hear him sigh and match my pace, trailing three feet behind. "This isn't pretending like it didn't happen, you know."

I stop abruptly. He almost crashes into me, pulling himself to a stop at the last possible second. He's wearing a flannel today. Something that looks buttery soft and warm, sleeves rolled to his forearms. A mix of pale blue and cobalt that matches his eyes. Damn it. I don't want to be noticing his eyes.

"Give me my phone, please."

He clasps his hands behind his back. "No."

"No?"

"Mm-hmm. My answer is no."

I resist the urge to stomp my foot. Charlie reduces me to the most reactionary version of myself. "Why is your answer no?"

"Because I want to talk to you, and if I give you your phone, you're going to run off through the trees. Again."

He's right. But he's also wrong. Because I don't need my phone to run away. I spin on my heel, prepared to do just that, when he curls his fingers around my elbow, gentle this time.

"Nova," he says, exasperated. "Wait a second."

I keep my eyes on our shoes. "I already told you, I don't want to talk about it."

Two days of clarity didn't change that for me. It's only made the burn of embarrassment worse. My cheeks flame with heat the longer I think about it, the band around my lungs pulled tight. I want to forget it ever happened, and I can't do that if Charlie keeps bringing it up.

"We need to talk about it," he insists.

Resigned, I tip my head back and meet his eyes. He looks serious, if not confused, dark eyebrows furrowed in concentration. He lifts his hand and taps his thumb to the edge of my frown.

"What's this face for?"

I push his hand away. "I don't want to talk about it," I say again.

"Why not?"

"Because I don't want—" I huff out a breath. "I don't want to be a joke."

It comes out more vulnerable than I'd like, a wobble at the edges that frustrates me. His lips twist down in a frown to match mine.

"Who said you're a joke?"

He did. When he laughed in my face.

"I'm sorry, okay?" I kick at the loose rocks by my feet. "I shouldn't have asked you for . . . what I asked you for. I was caught up in the moment, and I misread the signs between us. I'm sorry I shocked your delicate sensibilities, or whatever, but I don't want you to dangle it over my head. It makes me feel stupid and I hate feeling stupid. So, let's just . . . agree to move on."

He stares at me for the stretch of three heartbeats, his face unreadable. "You think I'm making fun of you?"

"Aren't you?"

"No," he says simply. He combs his fingers through his dark hair, dragging his hand over the back of his head to squeeze his neck. "No, I'm really not."

"You said no," I supply quietly. "You laughed at me."

"I didn't—Nova. You gave me twenty seconds to respond before you tried to take it back. And I didn't laugh at you."

"You told me to ask you again."

His eyes flare, a comet streak across midnight-blue skies. He takes one step closer to me, the toes of his boots pressed up against my Converse. I have to tilt my head back to keep staring at his face. Sometimes I forget how tall he is. Besides our dance through the trees, I'm not sure we've ever stood this close to one another.

"Because if that's something you want, that's what I need to hear from you. I'm not laughing at you. I'm not making fun of you. I need you to be sure. I need to know that it's me you want and not a random roll in the sheets."

I blink at him standing above me and try to weigh the truth of his statement. I sift through the cloud of my embarrassment and look at our dance together from another angle. I wanted it to be easy, something quick and fun to crack loose all the brittle parts of myself, and I didn't—I didn't give Charlie much of a chance, did I?

I asked, and Charlie tripped over his own feet. He asked me to clarify, and I thought the very worst of him. And then I—

Well, I ran away.

"Oh," I say, at a loss for anything else.

We stand together, watching each other in the small alcove of trees. It smells like pine and sap and something warm and delicious from Layla's bakery. Charlie's aftershave and my coconut conditioner. At some point, he looped his fingers around my elbow again, his thumb tracing over the worn leather of my jacket.

"I thought you were making fun of *me*," he explains quietly, eyes on mine. All I hear in his voice is honest sincerity, a touch of bashful restraint. A smile twitches at the corner of his mouth, a shallow dimple flashing in his cheek.

"Why?"

"Because I didn't think that was something you wanted from me," he answers simply. "I thought you were—" He coughs on the edge of a laugh. "I thought you were making some sort of commentary on my love life, not extending an invitation. I am—honestly, Nova. Of course I'm interested. Very enthusiastic, actually. Flags, confetti. Exclamation point." He closes the space between us, dipping his head to hold my eyes. "But the ball's in your court here, yeah? You ask me again if that's what you want."

"I'm not looking for a relationship."

He shrugs. "Neither am I. But that's not what we're talking about, is it?"

"To be honest, Charlie, I'm not really sure what we're talking about."

A slow smile unfurls across his mouth. His eyes slip to my mouth and hold. "You keep telling yourself that."

Yeah, I know what we're talking about. His big body pressed tight to mine. Grasping hands and sweat-slicked skin. The want hasn't faded from the other night. I thought it might, buried as it was beneath the burn of my embarrassment. But it's still there. A low buzz. A gentle but insistent hum.

I want Charlie.

I tilt my head to the side and consider. "Why don't you ask me?"

"Because I want you to do the asking," he says again. I'm not used to seeing this shade of Charlie. The arch of his eyebrow. The gentle but serious patience in every line of his face. The flannel. He wants me to make the decision. "Like I said, you can think on it. I'm not going anywhere."

He takes two steps back, widening the distance between us. He reaches for my hand and curls his fingers around my wrist. He opens my palm and drops my phone in it. I notice he's given me a new wallpaper photo. A close-up picture of his face, smile lines by his eyes, cup of coffee to his mouth. He must have taken it as soon as he got home from the wedding, those damn suspenders in the very edge of the shot.

"For your viewing pleasure," he explains. "I went back and forth between that and me shirtless in front of the mirror, but this felt more appropriate."

I roll my eyes and slip my phone in my back pocket. "Thank you."

"I can send you that shirtless picture, if you want."

"Noted."

He grins, back to the aloof version of himself that I'm used to. "I also have this." He dangles a white paper bag in front of my face.

"What is it?"

"A cupcake."

"I don't want a cupcake."

He sighs and thrusts the bag into my chest. "Layla told me to upsell the cupcakes, so you're getting a cupcake."

"But this isn't you selling it. This is you giving it to me."

"I'll pay for it."

"I don't want the cupcake."

His jaw clenches and releases. I like it probably too much. "Take the cupcake. The cupcake is here for you. You asked for the cupcake before, remember? But the cupcake was being stupid and didn't say the right things."

A laugh bursts out of me, loud in the stillness of the trees. What an absolutely ridiculous situation I've managed to put myself in. Charlie blinks, his shoulders finally relaxing with a slow exhale. His lips quirk at the corners.

"Okay, I'll take the cupcake." I close my hand around the top of the bag, and the band around my chest loosens. I peek inside. Chocolate hazelnut. I hope it has a ganache filling too. "What are you doing here anyway?" I ask into the bag.

"Are you asking me or the cupcake?"

"I'm asking you."

"Oh." He messes with the cuff of his flannel, fingers rubbing over the soft material. "I wanted to talk to you."

I unroll the top of the bag from where he crushed it with his hand and slip my fingers inside, swiping through the top of the cupcake. I pop my thumb in my mouth and chocolatey-hazelnut goodness explodes on my tongue. I make a faint sound. Charlie's eyes go hazy. He sways to the side.

"I meant here. On the farm. What are you doing on the farm?"

"What?" he asks, voice somewhere far away.

"Charlie."

"What?" he asks again, yelling a little bit.

I fold the top of the bag over again. I'll eat the cupcake later. "What are you doing at Lovelight? I thought you were supposed to be back in New York."

"Oh." He hitches his thumb over his shoulder, still looking a little dazed. "I work here now."

"At . . . the bakehouse?"

He tips his head back and forth. "Kind of all over, I guess. Wherever Layla and Beckett need me. I'm taking over for Stella while she's on her honeymoon."

I didn't realize she was going on a honeymoon. Last I heard, she and Luka were planning on sticking around for the harvest and holiday season before doing something together in the spring.

"Wedding present," Charlie explains, seeing the question on my face.

"That was generous of you."

He kicks a loose pebble with the toe of his boot. It goes bouncing down the path. Somewhere on the other side of the trees, two ladies laugh, voices drifting closer to the bakehouse.

"She deserves it. Deserves more than that, but this is a good start."

"And New York is okay with you being here?"

"My work is fine with it." He closes the space between us again, and I shuffle backward until a pine tree branch pokes at the space between my shoulder blades. "I'm more interested in what you have to say about it."

"I'm fine with it." I clutch my cupcake to my chest. "Why wouldn't I be fine with it?"

"Because," he says, his hand reaching so he can toy with the zipper of my jacket. He tugs it up and then down. Up again. "Now you can't avoid me like you were planning to."

"I wasn't planning on avoiding you." I lie through my teeth.

"Mm-hmm. That's why you sprinted from the bakehouse as soon as you saw me."

"I didn't sprint."

I walked at a very brisk pace. There's a difference.

He hums, amused. "Well. Get used to looking at this pretty face, Nova. I've got a feeling we'll be seeing a lot of one another."

I HAVE THIRTY-FOUR emails and sixty-two text messages waiting for me when I finally check my notifications. Charlie's smiling face stares up at me from my screen, and I have to swipe my thumb along his jaw to unlock the device.

It feels like a personal attack every time.

I prop my feet up on the corner of my desk in the back of the empty tattoo studio and look through my messages. Most of them are from my family the night of the wedding, trying to figure where I wandered off to. Some are automated messages from a few job boards I have listings on. And twenty-seven are from Charlie, starting around the same time I found Nessa in the trees.

No shirtless pictures though.

Unfortunately.

> CHARLIE: Nova, come back.

> CHARLIE: Don't use this as an excuse to never talk to me again. I can be persistent. You know that.

I snort a laugh and scroll some more.

A note that he found my phone in the field. A stupid joke about Montgomery's dancing at the reception. A hello in the morning when he woke up the next day and a grainy, blurry photo of a coffee cup on his kitchen counter. A description of the bagel he had for breakfast. Another photo of two different kinds of flannels laid out on top of his bed.

> CHARLIE: I know I have your phone and you won't see these until later, but which one do you think brings out my eyes?

All the reasons I wanted to take him home in the first place come roaring back. He's funny. He doesn't take himself too seriously. He makes me feel wanted and he . . . he's hot as hell. Pressed chinos notwithstanding.

I could set the terms and he would respect them. I know he would. It would be convenient, certainly. Especially since he's staying in town. I could use the outlet.

And if the attraction spinning between us in a thick syrupy haze is any indication, it would be good. Better than good. Maybe with Charlie out of my system, I'll be able to focus on the things I should be focused on.

All I need to do is ask him again.

> **CHARLIE:** Did I tell you how beautiful you looked in that silver dress? I can't remember.

> **CHARLIE:** Sometimes I think you're the most beautiful thing I've ever seen.

I bite my bottom lip and tap my thumbnail against the edge of my phone case.

> **CHARLIE:** Also, one hundo percent down for a night of hot, passionate sex. For the record.

> **CHARLIE:** With you. If that wasn't clear.

> **CHARLIE:** Ready when you are, Nova girl.

7

CHARLIE

"WHERE ARE YOU?"

I glance around Stella's office. There are haphazard stacks of paper on every flat surface, manilla envelopes in precariously leaning piles. Four days here and I still haven't figured out what system this is all organized by. I'm starting to think it's more of a toss it up and hope for the best situation.

That's not what my dad is asking though. There's one question on his mind, though he'd rather meander through pointless small talk than just ask it.

Why aren't you in New York?

"I'm working remotely," I tell him, shifting my laptop three inches to the left and almost sending a stack of pine-scented air fresheners to the ground. I wedge my phone between my shoulder and ear and collect them, opening the top drawer to shove them inside. Except there are about seven thousand more air fresheners in this drawer, and I couldn't wedge in another if I tried. I drop them in my lap. "Where are you?"

He hates when I'm deliberately vague. He also hates when I'm conversational. I'm pretty sure he hates me on principle, but that doesn't stop me from answering his phone calls, some stupidly hopeful piece of my head and heart wondering if this time might be different.

"I'm at the house," he says, sounding distracted.

The house he shouldn't have a key to because my mother kicked him out almost two years ago before starting her rediscovery journey. She's been traveling all over the globe for the past year, some sort of *Eat, Pray, Love* thing happening.

I'm happy for her. I'm also . . . frustrated that I'm the one left dealing with this dumbass.

"Why are you at the house?"

"Relax. Your mother is in Cape Town. Or something." I hear the clink of glass on the other end of the phone. I guess eleven in the morning is a fine time to start drinking.

I pinch the bridge of my nose. "You're not supposed to be there, whether mom is there or not. She wouldn't like it. I don't like it. You have a house. Go there."

He makes a huffing noise that more or less conveys the sentiment *I don't care what your mother does or does not like.* He's made that abundantly clear. He dragged his feet through the entirety of the divorce proceedings and fought my mother on every little detail.

And apparently, has not returned his house key.

I make a note to change the locks.

"I came to grab a few things from the office. Her lawyer is here, making sure everything is to her satisfaction."

My shoulders relax. A chaperone makes me feel slightly better. Still changing those locks though.

"And you decided to make a stop at the liquor cart?"

He doesn't answer me. "Where are you, and why are you not at the office?"

"I'm working remotely," I say again. My dad and I have never had a good relationship. My entire life, I've been running to reach his insurmountable standards. I've always thought if I could just work a little harder, be a little smarter, he might notice. He might be proud. But every time I jump, he cuts me at the knees.

But I can't stop myself from trying. For whatever reason.

"I heard you the first time you said it," he grunts. "I'm asking why."

I sigh and rub my palm over the back of my neck, reclining in Stella's chair. It squeaks ominously, then jerks me to a completely prone position with a quick jolt. I blink up at the ceiling. "I'm helping Stella out for a few weeks."

He's silent for so long, I have to glance at my screen to make sure we're still connected. I crank the desk chair back to a reasonable position.

"A few weeks?" he finally manages. "What could she possibly need help with for weeks? You need to be here, managing your clients. I heard from Wes Billings, you know. He isn't happy with your performance."

Wes Billings hasn't been happy with anyone's performance for the past six decades.

"Did you forget you have responsibilities here?" he continues. "A job?"

Because that's always what's been most important to my dad. Not family. Not relationships. But the job, the clients, and how much money he can rake in. His reputation and what the industry thinks of him.

"I am aware I have a job, which is why I made arrangements to work remotely."

Beckett appears in the doorway, rapping his knuckles against the frame, one of his cats draped over his shoulder. I pull my phone away from my ear and place it flat on the desk, the tinny faraway sound of my father delivering a lecture weaving in and out. I tap mute as Beckett slips into the chair across from me.

"Everything okay?" he asks as my father's voice picks up volume and speed. I want to fling my phone through the window. I want to bury it beneath all of Stella's air fresheners.

"Everything is fine. He'll be going on for a bit. Thanks for coming over."

Beckett nods, kicking out his legs. The cat on his shoulder nudges the side of his head with her nose and then scampers down his arm to his lap. Prancer, I think. Or maybe Comet. It's hard to tell which cat is which between the four of them. She curls up in a tiny ball, and he rests his palm on her back. He looks relaxed, content.

Maybe I should get a cat.

I pick up my phone again.

". . . your job is what you should be focusing on. Your legacy. Our legacy."

He didn't seem so concerned with his legacy when he was acting like a giant asshole around the office. "Got it. Listen, Dad. I've got to go. A work thing just popped up."

Beckett's face scrunches in confusion.

"What sort of work thing?" my dad bellows.

An intervention between the tree farmer and the baker because they're still not speaking to each other, and my toxic trait is wanting everyone to get along all the time.

"I can't share client details," I deflect.

He sighs. I can picture the exact face he's making. Disappointment and exhaustion, the baseline of our relationship.

"You need to get yourself together, Charlie. You're embarrassing me."

I press two fingers to the bridge of my nose and ignore the familiar burn of frustration. That's nothing new either. It's the role I've always managed to fill perfectly for my father. The family embarrassment. The wayward child. It doesn't matter how much money I make or how well I do, he'll always just see me as his too-loud kid that got in trouble with teachers for talking too much and could never quite figure out how to hand in his homework on time.

I'm a grown man. The fact that my father can still reduce me to second-guessing and overthinking is ridiculous.

"Noted," I manage. "Luckily that's something we're both familiar with. Next time you need to reach me, get in touch with Selene. She can slot some time on my calendar."

"Charlie, you need to—"

I hang up the phone and toss it in the same drawer as the pine-tree air fresheners. Only to pull it out again and set it face down on top of a stack of papers marked **PUMPKIN SZN**. I don't want to miss a text from Nova. If she decides to text.

She hasn't in the past four days, but like I said, I can be patient.

Beckett clears his throat on the other side of the desk. The cat kneads her tiny little feet into his thigh.

"Do you want to talk about it?" he asks, only managing to sound slightly hesitant.

"Not particularly." I cross my ankle over my knee and almost knock down another stack of files. This office is going to give me hives. "It was my father's weekly check-in to make sure I'm not a smudge on the family name."

Beckett gives me a look and adjusts his hat so it's backward, dark blond hair peeking through the snapback. "Your dad sounds like an asshole."

I laugh. "Not only does he sound like an asshole, he is one. You have impeccable hearing, by the way."

"A lifetime spent listening," he says easily enough. "Or a lifetime spent with three sisters."

One of which I've been flirting with. Very poorly, if her lack of communication is any indication. Luckily, I'm saved from responding by Layla appearing in the doorway, a tray clutched in her hands. She stops abruptly at the threshold and looks at Beckett. Her eyes narrow.

"You," she seethes.

So much for this meeting going smoothly. "Come in," I say easily. "Sit down. We're having a meeting."

"What sort of meeting?"

"A necessary one." I point at the empty seat next to Beckett. "Take a seat."

She remains standing, hands tightening at the edge of her foil until it's bent beneath her grip. "I'll stand."

Beckett sighs. "Layla, come on."

Her head snaps in his direction. "Do you have something you'd like to say to me?"

He swallows heavily. "We're still doing this?"

"Yeah. We're still doing this." She rips back the top of her container and extends it in my direction, not looking away from Beckett for a second. "Here, Charlie. Would you like a slice of zucchini bread?"

Zucchini bread happens to be Beckett's favorite. He makes a pained noise as the tray passes in front of his face, fingertips at the bridge of his nose. I shrug and decide this really can't get any worse. I might as well have a snack. I pluck out a piece with what must be ten thousand chocolate chips and take a bite.

Beckett looks offended.

"All right," I say around a mouthful of crumbs. "This is your opportunity to get it all out in the open. No more fighting after today." I gesture toward Layla. "You first."

She drops her tray on the empty chair and crosses her arms over her chest. "No, thank you. I have two more batches of apple cider donuts to make this morning—"

Beckett shifts in his seat. Layla doesn't even glance at him.

"—and I'll know if someone sneaks into my kitchen to steal them. I'm too busy to have this conversation."

"Layla," Beckett sighs. "I'm sorry I didn't let you make my wedding cake. You could—" He drags his palm along his jaw with a long-suffering look. "You could make it now, if you wanted? I'm sure it would be amazing."

The compliment falls flat. Layla turns her head slowly, narrowing her eyes. "You think you deserve my cake? After everything?"

He drops his head back against the chair and sighs at the ceiling. Prancer hops off his lap and darts beneath the desk. "I'm trying here, Layla. I really am. I hate fighting with you." He glances at the discarded zucchini bread and swallows heavily. "What can I do to make this better?"

She watches him for a long minute. Tension blankets the room. Part of me wants to leave, but another part of me is afraid of what might happen if I do.

Finally, Layla's shoulders curl forward, defeated.

"I didn't even know you were thinking of proposing," she says. "You didn't tell me. You told me about Clarabelle biting through her fourth leather leash, and you told me about the duck's feeding schedule, but you never once mentioned that you planned to make Evie your wife." She sniffs. "I should have been there. With a cake and a very tasteful speech. But instead, you snuck off in the middle of the afternoon and got married by some—by some hot dog cart vendor."

Beckett blinks, shifts in his chair, and then clears his throat. He looks uncomfortable and for good reason. No one likes to see Layla cry. "He didn't marry us. He was just the witness."

"Who was?"

"The hot dog cart vendor."

"Whatever." She turns her face away. "I don't care."

She very much does care. It's why the three of us are sitting in an awkward silence that's only interrupted by Beckett's cat digging her nails into the wood beneath Stella's desk.

"Layla," Beckett says. "I'm sorry I didn't say anything. It was . . . it was a spur of the moment decision." Layla snorts, but Beckett sits up in his seat, hand messing with his hat again. "Really. It was. I didn't even propose, I just—I woke up and saw her in the kitchen making coffee. Her socks were mismatched, and she had this line from her pillow on her cheek, and I don't know, I asked her to marry me. I didn't even have a ring. Or a plan. Obviously."

Layla glances at him, weighing the truth of his words. "Where did that fancy emerald come from, then?"

I reach across the desk and pull the tray of zucchini bread on my lap, captivated.

The tips of Beckett's ears turn red. "There was a pawnshop down the street from the courthouse."

I groan. "You got your wife a ring from a pawnshop?"

Beckett shrugs and looks down at his boots, fingers plucking at some of the stuffing that's squeezing out of the beaten-up cushion he's sitting on. Stella really needs to replace the furniture in here. "Neither of us wanted to wait. She said it didn't matter."

Layla reaches out and smacks him in the arm.

Beckett curls his body away from her. "What the hell?"

"Goddamn it, Beckett! I can't be mad now! That's romantic." She rounds the chair and collapses in it, the velvet material making a weird wheezing noise. "It's also perfect for the two of you. I'm just upset I wasn't there." She points her finger in his face. "I should have been there."

He slaps her hand away. "That's fine."

"I still want to make the cake."

He perks up. "That is definitely fine."

I clap my hands together behind the desk. Mending bridges. Repairing relationships. Ordering . . . hay. This meeting is officially a success. I am ten thousand miles away from my other life, where everything is shiny, and my phone doesn't stop ringing, and my brain hops from one thing to the next without taking a damn second to breathe. Where I sit alone in an office and watch the world spin out below my feet.

There are things I like about New York. I like the anonymity and the looming expanse of it all. I like my apartment and the way it's never truly dark, the glow of the city at night like a million fallen stars just outside my window. I like the subway beneath my feet on cold mornings and coffee in little blue paper cups, warm between my palms. Hot dogs in wax paper and the press of the crowd during the morning rush, everyone moving together. I like losing myself, but sometimes—

Sometimes I think I miss being known.

I miss having a place I fit. People who remember that I like zucchini bread with extra chocolate chips. An overstuffed chair covered in horrendous green velvet, one of the arm rests wobbling every time I try to rest my chin in my hand. A cat weaving between my legs while I try to figure out how I can get Beckett to agree to a dinner where he may or may not be the center of attention.

Layla pats the top of my hand. "Hey. Where'd you go?"

I drag my hand over my face. "Nowhere." Everywhere. "Sorry, I'm here. I'm listening."

I was diagnosed with ADHD as a kid after my parents dragged me to a staggering amount of doctors to "fix the problem." My dad's words, not mine. If my dad could have paid money for all of it to go away, he would have. He still sees it as his biggest failure as a parent, this thing that means my brain works a little bit differently than everyone else's. As a kid, I was overactive. Talked a mile a minute. Had trouble focusing and engaging with others while my brain was going at a sprint. I'd forget where I put my stuff and forget where I was supposed to be at certain times. I'd get anxious and then sad and then sad about being anxious.

As an adult, it's easier. I've learned to work with my brain instead of against it. But I still drift from time to time.

Layla smiles at me. "Do you want me to repeat what I just said?"

"Yes, please."

"We were discussing the harvest festival."

I frown. "What harvest festival?"

Beckett leans forward, and Layla finally allows him to scoop up some crumbs from the tray with his fingertips.

"Every year the town throws a harvest festival," he explains. "But they're trying to make a big thing of it this year. Make it a destination event or something. Stella is on the committee."

My knee works up and down beneath the desk. Prancer darts out and finds her spot back on Beckett's lap. "Neither of you mentioned this during our planning. Did you?"

We had several weeks of covert meetings over FaceTime as we tried to figure out the logistics of me taking over management of the farm while Stella and Luka went on their honeymoon. I don't remember hearing about a committee, but sometimes it's hard for me to keep track of the details.

Beckett shrugs. "It slipped my mind."

Layla fusses with the edge of her skirt. "Mine too."

I dart my eyes between them. "Why are you guys being weird?"

Layla's *"We're not being weird"* overlaps Beckett's *"You're the one who's being weird."*

I frown at them. They exchange a glance.

Layla sighs. "Neither of us . . . want to be on the committee."

Beckett crosses his arms over his chest. "If you make me be on this committee, I will quit on the spot."

"Please don't do that." I scratch at my jaw. I have no idea how to plant . . . anything. And Stella would be pissed if she came back to a farm without any farmers. "What's wrong with the committee?"

"They meet on Thursdays," Layla explains. "Thursday is deep-dish pizza night at Matty's. Caleb doesn't like to miss it."

That makes sense. The man loves his deep-dish pepperoni.

I look at Beckett. "And you?"

He arches a single eyebrow. Ah. Of course. Beckett doesn't like talking to most people. I can imagine a town committee meeting might push him right over the edge.

"Does this mean . . ." Hope flares. "Can I be on the committee? Can I take Stella's spot?"

Layla blinks at me. "You want to be on the committee?"

"Of course I do. Why wouldn't I?"

Fuck, I've been trying to get on an Inglewild town committee for years. The drama is always excellent, and I'm tired of hearing about it from the phone tree.

My phone blinks with a message on the desk. I pick it up, expecting a schedule update from Selene along with a string of colorful commentary about fielding calls from my father. But I almost fumble the damn thing when I see Nova's name. I glance up at Beckett, but the tray of zucchini bread in his lap has his full attention. And Layla's occupied with her phone, probably texting Caleb something pornographic about croissants.

It's a good thing too, because I almost fall out of my chair when I see what Nova's sent.

A picture of her in front of a long mirror, one hand on her phone and the other on the buttons of her shirt. She's clearly undone a few for the sake of the photo, the rose between her breasts on full display. One shiny black fingernail traces the stem of it.

> NOVA: You gave me a new wallpaper. It seemed fair
> that I send you one back.

I immediately save the picture to my phone. And then glance at Beckett again.

He's talking to Layla about adding more chocolate chips to the zucchini bread, not concerning himself with the wheezing sound that probably just left my mouth.

Thank god.

> CHARLIE: Have we unlocked sexy texting? Is this a
> thing we do now?

> NOVA: You started it.

Didn't realize that the picture I set as her wallpaper did it for her, but good to know.

> CHARLIE: I'm enjoying this development.

> NOVA: I bet you are.

> CHARLIE: Anything you want to ask me? While we're both here?

> NOVA: Yeah.

I watch the three dots on my phone with laserlike focus.

> NOVA: Did you see Ms. Beatrice is doing brown sugar lattes?

I hide my smile in my fist, knuckles rubbing roughly against my jaw. Nova Porter is a *tease*.

> CHARLIE: Cruel woman.

> CHARLIE: And no, I didn't. Appreciate the info.

> NOVA: 🙂

"Everything okay?" Beckett asks.
I keep my head ducked. I'm grinning like an idiot. "All good."
I'm better than good.
Nova is flirting back.

8

NOVA

"WHAT DO YOU have against pumpkins?"

"I've got nothing against pumpkins. I just don't think we should fill the fountain with them." A pause. "How do you even fill a fountain with pumpkins?"

"You stack them, you idiot. I saw a picture on Pinterest. It looked very artistic."

"You're on Pinterest?"

"I like art."

"What do you know about art? You can barely write your name."

"Art is in the eye of the beholder. Right, Nova?"

I ignore Gus and Montgomery's bickering and flip another sheet of paper over in my stack. I decided to print résumés for the receptionist position, because apparently I'm a sadist. I thought it would be easier than a screen, but the giant stack of paper just makes me feel like I'm on a hamster wheel that leads to nowhere while simultaneously destroying a forest of trees. I feel wasteful and I feel like I'm behind on everything.

And still distracted by Charlie. Exceedingly distracted by Charlie, actually, since we *unlocked sexy texting*. I've gotten a string of pictures over the last day and a half. Charlie in a thick white cozy-looking sweater. Charlie with a chocolate hazelnut cupcake halfway into his mouth. Charlie's boots standing by a pine tree. A ladybug on the tip of his thumb. A close-up of his face, absolutely delighted by the lady-bug on the tip of his thumb. A seven-second video of him yelling into the phone about the ladybug on the tip of his thumb. A full body shot of him in front of the bathroom mirror at the farm guesthouse, the top three buttons of his shirt undone, his finger at the buttons the same way mine were in the photo I sent him.

I wanted to see what Charlie might do if I push. I guess now he's doing the same.

"That's not true. Some art is crap. I went to an exhibit at the Vi-sionary Art Museum—"

"You what?"

"—and there was a giant pink poodle. A poodle. Made of tulle. I'm pretty sure it had wheels. How is that art?"

Gus gasps like Montgomery just pulled out a knife and stabbed him directly in the heart. "I know you're not talking about Fifi."

"Who the hell is Fifi?"

"Fifi is a kinetic sculpture at the Visionary Art Museum in Balti-more," I offer without looking up. "And I don't understand what she has to do with pumpkins in the fountain in the middle of the town."

I'm starting to regret signing up for this committee. At the time, I thought it would be a good way to integrate myself with local busi-nesses. I grew up here, but I want people to see me as more than little Nova Porter, the girl who used to spray-paint the sides of barns in middle school.

I want people to see me as a serious business owner. This might not be my first official studio, but it's the first one that truly feels like mine. My studio on the coast is part of a co-op with other artists, an open space we all share. I rented my chair in the back corner and worked my client base through the co-op system. This studio is all me. My first actual location.

Ink & Wild in Inglewild. The place I grew up. The tiny, little town that I love with my whole heart.

"I'm talking about art!" Monty shrieks, and I wince. I may love this town, but I do not love this committee. I hold a lot of regret in my heart every other Thursday at 6:30 p.m.

I collect my paperwork in a neat stack and set it to the side. In addition to Gus and Montgomery, the harvest festival committee consists of Ms. Beatrice from the café, Stella from the farm, and Alex Alvarez from the bookstore. Ms. Beatrice showed up to the first meeting, listened to Gus and Montgomery bicker for six minutes, gathered her bag, and walked out of the room. She hasn't been back since.

"Enough about the pumpkins." It comes out harsher than I intended. Alex glances up from the beaten-up paperback in his lap and pushes his glasses up his nose. Montgomery presses his hand to his chest like I've offended him. "We just—we don't need to worry about art installations right now. Gus, did you get the proper permits from Dane?"

He leans back in his chair and takes a giant bite out of a slice of pizza. It's deep-dish night at Matty's, and I can't believe I have to eat it in the tiny back room of the bookshop with these lizards.

"Permits are distributed by the fire department."

I try to channel a patient version of myself. "Did you get the proper permits from the fire department?"

Considering he and Monty are two-thirds of the fire department and they're both on this committee, it shouldn't have been difficult. Gus holds his hand out to Monty, and they give each other a very aggressive high five.

"Approved."

"All right." I don't ask any additional questions. "Alex, did you get food and drink set?"

He places his book to the side with obvious reluctance. I get a brief glimpse of a woman on the cover in a blue dress, her skirts hiked up as she dashes away. He notices me looking and quickly flips it over.

"Halfway there. Most people are happy to participate. It's just formalizing things from a potluck to actual booths with food available for purchase. And convincing Cindy Croswell she can't serve chili out of a crockpot."

"Man, I love her chili." Gus frowns. "What's wrong with the crockpot?"

"She can't serve her chili out of a crockpot in her minivan. That's what's wrong with the crockpot."

Gus opens his mouth to argue, but he's cut short when the door to the back room swings open. It slams into the table, making him shriek.

"Sorry about that." Charlie's low voice is colored with hesitation. He takes two steps forward, the warm light from the bookstore spilling in with him. "Is this—" He leans back to look at the sign on the door that says DO NOT ENTER with a tiny skull and crossbones. Some of my finest work. "Is this the harvest festival committee?"

"Sure is!" Montgomery manages with his head buried in the last remaining pizza box. "We were just debating chili."

"We were not debating chili," I say. Charlie's head snaps in my direction. He looks more like Investment Banker Charlie tonight, a light blue chambray shirt tucked into navy slacks. The top two buttons undone. A caramel-colored coat with the collar up. His whole face brightens like he's just been handed his very favorite toy.

I frown.

"Hey there, Nova. I didn't know you were on the harvest festival committee."

The door slips shut behind him and he attempts to climb around Alex. I don't know why we insist on meeting in the back storage closet of the bookshop. It's not like we're doing anything clandestine. There's not enough room for three people back here, let alone five and some pizzas.

"Alex is also on the harvest festival committee," Alex says as Charlie lifts the back of his chair so he can get around him. Charlie's arms flex beneath the line of his coat, and I have to stare down at my notepad. "Gus and Montgomery too."

"Yeah, I see you." Charlie glances at Alex's book. "Kleypas? Nice, dude. I told you you'd like it."

I don't know what to do with the information that Charlie recommends historical romance to his friends. He finishes climbing around Alex and grabs the only available seat in the tiny room. It screeches as he drags it across the floor, right next to me.

"Hiya, Charlie. You want a slice?" Montgomery extends a half-eaten piece of cheese pizza in his direction, but Charlie doesn't spare him a glance. He's too busy grinning at me, slipping that soft-looking coat off his shoulders.

"I'm good. Thanks, Monty."

Monty shrugs and takes a bite. "You taking over Stella's spot on the committee while you're overseeing the farm?"

"Yep." He collapses in his chair, his thigh pressed tight to mine beneath the table. I try to move away but there's nowhere to go. He ducks his head so his mouth hovers at my ear, his arm stretched over the back of my chair as he arranges himself. He is way too big for this tiny room. "Catch me up on what I missed?"

I stare at him, mind blank. The only thing we've talked about is pumpkins and chili. None of it is relevant and I'm too busy staring at all the minuscule differences in his appearance. Farm life has been good to him. His hair is ruffled from the wind, a slight curl behind his ears, where his hairline meets his collar. He hasn't shaved in a couple of days and scruff shadows his jaw. A slow smile works its way across his mouth the longer I look, his eyes crinkled in amusement.

"Well, we were—" My words are swallowed up when he reaches for the collar of my oversized sweater, adjusting it so it's flat against my collarbone. His thumb gently traces the edge of an inked flower petal before he drapes his arm over the back of my chair again. Half a second, barely a touch, and my bones feel like they're buzzing. I swallow and try again. "We were—"

"Nova was yelling at us," Montgomery says. "She says we can't serve chili out of the back of a van."

"That makes sense," Charlie replies, eyes still stuck on me. Specifically, the tattoos that dance along my collarbone and curl over my shoulder. He swallows and turns to face the rest of the room. "Is that an integral part of Cindy's recipe? The van aspect?"

I snort. I sometimes forget how much Charlie knows about Inglewild. He might live in New York, but he certainly has his thumb on the pulse of town happenings.

The rest of the room dissolves into conversation about meals served out of vehicles, and my mind drifts, pen doodling at the edge of someone's résumé. I'm painfully aware of Charlie next to me. The heat of his body and the smell of his cologne. It smells like something clean. Soap and cedar. Fresh laundry and the woods right after it rains. Leaves beneath your boots and wind in the trees. Every time he shifts in his seat, his thigh nudges mine.

I am distracted.

A running theme with Charlie.

"Nova?"

I blink and glance up. Everyone is looking at me, various degrees of amusement on their faces. Montgomery cocks a smug eyebrow. "Look who isn't being productive now," he mutters.

"Shut up." I lob my pen across the table only to miss him by a good seven inches. "What were we talking about?"

"Have you done your business sweep? Finalized the silent auction contributions? Asked who wants to sponsor the pumpkin sculpture?"

"Enough about the pumpkin sculpture." I wince. I haven't done any of those things. When Stella was here, we were planning on splitting it down the middle. But it fell on the back burner with . . . everything else on my plate.

"I can do it this week," I offer quickly, ignoring the yawning pit in the center of my chest. I hate missing things. I hate falling behind. I'll just have to adjust a few things on my schedule and figure out how I'm going to visit all the town's small businesses instead of half. Maybe

I can . . . add seven hours to each day. "I'll make a spreadsheet and bring it to our next meeting. I'm sorry."

Montgomery chews on the end of a pizza crust. "Don't worry about it. We have time."

But that only makes me worry more. I said I would do it and I haven't. I add it to my mental list, trying to ignore the thought that whispers I'm doing too much. That spreading myself this thin means I can't do anything well.

Charlie adjusts his arm on the back of my chair and his knuckles graze the back of my neck. I shiver, then push myself into it. His body goes rigid next to mine. All of my spinning thoughts quiet and dim. I tuck everything away until it's manageable again.

I can do it. I'm capable of doing it.

He leans closer under the guise of stealing the pen I didn't lob across the room. "You talking about spreadsheets, Nova girl?"

I tuck my chin to my shoulder and glance up at him. "I don't know if you know this about me"—I lick my bottom lip just to mess with him, wanting to see what pretty color his eyes flash in the muted light of this tiny room—"but I love a good spreadsheet."

He groans, a soft unconscious sound from the very back of his throat. "Do you like torturing me?"

I smile at him. "So very much."

He grins and leans back in his chair, widening the space between us and pretending to listen to whatever it is Alex and Montgomery are arguing about. A dunking booth made of . . . apple cider? Charlie's knee nudges mine.

"For the record," he says. "I like it too."

I STAY BEHIND as everyone files out of the room, an old cracked binder open on the table in front of me. It's probably from 1958. Every small business has their own dedicated sheet of white paper with an address and contact information listed. The first page is the theater that used to be on the corner of Albermarle and Park Street. It's a brewery now, but they still play movies every other Sunday.

This binder is a tiny history of Inglewild, each page accompanied with handwritten notes from whoever put it together. Things like: *Get the strawberry jam, not the apricot* and *Avoid the third step down; it's rickety because Barb is too cheap to fix it. Best bagel sandwich I've ever had* and *If you get there before four on Saturday, you can snag a good table.*

Some sheets are faded and yellowed with age, and others are crisp and white. I flip to the very back and trace my fingers over the latest addition—a logo I drew myself of twisting, crawling flowers. *Ink & Wild* in long slanted letters. No notes yet, but I hope that changes soon.

"Alex is closing up." Charlie stands in the doorway with his shoulder propped up against the wood, one hand braced on the frame and the other in the pocket of his coat. "Let's get you home."

I close the binder with a sigh and raise my arms above my head. I've been sitting too long today. "You don't have to walk me home."

"Obligation has nothing to do with it," he says with a small smile, eyes fixed on the line of my arms above my head. His gaze drops back down to mine. "I'd like to."

I can hear Alex puttering away in the shelves, flicking off lights and straightening books. He calls something to Charlie and Charlie laughs, low and deep. It rolls over my shoulders and settles at the small of my back. A gentle touch nudging me forward.

"Watch it," he says over his shoulder, "or I'll tell Abuela."

"Snitch." Alex snickers, finishing an ongoing argument. He winks at me over Charlie's shoulder. "Good night, Nova. Make sure you lock up when you go."

He disappears up the steps that lead to his apartment above the shop, and it's just me and Charlie and a single string of globe lights at the front of the store. I watch him watching me in the open doorway.

Strong shoulders. Long legs. Loose limbs. I don't think I've ever seen him so still.

"All right," I say, tilting my head. "You can walk me home."

"Thank you."

"You're welcome."

I stand and shrug on my coat, one of the sleeves twisted at my wrist. "What?" I ask, struggling harder the longer he stands there watching me.

He blinks once. Slow and heavy. "What, what?"

"Why are you looking at me like that?"

"Like what?"

Like he's just won some argument I wasn't aware we were having. He steps forward and wraps his hand around my forearm, lifting my sleeve and untwisting it with careful fingers. My hand pokes through, and he grabs it.

His hand is so much bigger than mine, my inked fingers a sharp contrast to his unmarked skin. He presses our palms together, comparing their size, his thumb tap-tapping at the side of my palm.

"I'm just looking at you." He lets my hand go with a squeeze. "Don't get a big head over it." He smiles, those damn lines by his eyes crinkling, and nods his head toward the door. "Let's go."

IT'S COLD WHEN we step out the front door, a gust of wind spiraling its way down Main Street and straight into my too-thin jacket. Clouds roll overhead, thick and luminous in the dark night sky. Everything glows gray and I hunch my shoulders, trying to curl against it.

Charlie peers down at me, face half hidden from behind his collar. Cheekbones and dark eyebrows. Windswept hair. "Want my coat?" he asks.

I give him a look and he laughs. "All right, no coat." He swings his arm over my shoulder and tugs me close instead. He's like a space heater beneath all that thick wool, and I give in to temptation and burrow myself closer. His body tightens in surprise as he gently urges us in the direction of my house, but I wrap my arm around his waist to turn us the opposite way.

He stumbles over the change in direction but quickly corrects. His eyes dart toward the pizza shop at the end of the street. "Didn't we just have pizza at the bookshop?"

"No pizza." I pull my arm back from around him and clutch the business binder to my chest. "I need to stop by the tattoo studio and drop this off."

And reassure myself that it's still real, still standing, and everything is in the proper place. I have trouble sleeping if I don't check in on it at least once a day, the culmination of years of hard work and the foundation for all my hopes and dreams.

Charlie has been by the studio plenty of times to drop off paperwork or to flirt with me, so I don't think too much about it as I fit my key in the lock. He stands at my back, doing his best to block the wind while I fumble with the keys. I can feel the warm puff of every exhale against the back of my neck. The brush of his heavy wool coat. It isn't until I elbow my way inside and flick on the lights that I realize he's the first person to see the finished product. The tattoo studio of my dreams. The first one that is wholly mine and mine alone.

Beckett has been nagging me for ages, but it hasn't felt ready yet. Too much of my head and heart poured into this tiny space for him to wander around before everything is perfect. I want so badly for Beckett to like it. Him more than anyone else. He invested in me first, and I couldn't bear it if he didn't like it.

"You put the lights up," Charlie points out, a smile in his voice. "And the flowers too."

My heart trips over itself and my palms turn clammy as Charlie strolls past me into the open space, head tilted to the side as he takes it all in. I want to grab him by the back of the coat and drag him into the alley. Clap my hands over his eyes and scream at the top of my lungs.

Charlie tips his head back to look at the ceiling and the oversized baskets of greenery that hang from the exposed beams. Eucalyptus and pothos and ivy overflowing in a canopy of green. An entire floor-to-ceiling wall of plants at the back of the studio, succulents peeking through a veil of cascading ferns. Living walls between each tattoo station, bursting with greenery. It turned out exactly as I planned it. Plants everywhere. The wild part of Ink & Wild.

"It's not what I expected," he says quietly.

My stomach drops as I walk over the reception desk, dropping off my binder and paperwork. I slap a sticky note on top and ignore my shaking hands, scribbling out a note to call the top three candidates tomorrow. "What were you expecting?"

Oblivious to my nerves, Charlie wanders around the space, hands behind his back. He stops in front of the display wall where I've re-created all my favorite tattoo designs in delicate white paint on giant gilded mirrors. I had to borrow Beckett's flatbed to get them. Drive three towns over and pull them out from beneath a stack of crab pots at a flea market.

Charlie gently traces the edge of a leaf with his finger and glances over his shoulder with a grin.

"I don't know. Something cool, obviously. But this is . . . I can't believe you keep saying this place isn't ready. It looks ready. It looks incredible," he says. He turns back to the largest of the three mirrors and points at a snake twisting around the thorns of a rose. "I want this one."

Relieved, I meet him at the mirror. In the reflection, our differences are almost comical. The top of my head just barely reaches his chin. His knee-length wool jacket is probably designer, and I got my oversized bomber from the back rack of a Goodwill. He catches my eye and grins.

"What do you think?" He holds up his arm, flexes, and smacks the inside of his bicep with his palm. "Right here."

"You're not getting that."

His bottom lip juts out in a pout. "Why not?"

"I thought you wanted a Taz. That character from Looney Tunes." I make a whirling motion with my finger and poke him once in the center of his chest. "Right there."

"Can I not have multiple tattoos?"

I step into his space and let my finger drag down the buttons of his shirt. Flirting with Charlie is fun, and a solid distraction from the anxieties bubbling up in my chest. "Maybe if you're a good boy, I'll pick out something special for you."

He makes a low sound of interest and wraps his hand around my wandering finger. "Is that what you like? Good boys?"

A laugh slips out of me, even as heat curls low in my belly. Temptation, anticipation. I don't know which one it is, and I don't really care. "I like lots of things. Is that what you want to talk about?"

He eyes me. "If it's what you want to talk about."

I roll my eyes with a huff. Around and around we go. Charlie and I have been playing chicken with each other since a slow dance beneath the stars. I step backward, over to the reception desk, widening the space between us.

Charlie drags his hands through his hair. "I could help you."

I don't glance up from the reclaimed-wood desk I stole from a barn at Lovelight Farms, my attention occupied by a bound leather appointment book, oversized with pale pink pages. The first two weeks of appointments are already full, and that's a different sort of pressure entirely.

I want to do well. I want to be worth the investment.

"What can you help me with?" I mutter.

"With the business thing . . . for the harvest festival. You were supposed to split it with Stella, yeah?"

I look up at him, still standing by the wall I painted, his hands in his pockets and an earnest look on his face. Charlie, waiting for me to say something. Charlie, waiting for me to accept the help he so freely offers. Charlie, waiting for me to flirt with him some more or to ask for space. I know he'd accept whatever it is I want from him, and it's that, I think, that makes my decision for me.

I snap my appointment book closed. I want this itchy, anxious feeling out from beneath my skin. I want to set everything resting on my shoulders aside, just for one night. I want my mind to go somewhere else.

I want to know what his hands feel like on my body. I want to make a selfish choice.

"Yes," I tell him.

"Yes?"

"I would like your help."

A bemused smile curls his lips. "Okay."

"With the business thing and with another thing too."

He nods, confused. "All right. I'll help you with whatever you need, Nova. You know that."

"Good, because I'd like you to walk me home." I swallow down the butterflies. "And then I'd like for you to stay."

9

CHARLIE

I DON'T KNOW how I ended up in Nova's kitchen with a jar of peanut butter and a bag of marshmallows, but I'm not exactly mad about it. Nova stares at me from the other end of the table with her chin in her hand, a wildly arousing combination of impatience and amusement etched across her face. Her left eyebrow ticks up every time I pull a new marshmallow out of the bag, and I wonder how much I can get away with before she kicks me out of her house.

I like pushing her buttons. She makes the cutest faces when I do.

"Good 'mallows," I tell her, mouth half full, cheek bulging. It's not my normal seduction routine, but nothing is normal when it comes to Nova. "Thanks for the snack."

"You grabbed it yourself," she drawls, leaning back in her chair. She took off her jacket in the entryway and I can't stop looking at the slope of her bare shoulder or the inked lines that dance down her skin. Twisted vines. Flowers bursting from in between.

I could spend all night learning the art that decorates her body. I just might.

But she needs to ask me first.

She still hasn't asked me.

I dip another marshmallow into the peanut butter. Nova sighs.

"Charlie."

"Hmm?"

She sighs again and I roll my lips against my smile. "What are you doing?"

I pop the marshmallow into my mouth. "Waiting for you to ask me a question."

Also waiting for her to change her mind. I don't want to pressure her. I don't want to make assumptions about what she does or doesn't want.

I want to hear the words.

"This is the longest buildup to a one-night stand I've ever had in my life." She sighs.

"Is that what we're doing?"

She is unamused. "Charlie."

"You know what I want to hear," I tell her. Though her repeating my name like that in that sassy tone of hers is sort of doing it for me too. I busy my hands with closing the jar to the peanut butter while Nova pushes back her chair.

The screech of it is loud in the quiet of the kitchen. My throat tightens as she moves around the table. Is she going to ask me to leave? Is this the final straw? Have I pushed too hard, asked for too much? I'm still not clear on why Nova wants anything from me.

But instead of grabbing my jacket off the hook in the hall and tossing it in my face, Nova pads over to me in her sock-covered feet and props her hip against the table at my side. The edges of her skirt brush against my fingertips, and I have to tilt back in my seat to get a good look at her face.

Her cheeks are pink, her eyes are dark, and her hair is a deep golden tangle in the light from above the stove.

I don't think I've ever seen her look more beautiful, and I've done a whole lot of looking where Nova Porter is concerned.

"Charlie," she says, her voice a honeyed rasp, "would you like to stay for a night of hot, passionate sex?"

She's done teasing, I guess. I swallow hard and shift in my chair. "I would. Thank you for asking."

She lifts herself up, sliding back on the table in front of me. Her knee nudges the bag of marshmallows. Her foot taps the side of my chair.

"I need to tell you something first." I clear my throat, staring hard at where her skirt rides higher against her thighs. "Before our night of hot, passionate sex."

Her eyebrows climb her forehead. "If you tell me you want me to bark like a dog while we do it, we're going to have some problems."

A laugh sputters out of me and I rest my hand on her thigh. I spread my fingers wide and squeeze gently. She shivers.

"No. I don't want you to bark like a dog. Do you want me to bark like a dog?"

She shakes her head. The color in her cheeks deepens with my hand on her.

I blow out a deep breath. "I did bribe the DJ."

Her forehead creases. "You what?"

"I did bribe the DJ. The night of the wedding. I told him if he saw me dancing with you, he should immediately change the song to a slow one."

"Ah." Her face lights up, delighted. "How'd you know I'd dance with you?"

I squeeze her thigh again. "I'm a persistent man."

"That you are."

She leans back on her palms, legs tipping half an inch wider in front of me. My heart trips over itself before cranking into double-time. It's entirely possible I won't survive the night.

"It leads me to my next point," I manage from a throat that feels too tight. Christ, the look of her. She's temptation wrapped in ink and a cozy-looking sweater, her socked feet swinging back and forth. I bet if I pushed her knees wider, I could see what color underwear she's hiding under that pretty skirt.

She arches an eyebrow. "Which is?"

I forget what I was going to say. "What?"

"You were going to confess another deep, dark secret."

"That's right." I rub my thumb over her tights. "I wanted an excuse to touch you. That night. That's why I wanted a slow song."

A smile hitches the corner of her mouth. "You're touching me right now."

"Yeah, that's the thing about it. I touched you once, and I only wanted to touch you more. I want to keep touching you. I want to make you feel good." I'm hanging on by a thread here. I slip my hand higher until it's beneath her skirt. Her skin is warm, her tights smooth beneath my palm. "I want a lot of things, Nova."

I want to hear her say my name again. I want to hear her beg it. I want to unravel her so thoroughly, she knows exactly what it feels like to be undone. I want to leave my mark on her, not just with my mouth and with my teeth, but with the memory of this night and all the delicious things I plan to do to her. This might be a one-night stand, but I want her to think about me tomorrow. I want her to think about me for a while.

She swings her legs back and forth. "Well, I can't say I don't like the direction of your thoughts." Her tongue wets her bottom lip, and I track the motion, a thrill of heat zipping up my spine.

My fingertips brush something lacey at the top of her thigh. I glance down at my hand and rub my thumb back and forth, considering. When I flip up the edge of her skirt to take a look, she laughs at whatever dumbstruck expression paints itself across my face.

Thigh highs.

She's wearing thigh highs.

I pull my hand back from her thigh and drop it to safer territory down by her ankle, letting my forehead fall against her knee. I rock my head there, back and forth, and try to get control of myself.

"I need a minute," I mumble.

"Take several minutes. I didn't mean to send you into a tailspin." She combs her fingers through my hair.

I squeeze her ankle. "Sure you did," I mumble.

This is good. This is great. One night and maybe I'll be able to knock Nova out of my head a little bit. I'll get rid of whatever this little infatuation is, and we can both exist in this town with the people we love without all of this . . . tension spinning circles and making me dizzy. No more back and forth. Just peaceful coexistence.

Nova taps her fingers down my neck. "Would you like to set some rules? For tonight?"

"Well, we've already established we won't be barking like dogs." I lean back. "What sort of rules did you have in mind?"

She shrugs. "I don't know. I don't think I've ever known a one-night stand the way I know you. Will rules make you more comfortable?"

I drop my chin to her thigh and gaze up at her along the lines of her body. She falters at the implication of the position, her eyelashes fluttering.

"Ah," I grin and tuck a quick kiss to her kneecap. Her leg jumps. "You like my head between your legs, Nova girl?"

She flicks me in the forehead. "Don't distract me. Rules. Let's hear them."

I rub at the spot between my eyebrows. "I don't know. You're the one who brought up rules."

"Should we . . . not kiss?" Her whole face scrunches up, a little wrinkle between her eyebrows. "Is that too much?"

I snort. "You trying to *Pretty Woman* me, Nova?"

"What? No. I don't even know what that means."

I lean back in the chair. "Do you like to be kissed?" I ask.

She watches me, evaluating. Her tongue peeks out at the corner of her peach-pink lips and I shift my legs. Her gaze slips down my neck, taking inventory. It lingers on my shirt, the spot where I have two buttons undone. Heat rolls down my spine.

"Yeah," she says, her eyes snapping back to mine. "I like to be kissed."

"Then I'll be kissing you."

She nods. "Good."

"What else?" I ask. My restraint is a quickly fraying rope. I want to flip up her little black skirt and inspect the tops of her lacy thigh highs again. I want to know if her underwear matches. I want to see that rose between her breasts and uncover the rest of the art I know she's hiding. I want to trace it with my teeth and then my tongue. My hands too.

Her chest rises and falls with her breathing, her oversized sweater slipping down her shoulder until it catches in the crook of her elbow. I lean forward and hook two fingers into her collar, tugging down until I catch a glimpse of beige lace. I swallow and adjust her sweater so she's covered again.

"Your bra has butterflies on it," I say, my voice grim. I am completely and totally fucked.

She blinks at me, her eyes heavy. "It does."

"Little ones."

A smile curls the edge of her mouth. "Yep."

"What else, Nova?"

"What else . . . has butterflies?"

Christ. Now I'm imagining tiny butterflies on her underwear too. Maybe the tops of those thigh-high-tight-sock-things she's wearing. "No. What other rules do you want to discuss?"

"I don't know, the rules were for you."

I nod and drag my palm against my jaw. "Okay. Let's make it easy."

I stand and the chair tips over behind me. I plant both of my hands on the table by her hips and lean forward until my forehead is pressed to hers. She grabs my arms and the jar of peanut butter rolls off the table. After all of our half touches, this feels like jumping into the deep end. Swinging from the edge of a rope and flipping head over heels into crystal clear water.

I gently grab her face with my hand, holding her steady. I trace my thumb over her bottom lip. "I'll take care of you. You'll take care of me. We'll do what feels good, and if you get uncomfortable, you let me know. We don't need rules for that."

She nods and her nose brushes against mine. "Okay."

"Okay," I repeat. "I do want one thing though."

She smiles, her mouth a millimeter away from mine. "I want more than one thing."

A laugh slips out of me. Yeah, I do too. But I want this one thing more than I want all my fantasies combined. It's not worth it to me otherwise. "You'll talk to me tomorrow. You won't hide from me. I refuse to be a regret, Nova."

She leans back slightly, just far enough so that her eyes can peer up into mine. Understanding flashes there. "Of course I'll talk to you. We'll still be friends tomorrow. This is one night. We'll get it out of our systems and everything will go back to normal, yeah?"

Relief is a swift undercurrent to the anticipation making my skin feel hot. I slip my hands beneath her thighs and lift. She makes a cute little squeak and wraps herself around me.

"Good. Let's go."

10

NOVA

CHARLIE SCOOPS ME off the kitchen table like a stack of mail, both of his big hands under my thighs, squeezing just shy of too tight. His eyes dart between the hallway and the oversized sectional that takes up a majority of my living room, jaw clenched.

"Bedroom or couch?" he asks.

I shrug and sift my fingers through the hair at the back of his head, nails scratching. His big body tenses and then releases beneath me. The couch has its benefits—proximity being one—but I want room to move. I want to spread out against my buttery soft sheets and feel his weight tucking me down into my mattress.

"Bedroom," I answer, like he's not already moving in the direction of the stairs. He kicks off his boots at the bottom with enthusiasm, one hitting the edge of my couch, the other tipped sideways. But he doesn't care, too focused on powering us up the steps, the hands on my thighs shifting until he has my bare ass cupped in his palms, fingers squeezing every other step like he can't quite help himself.

"What kind of underwear are you wearing?" he grits out, sounding furious. His socked feet move faster up the stairs, and his fingers go searching until he finds the thin lace band at my hips. "Jesus Christ," he mutters.

I expected this part to feel weird. Something about being too familiar and knowing the details of him—like how he eats his breakfast pastries in three giant bites. Or how he color codes his spreadsheets at fifty percent opacity. I don't think I've ever known the spreadsheet preferences of a bedroom partner before.

But it's good. It feels good to be wrapped around him like a vine. Better than good when I feel the press of Charlie's hard cock between my thighs. He's thick and big and hitting me exactly right on every step up, and we haven't even started yet. I curl my hands around his shoulders for leverage and roll my hips, delighting in the way he stumbles up the last three stairs, almost dropping me completely.

He props me up against the wooden banister at the top and eyes the four closed doors like one is the gateway to Narnia and the others are a highway to hell. I lean forward and catch the tip of his ear with my teeth, the exact spot that flushes red every time I say something that shocks him.

He sucks in a sharp breath. "Which door, Nova?"

"Pick one and find out."

He makes a grumbling, groaning sound. I don't think I've ever seen him so out of sorts. His hands squeeze my ass again. "Now is not the time to be cute."

"Why? I'm having—oh."

Charlie drags me up his torso, one arm under my ass while his opposite hand cups gently around my jaw. He grips me there, and I get a glimpse of bright, burning blue before he yanks my mouth to his and kisses me.

It's to shut me up, I think, or to force me to make a decision. But it doesn't work because Charlie is kissing me like he can't wait another second for it. Like he's mad I've already kept him waiting this long. His mouth is hot and wet and lush and—usually it's slower than this. Kissing someone for the first time. It's a tease, a tentative give and take. I'm used to partners who slowly try to figure out what I like, and what they like, and how we can fit together.

Not Charlie. Charlie kisses me like he's had a plan on how to do it the entire time he's known me. He slots my bottom lip between his and sucks, catching it with his teeth and then soothing with his tongue. I open my mouth to his, and my hips punch forward for friction, my arm tossed over his shoulders, trying to pull him closer. We slide our tongues together like we can bicker like this too, starting out forceful but settling into something slow and thorough. A wet, obscene press of our mouths that has me moving against him as much as I can, desperate to ease the tension between my legs.

Charlie stumbles his way over to a wall and presses me there, the force of our impact stealing the air from my lungs. A painting tumbles to the floor. Another tilts precariously to the side.

Charlie ignores it. So do I.

The hand on my face shifts and his thumb finds my jaw, pressing until I open wider for him. He guides me exactly how he wants me, a pleased sound rumbling in his chest when I go pliant against him. His palm slips down my neck, fingers fanned out, his thumb resting gently against the frantic flutter of my pulse. He holds me there, his hand cupped against my throat, his touch devastatingly careful.

I want him to stop being careful.

"Nova," he pants into my mouth, his other hand fisting in the material of my skirt. "Tell me which one is your bedroom."

"Or what."

"Or I'll fuck you on your hallway floor."

There's a deep clench between my legs, a flood of electric heat down my spine. I drop my head back against the wall and grin. His hand flexes against my throat, his thumb gliding up and then down. "That's not the deterrent you think it is," I tell him.

"Nova."

I tug on the ends of his hair and drop a kiss to his mouth. His bottom lip is swollen and I bet mine is too. I don't think I've ever been kissed so thoroughly in my life. "Kiss me again, first. Just—real quick."

I can't stand the idea of not doing it again, immediately, over and over. Kissing Charlie has taken all the cluttered thoughts in my brain and tossed them to the wind. I'm nothing but sensation. Shades and colors and hot, liquid feelings.

He gives in to me, finding my mouth with his, the hand collared around my throat holding me still as we move together. I catch his bottom lip with my teeth and a pained sound echoes somewhere in his chest. I want to reduce him to cinders. I want us both boneless and stupid.

"You taste like cherries," he mumbles, nose digging into my cheek, mouth pressing sloppy, wet, distracted kisses along the line of my jaw. I tip my head up to give him more room, looping my legs tighter around his waist.

"And you taste like peanut butter," I breathe.

Peanut butter and dark chocolate. Whatever spiced cider he was drinking at the bookshop. I roll my hips into his, and he pushes back, friction exactly right for a half a heartbeat. Then he angles himself away and tugs me off the wall, my body clinging to his.

"Bedroom, Nova," he grunts again, just below my ear this time. "Which one?"

"Last on the left," I manage, voice airy and tight. I scratch my nails down his neck and his teeth bite at the curve of my shoulder.

He turns to the right instead and almost sends us both tumbling into a linen closet. I shriek and wrap both arms around his shoulders as pale blue hand towels and a bath mat shaped like a succulent tumble down around us. I think a box marked **CHRISTMAS DECORATIONS** lands on his foot.

"I said the left." I laugh, trying to direct him with my hands in his hair. We're an overeager pinball, pinging back and forth between light-up bumpers. Colors and sound and a high-pitched *ding, ding, ding* echoing in my ears.

"You have too many doors," he mutters, spinning and finally finding my bedroom, nudging his way through the door and kicking it shut with his foot. He tosses me on the bed, and a few pillows slip off the edge as I bounce, my hair half in my face. Charlie plants one knee on the mattress and climbs after me. Moonlight from the gap in my curtains illuminates the hunger in his eyes, the smooth cut of the muscles through his shirt.

"Nova," he says as he situates himself between my open knees, his palms braced on the bed by my head. One hand lifts to brush the rest of my hair off my face. "I don't know what to do with you like this."

"You don't know what to do with me?" I shimmy beneath him, spreading my legs wider to make room for him, my skirt inching up my thighs. The very tops of my tights are visible, a strip of black lace with dainty butterflies stitched overtop. "I find that hard to believe."

Charlie inhales a deep breath through his nose.

"I don't know what to do with you being so agreeable," he tells me. He shifts closer and lifts himself to his knees. His fingers catch the edge of my skirt and he lifts, his tongue appearing at the corner of his mouth. "I like this."

"What? The tights?"

He nods, then shakes his head, then nods again. "The tights, yeah, but I was talking about your art." His thumb traces the curve of the sun at my hip, its bright, golden rays shining down to a garden in bloom across the top of my thigh. The tights are an afterthought. I love that he called it my art and not my ink, because that's what I think of it too. All the things that swirl around in my heart painted across my skin.

"Oh. Thank you."

He huffs a laugh. "See? That's what I mean." His hand drifts to the other side of my skirt, lifting it until he can see the heavy storm cloud inked on my opposite thigh. A crescent moon peeking out from behind. "I don't think you've ever agreed with me on anything."

"Well—" I lose my train of thought, focused instead on the way he's inching my skirt even higher. He tucks it up until it's a black band around my waist, pretty beige underwear to match my pretty beige bra. Butterflies here too.

Charlie sighs like he's endured something.

"I like your butterflies," he says, voice rough.

"So you've said."

"Have I?" he asks, his eyes not moving away from the way the lace stretches over my skin. "It bears repeating."

I toy with the edge of my high-cut underwear. "They were very expensive."

"A worthwhile investment."

I grin up at him. "Thank you. I think so too."

He blinks down at me and his hand curls around my thigh, squeezing once. "Do you usually wear pretty underwear like this?"

I nod. "Yeah. Usually."

I like the way it makes me feel. I like putting on something just for myself. I like the dainty fabrics and the different colors. I like looking at myself in the mirror when I get dressed and seeing the lace draped over my intricate designs. It makes me feel powerful. It makes me feel strong.

Charlie makes a sound. "I'm going to have a hard time with that."

I glance at his pants and the thick, hard line of his cock pressing against his fly. "It looks like you're having a very hard time."

He ignores me, his grip abandoning my thigh for the hem of my sweater instead, slipping beneath to curl around the bottom of my rib cage. He squeezes once. "Knowing that you like to wear stuff like this underneath your clothes, thinking about it, wondering what it might look like—" He breathes in deep through his nose. "It'll be a miracle if I focus on anything else ever again."

I tip my chin. "Sorry for the inconvenience."

"I'm not," he replies without a lick of hesitation. His eyes flick to mine and hold. We stare at each other in the stillness of my bedroom, and I'm delighted by how easy this is, how good it feels, having

Charlie like this. A half smile tugs at one side of his mouth. I think he feels it too. "All right, Nova girl. How do you want me?"

I arch an eyebrow. "Do you need instruction?"

He shrugs and starts undoing the buttons of his shirt, fingers working nimbly against the light blue material. "I don't need it, but I like it. I'd like to hear you tell me what you want."

A surge of heat bursts like a rocket in the middle of my chest. I don't know if I've ever had a partner willingly hand over control before.

Charlie pulls off his shirt with a roll of his shoulders, his torso flexing as he tosses it to a far-off corner of my room. I sit up beneath him on my elbows so I can get a better look. I've always known he was strong. Those suits he wears are tailored perfectly to his body, hugging the curve of his biceps and the span of his shoulders. But his body is . . . it's something else, seeing it like this.

He's all smooth, unblemished skin. A dusting of dark hair in the middle of his chest down to his belly button. His belt is undone, his pants hanging low on his hips, a cut line of muscle angling in. I run my fingers there, back and forth—until he tips his head back and grunts up at the ceiling, his throat working in a heavy swallow.

"What if I just wanted you to watch?" I sit up farther to drop a kiss to the center of his chest, then rest my chin there, staring up at him. He drops his head back to look at me. "Would that be okay?"

His eyes flash. Lightning in a storm. "That would be very okay." He scoops all of my hair up in his hand and then releases it, watching the strands fall over his fingers. "Is that what you want? Do you wanna show me how you like it first?"

The idea has its merits. I'd love to test all that meticulous control of his. But I think I want something else more.

I tap his thigh and slip from the bed, pointing at the headboard until he follows my wordless command with a gruff chuckle. He crawls his way up there, hair a ridiculous mess, shoulders flexing. He collapses into my pillows, legs sprawled, looking like every indecent thought I've ever had. He flicks open the top button of his pants and tucks his arm behind his head.

"This is more in line with what I expected," he says.

"What?" I shimmy out of my skirt and toss it in the same direction as his shirt.

"You, bossing me around." He watches with interest as my hands curl in the hem of my sweater. I tug it over my head.

"Glad I could meet your expectations." I prop one foot up on the edge of the bed and reach for the top of my tights. Charlie sits up.

"Don't," he says.

My hands still. "Don't, what?"

He drags his hand down his jaw, palm working at the scruff he's started sporting since he started farm life. I like it. It suits him.

I want to feel it between my legs.

"Leave the tights on," he says, voice low. His eyes dance their way up my body until they hold mine. "Please," he adds.

"So polite." I leave them where they are and crawl back on the bed. Charlie watches me move up his body. He curls his hands around my hips when I finally settle in his lap, thumbs tracing indistinct shapes against my waist. I peck a kiss on his waiting lips. "Such a good boy."

Charlie makes a low rumbling sound, the hands on my hips clenching tighter. "Nova. You need to tell me what you want."

My lips brush over his again. "Or what?"

"I don't know," he breathes against me, eyes shut tight. I like this unraveled version of Charlie so very much. "I didn't really think through the second part of that statement."

"How about this?" I wrap my fingers around his wrists and guide his hands up to my breasts. I place them there, over my lace bra. He peeks open one eye, and then the other. I smile at him. "Because you like my rose."

"I love your rose," he tells me. "I might love these more though."

He squeezes my breasts, testing their weight, his thumbs rubbing circles over my nipples through the material of my bra. My back arches and he drops his mouth to my neck. "That silver dress almost killed me, Nova."

I laugh and shift in his lap, chasing the friction. There's an ache low in my belly. A thrumming right beneath my skin. "You already know how I feel about the suspenders."

"Should I have brought them?"

Maybe next time, I almost say, but I bite the words back. There won't be a next time. There will be only this time. Just once, to get it out of our systems. Then we can go back to spreadsheets and taxes and meaningless flirtations over cider while Montgomery and Gus bicker about pumpkin displays.

But I don't want to think about that now. I only want to think about Charlie's fingers urging the strap of my bra over my shoulder, carefully peeling the lace cup down until there's nothing between his mouth and my skin. He presses a kiss to the rose between my breasts, licks a hot stripe across it, and then pulls my nipple into his mouth. My body shivers and my hips press down, the zipper of his half-open pants biting into the soft skin of my thighs.

"Charlie," I whisper.

He doesn't bother pulling down my bra on the other side, just catches my nipple with his teeth through the gossamer material. Impatient. I grind down on him, hips circling.

"I don't think you need direction," I say, sounding winded. My room is silent except for the wet sounds of his mouth, my panting breaths, the soft swish of my thigh highs against the comforter as I try to climb higher on his lap. I want to give him more of me. I want his big body to spread my thighs wider. Charlie helps, his mouth still working at my breast while his hand guides my hips in a smooth rhythm.

"Take off your pants," I breathe out, hand slipping in his open fly. I curl my hand around him as best I can with the angle and his entire body goes rigid before melting into smooth, languid lines. He watches me with heavy eyes as I stroke him once. Twice.

"It's hard to take off my pants when you're doing that."

"Do you want me to stop?"

He presses his hips into my touch. "I didn't say that."

I could watch him like this forever, I decide. Chest heaving, hair sticking up every which way. Cheeks flushed pink and his hands clenched into fists on top of my thighs. He moves with me, body chasing mine when I pull away, relaxing back into the pillows when I squeeze.

I rub my thumb over the tip of his cock and his body jolts. He tips his head back into the pillows, eyes closed. His eyelashes are a dark fan against the slope of his cheekbones. If I were painting him, he'd be streaks of purple in the muted moonlight. Loops of lavender in between.

"No more teasing," he says from between clenched teeth.

I give him another long stroke with my hand. "I believe it's called foreplay, Charlie."

His eyes blink open, and he leverages himself up beneath me until I'm flipped back, a squeak of surprise that I'm not entirely proud of tossed over his shoulder. He grips my thigh and tugs it wide, his hips slotting in between. He grinds against me and I grasp at his shoulder blades.

I feel the rumble of his chuckle against my breasts, his breath a hot puff against my neck. He leans up and sucks a kiss right below my ear, sending shockwaves all the way down to the place between my thighs where he's hard and heavy against me.

He props himself above me with the palms of his hands, arms flexing, his forehead pressed to mine, face angled down so he can watch our bodies move together. I look too, a moan caught in the back of my throat when I see the way his body looks pressing mine down into the mattress. The way my knees hug his hips, my skin flushed. All my ink pressed up against his pale, smooth skin.

"I can't wait to watch how you take me, Nova." He rolls his hips against mine, his cock hitting just right. I could come like this and he knows it. His smile is all predator, his easy charm replaced with something else. Something a little darker. Desperate. He leans forward and drops his mouth to mine.

"No more teasing. It's my turn now."

11

CHARLIE

THERE'S A PAINTING on the second floor of the Metropolitan Museum of Art, back in the corner of the twentieth-century European section. A woman brushing her hair. Pale pink flowers exploding from the window behind her, and her golden waves draped over her shoulder.

Nova looks exactly like that painting as she moves beneath me, her hair loose, flowers on her skin instead of the sheets behind her. Pleasure makes her light up like a solar flare, her body rocking against mine eagerly.

"Where do you need me?" I ask her, my voice rumbling out of me in a rough growl. I press my palm to her hip and let my thumb trail beneath her belly button to the heat between her legs. "Do you need me right here? Hmm?"

I can't believe I get to see her like this. Bra twisted beneath her breasts and those damn sock/tight things slipping down her thighs. I want to take off her clothes until she's nothing but bare skin and delicate ink. I want to leave everything exactly where it is.

I want too much, all at once.

"I thought you said no more teasing," she breathes into my ear, the rasp in her voice making everything inside me pull tight. Christ, I can usually hold myself together better than this.

Not with Nova, apparently.

"It's called foreplay," I tell her with a laugh, my hips still grinding against hers. We've barely touched and it's already the best sex of my life. I'm honestly afraid of what might happen if I take my pants off.

She lets out a low sigh and her eyelashes flutter against her cheeks. She moves against me harder, her leg curling around my thigh. I nip at her jaw. "You gonna come for me, Nova girl? So soon?"

"Don't sound smug."

I'm not smug, I'm captivated. She blinks open heavy eyes and watches me move over her.

"Put your mouth back on me?" She threads her fingers through my hair and guides me to her chest. I go very willingly, nuzzling at the rose on her sternum before dragging my jaw against her breast. I pinch her nipple between two knuckles and she makes a gasping sound.

"God," she breathes. "That's—um. That's very good."

I make a half-moon with my teeth just below her rosy nipple. I like leaving my mark next to all the others. Her back arches up. I grin. "Are you going to thank me for it?"

She smiles, tilting her head against the bed. We've somehow managed to flip ourselves so we're almost hanging off the bottom, our legs up by the pillows. We're impatient, grasping for one other. Shifting and rolling and tugging at whatever clothes are left. I brace one of my socked feet on the floor so I can drive into her harder, moving above her like we're already fucking.

Her hands slip from my shoulder blades to my biceps, gripping me there. "You'd like that, wouldn't you?"

I laugh and reach under her for the clasp of her bra, frustrated with the twisted lace. It gives and I fling it over my shoulder. "I like everything you do, Nova."

Her face softens at that, a pleased little smile that's completely at odds with that flushed and panting picture she makes beneath me. I slip my hand back between us to the front of her underwear, and her smile tumbles into a rough laugh.

"Thank you, Charlie," she breathes right against my ear. She tips her legs open wider, and I nudge her underwear to the side, touching where she's warm and wet. I make an embarrassing noise when I feel her, but I don't care. It's Nova. She's already seen me moonwalk in a reindeer costume at the tree farm during the holiday season. I'm not trying to impress her.

I'm just trying to make her come.

"You're so wet. Is all of this for me?"

She hums, eyes closed, hips moving into my touch. "I'm thinking about John Stamos."

I grin. "He must be doing it for you, then."

Nova's eyes blink open, gazing up at me. "Yeah," she breathes. She reaches down and curls her hand around my wrist, urging my hand harder against her. Her hips rock into me, controlling me from below. Taking her own pleasure.

It's hot as fuck.

"Yeah, he's doing it for me."

I slip two fingers into her and she sinks her teeth into her bottom lip. I rub my thumb at her clit, rough circles that have her shutting her eyes again.

"Nuh-uh." I move my thumb away and she whimpers. "Eyes, please."

She lets go of my arms, dropping hers above her head and gripping the bottom edge of her bed frame. Her fingers flex around the metal. I reward her with my thumb back where she wants it.

"Who would have thought—" Her breath catches when I change the tempo of my strokes, little taps that have her feet scrambling against the bed. "God. Who would have thought you'd be so bossy?"

"Not bossy," I mumble, watching the pink that blooms on her cheeks slip down her neck to the curve of her breasts. Her red rose looks like it's glowing. "I just want to watch you come."

She nods. "Okay."

"Okay." I shift down onto my elbow above her, hovering with my mouth over hers. Her whole body is trembling beneath mine. "Do you think you're close?"

I drop a chaste kiss to her bottom lip and move my hand faster against her. Another finger. More sloppy circles. She doesn't answer with words, just a sharp inhale through her nose.

"Yeah." I smile. "Yeah, you're close."

"Again with the"—she moans—"smug. It doesn't suit you, Charlie."

"Sure it does." I drop a kiss to the corner of her mouth, the curve of her chin, the secret little spot I've discovered below her ear. "I want it so bad, Nova. Probably more than you do."

She laughs, fingers curling tighter around the edge of her bed frame. Her knuckles strain white. "I don't know about all that," she moans. "I want it pretty bad."

I nod into her neck. "I can feel it," I whisper. "I can feel you. You gonna take it?"

She grabs the back of my neck and pulls. My body goes tight like she's got that hand on my dick instead. She tips her chin up and watches me with half-closed eyes, a flash of blue-green gray. Storm clouds gathering.

"You gonna give it to me?" she breathes, her lips curled in a smile.

"I've already told you. I'll give you anything you want."

I keep my hand steady against her, the other shifting up to sink into her hair spread across the comforter. She liked that earlier, when I tugged on her hair while we kissed. I loop it around my fist and urge her face closer to mine.

"You need me to put my mouth on you again?" I suck a wet kiss beneath her ear. "Want me to get on my knees?"

She laughs, something winded. "I think I'd like you on your knees."

I nod. "Yeah, I bet you would. I'd pull you right to the edge of the bed so you could watch. Keep you close so I could still touch these pretty tits." I drag my teeth up her neck and bite the lobe of her ear. "Come on, Nova girl. Tell me what you need."

She doesn't need me on my knees. She doesn't need anything but a rough roll of my thumb against her clit and my words in her ear, listing out all the things I want to do to her. All the fantasies that I've stocked up in my chaotic brain, tumbling free in rough pants against her ear.

She comes with a whimper of my name, hands curled into fists and her face tucked to the side. I nudge her back to me with my knuckles at her chin, watching her crest and break.

"No," I say quietly. "Keep looking at me."

She moans as she trembles through the rest of it, her gaze fixed on mine. She's beautiful. More than that. If I had the right words, I'd use them.

"Get a condom," she orders me, flinging one limp hand in the direction of her nightstand. I practically fall off the bed following her direction, yanking the drawer completely out. A notebook and a couple of pens spill out across the floor. A box of tissues and a strip of condoms.

I grab for it and fling them on the bed.

"That seems ambitious," she tells me, still blissed out and boneless across the edge of the bed. Her pretty underwear is twisted around her hips, one of her thigh highs scrunched below her knee. Messy hair and a hickey on her neck. I want to take a picture of her just like this and keep it in my wallet. Maybe blow it up and wallpaper my entire apartment with it.

"You said one night," I say, crawling back to her. I grip her ankle and tug until she's beneath me. "You didn't say one time."

Her eyes light up, delighted. "I guess that's true."

I grunt as I attempt to shimmy out of my pants without getting out of the bed. Her hands try to help, then get distracted and slip into my boxer briefs instead. I drop my forehead to her collarbone when she grips my cock. "Nova, I'm barely hanging on here."

"I know. I like it."

I move my hips into her touch for all of thirty seconds before it feels like too much. "Okay. Okay okay okay. Give me a second."

I tumble my way off the bed again, an absolute mess, and kick my way out of my pants. I slip off my briefs and turn back to her. Nova is watching with her knees tucked to her chest, her underwear on the floor, her hair pulled over one shoulder. She's lazy in her perusal of me, taking her time, holding me where I stand with her eyes.

"You're, ah—" Her eyes flick back to mine and hold. She swallows. "You look good," she finally says.

"Effusive praise." I laugh. Her tongue skirts her bottom lip as I walk over to the bed, the tightness between my legs almost unbearable. This will probably last all of twenty-six seconds. I want her so badly I'm vibrating with it, all the way down to my bones.

I loop my hands around her ankles and then make sweeping brushes of my palms against her calves. I can't get over her in these tights. I don't think I ever will. "How would you like me?"

"Back to this, huh?"

I nod. Yes, back to this. I want to do exactly what she wants. I want to be everything she needs. Fuck getting out of her system. I want to be so far in her system I'm all she ever thinks about.

"It worked out so well the last time," I manage.

"Up here, then." She points at the headboard. One edge of her fitted sheet has come off. All her pillows are on the floor. I follow her direction and sit with my back against the black wrought iron frame. She shifts up on her knees and follows me.

I grab her hips in my hands, hissing through my teeth when she perches herself just below my cock.

"Hello," she says, like we're out at a picnic and I'm not a second away from spilling all over her stomach.

"Hi," I grit out. I grab for one of the condoms, but she plucks it out of my hand before I can roll it on. She tears the wrapper with her teeth, then glides it over me with her palm. I think I might die. I tilt my head back and watch her with hazy, unfocused eyes. I can't decide what I want to watch. Her hand around my cock or her inked thighs flush against my hips. The flutter of her pulse in her neck or the bare swell of her breasts, pink nipples a tease through the cascade of her blond hair.

I settle for those blue-green eyes, narrowed in amusement as her hand works me. I think she likes watching me suffer.

I know she does.

"How are you doing?" I ask, attempting to hold on to the thread of conversation.

She snickers. "About to be better." She gives me another pump with her hand, then lifts herself on her knees. I grip the slippery material of the tights on her left thigh like I'm holding on for dear life. "How are you doing?" she asks with a tip of her chin.

"I'm—" The rest of my answer disappears as she sinks down, taking me inch by inch. She rocks her hips back and forth slowly, a deep exhale with every slow, sinuous movement. She has to stop halfway, her breathing harsh and her hands trembling.

It's a relief that she feels it too. This . . . overwhelming . . . everything.

"You can take it," I murmur. My chest is heaving and my fingertips are pressing bruises into her skin. She presses down another half inch. "There you go. You're doing so good."

She makes a sound. A huff or a laugh or a moan or a combination of all three. I can't really tell. "*You're* doing so good," she says back. Her fingertips trace shapes against my chest and she swivels her hips. "So patient."

"Not really." I laugh. I toss my head back and grip her ass in my hands when she nudges the rest of the way down, her hips flush to mine. I think about obscure tax forms. Deposit minimums. The return rate on that one stock I've been monitoring for two weeks.

I'm close already and all she's done is let herself sink down on me.

"Charlie," she whimpers, and something in my chest breaks off. I can't get a deep enough breath. "Charlie," she says again.

"I know," I groan. I squeeze her ass and move her over me. Fuck. She feels incredible. My body is a lightning storm of sensation. Electric bolts of pleasure between my legs and in the backs of my knees and at the base of my spine. "Fuck, Nova."

She nods and curls her fingers around my jaw. She tugs my face to hers.

"Kiss," she slurs. "Kiss me while I fuck you."

I nod. "Yeah, okay. Good. That's good."

I catch her mouth with mine as she starts to move, a gentle back and forth that somehow manages to wind me up even higher. My hands itch with the need to take. To push until we're both mindless with the pleasure spinning cobwebs around us. But I like that she's taking what she wants from me. Getting exactly what she needs from my body beneath hers.

"It's good," she tells me. "You feel good."

"You feel better," I mumble somewhere in her neck. I wrap my arm around her and drag my palm up her spine, anchor my fist in her hair and tug her head back until I can get more of her under my mouth. I trace the stars inked behind her ear with my tongue and her hips grind harder. "Can you go faster, Nova girl? I'm losing my mind."

"No," she says simply. She drops her head to the side and her hair tickles my thighs. She sighs so prettily, I'm suddenly right at the edge. "I want you to come like this. Nice and slow."

I push my hips into hers. "Inside you?" I grit out. Just the thought of it has everything curling tighter.

She hums. "Mm-hmm."

"Are you close?"

The ghost of a smile slips across her lips. "Yeah. Yeah, I really am."

I push up with my hips while she grinds down, a smooth, rolling pressure that builds and builds and builds. I shift farther down the mattress and prop my knees up behind her so she can lean back, thumbing at the place between her legs when she does. I stare hard at the rose between her breasts. The light sheen of sweat on her skin and the way her chest bounces with every smooth movement.

She shivers and I grin. "John Stamos again?"

She presses her palms flat to my clenching abdomen and chases my touch, grinding harder but keeping that same slow, deep rhythm. "He's really good with his hands," she gasps.

I laugh and then groan at a particularly rough roll of her hips. My thumb works faster against her. Everything feels like it's glowing iridescent, starlight dancing at the corners of my eyes. "You gonna come for me again, pretty girl?"

She nods and leans forward, trapping my hand between us until all I can do is nudge her gently with my knuckles. I cup my other hand around the back of her neck and hold her close. I want her mouth on mine when she comes. I want to feel the tremble that starts in her legs and rolls all the way up.

"After you come for me," she says, and then she kisses me, a messy biting thing that has me groaning into her mouth. Desperation fuels me, the edge suddenly looming before me, my orgasm within reach. I hold her still with my hand at her neck and move her the way I need, triggering my orgasm in three rough jerks, a cascade of golden sparks. I grunt into it, a breathless, wordless exaltation of her name as I spin out of orbit.

When I manage to scrape the pieces of myself back together, Nova is still draped above me, little restless swivels of her hips against mine. She hums, pleased, when I shift my hand, fingertips rubbing. I touch her carefully until her legs are shaking at my hips, my body still inside of hers. That delicious, perfect tremble clutching tight.

"Like this?"

She nods, nose digging into my cheek, her mouth open against my jaw. Her teeth scrape and her hands curl into fists against my shoulders. "Almost there."

"That's it." I brush a kiss to the corner of her mouth and she moans. Goose bumps pebble her skin and I smile. "C'mon, let's see it."

Her eyes narrow and she comes with a sharp inhale, her nose digging into my collarbone. Her hands clutch at whatever piece of me she can reach, and I cling to her just as tightly.

We lie there together afterward, sprawled across the middle of her bed. One of my legs is numb. Nova's right arm is hanging completely off the mattress. Another corner of the fitted sheet pops up, and I think I left the bag of marshmallows open on the table downstairs. I blink up at the ceiling. I have no idea what to do with myself. I have no idea if my body is still in one piece.

"I've got bad news, Nova."

I deliver it in staccato bits. I can't figure out how to catch my breath.

She lifts her face from my neck and rests her chin on my chest. Her cheeks are pink and some of her hair is stuck to her jaw. "What's that?"

"I'm not sure that worked anything out of my system."

"Oh?" She lifts herself off me and slips to the bed at my side, one hand propped beneath her head. I match her position and trace the flowers on her thigh with my fingertip, all the way over her hip and back down again. "Should I be a little bit mean? See if it helps?"

I shrug. "Might as well try it."

"That was the best you've got?" She snaps, voice sharp. "If I wanted a mediocre lay, I would have picked someone up at Applebee's."

I groan and flop back on the bed, my arm thrown over my eyes. My cock gives an eager twitch against my thigh.

Nova bursts out laughing.

"It didn't work," I mutter, peering at her from behind my bicep. "In fact, I think it's worse now."

She curls up with a pillow. "Does Applebee's still exist?"

"I don't know. You're the one hanging around them, looking for prospects."

"Prospects," she snorts. "I'm not trolling through the streets, Charlie."

"Thank god for me, you're just trolling through tree fields." I press a quick kiss to her shoulder, think about it, then lean forward again and drop a wet kiss to her neck. She squeals and rolls, and I follow her across the bed. I catch her mouth with mine and she laughs into me, hands clutching my back. We kiss for a long, languid stretch of time, her foot rubbing up and down the side of my leg and my fingers tangled in her hair. It's probably how we should have started all of this, if I contained even an ounce of patience.

"What were you saying about one night, not one time?" she asks quietly.

I lean up on my elbows above her, then glance over my shoulder at the bottom of the bed. There are six condoms left.

"I need another snack first." I drop a quick kiss to her mouth, then push out of the tangled sheets. I need carbohydrates. Electrolytes. Maybe an espresso from the fancy machine on her countertop. If I only get one night with Nova Porter, I'm going to make it fucking count. "Be right back."

I get rid of the condom in a wad of tissues and grab my boxers off the floor. Nova watches me from the bed, limbs loose and tangled in the sheets. Curved halfway on her side, I can see a peony blooming across her rib cage, the same petals as the ones drifting across her shoulder blades. She nuzzles farther into her nest of sheets, some of her hair falling across those gemstone eyes.

I stop and stare, and then stare some more.

"Bring back the fudge stripe cookies that are in the cabinet," she orders.

I shake myself out of my stupor and give her a tiny salute. "Yes, ma'am."

I'm halfway down the hallway when she shouts, "The peanut butter too!"

12

NOVA

I WAKE UP to Charlie sitting shirtless at the edge of my bed.

His pants are undone and low around his hips, a cup of coffee in his left hand. It's a good look.

Unfortunately, it is also way too early.

"What time is it?" I slur. The room is still dark and my body feels like it was hit by a Mack truck. I am sore in places I didn't even know I had. "Didn't we fall asleep like twenty minutes ago?"

I usually don't let casual sex partners spend the night, but Charlie passed out immediately after our last round, face down on my mattress with his arm flung over my waist. He looked so peaceful, and he didn't wake up when I dug my finger into his rib cage, so I allowed it.

"Close," he replies, voice low and raspy. It's the same way he sounded last night when he had his mouth at my throat, asking me if I wanted to come. Fabric rustles and the weight by my legs shifts. "It's early."

I squint open one eye in interest and watch as he attempts to button his shirt. It's horribly wrinkled, and he's missing one in the middle, but he endeavors. I stare at the inch of bare chest I can just barely make out in the predawn light, legs shifting beneath my mountain of blankets when I see the hickey at the base of his throat. There's an entire line of them all the way down his torso, two right at his hip. He had sunk both of his hands into my hair and watched me with his jaw clenched tight when I put them there, his entire body trembling beneath my touch.

Then I put my mouth on his cock, and he bit out my name like a curse.

Last night was . . . good. I am immensely proud of myself for the idea.

"I'm heading out." He finishes with his shirt and drags his hand through his hair, a massive yawn tipping his jaw open wide. His body slumps and he rubs his palm over his chest. "But I didn't want to leave without saying goodbye."

"Bye," I mumble, wiggling farther down in the blankets. I don't remember putting the blue knit quilt on the bed last night. I don't remember grabbing the pillows either. But I am sufficiently tucked in, everything just where I like it.

He huffs a laugh. "It's like that, huh?"

I grin into my pillow. "Help yourself to some coffee."

"Already made some," he says, voice still rough at the edges. "I'm taking a cup."

"That's fine."

"It's my souvenir glass."

I snicker into my pillow. "Bring it to the shop later and I'll etch it for you. 'Nova Porter rocked my world.'"

He laughs again, louder this time, a rumble in the stillness of my bedroom. He leans forward and slaps my ass through the blankets. "Hell yeah, she did. Maybe that's the tattoo I'll get."

His hand settles on the curve between my thigh and my ass, thumb rubbing back and forth as he yawns again. Everything is muted in the way early morning quiet always seems to be, geese squawking outside my window and the rickety creek of the iron gate on the side of my house that never quite latches right. The floorboards groan and my legs swish beneath the blankets, bare now, my thigh highs draped over the edge of the bed like an ad for debauchery.

"How are you getting back to the farm?" I ask, half into my

pillow. I imagine Charlie trudging his way down the side of the long dirt road that leads to Lovelight, shirt unbuttoned and my mug of coffee in his hand. A very long walk of shame. "I can drive you if you need me to," I offer.

"No, no." He squeezes my leg. "I left my car at the bookstore last night. I'm gonna head over there now and drive back. Should be early enough."

"Early enough for what?" I frown at him, but he's busy looking for something underneath my bed. He emerges with his belt clutched in his hand, some of his dark hair sticking straight up on the left side. It's unfairly adorable for a man who made my legs shake so bad I could hardly shuffle to the bathroom last night.

"To avoid your brother," he explains. "He starts his work around five."

"Oh."

Charlie watches me as he threads his belt through the loops. "I figured you wouldn't want anyone to know," he says.

I shrug and shift beneath my blankets again, everything fuzzy and far away.

"That's fine. Whatever you want." I can keep a secret. But I've lost the will to hold on to this conversation. I'm exhausted. Bone weary. My eyes slip shut, already drifting again between asleep and awake. I listen as he moves around the room, collecting his things from the chaos we created last night. Socked feet against the floor. The metallic clink of his wristwatch. The gentle thud of the coffee mug against my dresser and a poorly muffled curse when he stubs his toe on the edge of it.

It's a nice soundtrack. It doesn't give me the itch that usually blossoms bright with someone in my space. I just feel . . . content, I guess.

Sleepy.

"Key's under the mat," I slur, words heavy. I'm going to sleep for ages. "Lock up when you go."

Warm lips brush against my forehead, fingertips chasing. My hair is tucked behind my ear and knuckles nudge once at my cheek. "You got it, Nova girl."

And then I'm asleep.

"YOU'RE FREAKING ME out."

"Why?"

"Your face," Nessa says immediately. "It's doing something."

"What is it doing?"

"I don't know. This dreamy, stare-off-into-space thing." She drapes herself against the tattoo chair she's claimed as her own and contorts her face into something ridiculous. "Like that. You've smiled more this morning than that time Dad made four different types of pierogies for dinner."

"Fuck, I love pierogies."

"I know!" Nessa points at me furiously like I've just confirmed something. "Which is why you're freaking me out."

Charlie left a Post-it note on my coffee pot before he left this morning, a scribbled "Thanks for blowing my mind" with a smiley face that had me grinning into my mug, robe wrapped tight around my middle. I found my key in the middle of the hallway floor too, another note scribbled on the back of a receipt from Ms. Beatrice's that he must have found in his pocket. This one said, "Stop leaving your key under your mat" with a frowny face. I guess he shoved it through the mail slot on my front door after locking up.

"I'm just having a good day," I tell my sister. The marathon sex session last night certainly helped. My body feels boneless in the very best of ways, a pinching ache every time I sit. Probably from the last time, when Charlie bent me over the side of my bed and fucked me so hard I thought we might break the frame.

I press my palm to my cheek and glance over the top of my laptop. Thankfully Nessa is occupied by her phone. When I showed up to the studio this morning, she was waiting out front, sitting on the step. She said she needed something to do, and I said she could organize the tattoo stations.

Not that she's doing that currently.

"Everything okay?" I ask.

She blows out a heavy breath and tosses her phone to the side. "Can I set you up with someone?"

"What?" I laugh. "Why?"

She tilts her head. "Because I need something to do."

"Then organize the stations like I asked you to."

"I need something better to do. Come on, Nova. Please? My life is falling apart, and this would make me happy. I promise not to set you up with a loser."

"Your life is not falling apart," I murmur. I scroll through my email without seeing a single thing. "And I told you. I don't have time for a relationship right now."

I'm stretched thin enough. I cannot make myself available for another human being. Relationships require work, time, and emotional availability. I am equipped for exactly none of those things at this point in my life.

The casual sex I had last night is all the intimacy I need.

I think of Charlie with his hand between my legs, and my entire body flushes hot.

"Fine," she pouts. "Can I have a tattoo, then?"

I'm getting whiplash from this conversation. Nessa has never once expressed an interest in having a tattoo. "Of what?"

"Maybe some ballet slippers?" She traces two fingers along the inside of her arm. "Right here?"

I close my laptop with a frown. "You're serious?"

She nods, eyes misty. "There were strict regulations about tattoos in competition, but I figure I'm not competing anymore. And everyone else in the family has your work. It's about time I do too."

"Ness." I wander my way over to her and nudge her with my hip.

I collapse on the tattoo table next to her and hope to god it holds us both up. I can't afford a new one. "Did you make a decision?"

She nods and wipes her hand under her eyes. "Yeah. I formally dropped out of the competition circuit. I don't even know why I'm crying. I've been thinking about it for a while."

I prop my chin against her shoulder. "Because it's a big change. And Nathan kind of forced your hand."

She sighs. "Nathan sucks."

"Yes, he does."

"I'll probably let you key his car."

"Excellent. I'll let Beckett know. He had some ideas."

Vanessa shifts to look at me. "You told Beckett?"

"It may have been discussed in the sibling chat."

"The sibling chat?" She narrows her eyes at me. "Is there a sibling chat I'm not a part of?"

There are multiple sibling chats with rotating members depending on who we're talking about. I'm sure there's a sibling chat that I'm not a part of.

"I'll give you a tattoo," I deflect. "But it can't be today."

Nessa frowns. "Why not?"

"Because I want to think about what I'm going to draw, and I want you to think about it for more than ten seconds."

"Did Beckett think about any of his for longer than ten seconds?"

"No." But I'm older and wiser now, and I'm trying not to depend on my siblings for things. Beckett invested a lot in me when I was younger, more than I deserved. I'm not going to make that mistake again. "I also have someone coming in for an interview in the next fifteen minutes."

"Oh. That's fair. I guess you don't want my bare ass on your table when someone walks in."

"Bare ass? I thought you said you wanted it on your arm."

"It's a developing situation."

I leverage myself up and off the chair. Nessa stays sprawled across it.

"Apparently." I laugh.

My laptop pings from the table with an incoming email. I rub my palm across my forehead when it pings another two times, rapid fire.

"That sounds urgent," Nessa calls.

I keep rubbing my forehead, ignoring the fuzzy spots at the edge of my vision. Lack of sleep and too much caffeine are pressure points for my migraines, but I took some of my medication before I left the house, and I'm chugging water like it's my job. It should be enough to keep me functioning.

"Everything is," I sigh. Everything is urgent. Everything is required. I'm still waiting on a couple boxes of supplies. I need to hire at least one person to manage administrative needs, and ideally, I'd like to hire another artist to take overflow clients. I need to finish doing the setup for the soft launch private party in a couple of weeks, and I need to figure out how to hang the damn sign in the back.

I crack open my laptop and hold my breath, certain I'm about to be reminded about something else I forgot. But it's just an email from Charlie.

I click into it, ominously titled **THE PLAN**.

It's a blank email with a spreadsheet attached. Color coded, of course, with all the businesses in town. I frown at it and fish out my phone.

> NOVA: Did you mean to send me this attachment?

> CHARLIE: Course I did. I told you I'd help with the business visits. Selene helped me with the color coding. Isn't it nice?

> NOVA: Selene?

> CHARLIE: She's my assistant.

> CHARLIE: At work. I swear I've mentioned her before.

He sends a string of emojis, three little yellow faces with smirking mouths.

> CHARLIE: Why? Are you jealous, Nova girl?

I scoff.

> NOVA: Hard to be jealous when I can still feel you
> every time I sit down, Charlie.

> CHARLIE: Fuck.

> CHARLIE: Fuck.

> CHARLIE: Nova, you can't say things like that. Your
> brother is going to wonder why I have a boner while
> he's talking about fertilizer.

> NOVA: 😈

"You're making that face again," Nessa offers from her chair. I slip my phone into my back pocket and try to rearrange my face into something that isn't . . . whatever it's doing. "And I think your interview candidate is here."

I turn to look over my shoulder. Jeremy Roughman, recent Inglewild high school graduate and probably the most irritating teenager on the planet, is standing in front of my locked door. He's wearing a full suit, briefcase in one hand, and his usually messy blond hair is combed back with what looks like industrial grade gel. He looks like a car salesman, or a . . . beleaguered divorcee.

"No," I whisper.

Vanessa snickers. "Yes. Did he catfish you?"

He definitely didn't put his legal name on his résumé, that's for sure. He does not look like Megan Culver, Salisbury 2012 graduate, with extensive experience in customer service. "Maybe I got the résumés mixed up."

Jeremy knocks again. I don't know why. He can see right through the glass door to the both of us, staring at him. He gives a little wave.

Vanessa waves back.

I sigh.

"What am I supposed to do?"

"Let him in, probably."

I shuffle my way over to the door and inch it open. "Jeremy."

He clears his throat. "Ms. Porter."

I frown at him. He's never called me that in his life. "What can I do for you? Are you selling bibles?"

"No." He thinks about it for a second. "Would you want one if I was?"

A smile twitches at my lips. "No, I don't think so."

"Cool. Okay. Well." He adjusts the sleeves of his suit. It's cut too small, his long arms poking out from beneath the cuffs. I also think the T-shirt he's wearing beneath his button-down has a mermaid on it. Or something . . . mermaid adjacent. Jeremy tips his chin up. "I'm here for an interview."

I lean my hip against the doorway. "Did you fake your résumé, Jeremy?"

"What? No! I haven't even given you my résumé yet." He pops open his briefcase and a store-bought bag of pens, a newspaper from three days ago, and a roll of Life Savers tumble to the ground. He ignores all of it and pulls out a sheet of paper. "Here we go."

I take it from him, but don't look at it. "How'd you know I had an interview scheduled this morning?"

He shrugs.

"Jeremy."

"Yes?"

"How did you know?"

"Luck," he offers, his voice a shade too innocent. "Perhaps the stars aligned?"

Vanessa snickers from somewhere behind me. I sigh. "Jeremy."

"Fine! I saw her at the café, okay? Your candidate, or whatever. She was getting a latte from Ms. Beatrice and asked for directions to the tattoo studio. She said she was here for an interview."

"And where is she now?"

He scratches behind his ear, a blush coloring his cheeks. "She had to leave."

"Why?"

"Because I told her the interview was canceled."

Vanessa guffaws. I'm glad one of us finds this amusing.

"Jeremy." I sigh. "Why did you tell her the interview was canceled?"

"Because I need a job."

"Aren't you working at Ms. Beatrice's place?"

My entire life, the cantankerous Ms. Beatrice has owned the café on the corner of Main Street. She specializes in coffee drinks that are, frankly, life-changing. But you have to endure her surly attitude to snag one. She has also never deigned to name the place. Most people either call it Ms. Beatrice's or the café. I think someone tried to put a sign up once, and she had it ripped down by the next morning. The green-striped awning over the doorway still hasn't recovered.

"I need a career," Jeremy emphasizes. He shifts his feet, scratches at the back of his neck, and fiddles with the handle of his briefcase. "Also, unrelated, but she fired me."

"For what?"

"For something I don't want to discuss with a prospective employer," he rushes out.

I tap his résumé against the palm of my hand. "Were you caught in the alley making out with one of the customers again?"

His cheeks flame pink. "It was one time," he mumbles.

It was three times, and it was discussed at length during a town meeting. It also made the printed version of the phone tree newsletter. I stare at Jeremy. "Did you do something weird to the coffee?"

I hope not. I'll never recover. I get lattes from the café three days a week.

He sighs and rolls his eyes to the sky. "I was giving out free drinks to people."

"How many people?"

"A lot of people." He scratches his finger behind his ear. "I might have been . . . writing my phone number on take-out cups."

"Whose take-out cups?"

"Everyone's take-out cups."

"Ah."

He hums, shoulders curved in. "Ms. B said I needed to stop shooting my shot with everyone who walked through her door. So she fired me. And if I don't find a job, I won't be able to afford my rent."

"Don't you live with your parents? Aren't you going to NYU at some point?"

"I'm taking a gap year. And my parents started charging rent when I graduated. They said it builds character. Look, can I come inside? People are staring."

One person is staring. Gus is standing in the open door of the fire station two blocks down, eating a bear claw and watching our entire interaction. He waves happily when I glance over at him.

I wave back. This town, I swear to god.

"You worked for my brother, didn't you? You really want to work for another Porter?"

He shrugs, apathetic. "It was a good learning experience."

According to Beckett, it was certainly an experience. "Why do you want to work here, Jeremy?"

"Because I have no idea what I want to do," he says quickly, somehow sounding more like an adult than I've ever heard him before. "Because I'm tired of people thinking I'm some screw-up kid. I don't even have to be a receptionist or whatever. I can do small things around the studio. Whatever you need help with. I just want—" He rolls his shoulders back and tips his chin up, confident. "I'd like to explore doing different things before I have to settle on one thing for the rest of my life."

All right. Rest of his life seems a little dramatic, but I understand what he's going for. "You want to explore reception work?"

He shrugs. "Reception work. Tattoo stuff. You know. All of it."

I watch him carefully. He seems earnest enough. And I know what it feels like to be buoyed by all the excitement of graduation until you float down and you're left with nothing but stark terror at the wide-open world in front of you.

"I'm also really good at social media," he adds.

Yeah, I've seen what he does on social media. "Good" is probably a stretch. I step back and hold open the door. Jeremy's whole face lights up. I hear a single clap somewhere behind me. Nessa again, letting her opinion be known.

I ignore her.

"We're still going to have an interview," I tell Jeremy. "And I'm still going to think about it."

"Okay. That's fine."

"I'm going to want references."

He winces but nods again. "That's fine too."

I sigh and let him the rest of the way in. Maybe this can be my good deed for the . . . year. Maybe this good karma will carry me right through to a successful launch. What did Vanessa say I have? A bubble-wrapped heart? Maybe this is the first step to unwrapping some of it.

"Do you think I could get some tattoos for free?" Jeremy asks.

I shut the door behind him. "Don't push it."

13

CHARLIE

"I THINK YOU'RE trying to kill me," I wheeze.

I bend at the waist, my hands on my knees. The shovel I'm supposed to be using is discarded at my feet.

Beckett knows. He has to. There's no other explanation for why I'm standing in the middle of his backyard shoveling dirt just as dawn is breaking over the horizon. I didn't think he saw me when I drove back to the farm the other morning, but maybe he did. Maybe something about me currently says, *I had life-altering, mind-blowing sex with your sister two nights ago, and I don't regret it.*

And now he's brought me to the field behind his house to slowly kill me with aggressive manual labor.

I shouldn't have slept over at her house, but she rendered me unconscious after our last go. I couldn't have moved if someone paid me to do it.

Beckett snorts. "I'm not trying to kill you." He drives his shovel into the ground at his side and crosses his arms over his chest. He's not even sweating. "You're just digging weird."

"How could I possibly be digging weird?"

"You're lifting with your back."

"I'm not," I answer automatically, but the gasp in my words saps some of the strength from the statement. I'm digging weird because

I'm still sore from everything Nova and I did to each other. I walked with a limp for half the day yesterday.

I lean back up and look around the wide, open field. Everything is cotton candy pink, a furious orange burning closest to the tops of the trees. And I can't even enjoy it because Beckett is trying to kill me. "What are we—do you even need a fence here? Is this some sort of hazing ritual?"

"No." He drags his knuckles against his jaw and squints into the distance. "I told you, I'm not fucking with you. I need to build a fence."

"For what?"

"For the cows," he says simply, like the answer is obvious. He called me at five in the morning while I was working on the financial projections for one of my clients and told me he needed me in the field behind his house. When I arrived, he handed me a shovel, pointed to a spot on the ground, and told me to dig. For a while there, I thought he had me digging my own grave.

"Clarabelle is getting a fence?"

He nods. "Clarabelle and Diego."

"Who is Diego?"

"Another cow."

"You're getting another cow? I thought Evie put a hold on the animal adoption."

She had to. Beckett was getting out of control. He adopted an entire family of cats, two ducks, and a cow in the span of a single year. Evie told him he had to stop or build them a bigger house. He pivoted to gifting rescue animals to his friends instead. Caleb got a dog and Layla has an entire coop full of rescue chickens. He tried to get me to adopt a fox last summer, New York apartment be damned. I'm not sure how Luka and Stella have avoided it, though Beckett has seen the state of Stella's cluttered house. She'd lose an animal in there.

"Wedding gift," he explains. Right. The cow. "Evie found him on a farm outside of Durham when she was down there for work. Little guy is a miniature and was being starved half to death at some rogue petting zoo. He's at a rescue now, but we're going to drive down in a week or so to pick him up."

Evelyn travels frequently for her work with the American Small Business Coalition, lending a hand to start-up businesses all over the country. And apparently . . . finding miniature rescue cows for her husband.

"That's nice." I glance around the field. By the looks of it, we have about forty-two thousand fence posts left to dig. God help me. "If he's a miniature, does he need a yard this big?"

Beckett shrugs at me. "I figured we'd mark out the space whether he needs it or not. Clarabelle ended up in Layla's backyard a couple of weeks ago and almost gave Caleb a heart attack. Best to have the fence, I think."

I wipe my hand across my forehead. "All right."

Beckett's eyes narrow. "You okay?"

"I'm fine." Chronically overworked and stressed out about Beckett finding out I had a one-night stand with his youngest sister, but I'm fine.

"Is it your dad?" he presses.

"What?"

"Your dad. Did he call you again?"

I grab my shovel and wander over to the next spot Beckett has marked. I forgot he heard that conversation. "No, he hasn't." I don't expect he will either. His preferred method of communication is more indirect. He likes to shoot the shit with my clients at his country club, plant a few seeds of dissolution, then wait for me to call in exasperation.

I finally got ahold of Mr. Billings and had to talk him down from reallocating his entire portfolio. It seems like half of my other clients are in a similar state of distress. I wish I knew what my father was trying to accomplish. But I'm trying a new thing where I don't give my dad headspace he hasn't earned. It's a work in progress.

Beckett hums, watching me dig my silly little hole. I glance up at him. "Are you going to help, or . . . ?"

He frowns at me. "Is this too much for you?"

"The fence? Yeah, probably. I haven't been to the gym since before Stella's wedding, and apparently I was doing the wrong things when I was there." My biceps are tired. Though that could be Nova's fault—specifically when I held her up against the wall of her bedroom, eliminating the height difference between us, her legs curled high around my waist and my mouth at her neck while I—

"I'm not talking about the fence."

"Oh." *Stop thinking about his sister in front of him*, my mind begs. *Stop it*. But my brain has never been great at doing what I ask of it, and Nova has wedged herself firmly into my thoughts. Her and her smile and her butterfly lingerie.

So much for working her out of my system.

I blink and then blink again. "What are you talking about?"

"The farm," Beckett says. "Is running the farm too much while you're still working the job in New York?"

"Why?" Unease bottoms out my stomach. "Did I forget to do something? I ordered you that fancy fertilizer, right?"

"No, no. You did. I got the invoice. You've been doing great for us. It's not that." Beckett adjusts his hat, discomfort in the rigid lines of his body. "You've just been . . . working a lot. No one wants to see you run yourself into the ground trying to make other people happy."

"I'm not. I'm managing." I've had to stay up late and wake up a little earlier, but there's nothing I would change about the situation. Client needs are still being met in New York. Selene is filling in the gaps. Farm operations seem to be running fine here, and I even managed to put together that spreadsheet for Nova. I know all of this was my idea, and I know I probably wasn't the first choice to take over for Stella, but I think I'm holding it together nicely. "Everything is fine. I'm doing fine."

"Fine," Beckett snorts. He grips the handle of his shovel. "Christ, you sound like Nova."

Awareness makes my skin flush hot. Her name is a blinking neon sign. I feel like I'm being painfully obvious when I ask, "How so?"

"Her studio. She hasn't stopped since she bought the place. She's doing too much, but she keeps saying she's fine."

I drive my shovel into the ruddy earth. Comparing me to Nova is laughable. She is wildly out of my league, brilliant and kind and driven and a million other things that make her shimmer and shine. While I am doing the bare minimum and cashing in on a position awarded out of nepotism. "Nova wouldn't lie to you. And the studio is important to her. She wants it to do well."

He grunts again, eyes fixed on some far-off point. The creaky weather vane on top of his house grates in the morning breeze. A light turns on in the kitchen. Evelyn appears in the window with her long hair tied in a ponytail and a cat on her shoulder. She squints through the glass and waves when she sees us. We both wave back. Mine looks weird because I can't lift my arm above my shoulder.

"She's doing the thing she loves best. Look at her work." I nod at the tattoos that peek out from the rolled cuff of his flannel. "Do you think she should be doing anything else?"

He rubs his thumb over a maple leaf on his wrist. "I just worry."

"Well, don't." I nudge him with the tip of my shovel. "If she finds out you're babying her, she's just going to get pissed. You know that."

Beckett's eyes narrow. "Are you going to tell her?"

I hold my hands up, palms out. "Absolutely not. I don't have a death wish."

His shoulders relax with a sigh. "That reminds me."

A laugh bursts out of me. "Oh, good. I'm glad 'death wish' reminded you of something."

He shoots me a look. "Mom wants you at dinner tonight."

"Family dinner?" The entire Porter clan has family dinner once a week. I've always been deeply envious of their desire to spend time together. Also, his mom makes the best broccoli cheddar casserole I've had in my life. "Isn't that for . . . family?"

It takes Beckett a second to answer. He's distracted by the sight of Evelyn on the back porch, wearing an oversized hoodie down to her knees and a pair of muddy rain boots. She has a cup of coffee in one hand and a watering can in the other, tending to the plants that crowd the ledge.

"I don't have the heart to tell her she's overwatering them," he mutters quietly. "They'll be dead in a week." He sighs and shakes his head, a smile edging at one side of his mouth. "And yes. Mom wants you at family dinner. She said she's worried about the things she's hearing on the phone tree."

I stand straight. "The phone tree? I haven't heard anything from the phone tree since before the wedding."

It's been like a gnat buzzing in my ear. Usually, I get at least seven texts a day. I even tried starting my own message chain, but I got a disconnected voice mail from Matty that sounded suspiciously like Gus's voice when I dialed the number. The phone tree has been inactive. I can't figure it out.

Beckett grunts. "Lucky you."

"Have you heard anything?"

"I heard about the brown sugar lattes, if that's what you're referring to."

It is not. I narrow my eyes. "Have I been kicked off the phone tree?"

I better not have. I've earned my spot. I pass on messages faithfully no matter what I'm doing. I once stopped a client meeting so I could lock myself in the bathroom and call Matty about the two-for-one sale on fish tacos at the little stand by the coast. I take it very seriously.

"You can ask my mom about it." Beckett tosses a shovelful of dirt over his shoulder. It narrowly misses my shoes. "At dinner."

I prop myself up with my shovel. Nova and I have texted a few times since I rolled my way out of her bed, but I'm not sure where this falls on the *how to behave after a one-night stand* spectrum.

"Will, ah—" I scratch at my chin. "Will your sisters be there?"

Beckett doesn't look up from his shoveling. "At family dinner?"

"Yes." I drag out the word until it's seven syllables long. I am not doing an excellent job of playing it cool.

Beckett grunts. "Yes. My family will be at family dinner."

"And your mom wants me there?"

"That's what she said."

"You're sure?"

Beckett straightens with a huff, thoroughly done with this conversation. He nudges his hat up so I can appreciate the full force of his glare. "You can come willingly, or you can disappoint my mother when I drag you in through the back door. Those are your choices."

There's an implication with the second choice. That disappointing his mother will result in another action as well. Potentially with the knuckles of his left hand.

"I'll come willingly."

Beckett goes back to digging his hole. "Good."

I'M FIDGETING.

I'm fidgeting and I can't decide which book to buy. What sort of book says, *Thank you for having me over to your home for family dinner, I don't know what to do with an invitation like this, but I'm grateful all the same*? A thriller? A paranormal romance? Something nonfiction?

"Why don't you just bring flowers?" Alex calls from behind the counter, his nose buried in another regency romance. He's barely said two words since I strolled in here.

I pick up a copy of a book with a giant cat on the cover and flip it over, skimming the back. It might as well be in a foreign language. Nothing is resonating right now. My brain is static, my thoughts tumbling over one another. I've sufficiently overthought this dinner invitation to death.

"I want to make a good impression. Any dope can bring flowers. Mrs. Porter likes books."

"You bring my grandmother flowers all the time."

"That's because your abuela loves flowers and you should bring people the things they like." Alex makes a face behind his book. "Don't pout because your grandmother likes me better."

I decide on the cat book. At the very least, she'll appreciate the cover. At the worst, she can drop it in the Little Library I know she has outside of the salon she works at. I whistle and toss the book across the room. Alex catches it right before it smacks him in the face and rings it up.

"Make a good impression," he mutters. "Like they don't know exactly who you are."

That's the problem, I think. The Porter family does know exactly who I am. I am fun-loving, always-loud, sometimes-takes-trivia-night-too-seriously Charlie. I am the guy who is here to have a good time.

But I'd also like to be the guy that earns a spot at the table by being thoughtful and kind. I'd like to maybe not be a giant joke of a human being all the time. Coincidentally, I'd also like to be the guy that one particular Porter doesn't have regrets about.

Maybe I should bring her a book too.

I stroll over to the counter and lean against it. "What's gotten into you?"

"What do you mean?"

"You've been grumbling and growling since I walked in here."

"Have not."

"Have too."

"Have not."

I give him a look and snatch the book out of his hands. "Don't underestimate how far I'm willing to take this, Alex Alvarez. You're a certified grump right now. What's going on?"

Alex sighs and collapses in the old leather chair he keeps behind the counter. It creaks and groans beneath his weight. "Abuela made you tres leches."

"You're mad about tres leches?"

He sighs. "Among other things," he mutters under his breath.

I scratch my eyebrow. "Yeah. She made me tres leches." She had Caleb bring it to me. When I peeled back the foil, it was missing the entire left corner. He had cinnamon clinging to his collar and a glare on his face when he handed it to me, utterly unrepentant.

"She usually makes it for me," Alex grumbles.

I grin. "Luckily, I know how to share."

Alex raises both eyebrows. "Is that so? I seem to remember you screaming and shoveling carnitas in your mouth the last time she brought you leftovers and I asked for some."

That's fair. I did do that. But I only have lunch dates with Abuela once a month and he can see her whenever he wants. She's his grandmother. I've inserted myself into the Alvarez family with the same lack of grace I seem to do everything else, but I can't feel bad about it. Not when I get tres leches.

"There's some left. I'll bring it to the next harvest festival meeting."

"Ah yes, the harvest festival committee." Alex's dumb face slips into something smug. "I heard you volunteered to help Nova with her business visits."

"Where did you hear that?"

Alex shrugs. "The phone tree."

Goddamn it. I knew it. I slap both hands on the counter. I knock over a cup of pens and a haphazard stack of novelty Post-it notes. "Why the hell am I not getting phone tree messages?"

Alex picks up his book and flips through the pages, trying to find his place. He dog-ears the corners every time he stops, like an absolute barbarian. "The text chain is on hiatus. Barney over at the farm ran out of minutes."

"You don't need minutes to text."

Alex waves his hand over his head. "You know what I mean."

I have no idea what he means. "How are you getting information if the phone tree isn't working?"

Alex's eyes flick up from the book, then back down again. He turns two more pages, then flips back three. "I never said the phone tree isn't working."

He's being deliberately obnoxious. I glance at my watch. I don't have time for this. I'm already cutting it close to dinner, and I won't be late because Alex doesn't feel like being forthcoming. I grab the book and shove it under my arm.

"We're talking about this later," I grumble.

"Sure." He nods, not looking up from his book. "Tell Nova I say hello."

"I'm not having dinner with Nova."

He flips another page. "She will presumably be there."

"Yes."

"Then tell her I say hello."

"Why are you saying it like that?"

A smirk tugs at one side of his mouth. "Like what?"

"I don't have time for you." I start toward the door, then change my mind and turn back. "You've just lost your chance at tres leches."

Alex drops his book to the counter and gives me an affronted look. "What? Why?"

"Because of your attitude." I open the door. "You don't deserve it."

THE PORTER HOUSE sits right at the edge of town, a sprawling rancher with a wide wraparound porch and crisp white shutters. A giant garden out front overflowing with wildflowers and tomato plants. I park behind Beckett's truck and hustle my way up the ramp they built for Mr. Porter's wheelchair, a bottle of wine under one arm and the book with a bouquet of flowers in the other. The book by itself felt stupid halfway through town, so I went back to Mabel's and grabbed a bouquet. We ended up talking for fifteen minutes about posies and peonies, then a client called when I was in my car, and I spent another seven minutes sitting on the side of Main Street talking them down from reallocating half of their savings into a different investment portfolio.

More of my father's handiwork. An indirect punishment, probably, for cutting our call short the other day.

The door opens before I can knock, and Nova stands in the threshold. The last time I saw her she was sleep-mussed and perfect, naked in her bed with her blankets pulled to her chin. Now she's standing with her hip against the door, her hair twisted back in one long braid and a simple white fuzzy-looking sweater draped over her frame. Dark jeans and wool socks.

Affection, warm and surprising, fills my chest. She looks cute as fuck.

"Hey," I call, trying to pretend I didn't just trip up the ramp at the sight of her. "Were you waiting at the window?"

"In your dreams." She shivers in the cold air, socked feet shuffling in the entryway. "I saw your headlights in the driveway and it took you a while to get in here. I was starting to wonder about you."

I give her a wink as I drag my boots against the welcome mat. "I love it when you wonder about me."

A smile teases at her bottom lip. She passes her fingers over it like she's trying to hide it. "Get in here, Romeo. It's cold."

She ushers me in and shuts the door, pressing her back to it, hands tucked behind her. I watch her as I slip out of my jacket, glad to have her alone for a minute whether she was waiting for me or not.

"I meant to text you," I say quietly, keeping my voice low.

"About what?"

"Tonight."

Her face twists in confusion. "What about tonight?"

"I wanted to ask if you were okay with this. After . . . everything."

"Everything, huh?" She presses up on her toes to glance over my shoulder, then falls back to the flats of her feet. Checking, I think, to see if anyone is within hearing distance. A coy smile curls her lips. "Have I been on your mind, Charlie?"

That feels like an understatement. She's been circling there. I was buttoning my shirt this morning and caught a glimpse of a hickey on my hip in the mirror. I stared into space for thirty-eight seconds, half hard, the desire to be back in that bed with her so fierce it felt like a fist in my chest.

I halve the space between us until she has to tilt her head back to hold my eyes.

"I told you," I tell her, voice low. "Alarming frequency and incredible detail." I reach for the braid hanging over her shoulder and tug lightly. "Even better detail now." Her eyes flash and a smile kicks up one side of her mouth. I drop her braid. "You sure it's okay I'm here?"

"Of course it's okay. We said nothing would change, Charlie. You're allowed to come to dinner at my parents' house."

"I know what we said, but I don't want to intrude," I murmur.

I don't know the protocol for how to interact with a one-night stand that is also your friend. I've never had to do it before.

She watches me for a long moment. Farther back in the house, someone laughs. A chair screeches across the floor and utensils clink against plates. Family. Or what I've always imagined it might sound like, anyway.

"You're not intruding," she finally says. She glances at the book and bouquet in my hand and tips her chin up. "Did you bring me a present?"

"Absolutely not." I move them out of reach. "They're for your mom. Why? You want me to bring you flowers, Nova girl?"

It's easy to fall right back into the parts we play with one another, but then again, most things are easy with Nova. I think there was a part of me that was worried she'd put space between us. Maybe pretend the other night never happened.

But she isn't avoiding me, and she isn't acting any differently.

She's still Nova.

Relief relaxes my shoulders.

She grins at me. "I like buying my own flowers."

I laugh. "Yeah, you do." Unthinking, I reach forward and drag my knuckles along her rib cage. I know this piece of her now, the ink that's underneath this sweater. The flower on her ribs and the petals that float down her back. "Good at drawing them too."

"I like to think so."

Something heavy floods the space between us as I let my hand drift over the soft material of her sweater. Her breath hitches as my hand strays higher, knuckles ghosting closer to the curve of her breast. I wonder if she's wearing something lacey and delicate beneath. I bet she is.

Our gazes hold. This close, she's more color than shape. Sea-glass green and blue so deep it almost looks black. Tidal pools as the surf rushes in. A million treasures hidden beneath the surface.

Dishes clink together farther in the house and another burst of laughter slips down the hall. I pull my hand back and clear my throat, then thrust the bottle of wine in her hands.

"Here."

"Oh. Is this for me?"

"Also no. But you can carry it into the kitchen."

She laughs and pushes off the door, nudging my shoulder with hers on the way to the kitchen. It does something stupid to the inside of my chest.

"That's very generous of you."

"I'm a generous man."

She turns to glance at me, braid swinging between her shoulder blades. "I know for a fact that you are."

"Nova," I choke in warning as we both step into the kitchen. I glance around the open space, waiting for Beckett to descend on me with a steak knife. The last thing I need to be thinking about in a room full of her family is Nova's preferred interpretation of generosity. "Behave."

She snickers and places the wine on the island. Something that smells like thyme and butter is simmering on the stove, a basket of rolls on the counter. Oven mitts lie discarded next to the sink. Nova reaches for the bread basket and nods toward the back of the house. "Relax. Everyone is in the sunroom for dinner."

"The sunroom?" I frown.

Nova shrugs. "Mom likes to eat under the stars and Dad likes to make her happy. Beckett installed a fireplace last winter. It's nice."

It's better than nice.

A large stone fireplace anchors one side of the sunroom, the dancing flames reflected in the glass windows on every side. The whole space is glowing, both with the light from the hearth and the globe lights strung along the ceiling. Night presses in from the outside, condensation ringing the bottom of the glass in a halo of clouded white. And in the middle is a long wooden table, filled with bickering Porter siblings. Someone shouts something about asparagus and there's an answering ruckus. A wooden spoon flies across the table.

I don't think a single person notices when Nova and I walk in.

Nova steps past me and drops the rolls in the middle of the table, grabbing two quickly off the top before her siblings can descend on it.

"Look who I found lurking in the driveway," she announces.

Mrs. Lucy Porter looks up from the head of the table, an easy smile on her face and her chin in her hand. I hand her the flowers and bend so I can press a kiss to her cheek. "Sorry I'm late. I got caught up." I hesitate, then hold up the book. "I also stopped to get you this."

She makes grabby hands. "For me?"

I nod and catch Nova's eye on the other side of the table. She rolls hers and mouths *Suck-up*.

I shrug. It's true. I'm happiest when the people around me are happy. I'm uncomfortable when there's tension and I want to be liked. I've never seen any of those things as a bad thing.

"Sit, sit." Lucy gestures to the chair next to her. "Sorry I couldn't keep these barbarians from eating. Harper turns into a harpy when she's hungry."

"It's mac and cheese night," floats up from somewhere near the end of the table. It sounds like there are three different conversations going on, at least one of them at a decibel level that seems unnecessary for indoors. Harper and Vanessa are gesticulating wildly with their hands, and Mr. Porter is using his steak knife to illustrate something on the table. Evie is half standing from her chair, leaning over Beckett to nod and point. Nova tears apart a dinner roll and watches the back-and-forth with narrowed, calculating eyes. There's a phone propped up against a half-empty dutch oven casserole dish, Evelyn's dad in the tiny picture, his hands folded under his chin and his glasses low on his nose.

It looks like the floor of the stock exchange . . . but more aggressive.

"They're talking about the last episode of *Real Housewives*," Lucy explains.

Beckett, sprawled in his chair on the other side of her, doesn't look up from his plate. "It's been forty-five minutes."

I study him carefully. There's a reason he chose a job where he spends a majority of his time in empty fields. "Hanging in?"

He nods and gestures at his ears. He's wearing foam earplugs, sensitive to the level of noise in this tiny room. "Shockingly, I can still hear everything that's going on."

Lucy pats his bicep. "You know how the girls get when they're all together."

Beckett grunts.

It's not just the girls though. Mr. Porter and Mr. St. James seem to have a lot of opinions about the women of New Jersey. They gang up against Harper and Vanessa, exchanging an air high-five through the phone after a very detailed and obviously rehearsed closing argument.

"Is your dad a lifelong fan of the housewives?" I ask Evelyn.

Evelyn rolls her eyes. "This is a recent development."

"Perhaps if you and that husband of yours decided to communicate with your families better, we would have found common interests sooner," comes the tinny voice from the phone. Evelyn's dad presses his glasses up his nose with both eyebrows raised. I guess Layla isn't the only one salty about missing the wedding.

"It's my fault, Mr. St. James," Beckett pokes his head into the frame, the tips of his ears red. "I couldn't wait to marry your daughter."

The table releases a collective groan. Nova boos and tosses a piece of her roll at Beckett's forehead. Evelyn beams behind Beckett, and her dad chuckles on the other end of the phone.

"You're not sorry."

"No," Beckett ducks his head. "I'm really not."

Lucy passes me various dishes to load my plate and I sit back and observe. I have no idea what's going on, but it's clear that everyone is enjoying themselves. Mr. Porter tilts the phone so he can continue his conversation with Mr. St. James. Not just a family born but a family made too.

Nova keeps to herself, adding a quiet comment every now and again that sends everyone into a fit of laughter. My eyes keep cutting back to her—that damn braid over her shoulder and a peek of ink at the collar of her sweater. I'm looking at her more than I should. I know I am. But I want to know what makes her laugh. I want to catch all of those reluctant smiles, right as they bloom across her face. Pink on her cheeks and that scrunch in her nose.

"So, Charlie." Lucy rests both hands on top of her brand-new book and fixes me with a look. The kind of look that someone perfects after they've raised a flock of children and taken exactly none of their shit. "Tell me how you are."

"I'm good," I tell her, reaching for another heaping spoonful of something that smells like buffalo sauce and heaven. Her face twists in comic disbelief and I laugh. "I heard this might be a welfare check."

"Is that so?" She turns her face to her son. Beckett keeps pushing his noodles around his plate. She sighs and rolls her lips. "I just wanted to make sure you're doing okay. You've taken on quite a bit."

I shrug. "The farm basically runs itself. I mainly eat cinnamon rolls at the bakehouse. And occasionally dig fence posts."

"That's not true." Beckett spears a piece of broccoli with his fork. "You organized Stella's filing system. Which hasn't been a filing system since I've known her."

"And you charmed Layla's dairy vendor into lowering their prices," Evelyn adds, chin on Beckett's shoulder. "You also patched the hole in the roof on the tractor shed."

I almost killed myself doing it too. I don't know what made me think I was qualified to replace shingles, but it didn't stop me from climbing on top of the damn thing. I slid halfway down on a skid and managed to catch myself on the weather vane shaped like a candy cane. I've never been more glad for Stella's impulsive thematic purchases.

"Do you like the work?" Lucy asks. "At the farm. Is it something you enjoy?"

"It is." I like waking up and hearing birds in the trees. I like standing at the back window of the guest cottage and watching the fireflies dance. I like walking over to the bakehouse and having a cup of coffee with Caleb while Layla bustles around the kitchen. I like working the register and knowing every single person who walks through the door. I like bothering Beckett into talking to me. I like feeling like I belong, even if it's not exactly the truth. "It doesn't feel like work at all."

"The best sort." Lucy smiles, rubbing her fingertips against her nose the same way Beckett does. "Maybe you should consider a career change."

"But then what would I do with all of my suits?" I grin and take the salad bowl Evie offers me. "Nah, this is temporary. I'm just giving Stella the break she deserves."

"And what do you deserve?"

I pause with my fork halfway to my mouth. Conversation on the other end of the table has resumed, picking up volume. Evelyn is draped over Beckett's shoulders with both of her arms wrapped around his neck, their fingers threaded together, both of their attention fixed on Harper and whatever point she's trying to illustrate with a bowl the size of her head curled in her arms.

Lucy's doesn't waver, her chin resting against her knuckles.

"What do you mean?" I ask.

"What do you deserve, Charlie?"

"I—I don't know." I laugh. I try to deflect from how lost I am with that question. "I certainly don't deserve this dinner, I know that."

I'm not just talking about the buffalo mac and cheese that tastes so good it should be illegal. I'm talking about the invitation, sitting here. Having a place carved out for me, no matter how temporary. Handed dishes and asked questions and folded into the easy interaction of a family that loves each other. It's like sitting in front of a fire and feeling the brush of warmth. Being here at the edge of it has me feeling homesick for a place I've never been.

Lucy's smile dims, understanding in the lines of her face. "Well then, maybe you should try to figure it out."

"Your mac and cheese recipe?"

At the other end of the table, Nova leans over Vanessa to stick her fork in Harper's bowl. All three of them descend into bright, cackling laughter. I yank my eyes away.

"No, Charlie." Lucy hands me another bowl. "How to accept things without wondering what you've done to deserve them."

14

NOVA

"WHAT'S GOING ON with you?"

I hand Beckett another dish, soap suds up to my elbows. He'd been quiet throughout dinner, more so than usual. He typically keeps to himself, especially when we're all together and loud, but something seems off tonight. He keeps shooting me concerned glances out of the corner of his eye like I'm about to collapse to the floor in hysterics.

Does he know what I did with Charlie? Is he mad about it?

Do I care?

"What do you mean?" he asks slowly, dragging the dish towel along the corners of the casserole dish.

"I mean you keep giving me puppy eyes." I turn to him and exaggerate a frown. "Like that. What's up?"

He gives me another quick, quiet look, his mouth turned down at the corners. I want to dig my finger into his cheek and scream *SEE*. But I don't. I just keep washing the serving spoon Harper was using as her own personal utensil and wait for Beckett to say something.

"When was the last time you had a headache?"

"Do you mean a migraine, or do you mean a headache?"

"Migraine," he corrects, voice lower like he's afraid to say the word too loud.

I wish my migraines felt like headaches. Instead, it's a full body experience. When I was a kid, Beckett and my sisters helped me through them. I don't think they've been able to let that go. They still see me as someone they need to take care of.

"Not lately," I answer, evasive.

Beckett isn't having it. "Nova."

"Probably a month ago," I sigh. It was actually three weeks ago, right before the wedding, and I was in so much pain I couldn't move from my bed for an entire day. My medication didn't help. I had to just lie there and wait for it to pass.

"Was it ocular?" he asks.

I shake my head. I didn't lose my vision this time. Just the pain and some general numbness in my hands and feet.

He huffs. "You're getting them more often."

I shift in front of the sink, running my hands beneath the water. I know exactly where this conversation is leading, and I have no interest in talking about how to manage my pain with my brother. I can't slow down right now. I can't push things off my plate. Everything that's there needs to be there, and I need to keep moving forward if I have any hope of achieving the goals I'm desperate for.

"I'm managing," I tell him. "You don't need to worry about me."

He grumbles something under his breath that I don't hear, dragging his cloth aggressively around the outside of a dish. It's a miracle the thing doesn't crack in half.

"Anything else bothering you?" I pour some more soap on the sponge shaped like a cob of corn. My mom has really committed to the agriculture theme in the kitchen. "Now's the time."

He sighs. "Vanessa mentioned she stopped by the studio the other day."

"She did. She harassed me about dating and tattoos, and then she left. I think she needed some company."

Beckett nods and holds out his hand for the next dish. "She said the place looked nice."

Ah, okay. Now I know what the issue is.

I haven't let Beckett see the studio yet. He's been asking for months, but I tiptoe my way around an invitation every time. It still isn't ready. I need to hang the light and I want to move some of the plants around. The workstations aren't quite set up yet and I'm missing a few chairs. I want everything to be perfect when he sees it for the first time.

"It's a work in progress," I explain, reluctant.

Beckett makes a frustrated sound and slaps the sink off with the palm of his hand. My fingers are still covered in suds. I try to turn the water back on but he nudges it off again. Apparently, we've reverted to the teenage versions of ourselves.

"What the hell, Beck?"

He flips the dish towel up over his shoulder and crosses his arms over his chest. "When do I get to see the studio?"

"When it's ready." I try to turn the water on again. Beckett nudges my hand away.

"When will that be?" he asks.

I flick off the soap and grab his dish towel, focused on drying my fingers instead of the look on his face. My honest answer is never. I don't think I'll ever feel ready for Beckett to see the studio. His approval means more to me than anyone else's, and while I know he'd give it without hesitation, I want to earn it. I want to deserve it.

Beckett has spent his entire life sacrificing for our family—for me. When my dad was left paralyzed by an accident when we were kids, Beckett dropped out of school to start earning an income to support our family. When I decided I wanted to be a tattoo artist, he offered to be my very first client. When I said I wanted to open my own studio in Inglewild, he went around town inquiring after properties and sending me real estate information, even though I know he hates talking to people. He has always believed in me.

And what have I done for him? How have I repaid all his sacrifices? I've put together a tattoo studio that isn't even finished yet. I'm fumbling along, barely holding it together. I'm terrified it won't live up to his expectations. I'm terrified *I* won't live up to his expectations. That'll he'll look around the space I've created and find it lacking in some way. That he'll regret entrusting so much to me.

"I'll send you some pictures tomorrow."

His frown deepens. "Why don't you want me there?"

"I do want you there. I just—" I tuck some of my hair behind my ear. "I need some more time."

"For what?"

"For the . . ." For everything to be perfect. For the gnawing ache in my chest to ease. "For the plants," I answer.

"The plants," he repeats. "What about the plants?"

I roll my lips together and think. "The ivy needs to grow."

"Nova."

"It's true. It hasn't started wrapping around the edges of the planters yet. I'm hoping those little vines will eventually drop down so it looks—" I do something stupid with my hand. I have no idea what I'm talking about. "So, it looks like you're in a jungle or something. Wild. Ink and Wild. Get it?"

"Yeah, I get it." Beckett is still frowning at me. "When will that be? When will the greenery finally be to your satisfaction?"

Charlie chooses that moment to stroll into the kitchen, his arms laden with cups and bowls and a giant ceramic dish in the shape of a tractor. He's grinning down at it like it's the best thing he's ever seen.

"Where did your mom get this thing? It's awesome." He rearranges the dishes in his arms so he can take a closer look, inspecting the tiny cats that are hand-painted along the wheel. He is blissfully oblivious to the standoff at the sink. "Was this custom made?"

I've been painfully aware of him all evening. If I thought having sex with him would suddenly make him less appealing, I've sufficiently proved that hypothesis incorrect during the course of this dinner. I kept sneaking looks at him in his pale blue button-up, collar undone. I found myself wondering if I pulled that collar down, if the hickeys I left would still be there. If maybe they're a deeper purple now. What colors they might turn if I put my mouth on them again.

I clear my throat. These are not thoughts I should be having about Charlie in my parents' kitchen while standing next to my brother. These are not thoughts I should be having about Charlie, period.

One and done. Out of our systems. That was the agreement.

"Yeah," I answer, grateful for the interruption, even if it's Charlie-shaped. I don't want to talk about the studio with Beckett anymore. He'll see it when he sees it. "Beckett got it for her for Christmas."

"Nice." Charlie glances up, smile faltering when he notices the way Beckett is trying to stare holes in the side of my face, arms still crossed over his chest. Charlie's eyes dart back and forth quickly as he reads the room, an unusual seriousness in the set of his mouth. "Everything good in here?"

His knuckles brush against my arm as he dumps the dirty dishes in the sink and he stays close after. A silent show of support.

"Yeah, everything is good." I flick the water back on. Beckett allows it.

"We were just talking about vines," Beckett says, voice dry as a bone.

"Oh, nice. The ones in Nova's studio? They look great."

My eyes slip shut. *Shit.*

"Beckett," I start. But he's already shaking his head, looking down at his boots. He doesn't look mad. It's worse than that. He looks hurt.

"Am I the only one you haven't let inside?"

"He just stopped by for a minute," I try to explain. "He was walking me home after the harvest festival meeting and—"

"It's fine," Beckett says. But it's not fine. He won't look at me and his mouth is set in a firm, frowning line. My stomach hollows out. The only thing I've ever wanted to avoid is disappointing my brother, and it seems I somehow managed to do it anyway.

"I, ah—" He puts down the dish he was drying and tosses the rag on the counter. He scratches roughly at the back of his head, a nervous tic that makes my heart squeeze in my chest. He glances at me briefly and then looks away again, like he can't bear the sight of me. A hot pressure burns behind my eyes. "It's your choice, Nova. I'll stop by after you open. Or . . . not. Whatever you want. Don't worry about it, okay?"

"Beck, I'm—" My voice catches in my throat.

He gives me another half-hearted quirk of his lips and leaves the kitchen. I listen to his boots against the creaking wooden floor, the gentle *snick* of the sunroom door opening and closing. Voices grow louder and then muffled again. I sigh and press the palm of my hand to my forehead. Some dish soap smudges on the bridge of my nose.

"What's your choice?"

I drop my hand and glance at Charlie. "Beckett hasn't seen the studio yet," I explain.

He frowns. "Why not?"

"Because—" I let my hands drift beneath the running water, soap suds slipping over my inked knuckles, down my wrist to curl around the tattoos there. "Have you ever felt the weight of someone else's expectations? I know he doesn't mean to, but his unfailing belief that I can do whatever I set my mind to just makes me feel—" Claustrophobic. Terrified. Undeserving. "It makes me feel like I can't fail. Like there's no room for it."

I release the confession like the end of a balloon string, watching it float up, up, up to the ceiling. I wish letting the words slip out of my mouth made me feel better, but I just feel empty. Exhausted and sad.

Charlie makes a low sound, fingers reaching for the end of my braid the same way he did back in the entryway of the house. He tugs once and that feels the same too, the curl of warmth that slips over my shoulders in response. "No one would care if you failed. Especially Beckett."

It's the wrong thing to say. The weight on my shoulders grows heavier.

"I would," I whisper. I can't make my voice any louder. "I'd care a lot."

"That's not what I meant, Nova."

I'm frustrated with myself. It's easy enough for that frustration to bubble up and over to the man standing next to me. I don't want to talk. I don't want to be comforted. I don't want the small, flickering lick of warmth that glows in my chest when Charlie presses closer next to me. I shouldn't want a damn thing from Charlie. It falls way outside of the lines we've drawn for each other.

I just want to finish these dishes and go home. Turn on a dumb movie and fall asleep to the sound of a laugh track.

"You can stop with all of"—I wave my soapy hand between us—"this."

Charlie lets go of the end of my braid. "Stop with what?"

"The emotional check-in. I don't need it." I grab the tractor plate and start scrubbing furiously at a spot of stuck cheese. "We're not—" *Together*, I almost say. "We aren't anything, Charlie."

He falls quiet next to me. There's nothing but the sound of the sink water and my brush against the plate. The pound of my heart in my ears.

"Friends don't make sure their friends are okay?" he finally asks.

A laugh sputters out of me. "Is that what we are?"

Do friends argue the way we argue with one another? Do they fuck each other and then pretend it never happened? Do they snark and twist and bite? I don't know what we are to each other, but it doesn't exactly feel friendly.

Charlie stills next to me, his body one tense line. He leans back until there's a perfect two inches of space between us, not a single point of contact.

"I thought so, but I guess not." I watch him drag his palm over his jaw from the corner of my eye. He huffs a disbelieving laugh. "I guess I'm just the guy you had a good time with. Noted, Nova. Thank you very much for clarifying my place."

That's not what I meant. "Charlie—"

"It's all good. You're right. This is what we agreed to." He gives me a tight smile and nods toward the same door Beckett just walked through. "I'm going to say bye to your parents and head out." He pauses. "I won't make the same mistake twice."

He leaves without another word, and I stare hard at the sink.

"Well," I tell the tiny painted cats judging me with their little black eyes, "I fucked that up."

15

CHARLIE

"WHAT DO YOU want to do about the Wyatt portfolio?"

I rub my hand against the back of my neck and squint at the spreadsheets that cover the entirety of the kitchen table in the guest cottage. I've been up since three in the morning catching up on New York emails and talking to Selene since six, trying to manage the shitshow that is my client base.

I'm going to have to talk to my dad sooner rather than later. If he thinks causing a bunch of middle-aged men to panic into changing their entire savings plans is character building, I have news for him.

It's irritating. And unprofessional. And stupid.

"Can we encourage him to invest in a rocket ship that will launch his adulterous ass into outer space?"

"Ooh." Selene leans back in my desk chair in my office on the other side of the computer and takes a long sip out of my coffee mug. "You're feeling spicy today."

She looks immaculate on her side of the screen. Neat, dark gray suit and a creamy white blouse beneath. Her dark hair is pulled into a tight ponytail, and she's wearing her usual thick, black winged eyeliner. She calls it her battle armor.

Meanwhile, I look like I've been to hell and back. I wince at my reflection in the top right corner. My shirt is on inside out and I didn't bother combing my hair before answering this video call. I think I have dried granola on my collar.

"Is it the beard?" she asks. "Has it given you a personality transplant?"

"I don't have a beard," I mutter. I drag my palm over the scruff that covers my jaw. "I have a light dusting of facial hair. A starter beard."

"The word *beard* was in that explanation. And don't say, 'dusting,' it's weird." Selene gives me a look and crosses her legs, sipping at her mug. "Are you breathing in too many pesticides down there?"

"No. I'm just in a bad mood." I slept like shit last night. My brain wouldn't stop turning over Nova's words. That sarcastic little laugh. *Is that what we are?*

Who knows what we are. Not friends, apparently. I don't get to care about her; I just get to fuck her. I guess when she said she wanted me out of her system, she meant out of her life too.

"All right." I blow out a deep breath and stretch my neck. No use making my bad mood worse by reflecting on it. "What else do you have for me?"

Selene stacks some folders, color coded with various Post-it notes, and drops them neatly in the complex organizational structure I keep behind my desk. I really should give the woman a raise. She keeps the show running.

"I have some advice."

I drop my head to my keyboard and bang it there twice. "No, thank you."

"You need to cut your father off."

I groan louder. "I know that."

It's silent on the other end of the computer. I lean up and rest my chin on the trackpad. The only part of me visible on the computer screen is the top of my hair and thank god for it. Selene doesn't need to see a car crash in real time.

Selene blinks at me. "I expected more of a fight, to be honest."

"I know he's causing problems, but I—" I have trouble with confrontation. I'm confident until I'm not, and I'd much rather do a bunch of extra work than talk to my father directly about what a pain in the ass he's being. I'm a people pleaser, through and through, and it doesn't matter that the person I'm trying to please is an asshole. All my brain recognizes is the itchy, uncomfortable feeling of disappointment. "That's exactly what he wants," I finally say.

"He wants you to cut him off?"

"No. He wants me to call him and give him the attention he's craving. He pokes and prods me until he gets it. He's a narcissist." Among other things. If I don't cave to his whims, he'll keep escalating until I do.

"So, what are you going to do?"

I press my fingertips to the base of my skull, trying to ease the tension headache I can feel brewing. My arms and back are tired from the fieldwork yesterday, and I'm just . . . I'm tired.

"I'll take care of it."

Selene raises both of her eyebrows. "When will you take care of it?"

God. She's been working with me for too long. She knows all of my avoidance mechanisms. "This week. I'll take care of it this week."

"Would you like me to pencil it in your calendar?"

A half-hearted smile curls the edge of my mouth. "What will it say?"

"It will be a blanket 'Do Not Disturb' titled 'Standing Up for Ourselves.' I'll schedule the call, an hour before to panic, and an hour after to decompress."

I snort. "That would be great. Thank you." I think for a second and drag my hands through my hair again. "Could you color code it blue?"

I SPEND THE rest of my morning buried in email hell, the notification on my calendar to call my father an ominous countdown in my periphery. I don't know if I can have it hanging over my head for the rest of the week, that blue block of pressure.

"Fuck." I sigh and pick up my phone, dialing the number I refuse to keep saved but know by heart anyway.

He lets it go to voice mail, because of course he does. I finally give in to him, and he keeps tugging me along.

"You've reached Brian Milford, independent financial consultant." I groan out loud. He shouldn't consult anyone about anything. "Please leave your name and number, and I'll get back to you."

The phone beeps. Words come tumbling out.

"This is Charlie Milford, and I'd appreciate it if you'd stop with the independent financial consulting. If you need attention, here it is. Call me back."

I place my phone on the table gently, even though I'd like nothing more than to hurl it out the window. I don't like getting angry. I don't like losing control of myself. I hate the rolling, roiling tension in my head and in my chest. My thoughts pick up speed until I can't pluck out a single one, just a constant stream of stressors and reminders and pieces of conversation. It's like shoving my head underwater at a concert, everything muffled with endless, indistinguishable sound.

You're missing things, my mind whispers. *Focus. You're falling behind. People are depending on you and you're falling apart. Again.*

I breathe in deep through my nose.

Out again.

I sit like that, breathing, for a while. My hands slowly relax from clenched fists and my thoughts slow to a trickle. I watch a brilliant red cardinal just outside the window, sitting on the edge of a bird feeder. He pecks at something on the ledge, spreads his wings, then flies off.

It would help if I opened the window. Fresh air always wipes away some of the fog in my mind. But I can't seem to make myself move from this chair.

Lucy asked me what I deserve and maybe this is it. Maybe this is exactly what I'm meant for. This chair in this kitchen in this house that I do not own. In a place I do not belong. With friends who are my sister's friends but who I've claimed as my own. So far away from New York and all the things that should be my responsibilities. The life I've built there, trying to edge my way out of my father's shadow.

While all I'm doing here is shrugging on a jacket that doesn't quite fit.

Nova's voice: *Is that what we are?*

I've got no fucking clue.

SOMEONE KNOCKS ON the door of the cottage around dusk. The only source of light in the kitchen is sunlight slipping through the windows, painting everything a burnt, dusty orange. The table is more organized, but my brain is not. I spent the entire day hyperfocused on crossing things off my to-do list, and I didn't stop for lunch. Time became a fleeting concept, a vague awareness.

I feel it when I stand and shuffle my way to the door, my body creaking and knees popping. I don't know who I'm expecting, but it certainly isn't Nova on the second step up to the porch, a box from Matty's in her hands and a cute black beanie on her head. Her blond hair is in loose waves around her shoulders, cheeks flushed in the melting daylight. She frowns when she sees me.

"You shaved your beard," she says.

I rub my knuckles against my smooth cheek. Sometimes it helps me restart when I rely on my routines. After my call with Selene, I did everything I usually do during a morning in the city, short a subway ride and an overpriced cup of coffee.

I skipped the suit too. I pulled on a Lovelight Farms hoodie and a pair of black sweatpants I think I've maybe worn twice. I don't have much need for athleisure in the city.

"I shaved, yeah." I nod at the pizza in her hands. "Are you delivering for Matty's now?"

She glances down at the box like she forgot she was holding it. Her fingers tighten at the edges.

"New side hustle," she says quietly with a quirk of her lips.

I resist the urge to fill the silence between us and lean my shoulder against the doorframe. She came here with something to say. I'm not going to rush her on it.

I'm also not going to make it easier for her.

She kicks at a crooked floorboard and blows out a deep breath. "I was a jerk last night."

I shrug. She was honest. She held her boundaries. That doesn't make her a jerk. "No, you weren't. I pushed you and I shouldn't have. You don't have to talk to me about anything. I know the parameters of our relationship."

I know my appeal. I'm the fun time. The break between more serious pursuits. The joke and the easy laugh. Nova made it perfectly clear what she wanted from me. I got carried away thinking I had a right to anything else. That she'd want me for anything else.

She blinks at me and climbs another step. I get a whiff of mozzarella and basil. My stomach rumbles in appreciation.

"I was a jerk," she repeats. "I shouldn't have said what I said."

"Which part?"

"The part where I told you we weren't friends." Her head tips to the side, watching me. I do my best not to flinch. "I was frustrated with myself, and I took it out on you. I thought I'd make it up to you with pizza." She lifts the box in her hands in silent explanation. "Can I come in?"

I fix a smile on my face and reach for something that feels familiar. "You never have to ask me to come," I quip.

She frowns, her face softening. "Don't do that," she says quietly.

"Do what?"

"That," she says again. "The performance."

I dip my chin to my chest, a falling sensation in the pit of my stomach. Like I've just stepped off a ledge and I can't tell where the bottom is. I sigh. "I don't want pity pizza, Nova."

"It's not pity pizza," she responds. "It's pepperoni pizza."

It's a fight to keep the smile off my face. I wish she wasn't so fucking funny. It would make a lot of this easier for me. "Cute."

She sighs and closes the remaining distance between us. She thrusts the pizza box into my chest. I stare down at her and raise both eyebrows.

"It's a thick crust, extra cheese pizza with double pepperoni. I got it because I know it's your favorite. And I know it's your favorite because we are friends. Now, I'd like to come inside and eat this pizza before it gets cold. With you."

"As friends," I clarify.

That half smile curls her mouth again. "Yes. You can tell me about your day and I'll tell you about mine. We'll do some planning for the harvest festival and I'll steal something to drink from your fridge. Then I'll drive home and see you later this week."

"Later this week?"

"Yeah. Later this week."

I consider it. Part of me is still tender about last night, but there's a bigger piece of me that's tired of sitting in this little house all alone.

"I'm picking what we watch on TV," I finally say.

Her smile slips wider before she tucks it back into place, lips pressed down against it. She rocks back on her heels on the rickety front porch, boards squeaking beneath her boots. "That's fine."

"And I'm going to eat your crust."

"That's fine too."

"I'm going to take up most of the couch," I warn.

I take up too much space, I want to tell her. *I'm loud and sometimes I don't know how to stop talking. I'm a lot and I know that. I can't figure out how to make myself fit, but I'm trying. I promise I'm trying.*

She shrugs. "I don't need much room to be comfortable."

I push off the door and open it wider behind me. Nova's smile cracks open. Something in my chest stumbles over it, and I have to remind myself, again, that Nova Porter is not for me. I've already gotten everything from her that I'm going to get, and I can settle for this, or I can have nothing at all. Those are my options.

"Come on in then."

She slips past me into the house, her arm brushing against mine.

"I hope you have hot sauce."

I watch her wander into the kitchen, holding the pizza box in one hand while she wrestles her way out of her coat. It's a tight feeling in my chest, seeing her in this space. Moving around it like she doesn't want to be anywhere else. I blow out a deep breath.

"Of course I do." I shut the door to the cottage. "I'm not a heathen."

WE SPREAD OUT on the couch with the pizza.

Nova burrows in the corner with her legs tucked under her while I spread out on the other side, my crossed ankles resting on the coffee table, my arm spread across the back. She drops a slice of pepperoni on a chipped plate with tiny Christmas trees along the edge and takes the box for herself, opening it on her lap.

"Did you not want a plate?"

"I have a plate." She holds the box up off her tucked knees and wiggles it around. I urge it back to her lap, not willing to spend half of my evening scrubbing grease stains out of Stella's couch.

"An actual plate."

"What do you have against cardboard, Charlie?"

"Nothing. I just like coordinating dinnerware."

She snickers as I scroll through the channels, looking for something for us to watch. I pause on the Home Shopping Network and she boos. I pause again on a show about dog grooming just to hear her laugh.

Her face lights up when I pause on the classic movie channel,

Katharine Hepburn filling the screen. I toss the remote on the coffee table and reach for the pizza plate I set to the side. She peers at me from behind the lid of her makeshift plate with a surprised look on her face.

"What?" I ask.

"What, what?"

"That look on your face."

She shrugs, one shoulder inching up to her ear. She drizzles some hot sauce on top of her slice and takes a massive bite. Tomato clings to the corner of her mouth. "You don't strike me as a classic movie guy," she manages around a mouthful. She swallows and swipes her thumb along her bottom lip, missing the spot of sauce completely. I am acutely focused on it.

"I think you'll find that I'm a man of taste," I manage.

She chuckles. "That you are."

Dinner is quiet as we avoid any conversational landmines. We watch TV and talk about inconsequential things. Gus and Montgomery and their desire for a pumpkin art display. Ms. Beatrice and her brown sugar lattes. Sheriff Dane and his husband, Matty, and whether or not Beckett will force them to adopt a dog sooner rather than later.

"I'm surprised he hasn't yet."

Nova nods. "I think Evie getting him that cow has settled him down. For now."

It's calming in a way that's usually difficult for me to find, sitting here on the too-small couch with Nova's knee nudging mine, the edge of the pizza box digging into my thigh—hot sauce passed back and forth and a beer split between two mismatched mugs on the table in front of us.

"So." I settle my mug on the arm of the couch, watching Katharine Hepburn spin around the room with a glass of champagne. "When can you pencil me into your schedule? For my tattoo."

"Still on that kick, huh?"

"It's not a kick. I really do want a tattoo." I roll my head against the back of the couch and poke at her knee. She nudges me back with her sock-covered foot and leaves it there, tucking it beneath my thigh when I don't protest.

She narrows her eyes. "What do you want?"

"I don't know."

"Where do you want it?"

"Don't know that either."

"Typically, in my professional experience, if someone doesn't know what sort of tattoo they want or where they want to get it, they're not ready for a tattoo."

I take a sip of my lukewarm beer from a mug shaped like a nutcracker and keep my eyes on hers. Her skin glows blue and gray in the light of the TV, her hair a silver wave over her shoulder. Her hat is on the table in the kitchen. Her shoes are stacked right next to mine.

"What would you pick for me?" I ask.

"A scorpion," she says, right away. "On your ass."

My smile feels stupid on my face. Too big. Too much.

"If you want to see my ass again, Nova girl"—I take another pull from the mug—"all you need to do is ask."

"I'll keep that in mind," she laughs. The look in her blue-green eyes is a flash of heat. Smoke over rolling water.

My brain trips right back to our night together with enthusiasm, remembering the way she spread out beneath me, one of her knees at my hip and her hands above her head. She had looked at me like that then too. The same sort of calculated interest. Like she's thinking about what she wants to do first.

One night, I tell myself. *Out of our systems. Don't impose. Don't be too much. Take what you're given and don't ask for more. Don't push.*

I clear my throat and look away. I take another sip from my mug just for something to do with my hands. "How did you decide what to give Beckett? He didn't know what he wanted, right?"

She shakes her head. A tiny frown line appears at the bridge of her nose. I want to press my thumb to it until it disappears. Chase away the thoughts that put it there. I've always been quick to empty everything in my head, but I think Nova holds on to too much. She keeps her thoughts and her insecurities and worries close, letting them buzz around her brain.

"No," she says thoughtfully. "That's a good point. He just told me to do whatever I wanted."

I remember what she said last night about the weight of someone else's expectations, how she feels the crush of it. "And you wanted to give him flowers and stars?"

On Beckett's left arm, he has a full sleeve of constellations and planets, swirling purples and blues from his shoulder to his wrist. And on his right arm, he has the forest. Flowers and vines and towering trees. All the things I now know are Nova's specialties, color and delicate lines and seamless, beautiful shading. Her work really is incredible.

"I wanted him to have the things he loves most with him wherever he goes." She blinks quickly and glances down at the pizza box in her lap. She picks idly at the edge of it. "Beckett gave up a lot to make sure the rest of us got what we wanted. He's always put himself last. It seemed like the least I could do."

I watch her face carefully, shadowed in the flickering from the television.

"Why don't you want him to see your studio yet?"

She traces the *Y* in MATTY. "I don't know."

"Yes, you do."

Nova huffs and gives me a look. I raise both eyebrows back.

"I just . . . I want it to be perfect." Quieter, she says, "I want him to be proud of me."

"You don't think he will be?"

"It's not that I don't think he'll be proud." She curls her fingers in the sleeve of her shirt and rubs it against her cheek. "I know he will be. I know he is. But I've never done anything to deserve that from him, have I? He's always just . . . given it. He let me do all of that work on his arms when I really shouldn't have been tattooing anyone. He dropped out of school and gave up on his dreams so I could have mine. I want him to walk in and feel like all of that was worth it. And I don't feel ready yet. There's some stuff I still want to do before he sees it." She peeks up at me and tucks her knees tight to her chest. "Is that dumb?"

"It's not dumb." I rest my hand against her ankle and trace the jut of the delicate bone there with my thumb. "But, Nova, you don't need to be perfect."

"Yes," she whispers, voice cracking. "Yes, I do."

I roll my lips against the desire to tell her that she's wrong. That doing her very best is good enough. That she deserves all the things she has. "Do you come to the farm because you have to?"

She cocks her head. "What?"

"Why do you visit Layla's?"

"Because that chocolate hazelnut cupcake changed my life."

I squeeze her ankle. "And why do you get your Christmas tree here? Every year."

"Because they're pretty trees," she answers, still bewildered. "And Beckett would murder me if I bought a fake one."

"Do you feel like you have to support this place just because your brother owns a piece of it?"

Realization softens her face. "No. I just like to."

I let myself trace her soft skin one last time before I let go, letting my hands rest in my lap. I widen my eyes in exaggeration. "Isn't that interesting?"

"Subtle, Charlie." She nudges me with her foot again and then withdraws, curling both beneath her. "I'm going to talk to him."

I nod. I'm certainly not an expert on positive family interactions, but I like the idea of Nova and Beckett getting along. "I think he'd like that."

"What about you?"

"What about me?"

She leans forward and plucks her mug from the coffee table, keeping her eyes on me as she takes a careful sip. "You're here an awful lot, Charlie, for a man who lives and works in another state."

I'm grateful for the low light and the flickering light of the television. "Too much?" I ask carefully.

She's quiet until I turn back to her. "No. Not too much. Not if being here makes you happy."

Being here makes me feel like . . . like the edges of myself that are too sharp everywhere else can be sanded down into something tolerable. Like I don't have to put on a show. All the things that hold me in place in New York don't feel as tight around my neck when I'm here. It's easier to breathe in air that smells like pine with a cup of coffee from Ms. Beatrice's and a croissant from Layla's.

"Yeah, being here makes me happy" is what I manage.

She nods to herself and turns back to the TV. She watches it and I watch her. Her ink looks darker against her skin in the muted light, like broad strokes of a paintbrush. A thumb smudged through wet paint. She smiles gently at something on the screen, and the questions sitting idle in the back of my mind bubble up. She's given me one of her secrets and I want the rest of them now. I want to know everything.

"What's it like?" I ask.

She turns back to look at me. "What?"

"Your work. Why did you want to be a tattoo artist? Why not something else?"

"Because . . ." Her eyes flick up and then back down again. "Probably because I like the permanency of it. The idea that someone, somewhere, is walking around with something I made painted on their skin." She smiles, bashful. "Our bodies are miracles, aren't they? It feels like the best sort of gift to be trusted like that. An honor, really."

"But you won't give me a scorpion on my ass?"

Her face brightens again, a laugh in her eyes. "No, Charlie. I won't give you a scorpion on your ass. Or a Looney Tune in the middle of your chest." She leans back against the arm of the couch and looks at me. Eyes lowered, comfortable in the silence that stretches between us. It's an honor to have this—this yawning quiet. This warm, settled feeling.

I'm aware of my heartbeat, steady in my chest. A *bum bum bum* that I feel in the palms of my hands.

"Think about it." I take another sip of my beer.

"About your ass?"

"Always about my ass. But also about what tattoo I should get."

She considers me, seriously this time. "I'll think about it," she says.

"Good."

That half smile again. She looks over my head to the window above my shoulder, then leans back over the arm of the couch to check the time on the microwave. Her shirt lifts, and I get a glimpse of the soft skin of her belly. The gentle curve of her hip. I know that skin. I've felt it under my hands, my mouth. I've had it pressed tight to mine, her gasping breaths in my ear. Laughter in the dark.

She had been so soft. Every inch of her.

I swallow hard and look away.

"I should get going," she says.

I nod and stand, stretching out my neck. "I'll walk you out."

She snorts and grabs the pizza box, collecting the remnants of our dinner and clearing it from the coffee table. "You could probably spread your arms and touch either end of this house with your fingertips. You don't need to walk me out."

"I'd like to," I insist.

She is right though. The house is tiny. More of a studio loft than anything else. Stella said she built it just in case anyone wanted to rent the place for a weekend on the farm, but as far as I know, I'm the only one who has ever stayed here. The first floor is open with a medium-sized evergreen couch dividing the living room from the kitchen, a small wooden table that's currently stacked with my work stuff. The stairs lead to a small open loft, a king-sized bed and a dresser at the top.

It's the back of the house that turns it into something special. It's all windows, just like Layla's. In the morning it's nothing but golden rolling hills and neat lines of Christmas trees. The smoke from Layla's off in the distance and the rumble of Beckett on his tractor. The house seems bigger then. Like it stretches all the way out to the fields and everything beyond.

Now it's just inky blue night, the stars a blanket above. A reflection of me and Nova in the dark windows.

I could bend down and pick her up. Make it easier for us to close the distance between our mouths and chase that hungry feeling burning in my chest until it's satisfied. I could lose myself in her, in the way she makes me feel, in the heat that I know is between us.

She still has some pizza sauce clinging stubbornly to the corner of her mouth. I reach for her without thinking, hypnotized by the look of her in the moonlight. My palm cups her jaw and her lips part as my thumb touches her mouth. She sucks in a shaky breath. Desire pounds out a drumbeat at the base of my spine. That warm, soft, glowy feeling in my chest tumbles easily into an inferno.

"Pizza sauce," I explain, rubbing once. My voice is a low rasp, grit at the edges. My fingertips slip into the hair just behind her ear, and I let my thumb trace the curve of her bottom lip, helpless not to. Her breath shakes beneath my touch, but I don't look at her eyes. I can't. I can only look at the petal pink softness of her mouth and my thumb at the corner of it.

What would she do if I slipped my thumb into her mouth? Would she make that whimpering, wanting sound—same as she did the other night? Would she let me drag it from her lips and trail it straight down over the column of her throat to that pretty red rose between her tits? Would she sigh my name? Would she like it?

Nova's face tips up, open and willing and—*fuck*—trusting. She looks like she wants me to kiss her. I want to kiss her. But I'm always seeing the things I want to see, and I can't trust that I'm what she wants right now.

I get it. I get what she said about trust feeling like a gift. Because right now with her looking at me like this, I want to earn that trust. I want to be worthy of it.

And I'm not going to push her. Not when she's been so clear about what she wants.

It feels like trudging through mud, but I step away from her. I grab the pizza box out of her hands and hightail it to the kitchen, putting more space between us. She doesn't say anything, and when I turn around again, she's tugging her beanie on her head. She gives me a smile and . . . I must have imagined it. Whatever it is that just happened. Because everything is exactly as it's always been between us.

No tension. No secret looks of longing.

Just me and Nova sharing some space.

"Thanks for the pizza," I tell her.

She nods and shrugs on her jacket. "Thanks for the movie."

I walk her to the front door and prop it open with my palm. She hops down the stairs to her car parked behind mine, a Chevy that is more or less seventeen times her size.

"I'll see you this week?" she calls.

I lean against the door. I feel like I need the support. "For what?"

She kicks her boot up on the footboard of the truck and swings herself in the driver's seat. She rolls down her window with three cranks of her arm. It makes me smile that she drives this old thing. I bet it was a hand-me-down from her dad or brother.

"We'll do those business visits," she says, bossy as ever. "Pick me up at the shop when you want to go."

"As you please," I yell back.

She smiles at me through the windshield. "Always."

I wave as she drives off. She rumbles down the path in her gargantuan truck, kicking up dirt as she goes, her red taillights disappearing around the bend. I stand there until it's just me and the moonlight, the slowly settling dust and the odd lightning bug, flickering in the darkness.

And for the first time in a very long time, I don't mind the quiet.

❖ 16 ❖

NOVA

I ALMOST KISSED Charlie in his kitchen.

I wanted to kiss him, and I have no idea what to do with that. It's been three days and I can't stop thinking about the look on his face. Earnest and tired. Vulnerable and honest. His thumb at my bottom lip and our faces so close, all it would have taken is one press of my toes to bring my mouth to his.

I liked it. All of it. The pizza and the talking and the movie and his hand around my ankle. It's the closest I've come to cuddling with another person in years and it was . . . nice.

Good.

Confusing.

But nice.

Jeremy knocks over something at the front of the shop with the end of the duster he discovered under a stack of boxes. He's been doing a whole lot of nothing since he showed up this morning.

"When is the grand opening?"

I close one file and open another, double-checking the numbers on my screen with the numbers on the sheet. Everything seems like it's in the right place, but instead of feeling calm and confident, I'm just paranoid that I've forgotten something. Especially since I've been spending most of my morning staring into space and checking my phone for texts from Charlie.

"We officially open October fifteenth. But we have a soft launch coming up." I glance up when Jeremy makes a confused sound. "A party for invited guests only," I explain. "Influencers and other tattoo artists so they can spread the word and hopefully bring in more business."

I wasn't sure about the concept at first, but I hit capacity for the event ten minutes after I sent the invitations. Layla is making little cakes shaped like succulents for people to snack on, and I rented a taco truck to serve food out front. Cake and tacos and tiny tattoos from a preselected offering list I printed out on fancy cardstock, *Ink & Wild* in looping print across the top. I pull the stack out of a drawer and trail my thumb over it. The tattoos I'm offering are all trademarks of my style—a bouquet with a trailing red ribbon, a hand holding a palm full of stars—color and delicate line work that I can replicate quickly and easily.

I'm excited for it. Excited and nervous. Charlie told me last night that I don't have to be perfect, but I do. I do. This needs to work. Not only because it's my dream, but because so many people have given up the things they've loved to get me here. If I fail now—if I lose focus for even a second—my house of cards could come tumbling down around me.

I wish it were easier to believe in myself. I wish it were easier to believe that all of this is going to stick around. That I've earned it. But imposter syndrome hangs over my head like a storm cloud I can't chase away.

I close the folder and dig my thumb into the middle of my forehead. Apparently even when things are going well, I'm going to panic. Awesome.

"Oh. Can I come?"

"To the event?" I ask. Jeremy nods. "Are you going to help?"

He shrugs. "Sure."

"Then, yes, you can come."

He shifts on his feet and dusts the edge of a mirror, looking at me out of the corner of his eye. "Can I get a tattoo?"

"No."

The door to the tattoo shop swings open and Charlie appears. Expensive camel coat with the collar turned up and a thick green sweater beneath. Awareness lights me up, a knot of anticipation low in my belly.

I scowl at him. He grins.

"Hiya, Nova girl. Did you miss me?"

Yes. Unfortunately, I think that's exactly what I've been doing.

"No." I tip-tap my way across the keyboard and pretend like I'm doing something important. "Why? Have you missed me?"

He strolls his way to the table and drops a folder and two cups of coffee on the edge. "Desperately," he says, still with that grin. He glances over his shoulder at where Jeremy is pretending to dust while I pretend to type. We really do make an excellent pair. Nothing is ever going to get done in this studio. "Are you aware that Jeremy is assaulting your tattoo displays?"

Jeremy huffs. "I'm dusting them."

Charlie's face collapses in confusion. "Why?"

"Because I work here," Jeremy says, sounding far too smug for someone who has been employed for less than seventy-two hours.

Charlie turns back to me with both of his eyebrows raised. I raise mine right back.

"What?"

Charlie picks up one of the coffees, opens the lid to peer inside, then hands it to me. "Nothing."

I reach for it and curl my palms around its warmth. It smells like cinnamon and pumpkin, my favorite Tuesday pick-me-up from Ms. Beatrice's. Charlie takes the other cup for himself and props himself against my desk.

"It doesn't look like nothing."

He shrugs and picks up one of my printed tattoo cards. "You've got an ooey gooey heart, Nova Porter."

I snatch the card out of his hand and put it back on the stack. "No,

I don't." Apparently, I have a bubble-wrapped heart. A stone heart, if my siblings are to be believed.

He hums and plucks up another one. "Yes, you do. You're a big ol' softie beneath all of those tattoos. But don't worry." He winks and goose bumps erupt across my skin like a shower of sparks. "Your secret is safe with me."

I might be safe with him, but I'm starting to think I'm not so safe from him. Not my secrets and not this feeling in my chest every single time he's around. Like someone is pressing down and pulling me up at exactly the same time.

I am cracked wide open, want spilling out and filling me to the brim. I don't understand how this happened. I don't have cravings and I don't do distractions. I don't go back for seconds.

But I think Charlie might be the exception to that rule. He was supposed to get out of my system, not burrow himself deeper.

He looks at the tiny tattoo card in his hand and waves it back and forth. "What are these for?"

"Exclusive influencer party," Jeremy answers from the front of the room. Christ, I forgot he was here. "You're not invited."

"Is that so?" Charlie ignores Jeremy completely and stares down at me, one dark eyebrow raised. "Am I not invited, Nova?"

"Do you want to be invited?"

"Depends." He taps the card against the palm of his hand. "Can I get a tattoo?"

"I don't know. Tiny Oompa-Loompas aren't one of the selections."

His navy eyes linger on one of the tattoos in the bottom right corner. It's a small peony, the petals in full bloom. A twin to the one inked across my ribs. His gaze flicks to me and the old T-shirt I have knotted at my waist, considering. I brace for myself for impact, but the flirty innuendo never arrives. He jerks his eyes back to the card in his hands and clears his throat. Like he doesn't want to be caught doing something he shouldn't be.

"I think I'd like one of these," he says, ignoring the suggestive comment wrapped in a bow that I dropped in his lap. I don't know if it's because Jeremy is here and clearly listening or because he's suddenly concerned with holding a boundary between us. But it stings.

Last night, I stood with my face tilted toward his and waited for a kiss that never came. This feels just like that. Like he's being careful to make the right choice when he has never once been careful with me. He hasn't been careless either, but he's been . . . open. Honest. Aggressively transparent with whatever is going on in that head of his. He's made excuses to be close and flirted his way through conversations.

And now he's standing on the other side of the table pretending to study a card and keeping his thoughts to himself. I thought that's what I wanted. Everything kept in neat boxes. But I don't like it at all.

I pluck the card from his hand. "No, you still can't get a tattoo."

"Got something special planned for me?"

I snort. "Sure."

A warning label, right at the hollow of his throat. *This man will upset all of your carefully laid plans. He will be your biggest distraction.*

"I'm going to hold you to that. In the meantime—" He drops the files tucked under his arm on the table. "Here."

"What's this?"

"It's Form 941 for your federal taxes. I didn't see it with your other paperwork."

"What other paperwork?"

"The paperwork on your kitchen table."

I take a small sip from the take-out cup. It's exactly the way I like it, down to the cinnamon sprinkled on top. "When were you going through the paperwork on my kitchen table?"

"When I was waiting for your coffee pot to brew," he says, lowering his voice to a gruff rasp. "While you were sleeping."

When I was naked in my bed, he means, and he was shuffling through my house in nothing but his pants, unbuttoned and low around his hips, bleary-eyed and messy-haired.

He taps the top of the folder. "You need to file that with the rest of your stuff."

I flick it open and look down at the top piece of paper. Charlie has already filled out most of the information, down to my business-identification number. The itchy, claustrophobic feeling from earlier comes roaring back, pressing against my shoulders.

"I can't believe I forgot something," I murmur.

"Yes. I can't believe you forgot this one document out of the seven hundred you need to complete in order to open a business in the state of Maryland." He leans over the desk and shows me the blank line at the bottom of the page. "Sign here and I'll send it in for you."

"You don't need to do that."

"I'm happy to."

I know he is and that somehow makes everything worse. That he'll bring me my favorite coffee and the forms I forgot to fill out and ask for nothing for himself. I wish I knew what he wanted. I wish I knew what I wanted too.

I sign the bottom of the paper and toss it in the top drawer of my desk. I'll send it myself. I don't need any more favors from Charlie.

He slurps at his coffee, purposely making it louder than it needs to be. "Has anyone ever told you that you're a stubborn woman?"

"With alarming frequency and incredible detail," I volley back. I give him a tight smile. He huffs a laugh and tips his head toward the door.

"You ready to go?"

"Go where?"

"Business visits," he explains. "You said you wanted to do those this week."

No part of me wants to walk with Charlie through town right now. I still feel too raw, too unfocused, too wobbly on the edge of . . . everything. But it's a thing that needs to be done, and I did promise.

"Sure," I sigh.

Charlie laughs. "What glowing enthusiasm."

I stand from my chair and grab for my coat. Charlie is pleased with himself, watching me struggle with the sleeves of my jacket with unbridled amusement. "Stop making that face," I snap.

"We've been over this, Nova girl. This is just how my face looks."

"Well, it's a dumb face," I grumble.

Charlie laughs, a flash of white teeth, eyes crinkling at the corners.

"Sure it is." He takes another slow sip of his coffee and winks at me. "That must be why you look at it so much."

I AM A mess.

I am grumpy and frustrated and far too aware of Charlie. The stretch of his shoulders beneath his coat and the smell of his cologne. The strong line of his jaw and the way he twists his big body to block me from the wind that keeps lifting my hair. He tries to engage me in conversation, and I grunt in response, too stuck in my own head.

This is why I don't date. This is why I don't do relationships. I should be focused on the harvest festival and the shop, and instead I'm worried about why Charlie didn't kiss me in his kitchen. I hate feeling like I don't know what I'm doing, and I've never had any clue when it comes to relationships.

I feel stupid. Childish. A silly girl with a crush.

We abandon any attempts at conversation by our second stop on Main Street, standing in the record shop like two people who don't even know each other. Charlie is charming and I am . . . not, flicking through a collection of eighties punk rock instead of trying to do what I volunteered to do. I'm just going through the motions, stuck in my own head and this weird tension that won't seem to break.

He's still holding strong to his infuriating level of careful. Careful to keep a polite amount of space between us. Careful to only speak when spoken to. Careful, careful, careful. He doesn't knock into my shoulder or tease me about his theoretical tattoos after our third stop. He keeps his head down with both hands gripped tight to some invisible boundary we never discussed. All of his touches are polite and brief, and while I'm busy trying not to think too much about any of it and why it feels like a sledgehammer in the middle of my chest, he's acting like Inglewild's prodigal son.

This is what you wanted, I remind myself. *This is what you told him you wanted.*

Everywhere we go, it seems like someone wants to talk to him. I've lived here my entire life, but he greets people I've never seen before with a smile and a handshake, asking after grandchildren and pets like everyone is a long-lost family member. The attention and well-wishes make him light up, and I'm the black storm cloud trailing after him.

"How do you know all of these people?" I grumble as Becky Gardener waves over her shoulder. I've been in and out of three stores while she and Charlie stood on the sidewalk and talked about bean dip recipes. He agreed to write his down for her and drop it by the daycare center. Something about Taco Tuesday. I really don't know. I'm still too confused on the how to investigate the why. Also, I don't care.

Charlie scratches once behind his ear and squints into the sun. He pulls a pair of sunglasses out of his pocket and slips them up his nose. I am quietly devastated once again by how good-looking he is, and then annoyed that I've noticed. I never used to notice.

Then he fucked me in twelve different positions across my bedroom and watched a Katharine Hepburn movie with me and now I can't stop noticing.

Charlie glances at me over his dark lenses. "I spend a lot of time in town, Nova. I know who people are."

But there's a difference between spending time somewhere and knowing the dates of dance recitals . . . allergy information and whose kids have been working on their T-ball swing. He knows details. He cares about them. He's invested.

"Why?" I ask. Charlie is here almost every other weekend, even before he committed to overseeing Lovelight Farms for Stella. "Why do you spend so much time down here?"

"Stella is here."

"You don't always see her when you come down."

A half smile tugs at his mouth as he pushes his glasses back up his nose. "Are you keeping tabs on me?"

"You're difficult to miss, Charlie. Especially when you're wearing a tutu and doing a keg stand at trivia night."

"It was ballet themed," he mumbles to himself, referencing the long-held, passionately defended town rule that all trivia nights adhere to a dress code related to the theme. He kicks at a loose rock on the sidewalk. "My friends are here," he says quieter, seemingly talking to his boots. "Alex and Caleb. Your brother. Luka."

"You don't have city friends?"

"I have city friends," he replies, but he doesn't sound too sure of that answer. He sighs. "I like it here."

"You like it here."

"Yes. I like it here." His eyes are unreadable behind the dark lenses of his glasses. "The food is good."

"You're visiting from New York and you think the food is good? Here?"

Ms. Beatrice has a decent breakfast and Matty makes some excellent pizza, sure, but it's not New York.

"That's what I said, isn't it?" His lips are twisted down in a frown. It's a strange look on his handsome face. Out of place. "What's with the inquisition?"

"I'm trying to figure you out."

"Well, best of luck with that. Let me know what you discover when you do." He nudges my shoulder with his and tips his chin toward Rooted, a tall, domed glass building at the very end of the block. Mabel's greenhouse is our last stop of the day. "Let's finish up. I know you've got other stuff you want to get to."

His comment sours my mood further. If I wanted to be doing

other things, I'd be doing them. For some reason that defies logical explanation, I wanted to do this with Charlie today. I wanted to bring him pizza the other night. I wanted him to kiss me in his kitchen, and I want him to kiss me now.

And it's making me a grump.

As we're crossing the street, I catch him reaching for my elbow, only to redirect himself and tuck his hand in the pocket of his jacket instead. It snaps the tether I'm keeping on myself.

"What are you doing?"

He blinks at me. "I am . . . crossing the street with you."

"With your hands," I clip. "What are you doing with your hands?"

He glances at his hands in his pockets like the explanation for my sudden outburst will be there. "My hands are in my pockets."

"I know they are. Why are they in your pockets?"

"Because it's . . . cold?" He answers my question with a question, his eyebrows furrowed in a confused slash. "What are we arguing about right now?"

I wish I knew. I wish I could figure out this tangled-up, twisted feeling making an ugly mess in my chest. This . . . want that won't go away.

"You keep—" I bite off the rest of my sentence, frustrated. I step up on the curb and tell myself to get it together.

Charlie pulls me to a stop on the sidewalk, tucking us both halfway in the alley between the duckpin bowling alley and the bar. It's the first time he's touched me with intention all day, and he immediately drops my elbow to tug off his sunglasses, hooking them in the front of his green sweater. It dips in the front, exposing the hollow of his throat. I stare at that tiny patch of skin instead of his face.

He ducks his head down and tries to meet my eyes. "What's going on with you?"

"Me? You're the one with the problem." I poke him hard in the chest. We somehow keep finding ourselves here, arguing about nothing. "You're different."

His lips flatten into a line. "No, I'm not."

"Yes, you are. You're . . ." I think about our conversation in my kitchen, the night all of this started. He told me he wouldn't fuck me if it would change things between us, but he's the one doing the changing. "You're hiding from me."

His jaw clenches tight. "I'm not."

"You are," I tell him. "You're acting differently, and I have no idea why."

"Nova."

"Don't 'Nova' me," I snap. It's making me feel like I'm imagining things and I'm not. I know that I'm not. "I thought we fixed things. Are you still mad about what I said at my parents' house?"

"I'm not mad," he mumbles, but he thrusts his hand through his hair, pulling lightly at the ends. "I was never mad, Nova. We're fine. Everything is fine."

"We are not fine." I cross my arms over my chest, tugging my coat tighter around me. The six inches of space between us might as well be a mile. "What's changed? Why are you acting like . . . this?"

"Like what?"

"Polite," I spit, like the word is personally offensive. He's acting like a watered-down version of himself. Like we were never friends to begin with.

"I know it's hard to believe, Nova, but I can be a polite, mature person."

"Not with me," I say. "With me, you're just yourself. You don't try to be anything other than Charlie."

And that's the painful rub of it, I think. The part that chafes. Last night in a kitchen that was too small to contain the whole of him, Charlie was more himself with me than he's ever been. He didn't try to shape himself into anything other than exactly who he is. An honest, kind man. No fancy clothes or quippy comebacks. No flirtation or innuendo. Just Charlie and the person he is beneath everything else. He dropped the performance.

And then this morning, he showed up at my shop and acted like it never happened.

"I'm trying to—" He huffs, eyes flashing. "I'm trying to do what you want."

"And what do I want?"

"I wish I fucking knew!" It explodes out of him in a rush, frantic energy crackling like bursts of static. "I wish I knew what you wanted, Nova. That would make all of this a hell of a lot easier."

"I want you to be normal with me."

"And what is normal, huh?" He drags his palm along his freshly shaven jaw. His gaze holds mine, frustration in the lines by his eyes. "What's normal for us, Nova? Sometimes we argue, sometimes we laugh, but most of the time, you can't stand the sight of me."

"That's not true," I tell him.

"Isn't it?" He steps closer until I'm pressed against the brick wall, his chest brushing against mine. I suck in a breath. "I like you, Nova, but I've got no fucking clue what normal looks like for us. I'm not being different on purpose. I'm just . . . I'm trying to hold myself together around you."

My chest feels fit to burst. Everything is hanging on by a thread. The shop, the fight with my brother, Charlie and all the things I don't want to be feeling. I'm being tugged in too many directions and it's all of my own doing. Why is this so hard for me? Why do I tuck myself in these carefully constrained boxes? Why do I put . . . all of this pressure on myself to be perfect in every single way?

Why do I feel like if I want too many things, I'm going to lose all of it?

My heart thunders in my chest. I tip my head back and stare at Charlie, letting go of all the things I should and should not be thinking and feeling and doing. I let myself be right here. In this spot. With him.

I let myself want.

"Well, stop it," I breathe.

Charlie looks at me, exhausted, one hand anchored against the back of his neck. He releases it with a sigh and props himself against the wall at my side, his palm against the brick, his long body slouched in exasperation. Loose lines and slumped shoulders.

"Sure, all right," he says. "What should I stop?"

"Stop holding yourself together," I tell him, and then I do exactly what I've wanted to do every single time I've seen him since he left me in my bed with a Post-it note smiley face and a hickey on my neck. I do the thing I told myself I wasn't allowed to do.

I press up on my toes, cup Charlie's face in my hands, and I kiss him.

17

NOVA

IT TAKES HIM a second.

I stand there on my tiptoes with my mouth pressed to his and I wait, both of my hands cupped gently around his jaw. I suck on his bottom lip, and he makes a sound low in his throat. I brush my tongue there and he shudders out a sigh.

Respond, I beg with my mouth against his. *Show me I'm not the only one who feels like this.*

My nails scratch through his hair and he shudders. I lean back to breathe, my nose brushing his, my eyes clenched tight.

I wait.

And then Charlie drags my mouth back to his and kisses me like he wants to devour me.

He's messy with it, desperate, the hand on the back of my neck trembling. But I'm just as needy, arching away from the wall to press my body to his, a moan whimpered into his mouth when he grips me tight and pushes me right back against the brick.

"Nova," he whispers against the corner of my mouth, a shaky exhale. "You said you wanted a one-time thing."

I nod and slip my hands up to the collar of his coat, tugging him closer. There's no space between our bodies but he's been circling just out of reach all day and I'm tired of it. I want to feel the heavy weight of him caging me in. I want him tucked against me until I can't breathe.

He gives in to my incessant yanking and slips closer, sliding his knee between my thighs and bracing his hand on the wall behind my head so my hair doesn't catch on the brick.

"I thought once would be enough," I explain quietly. "It usually is."

He leans back, dark eyes watching me carefully. His cheeks are pink and his bottom lip is slightly swollen. He looks dazed and confused and deliciously out of sorts. Like I've just told him it's raining pickles or I've filled out the wrong tax form.

"Once wasn't enough?" he asks. "With me?" A thin note of disbelief hums beneath his words. It's barely noticeable but there. I sometimes forget that for all his easy smiles, Charlie has insecurities too. Ones that are coming into focus the longer I look.

Something in my chest turns over and I shake my head. "It wasn't."

"Why didn't you say anything?"

I drop my head back against the brick wall and stare at him. "I was waiting for you to say something."

He blinks twice, still bewildered. "Were you?"

I nod. "Yes. I thought my intentions were obvious. It's why I've been so cranky this morning."

"It was not obvious, and you're usually cranky."

"Thank you, Charlie. You sure have a way with words."

"How did you make your intentions obvious?" he presses. "You told me at family dinner you didn't want to be friends, and now you're telling me you're mad I'm not kissing you. I'm trying to keep up here, Nova. But it's tough to follow."

I wince. "I know. I'm not being fair." I toy with a button on his coat. "I'm going to work on being honest with you, even if I'm not sure what it is I want. Here's the first thing, are you ready?"

He nods.

"Last night, in your kitchen, I thought you were going to kiss me. I wanted you to kiss me."

Something in his face softens. "I wanted to kiss you too."

I take a deep breath and tell myself to be brave. "I've thought about you every day since the night we had together."

"Of course you have," he murmurs. "I haven't given you a second to breathe. I wanted you to think about me."

"More than that," I whisper back. We're slowly moving closer together. My nose brushes his. "I've been wanting you, Charlie. I can't stop thinking about all the things we didn't get to do."

He squeezes my hand still caught in his, then lifts it and presses a quick kiss to my knuckles.

"Okay," he says, a knowing gleam in his eye. I've seen that look before. On a dance floor made of old rugs and in the stillness of my bedroom. A tease and a promise, all in one. "What should we do about it?"

I like that word so much. *We*. But I feel the implication of it like a pinch right in the middle of my chest.

"I want to bring you home with me, but—"

Charlie interrupts the rest of my sentence, swooping down and catching me in another kiss. He curls his fingers around my jaw and holds me to him, licking into my mouth. He's demanding and rough, his teeth scraping along my bottom lip. When he pulls away, we're both breathing heavily.

"Yes," he says. "That."

I squeeze my eyes shut tight, then open them with a sharp exhale. "I still don't want a relationship," I say carefully. I don't want this thing with Charlie to feel like something on my list that needs attention. I want to have this with him without having to worry about what it means or what comes next. It's selfish, but it's all I can manage right now.

My hands clench in the collar of his coat. I smooth it down, then twist it up again. "I know it feels like I'm leading you on right now, but I want to be really clear and—"

He cuts me off again, lips gentle this time. He brushes his mouth back and forth, a smile ticking at the very edge.

"I get it, Nova. I hear you." His hand brushes down my back, tucking me closer to his body and away from the wall, his thumb tracing over each bump of my spine through the material of my coat. "I don't care how we categorize what we're doing, as long as we can keep doing it."

My hands slip from his collar to his chest. "You want to keep doing it?"

"I do if you do," he murmurs.

"I do," I answer quietly. "But only if you're okay with that."

"Something casual?" he asks. I nod my head. His hand meanders down my back with large, sweeping strokes. "Yeah, I'm okay keeping it casual. I'm only here through the end of the month anyway. That probably makes the most sense for both of us."

I nod. "Yeah."

"No expectations," he says easily, a bright smile sweeping across his mouth. It never quite reaches his eyes, does it? "It's how I do my best work."

I frown at him. Keeping it casual has nothing to do with him and everything to do with me. That part of me feels broken, rusty with disuse. My bubble-wrapped heart.

"Maybe we can call it *business* casual," I say slowly.

His hands tighten on my hips. "What does that mean?" He laughs.

"Business casual," I say again, the idea growing on me. Yes, that's exactly what I want. Something casual but with parameters in place so neither of us can hurt the other.

I tuck my finger in the collar of his sweater and tug him closer. "It means this only lasts as long as we want it to. It also means . . ." I tip my chin up and nip lightly at his bottom lip. "It also means if I'm fucking you, no one else is."

I'm still figuring out what I do and I don't want, but I know for a fact I don't want to share Charlie with anyone else.

His eyes flash dark and his breath catches, an inhale that lasts an extra beat. I watch with interest as his tongue wets his bottom lip. I have no right to be possessive over him, but I am, and I think he likes it.

I think he likes it a lot.

"Are you using corporate speak to turn me on, Nova?"

"That was not my intention."

"The results seem to be in your favor." His fingers flex where they rest against the back of my neck. "Business casual," he repeats, thoughtful.

I nod, wrapping my arms around his waist beneath his coat. "That's what I can offer right now. What do you say?"

He tips my chin up with his knuckles and catches me in another kiss. I sway into him.

"I say we should go back to your place."

WE'RE PROBABLY CAUSING a scene.

Charlie and I aren't exactly being discreet as we speed walk down the street toward my house. He keeps his palm against the small of my back and I keep my hands buried in the pockets of my jacket, but we keep sneaking looks at each other.

"Of course I'll check out your thermostat," he yells when we stop at a crosswalk, the elementary school bus unloading for the afternoon on the other side of the street. "I'd be happy to."

I stare at him. "What thermostat?"

"The one that's broken," he yells again.

"What is happening right now?"

"I'm creating a plausible reason for why I'm going to your house in the middle of the afternoon," he says out of the side of his mouth.

"Do you really think anyone would care?"

"I can think of several people that might care."

He's right. This town cares entirely too much about what everyone is up to in their free time. This would be headline news for the phone tree. My hands fiddle with the zipper of my jacket. I yank it up and then down. Up again.

Charlie reaches over and closes his hand around mine, tugging my zipper up until it's tight against my neck.

"Nova," he says carefully, eyes straight ahead. "Enough with the zipper."

"Is my stained Blondie T-shirt tempting to you?"

His eyes slant down to mine. "You are tempting to me."

The bus drives off and Charlie steps off the curb. He doesn't wait for me to cross with him, two of my steps for every one of his.

"I don't think I've ever seen you walk so fast."

"I'm highly motivated," he tosses over his shoulder.

Motivated until we're on the same street as my house, and the entire sidewalk is blocked by a gaggle of geese, their dark heads bobbing as they waddle their way across the pavement. There must be a hundred of them, squawking and hissing at each other. We both stumble to a stop, Charlie's hand curled around my bicep as he tucks me halfway behind him.

"What the fuck is happening?" he mutters. "What the fuck is this?"

"It looks like a gaggle of geese."

"Is it every goose on the Eastern Seaboard?"

Possibly. It's certainly a lot of them. I think they're going for the fountain on the other side of the street. Charlie tries to step forward, and the one closest to us flaps its wings in warning. The goose right behind it hisses.

I grab the back of his coat and tug him back, my arm wrapped around his middle. "It's probably best to wait them out."

Charlie grunts and drops his head back, his jaw and the line of his neck in stark relief against the bright blue sky. I feel a swoop low in my belly.

"If we're waiting, you're going to need to stop staring at me like that," he mutters, glancing at me out of the corner of his eye.

"Like what?"

"Like you've got ideas."

I blink innocently and his whole face collapses into something serious and strained. Twilight eyes. Middle of the night, Charlie above me in bed eyes. Tense jaw and a lock of dark hair over his forehead. A man pushed to the very edge. The lovely, unrestrained version of Charlie. The one that was missing when he walked into my studio this morning.

"I have lots of ideas," I say, voice low. He makes a faint pleading sound. I laugh. "I told you. I can't stop thinking about all the things we didn't get to do." I trail a single finger over his knuckles. "Would you like to hear about them?"

He grabs my hand with his and starts to tow us through the geese. One snaps at my ankle, and I make an embarrassing squeaking noise, pressing myself closer to Charlie. His hand tightens on mine and he walks faster. "You can tell me all about your ideas at your house."

"If a goose bites me, you're not going to hear anything."

"Do geese bite?"

"I better not find out."

The geese don't bite, but they aren't happy with Charlie steam-rolling a path through them. I press my grin into the space between his shoulder blades as he grumbles and curses under his breath, his hand reaching behind him to anchor in the front of my jacket, keeping me close. Once we're free of the gaggle, Charlie tugs at me until I'm in front of him, marching us the rest of the way down my block and up my front steps like he can't wait a second more.

We collapse through my front door and immediately grab for each other, my hands pushing his jacket off his shoulders while his fingers yank at my zipper. Something tears, a button goes flying across the hallway, and I laugh into his chin. We are a blur of grasping hands and fumbling kisses, uncoordinated and messy and tripping over one another.

"You should have told me sooner," he mumbles against my mouth, one hand working at his belt, the other cupped around the back of my head. I sigh and slip my cold hands beneath his thick sweater, the material bunching at my wrists. I trace his sides, his chest, the smooth muscles of his abdomen. His body goes rigid and then relaxes, a string pulled until it gives. He abandons his pants and grips my chin instead, holding my face to his.

"What?" I gasp into his mouth.

"You should have told me you wanted me again." He drags wet kisses down my jaw to my neck, nipping at the curve of my shoulder where he yanks my T-shirt to the side. I arch and press myself harder to him. "I would have given you anything you wanted, Nova."

I know he would have. But I want him to take what he wants too. I guide him backward until the backs of his knees hit the couch in my living room, pushing at his shoulders until he collapses. He stares up at me, legs sprawled wide, his big body taking up a majority of the couch. His sweater is half pushed up his stomach, revealing a trail of dark hair beneath his belly button. I like him like this, loose leather belt and the press of his cock against his pants. Thoroughly undone. I drag my tongue along my bottom lip.

He pats his knee once. I grin.

"Oh yeah?" I ask.

He leans forward until he can tuck both of his palms behind my thighs. "Yeah." He yanks once and I go tumbling in his lap. I rest my elbows on his shoulders, my mouth hovering right above his as I get comfortable. I peck his nose once. Because I can. Because I want to. And because his face lights up when I do.

"Look at you being nice," he murmurs, palms dragging up the

backs of my thighs, fingers flexing against the curve of my ass. "Who knew you had it in you?"

"I'm about to have something in me."

A laugh bursts out of him, quick and delighted. "Nova Porter, what in the hell am I going to do with you?"

I trace my fingers along his jaw, down the line of his throat to the hollow between his collarbones. It's the best sort of indulgence to touch him like this after convincing myself I shouldn't. Like taking a bite of apple pie after committing to strictly salads. I want to sink my teeth right into Charlie.

He leans his head back against the couch and watches me with heavy eyes, my fingertips dancing down his chest to curl in the bottom of his sweater. I tug at it once and he lifts his arms with a smirk. I tug again until it's over his head and he's nothing but bare skin and smooth muscle in the hazy glow of my living room. He spreads his arms across the back of the couch as I perch in his lap, arm muscles flexing. I want to bite those too.

"How would you like me, Nova girl?"

My smile turns sharp and Charlie swallows hard, Adam's apple bobbing in his throat. I sink closer to him until our hips are pressed together and my mouth is a whisper from his.

"I like when you ask me that," I confess.

"I like asking it." His hands flex against the top of the couch. He's holding himself back, waiting for direction, and I like that too.

"I know you do." I grab the hem of my T-shirt and pull it over my head. My hair tumbles around my shoulders, and Charlie releases a breath like he's just been punched in the chest. I drag my finger down the rose between my breasts. "Would you like to touch me, Charlie?"

He's busy looking at the lavender lace against my skin, the demi-cup bra that barely covers me. It's fancy and impractical and I love it.

His tongue licks at the corner of his mouth. "Do you even need to ask that question?"

"You're not the only one that likes words," I say.

His eyes flick up to mine and hold, a flash of awareness that flares and fades like a single firework in an inky-black night sky. "Yeah, Nova. I'd like to touch you." He pushes off the back of the couch until we're nose to nose, his chest pressed tight to mine. One of his hands finds the middle of my back, fingertips spread wide. "Would you like to hear about all the ways I've thought about touching you since I left your bed?"

I nod and wrap my arms around his neck. His skin is so *warm*. "Yes, please."

His other hand finds the side of my face, fingers anchored in my hair. He guides my mouth to his and brushes a gentle kiss against my bottom lip. Another when I sigh against him.

"I've thought about kissing you a million times. Probably more." His thumb drags against my bottom lip, and I nip at it with my teeth. "I thought about that pretty flower between your pretty tits and kissing that too." He huffs a laugh. "How much do you want to hear?"

"Everything."

"Everything, huh?"

"Yeah." I take up the abandoned effort of his pants and slip his belt through the loops, tossing it behind me. He lifts his hips while I work at the button and zipper, the both of us shifting and wiggling and tugging to get them off. They stay trapped around one ankle when his hands settle at my hips, his forehead against the rose he likes so much, his breaths panting and heavy through delicate lace.

"I wanted to kiss you in my kitchen, and I wanted to peel off your sweater. I wanted to put you on your knees and wrap your braid around my fist. Fuck, Nova." Another breath explodes out of him. "Every time I look at you, I only want you more. I want to keep you in this lace and I want to rip it off. I want to fuck you until neither of us can move."

I thread my fingers through his and squeeze. "Okay."

He brushes his mouth over the petals of my red rose and looks up at me through his lashes. "Okay?"

"Mm-hmm, let's do that. All of it." I squeeze his hand again. "Where would you like to start?"

His eyes flash a shade darker, consideration in the set of his jaw. "I want to make you come."

My belly clenches tight, warm, liquid heat in the place where our hips are pressed together. I shift on his lap, then shift again when I feel the hard length of him pressing exactly right.

"I'm still wearing my underwear," I point out.

He tilts his head to the side and sighs happily, like he's just remembered and he's pleased by the fact. He fingers the strap of my bra, running his pointer finger beneath. He smiles at the tiny bow that holds it all together. "That feels like a challenge, Nova."

I force myself out of the lazy trance I've slipped into, rocking on his lap, chasing that dizzy, warm feeling and try to follow the conversation. "What does?"

He noses at my bra, lips barely grazing my nipple through the lace. "Do you think I can make you come with your underwear exactly where it is?"

I laugh. "Yeah, probably." I remember the last time we were together. How easy it was to lose myself with him. "Why? Are you having doubts about your abilities?"

"Nah." He plucks at that tiny bow again, twisting it back and forth. "I'm just feeling a little competitive."

"With who? Yourself?" I rock my hips against his harder, a rough drag that has his hand squeezing at my hip. He groans out something that sounds like my name and I feel it low in my belly. Behind my knees and tucked under my ribs. I like how he says it *so much*.

"It's good to have goals, Nova."

I snicker. "I bet I can last longer than you can."

"Is that so?" He tilts his head to the side. We haven't moved from the couch and I don't think we're going to. We're both too impatient. The friction is exactly right like this, his body beneath mine and my knees hugging his hips. I sink my fingers into his hair and change the angle, grinding harder in his lap. "Weren't you the one begging for me in the alley?"

"I wasn't begging."

He nips lightly at my ear. "It sounded like begging."

"We'll see who begs who." I roll my hips against his again. "How about we see who can get it done faster?"

He grins at me, delighted. "Oh, I like this idea." Both of his hands fall to my hips, helping me move against him. He drops his head back against the couch and watches me, blue eyes heated. "What will I win when I make you come?"

"Is my pleasure not enough of a reward?"

His grin tips wider. "I was thinking something more . . . material."

"Why does it sound like you want my underwear?"

He laughs, meeting my steady rhythm with a smooth roll of his hips. For a second, I lose track of the conversation and chase the friction instead.

"You always have the best ideas, Nova girl. But purple isn't exactly my color."

I keep rocking over him, my hands drifting over the lace that covers my breasts. "It's mine though. Isn't it?"

"It really is." Charlie's face goes a little bit slack, gaze focused on where my fingers dance over lace. I thumb at my nipple just to watch the way desire paints his skin pink, but it feels so good I do it again, driving myself down harder against him. He swallows once, and then swallows again, catching my hand with his.

"It doesn't count if you help." He tugs my hand to his bare chest and presses it there, his fingers threaded through mine. His other hand cups my breast, resuming my gentle strokes with his thumb instead. "What do you want?"

"What?" I breathe.

"If you win," he says. "What do you want if you make me come faster than I make you come?"

"You're serious?"

"For once," he nods, still with those maddening strokes against my breast. He tugs the cup down so it's tucked beneath, exposing the hard point of my nipple, pushing it up. He presses a careful kiss where the lace bites into my skin. "Yeah, I'm serious."

"For someone so serious, you're bending the rules." I arch my back and press myself harder into him. "You said you wanted to make me come with my underwear on."

He folds the other side of my bra down. "You're still wearing it, aren't you?"

"I guess you're right."

"Tell me what you want, Nova. If you win."

I consider my options. I'm having trouble concentrating when he's touching me like this, but I think that's the point. He shifts his hand and the sun catches against the watch on his wrist. Silver metal with a classic black face. I smile and let my head dip against my shoulder, hair curtaining us both. Golden sun beams and warm skin and cinnamon on the tip of my tongue.

"Your watch," I say, my hands mapping his smooth skin. "I want your Rolex when you come faster."

"We'll see." He pinches my nipple and my body bows over his. It's somehow better than I remember, being with Charlie like this. Everything feels amplified, electric. His arm curls around my waist, and he tips me to the side, pressing me down into the cushions of the couch. His hands fumble with the button of my jeans and then he's tugging them off in three rough yanks, my body moving down the couch with every pull.

"Someone is eager." I laugh.

"Don't act like you haven't been aching for it since I kissed you in the alley," he replies, face set in stern concentration, jeans tossed somewhere over his shoulder. He curls his hands around my ankles and drags his palms up, over my calves, behind my knees to the insides of my thighs. He traces all my tattoos with his eyes and then his fingers, gentle, soothing strokes that have me wiggling beneath him. I'm being memorized. Appreciated. Devoured.

His touch firms, and he lifts my leg, hooking my foot over the back of the couch. I lie there beneath him and let him move me how he likes.

"Did you think about touching me like this too?" I whisper, heart thumping wildly in my chest. The pressure between my legs is unbearable. I'll be lucky if I last a minute.

Maybe less than that when I figure out what he intends to do. Charlie lowers himself over me, tucking his broad shoulders between my thighs. His long body stretches out across the couch, and he drags a kiss that's more teeth than tongue to the inside of my knee.

"I've been thinking about this more than anything else."

And then he sets his mouth to me over the lace of my underwear. He keeps one hand splayed low against my belly and the other on the inside of my thigh, holding me still. I expected something fast, desperate, just as messy and unhinged as our kisses while we stumbled down the hallway. But he's slow and methodical, absolutely decadent in his thorough appreciation. The lace makes everything feel rougher, the scratch of the material and the heat of his tongue. I've never been consumed like this before. Never been so carefully worked over, every single minute movement of Charlie between my thighs intended to drive me higher.

And he does. Higher and higher even as I try to grasp at the edges of my control. He kisses me through the lace, and I watch him move over me, the hand on my thigh squeezing like he wants to hold as much of me as possible. His dark hair brushes against my belly, and I groan, sapphire blue eyes blinking up to mine while his mouth works me over. I make another choked sound, and he leans back, grinning into my leg.

"How're you doing, Nova girl?" His thumb works me while his mouth sucks a mark against the inside of my thigh, right next to an inked cluster of lavender. "Hanging in there? I haven't had my mouth on you for very long."

"I feel like I'm, oh—" I drop my head back against the couch and roll my hips into his hand, chasing that delicious tension. I'm definitely going to come faster. I'm already on the very edge, my leg trembling where he's hooked it over the back of the couch. "I can take it," I wheeze out.

"Yeah, you can." Charlie makes a pleased sound, working his mouth back up my leg to where his hand is still rubbing roughly through the lace of my underwear. He presses a kiss to the tiny bow on the front that matches the tiny bows on my bra.

"And I'm sure you'll make up some time," he grits out, voice low. His hand leaves my thigh, and I glance down my body, watching as he adjusts the front of his briefs. He strokes himself once and his eyelashes flutter against his cheeks. He opens his eyes and gives me a half smile. "Yeah. You're not lagging nearly as much as you think."

"That's good."

I don't really care. I just want more of this weightless, breathless feeling. I am boneless with want, all of my anxieties somewhere else entirely. It's just me and Charlie and all the things he makes me feel.

He seems to agree because he presses his mouth to me again without another word, his gentle, teasing rhythm slipping into something rough and desperate. He winds me up higher and higher, one hand sliding over my torso to my chest. He strokes his thumb over my rose, then grabs me roughly, pinching my nipple with two fingers. The bright burst of pain and the rough press of his mouth are enough to have me stumbling to the edge, the low grunt that vibrates between my legs sending me over it. Heat tugs at everything, a blissful pulse that rolls and rolls and rolls. I have to close my eyes against it. Have to curl both hands around the pillow by my head and squeeze so I'm not swept away.

Hands tug at my hips as Charlie rolls me over on my hands and knees. I go willingly, legs shaking and hair in my face. My body is suffused with tiny pinpricks of light. A sunbeam shot through cracked glass, rainbows spinning out across the room.

I vaguely register the sound of foil ripping, the shuffle of fabric being moved out of the way. Charlie tugs my underwear to the side and holds it there with his thumb, then pushes into me with a groaning, growling burst of breath.

"Fuck," he says. He holds himself still against me, his hands tight around my hips. "Fuck," he says again.

I'm all sensation. A blissed-out, half-delirious laugh tumbles out of me. He feels so good. Exactly right. Exactly what I've been needing. I reach back and grab his hand on my hip, needing to feel him. Needing to be connected to something while all of this golden light rushes through my body. His hand squeezes mine.

"You're gonna win, Nova girl," he breathes, his body moving against mine. He threads our fingers together at my hip and holds me tighter. "Fuck, you feel so good. And you look—"

His hand sweeps down my side, over the tattoos painted along my rib cage.

"You look so pretty I think I'm having a heart attack," he mumbles. He pulls out of me, groans, and then pushes back in half a second later. If he was trying to hold himself back, he's not doing a very good job of it. "You're definitely going to win. I'm going to last ten seconds, max."

Another laugh wheezes into a whine when he picks up his pace. I don't care who wins this stupid contest. "I think we've both won, don't you?"

He doesn't answer me with words. He just moves his body into mine, a smooth rolling rhythm that picks up speed and ferocity as the thread of his composure begins to unravel. He slaps one hand on the inside of my thigh, the snap of it urging my legs wider. I fall farther into the couch with a groan, my bare breasts rubbing against the soft material with every thrust.

I feel myself start to climb again and Charlie curses behind me, something pained and hungry, his hips abandoning their rhythm for something wilder, uncontrolled. My orgasm is sweet and surprising when it grabs me again, low tremors making me tremble in his arms, one of my knees giving out and sending us both tumbling to the couch.

I laugh and screech, body flailing, but Charlie yanks me up to him with my back to his chest, chasing his pleasure and drawing out my own. The angle makes him slide deeper, my legs spread wide over his. I throw my head back over his shoulder, and he cups his hand at the base of my throat, holding me to him, his breathing harsh in my ear. I'm surrounded by him in the best of ways, held safe and tight in the cage of his arms. I stroke my fingers across his forearm and encourage his fingers to press harder against my throat, and his body goes rigid against mine. He makes a sound against my ear, thumb tracing lightly over my pulse point. Relief. Disbelief. Bone-deep pleasure.

We collapse, Charlie half on top of me. His body is overly warm, and my underwear is a twisted mess, cutting into my hip. My left leg is almost completely numb.

I am quiet and thoroughly, wonderfully undone.

Charlie lifts his arm from around my waist and I grunt my displeasure. He snickers and brushes a quick kiss against the back of my neck.

"Hold on a sec," he explains. "You need to collect your winnings."

Something cold and heavy slips over my wrist. I squint open my eyes to see Charlie snapping the clasp of his Rolex. It looks obnoxious on my much smaller wrist, the weight of it too heavy, the band too wide. But I tilt my arm back and forth anyway, admiring the shine of it in the sunlight.

"It suits me," I muse.

Charlie props his head up on his fist, one of his legs thrown over mine. Our eyes catch and hold, and I get the distinct pleasure of watching his smile start at his eyes and slip over his face until his whole body is alive with it.

He drops himself back against the couch, face smooshed against my arm. He makes a deep, grumbling groan of appreciation. "It really does."

18

CHARLIE

I'M AN IDIOT.

A giant, stupid, ridiculous idiot.

I knew it couldn't last.

I knew I was swimming out of my depth, thinking I could have this one thing.

But I had hope. Hope that I could cling to the possibility of keeping this . . . this impossibility. I know I don't deserve it, but that's the thing about hope, isn't it? You can't reason with that little balloon in your chest.

"I think you're being a little dramatic about the cupcakes, bud." Caleb takes a bite of the cupcake in question. The last cinnamon apple streusel cupcake in the bakeshop. "The display case is half full. I'm sure you can find something else in there that you'd like."

I don't want anything else. "I wanted that cupcake."

Caleb shrugs, not a care in the world. "Well. That's too bad for you, isn't it?" He takes another bite, and I fight the urge to slap the entire thing out of his hand. "Maybe you should have gotten here earlier."

I meant to get here earlier, but I spent an hour and a half on the phone with my father, bickering about what he should and should not be doing. It was a long list. Basically everything he is doing, he should not be doing. He did not agree. We had an unproductive and frustrating conversation about it.

I wanted a cupcake to make me feel better.

A specific cupcake.

The one Caleb is holding the remnants of.

I drag my hand over the back of my head. Sure, Layla has other cupcakes in the display case, but I wanted this one. It's the one I woke up thinking about this morning. It's the one I've been thinking about all day. It's my favorite cupcake, and now all I'm going to be able to focus on is the fact that there's no more of that cupcake left for me to enjoy.

It's entirely possible I'm projecting.

I left Nova's house this morning before dawn, a thick cover of clouds blanketing everything gray. I woke up with her sprawled across my bare chest, her hair in my face and her legs tangled with mine. I tried to extricate myself without waking her, but every time I moved, she'd dig her cold toes between my thighs and grumble. A tiny, aggressive barnacle. When I finally managed to tumble out of the bed, she muttered something about biscuits, slapped my ass, and rolled to her side. She took all the blankets with her too, curled over her shoulder in a lump in the middle of her mattress.

This thing with Nova is unexpected. I've spent every day this week at her house or at her studio, enjoying the fuck out of business casual. I know I'm playing with borrowed time, and I know it's temporary, but I can't help the way I keep tumbling back into bed with her. I tried to limit myself, and all I managed to do was frustrate the both of us. So now I'm indulging. Over and over again. For as long as I'm here.

Caleb pops the rest of the cupcake in his mouth and I frown at him. Between this and the tres leches incident, he's on thin fucking ice. He's lucky his fiancée is in the back kitchen, probably playing with knives. I'm too scared of her to slap him around.

Caleb grins at me with his cheeks bulging like he knows exactly what I'm thinking. "I meant to ask," he says around a mouthful of food. "Where were you the other night?"

"The other night?"

"Yeah. You were supposed to watch the game with me and Alex. He tried calling you, but it went right to voice mail. Everything all right?"

It went right to voice mail because my phone was somewhere under Nova's bed and Nova was in my lap, my hands braced on her hips and my mouth busy with tracing every inch of ink I could find. I didn't realize my phone was missing until the morning.

That's how it goes with Nova. Every time I'm with her, it's like a vacuum of time and space until there's nothing but her smoky laugh and her dark blond hair. Careful touches and wicked grins. She reduces me to ash with the flick of her finger.

My phone buzzes in my back pocket, and I pull it out. Nova's name flashes across the screen. I glance up at Caleb, but he's busy staring dreamily into the display case, probably trying to figure out what to stuff his face with next.

"Yeah." I clear my throat and then clear it again. "Yeah, you know. Work stuff."

I swipe open the message.

NOVA: You left your shirt at my place.

CHARLIE: Did I?

It must have been the button-down she ripped off me the second I was in her bedroom. I slipped my sweater over my T-shirt when I left her house this morning, too tired to go hunting for it in the dark of her room.

NOVA: You did.

A picture comes through half a second later. Nova standing in front of that damn mirror in the corner of her room, my shirt dwarfing her small frame, a strip of skin visible from the hollow of her throat down to the lace underwear she has on. The rose between her tits framed perfectly. I bite the inside of my cheek.

Caleb gives me a critical look. "You're working too much."

I tilt my phone closer to my chest just in case he gets curious. "Yeah," I grunt. "Work."

Another picture appears below that one. The shirt is slipping down one shoulder, the swell of her breast a tease. Half an inch more and I'd see everything.

I type out a quick response.

> **CHARLIE:** It looks better on you than me.

> **NOVA:** Even better on the floor.

Another picture. Nova with her arm banded over her bare breasts in the mirror, my shirt crumpled at her feet. One leg crossed in front of the other, bruises in the shape of fingerprints on the curve of her hip. A sly smile, teeth clamped down on her bottom lip.

"Fuck," I whisper.

Caleb looks concerned now. "You all right?"

I tuck my phone in my back pocket and try to calm the hell down. If Caleb thinks I'm getting hard over Layla's croissants, he might dropkick me in the nuts. The promise of violence is enough to settle the blood rushing through my veins. I'm going to have the image of Nova in nothing but lace burned into my retinas for the rest of my life. When I'm lying on my deathbed, I'm going to request that exact picture projected on the ceiling above my head.

Maybe that's the tattoo I should ask for.

"M'fine," I mumble.

Caleb is dubious. "You don't look fine."

"I'm fine," I say again, doing my best to firm my tone. "I'd be even better if you didn't eat the cupcake I wanted."

He ignores me. "I don't understand how you're working two jobs."

I shrug and busy myself with a container filled with paper straws. I rearrange them until they're all at the same height. "Is it considered work if it's what you love?"

Caleb scoffs. "Do you love investment banking?"

No. In fact, I'm starting to think I hate it. But it's too late for me to pick a different path. I've firmly built my life around my career and everything I've accomplished in New York. These trips I make to Inglewild and Lovelight are a chance for me to catch my breath. Happiness distributed in increments. I'm afraid if I get too greedy for something more, it'll all go up in a cloud of smoke. Best to take what I can get.

"I love my paycheck." I reach over the counter and pluck a honey glazed bear claw out from the display case. I shove half of it in my mouth. "I love money, Caleb."

"See, I think that's something you like to tell yourself so you don't have to think too hard about it." Caleb crosses his arms over his chest and rests his hip against the front counter. "Look at you. You're not even wearing your watch."

Heat curls around the base of my spine and tugs. I'm not wearing my watch because Nova managed to unravel me in the space of two minutes. She won that thing fair and square, and I loved every second of it.

Layla elbows her way out of the kitchen, a pink scarf twisted around her ponytail, little strawberries printed all over it. She's holding a tray of mini pies that is bigger than she is. Caleb slips around the counter and grabs it before she can ask.

Layla gives him a grateful smile, wiping her hands on her apron. "Who is missing their watch?"

Caleb is busy gazing at the tiny pumpkin pies like they're the answer to his salvation. "Charlie is," he says without looking up.

Layla glances at my bare wrist, then up to my face. Her eyes narrow and her head cocks to the side.

"Is it a silver watch? Black face?"

I take another bite of bear claw and nod. "Yeah."

"Hmm," she says, mouth twisted to the side. A creeping feeling of unease pinches at the back of my neck. It's the same look she gave Beckett that day she walked into the office and realized she was ambushed. She's sizing me up, trying to figure me out. I swallow the rest of my pastry and try not to fidget under her attention.

"Why do you ask?"

"No reason," she says airily, but her face is telling a different story. Layla looks like she wants to take that scarf out of her hair and strangle me with it.

Her eyes dart to Caleb and hold, watching him place the pies in the display case exactly the way she likes. She chews on her lip. "I'm just wondering if I should make another thing of coffee or not," she says slowly, sounding stiff. She glances at me and hitches her thumb over her shoulder. "Help me with the machine in the kitchen."

It does not sound like a request. It sounds like an order. I know for a fact that she does not need help with the machine in the kitchen. I watched her make a three-tier cake two days ago with edible leaves that she placed with special tweezers. The coffee pot requires about an eighth of that attention and dedication.

I think she wants to get me in the back kitchen so there are no witnesses.

We stare at each other across the counter. Her eyes narrow, her head tips to the side, and . . . I know she knows. She knows what I've been doing with Nova. I have no idea how, but that devious little mind of hers has figured it out.

I shake my head. "No, thank you."

"It wasn't a suggestion. Help me with the coffee machine."

"I have a meeting, actually. That I should get going for."

"You can leave for your meeting after you help me with the coffee machine," she says between clenched teeth. I think she's trying to fake a smile. She's not successful.

Caleb finishes up with the pies and sets the tray on the back counter. "I can help you with the coffee machine," he offers.

She turns to look at him and some of the severity slips from her face. "Charlie can help me. You have that study group before homeroom this morning, remember?"

He glances at the clock on the wall behind the counter. "Ah, shit. You're right." He reaches down and collects his messenger bag, slinging it over his shoulder. He cups her chin with one hand and presses a quick kiss to her lips. "I'll see you later?"

"You absolutely will," she says, smiling. He lets his hand trail over her ponytail and the silky pink scarf twisted in her hair, tugging lightly. Her smile melts into something soft, and she clutches the front of his shirt in her fist, tugging him closer. I look away, fiddling with the straws again. Layla glued little cardboard pumpkins to some of them. I pick one up and twirl it between my fingers.

Caleb claps me on the shoulder as he rounds the counter. "You owe me a six pack," he calls, heading for the door.

"And you owe me an explanation," Layla says, a thin thread of warning in her tone. The door slams behind Caleb, and it's just the two of us, the morning rush over and the front of the small bakehouse mostly empty. There's no one to save me except Pete, sitting in the corner with a danish and a cup of coffee, reading the paper and minding his own business. Layla points to the door behind the counter. "Come help me with the coffee machine."

"I told Pete I'd sit with him and do the crossword."

"That's all right, young man," calls Pete, suddenly developing stellar hearing for the first time in his very long life. "I'm almost done."

Fuck. "Even eighteen across?"

"Even eighteen across."

Layla is still pointing at the door. "Coffee machine."

I swallow hard. "I really don't want to help you with the coffee machine," I whisper.

"Don't make me come around this counter."

"Fine. Okay. Fine." I move around the display case, careful to give her a wide berth, and push through the back door. It smells like cinnamon back here. Pumpkin and buttery, flaky pie crust. There's still some filling in the mixer on the corner of the long metal work desk. A collection of various silicone spatulas and a cooling rack, empty and waiting.

Layla starts collecting dirty items and stacking them in her arms. "Is there anything you'd like to tell me?"

Nova and I haven't discussed it, but I'm pretty sure telling people about our situation falls outside the lines of business casual. It doesn't feel right to lie to Layla, but I don't want to break Nova's trust either. It's our business. No one else's.

"The bear claws were good today," I say, trying my best to infuse my voice with as much enthusiasm as possible. "Did you use sea salt again?"

"Yeah, I used sea salt. It's a new recipe I'm trying where I put it in the glaze." She dumps her armful of dirty dishes into the sink with a clatter. "But I was referring to what you think you're doing with Nova."

I shrug and try to keep my face from doing anything weird. "Nova?"

Layla gives me a look. "Yes. Nova. This tall." She holds up her hand in front of her. "Blond hair. Pretty tattoos."

I have to bite the inside of my cheek against my smile. Her tattoos are *so* pretty.

Layla widens her eyes. "You know. Beckett's youngest sister."

"I know who Nova is, Layla. What are you asking?"

She turns on the water and grabs for the bottle of soap. "Why is Nova wearing your watch around town?"

This time I can't help my smile. It tugs at my mouth until I'm beaming at Layla across the small kitchen, a deep satisfaction settling in my bones. I didn't realize she was wearing it out of the house. She likes to taunt me with it when we're both naked, the watch and only the watch on her wrist. I think she likes to remind me of how easy it was for her to bring me to my knees.

But I like to remind her that I certainly make it worth her while when I'm down there.

"She won a bet," I tell Layla, rubbing my fist against my mouth, trying to scrub my smile away.

Layla arches a single eyebrow. "You bet your ten-thousand-dollar watch?"

No. I bet something, and that is the something that Nova said she wanted. She won the bet. She got the watch. I would have given her anything she asked for.

"It wasn't ten thousand dollars," I shrug. "And I have other watches."

"Interesting."

"Is it?"

Layla runs her soapy fingers beneath the water. "Very."

"How so?"

"That stupid smile on your face, for one." She shuts off the water and grabs a dish towel in the shape of a Christmas tree, drying her hands as she considers me, her mouth set in a firm line. "I don't think I've ever seen you look like that."

"What? Stupid?"

"No," she says. "Happy."

I feel it like a hand pressed flat to the middle of my chest, shoving me back. "I am happy," I manage around a throat that feels too tight. I don't know why that word bothers me so much. "I'm usually a happy guy, Layla."

I'm having fun with Nova. That's all this is. A release for the both of us. It's not what Layla is implying.

Layla hums, watching me as she dries her hands. "Okay."

"Okay, what?"

She shrugs and tosses the towel to the side. She pulls out a flat silver tray from the cabinet behind her and places it on the work table. She grabs a mixing bowl and drops it in front of me. "Okay. Just okay. You had a bet. She's wearing your watch. We'll leave it at that. Do you want to help me make some scones or do you need to go to your fake meeting?"

I take the bowl she hands me. Then the spoon. She reaches under the counter and sifts through some drawers before she emerges with a pale pink apron, ruffles at the edges. She tugs it over my head and then ties it at the small of my back. I still haven't moved an inch.

"It wasn't a fake meeting," I say.

It was absolutely a fake meeting.

"Sure."

I narrow my eyes. "Why are you being so nice?"

She reaches across the counter for the flour and drags it closer. It leaves a little streak of white across the tabletop. "I'm usually nice, Charlie," she tells me with no shortage of snark, echoing my earlier statement. But then she looks at me and her face softens. "Just . . . be careful, all right?"

I know what she thinks. It's written all over her face. She thinks what everyone else always thinks about me. She thinks I'm fucking around. That I'm using Nova to have a good time before I go back to my reality. But it's not true. I like Nova. If I won the watch bet, I was going to ask for another Katharine Hepburn movie night. Pizza on her lap and my legs on the coffee table.

Nova's making all the calls. She's setting the boundaries.

"It's not like that," I say quietly.

"Like what?"

I adjust one of the apron ruffles so it lays flat against my chest. "There's nothing going on."

Nothing that will last, anyway. There's no point getting all twisted up about it when we'll both be moving on in a couple of weeks. We'll have our fun, and that's that.

Layla smirks at me. "Oh, Charlie. Sweet, sweet Charlie. I was once as oblivious as you." She hands me a measuring cup, then a bag of sugar. "Now sift that into there. And find me some blueberries."

19

NOVA

"DO YOU THINK everyone sees the same colors?"

I lean my head out of the bathroom and look at Charlie. He's spread out in the middle of my bed in nothing but his black Calvin Klein boxer briefs, a bowl of chocolate-covered peanut butter pretzels resting in the middle of his chest. He digs one hand in the bowl and pulls out a single pretzel, holding it above his face as he stares at the ceiling.

I drag a towel through my wet hair. "What do you mean?"

"I mean, like, your walls are painted pink, right?"

I glance at my bedroom wall and then back to his prone body against my disheveled sheets. We actually made it to the bed this time, a rare occurrence despite how often Charlie has been in my bedroom over the past two weeks. He stopped by with some blank tax forms, spent thirty seconds pretending like he was here for a legitimate reason, then scooped me up, carried me up the steps, and tossed me on the bed. He made me come twice, then bent me over and took his own pleasure with both hands braced on my hips. I have three little bruises in the shape of his fingers against the curve of my waist. I think I like them more than my tattoos.

"They're more of a blush than a pink."

He leans up on his elbows and tosses a pretzel up in the air. He catches it in his mouth with a loud crunch. I have no idea why, but some part of me finds that wildly attractive. The part of me that's still blissed out and boneless, apparently.

Charlie notices my staring and winks. "All right. Blush. How do we know we're both seeing *blush*?"

I look at the wall and then back to him. "Because it's . . . blush?"

"But how do we know? Because we both describe that color as blush, right? But what if the blush I see is different from the blush you see?"

I toss my towel over the edge of the door and shuffle my way over to him, the back of my hand pressed to my mouth. "Is this what your brain does all the time?"

He grins at me, bright and boyish. "You'd be surprised."

I doubt that. Charlie is almost alarmingly transparent. He thinks he hides himself away, but I can read the lines of his body now. He sets his bowl to the side as I get closer and reaches for me. His hands open and close in a grabbing motion. *Come closer*, he's saying. *Come here.*

He cups his hands around my thighs and squeezes, tugging until I'm perched in his lap. I drag my fingers through his hair and yawn again, right in his face.

He frowns at me. "You're tired."

"I am."

"I'm taking up too much of your time."

"You're not," I argue. These stolen moments with Charlie might be my favorite way I've been spending my time lately. Everything else is deadlines and rushing and paperwork and crossing items off my list. But when we're together like this my brain is only focused on Charlie's warm body beneath mine and the delicious ache in my muscles. Unplugged.

I yawn again and Charlie sinks his hands into my hair. He rubs at the base of my skull, and I let out a deep, ugly moan. He snickers and circles his arm around my back, tipping me over into my bedding.

"You like that move," I grumble, my face half buried in a pillow.

He snorts a laugh. "You seem to like it too, Nova girl." He slips off the edge of the bed and tugs at the blankets trapped beneath my legs. I stare at the stretch and pull of the muscles in his torso and do absolutely nothing to help. He grunts and tries to yank at a blanket. It rolls me sideways and my legs go flailing.

"Easy," he says, dodging my foot. "I'm trying to burrito you the way you like."

"You are not doing a very good job."

"I'm doing a great job." He slaps at my knee and tries to pry a fuzzy gray blanket out from beneath my hips. "You're not exactly being helpful."

I snicker. "How so?"

"You're in my way."

A laugh bursts out of me, incredulous. "Oh, excuse me, Charlie. I didn't realize I was in your way as you try to swaddle me."

"Thank you." He manages to free my fuzzy blanket and he wraps it around my shoulders. "Apology accepted."

I stare at him as he fusses with the material, tucking it just right so it's under my chin. He is entirely focused on getting me cozy. I watch his face as he wraps the rest of the blanket over my shoulders. I guess he's been paying attention when I roll myself in my blankets every night.

My smile is half hidden behind a blanket that has tiny cats all over it. It's nice to be taken care of.

His phone buzzes across my dresser, and he sighs, shoulders slumping. I wiggle in my blanket cocoon and nudge him with my foot.

"Your dad again?"

He makes a vague noise of agreement. "Yep."

"Do you want to answer it?"

"Nope."

I frown at him. He sighs and yanks my blanket around me tighter. "I'm a grown man. I don't need to talk to my father if I don't want to."

The ringing on the dresser stops, and Charlie lets out a sigh of relief. "This is just a thing he does when he feels like he's not getting an appropriate amount of attention. It's been worse since—"

He lets the rest of that sentence drift off.

"Worse since what?"

He scratches at the back of his head and ducks down, peering at me. "You really want to talk about this?"

The way he asks the question—disbelieving and a little unsure—raps against the hollow in the center of my chest. Does he truly think I wouldn't care?

"I do."

He nods and collapses on the bed next to me. I go tilting to the side in the blankets, but he slips his arm around my back, holding me up. His hand squeezes at my hip, then slips down and gives the curve of my ass an affectionate pat through three layers of fleece.

"Since the divorce was finalized," he finishes with a sigh. His phone starts buzzing across the dresser again, and I can feel it this time, the wave of tension that makes his body pull tight. "I think he's lonely, but he's got a shit way of trying to connect with me."

Yeah, I've overheard some of their conversations. The first time I heard him talking to his father on the phone, I thought I was eavesdropping on a business meeting. There was no affection. No warmth.

"You don't deserve that," I tell him quietly, the words feeling clumsy on my tongue. I'm not good at comforting people, but I wish I was. I wish I could make the look on his face disappear.

Charlie rubs his hand across his jaw, keeping his face angled away from mine. "It is what it is," he says. He blows out a breath. "I can't be too hard on him."

"Why not?"

He shrugs and his phone finally stops that incessant rumble across the top of my dresser. We both stare at it, waiting for it to start up again. "I crave attention. I think I'm—" He swallows. "I think I'm more like my dad than I like to admit."

"No, you're not." The words tumble out of me before I can even register them as a thought. Charlie looks at me with amusement lighting his tired eyes.

"You don't even know my dad," he says.

"But I know you."

Charlie doesn't harass. He doesn't make people feel small to boost his own confidence. He might be loud and borderline obnoxious, but he's also kind. Thoughtful. He remembers things. He sees the details. He volunteered to work two full-time jobs so his sister could go on a honeymoon. He brought me printed tax forms in the middle of the afternoon because he knew I'd probably forget to fill them out.

I'm starting to think the jokes and the comments and the ridiculousness he wraps himself in is compensation for something else. A way to hide.

I wiggle closer, frustrated by the inability to use my arms. I suddenly hate this blanket burrito. "You're a good person, Charlie."

"That's all the orgasms talking," Charlie murmurs, nudging me with his shoulder.

"It's not," I argue. He turns his face toward mine and arches an eyebrow. "Okay, maybe a little bit. You give good orgasms, but that doesn't change the fact that you're also a good person." I knew it before we ever started sleeping together, and I know it better now. He huffs a laugh and my lips twist. "Do I need to list all of your positive qualities?"

A smile tugs at one side of his mouth. "It wouldn't hurt."

I wiggle one hand out from where it's trapped against my side. I flick up one finger. "You have excellent taste in watches." I lift another. "You have excellent taste in women."

"Both of those things are true." His half smile tumbles into a grin. "I am also smoking hot."

"Reasonably attractive, I'd say." I tuck my arm back in my blanket. I dip my chin until only my eyes are peering out of the top. "You're kind. You're invested. You're easy to talk to, and you go out of your way to help others. Why is it so hard for you to believe that you're a good person beneath all of that custom tailoring?"

"Because," he sighs, scratching his hand through his hair. He glances around my room, looking for inspiration in the large canvas print that takes up a majority of my wall. Wildflowers in bold strokes of color. A bright blue, cloudless sky. Charlie sighs. "I'm just pretending."

"Pretending what?"

"Everything." He swallows. "That I'm not a selfish person."

I snort and roll my eyes. "I don't believe you."

Charlie doesn't laugh. "You don't have to believe it. It's the truth. You think I came to Inglewild and volunteered to watch over Lovelight out of the goodness of my heart, but that's not true. I'm doing it for me. Because I wanted an excuse to be here."

I blink at him. "Wanting something doesn't make you selfish, Charlie."

"What about taking it?" His eyes drag to my lips and hold. His voice is a rasp when he asks, "If I take the things that I want, doesn't that make me selfish?"

I shake my head. We're not talking about the farm anymore.

"Not if it's willingly given," I whisper back.

A different sort of electricity flickers between us. Like plugging in a strand of lights that's been shoved in a box in the back of the attic only to find every bulb works. Bright and brilliant. Glowing gold.

Charlie's eyes flick back and forth between mine, a question in there somewhere. "Nova, I—"

A knock sounds at my door, quick and sharp. It cracks through my room, and my body goes tipping to the side again with a little bounce. Charlie steadies me with a palm at my side, frowning into the dark of my hallway.

"Did you order food?" he asks.

"No." I shake my head. "Did you?"

The door rattles with another impatient knock. A voice yells, muffled through the wood. "Nova!" Beckett calls. "I've had enough of you ignoring me. Open the door."

We both freeze, heads turned in the direction of my brother's voice.

"Tell me you moved the key under the welcome mat," Charlie whispers.

"I moved the key under my welcome mat."

A deep breath rattles out of him from somewhere in his chest. Relief, swift and sudden. I wince.

"I moved it underneath the potted plant on the other side of the porch," I rush to explain. "I give him three minutes before he finds it."

Charlie launches himself from the bed. "I thought I told you to move it."

My arms struggle with the blanket wrapped around me. "Just because you tell me to do something doesn't mean I'm going to do it."

"I guess not," he snaps. My front door rattles again, and Charlie drops to his knees, reaching under my bed for his discarded clothes. I don't even know how they got under there. It happens every time. My room almost consistently looks like it survived a bomb blast these days. "I'm not wearing pants, Nova."

I finally manage to free my arms from the blanket. "Then I suggest you put some on."

We collapse into a flurry of frantic movement and whispered arguing. I trip over the edge of the blanket and slam into the dresser. Charlie almost tears the arm of his shirt punching his hands through the sleeves. I listen for the door as best I can while Charlie mutters a string of obscenities under his breath.

He army crawls from beneath the bed again with his belt in one hand and his jeans in the other. His chest is still mostly bare, his shirt unbuttoned, a line of hickeys worked across his ribs in the shape of the little dipper. I was feeling creative earlier but now all I'm feeling is bone-deep frustration that I don't have a chain and lock on my front door. Maybe I'll start wedging a chair beneath the handle like I did in high school when my siblings lacked boundaries.

I hear the unmistakable sound of a key sliding into the lock. They still lack boundaries, apparently. I toss Charlie his sweater and it smacks him right in the face.

"Hide," I whisper.

"I'm a grown-ass man, Nova." Charlie strides across the room to my window with his jeans unbuttoned. "I'm not hiding."

"What are you doing?"

He yanks the window up with one hand.

"You can't climb out the window," I whisper, sounding hysterical.

"I can absolutely climb out this window," he whisper-yells back. "I don't want to die tonight."

"You said you're a grown-ass man."

"A grown-ass man who is terrified of your brother, yes."

"You might die when you fall out of my window."

Charlie winks at me, one leg thrown over my windowsill. Behind him, the moon hangs heavy in the night sky.

His lips tilt up at the edges. "But soft, what light through yonder window—"

"Oh my god," I mutter, spinning on my heel and leaving the room. I slam my bedroom door behind me. There's a shuffling at the door and then it opens.

20

NOVA

BECKETT APPEARS WITH a frown, his eyes immediately finding me at the top of the stairs. "Hey," he says, after an awkward stretch of silence. He holds up my spare key. "I let myself in."

"I can see that."

I haven't seen Beckett since our argument at our parents' house. It feels like a lifetime ago. It's probably the longest we've ever gone without talking to each other, including the time I told him he couldn't propagate garlic for shit and he didn't talk to me for an entire week.

He shifts on his feet and tugs his hat off his head, bending the bill beneath his palms.

"Is it okay that I'm here?" he asks.

My shoulders relax. "Of course it's all right that you're here." I make my way down the stairs. I wish he had shown up twenty minutes later and didn't know about my spare key, but there's not much I can do about that now. "Come on. I'll make us some tea and we can talk."

Beckett awkwardly follows me down the short hallway. We're usually comfortable in the quiet, but this is a different sort. His hurt was—and is—unbearable to me. I haven't reached out because I don't know what to say. And now I'm just as clueless as to where to start.

"I thought you were going to let me stand out there on the porch," he says quietly, peeking up at me. "When you didn't answer. And then

I got worried that maybe you were having a migraine. I'm sorry I just . . . burst in here like that."

"No," I sigh. "Don't apologize. I get it and I—I don't want to avoid you anymore, Beck."

He nods and adjusts his hat again, blowing out a heavy sigh. "Good. Because I hate avoiding you." Half of his mouth lifts up in a hesitant smile. "Don't tell your sisters, but you're my favorite."

"Obviously I'm your favorite. But I think—" Nervousness twinges in my belly, that touch of imposter syndrome that sits heavy on my shoulders making itself known. The idea that I can't make a single misstep without disappointing someone else. Him, in particular. "I think that's the problem, actually."

"What is?" Beckett asks, all traces of humor gone. He's alert, concerned, looking for the thing he can fix and make better. But I'm the one that needs to fix it this time.

"Your unwavering faith in me," I say quietly.

Hurt brackets his mouth, a punch right in the middle of my chest. "What do you mean?" he asks.

I nod toward one of the chairs at my kitchen table and busy myself with two mugs, pulling out the tea I know he likes. I consider it, then reach for the small bottle of whiskey. I need the liquid courage. I've never been great at sharing how I feel, especially with Beckett. The person I admire most in the entire world. I fill the kettle, set the bags in the mugs, and try to find my words. I try to find the root of this messy, uncomfortable pressure that sits heavy on my heart.

"Do you know why I wanted to open my shop here? In Inglewild?"

Beckett toys with the saltshaker in the middle of my table. "You said it was because you wanted to be closer to home."

I turn my cup in my hands, my palms pressed tight to the sides. "That's true. I do like being closer to you guys. I like seeing you more than every other weekend. But more than that, I think I wanted to— I wanted to do something that made you proud."

Beckett frowns at me. "I'm always proud of you."

"I know you are. I know. But I'm—" I stare hard at the tabletop and try to untangle the knot in the middle of my chest. I don't know how to explain it. "You've been taking care of me my entire life, Beck. That's who you are. You're a caretaker." He grumbles and I roll my eyes. "You are," I insist. "And you—I think you see the best version of the person I am. Or you see the person I could be. You never think I'm going to fail, and I think—I think sometimes that makes me feel like I can't. I don't want to disappoint you."

Even the idea of Beckett thinking less of me has tears pushing at the backs of my eyes. My throat feels too thick, my heart too heavy. Somewhere in the back of my mind, logically, I know that Beckett wouldn't be disappointed in me over a tattoo studio. That I could never have another client again and he'd be just as proud. But that's the point, isn't it? I want to earn it. I want to deserve it.

"Is that why you haven't shown me the studio yet?" he asks.

I nod. "I want it to be perfect before you see it. I don't want you to see it and regret the time and trust you've invested in me. I want it to live up to your expectations."

He gapes at me across the table. "What?"

And that's it, I think. That's the thing I've been terrified of this entire time. It's why I've been pushing myself so hard to be good at all of this. To do it by myself and succeed. Because Beckett has been quietly standing behind me this entire time, never asking for a thing in return. If he can do it all by himself, I should be able to, too.

"I wouldn't have any of this if it wasn't for you. And I don't—I don't know how I can ever possibly repay you for it." I take a deep breath through my nose and swallow hard. My voice is trembling. My hands too. I squeeze them around my empty mug. "If it wasn't for you, I wouldn't be opening my own place. I probably wouldn't be tattooing at all, and I—I never—" I have to stop again, and I force myself to look at him this time. To be brave. "You've always believed in me the most, Beck. You've blindly supported every whim, every idea, every project I've ever had. You don't think I can do anything wrong, and I think that's turned into me thinking I don't have the space to do anything wrong."

Beckett watches me, his face falling. "I've been putting pressure on you?" he asks. "Nova, this whole time . . ." He rubs his hand over his jaw. "This whole time, I've been hurting you?"

"No, that's not on you," I say quickly. Those are my own thoughts. My own insecurities that he inadvertently amplified. That's something I need to work through on my own. I just—"I don't want to disappoint you. I don't want you to see the studio and think I've squandered the chance you gave me. You've always worked so hard, and I've hardly worked at all, and it isn't fair that I've gotten the things I want when—"

"That's enough," Beckett says, his voice sharp at the edges. My words stutter to a stop, and I press my lips together to keep anything else from falling out. He looks serious and confused, the little line between his eyebrows that's a perfect match for mine appearing in earnest.

The other side of my coin.

My big brother.

"That's enough of that," he says again, voice gentling.

"Okay," I rasp, horrified when my lower lip begins to tremble. I stare hard at the wood grain beneath my mug and tell myself I'm not going to fucking cry.

The kettle begins to whistle on the stove. I stand, grateful for the chance to piece myself back together. I don't know what I expected from Beckett, but I didn't expect him to shut down the conversation.

I lift the kettle and pour the tea, steam curling around my wrists.

"How can you say that?"

I don't respond and he doesn't move to fill the space with an explanation. I shake my head, and I hear him shift in his chair.

"Hardly worked at all," he repeats quietly. "Nova. You've been working your ass off for years to establish yourself. I might have been—I might have been the first person to sit in your chair, but that was a favor to me. Not you."

"How do you figure?"

I turn with two mugs of tea in my hand and set them between us. Beckett pushes out of his chair, circling the table until he can collapse in the seat closest to me. He grabs my hand with his, the ink on his wrist a pair to the ink on mine. "I like all of this ink you gave me. It's always felt—" He sighs, staring hard at me. "You know I'm shit at telling you how I feel, but I'm going to try, okay?" I nod. "I volunteered to be your first client because I wanted to have your work first. The tattoos . . . they always felt like something special for just the two of us. I like that we're the only ones in our family that look like this. I like that I can say I have the first ever Nova Porter design." He swallows. "The things you have are because of you. Not me. I'm not the one who is filling your appointment books. I'm not the one busting my ass to launch a tattoo studio. All I did was believe in you. You were the one who was brave enough to try."

My fingers flex in his hand. "I know, but—"

"No buts," he says. "It's as simple as that. You've earned this. You've done it."

I sniffle. "It doesn't always feel like that though. Sometimes it feels like if I mess this part up, everything is going to disappear. It feels like maybe I won't get another chance."

"And how are you going to mess it up, huh? You gonna run out of ink? Your vines not gonna drop the way you want them to?"

I garble out a laugh. Beckett's face softens into something it only seems to do occasionally, that big heart of his right on his sleeve. He squeezes my fingers again.

"Some of that is my fault, yeah? I haven't listened the way you need and I'm sorry about that. I'm going to do better, but I need you to do better too. I know you've got no problems yelling at me, Nova Ray Porter. I need you to start talking louder."

"I will," I tell him. "I promise."

"Good." He leans back in his chair, still keeping my hand in his. "And don't take this the wrong way, but I don't give a fuck about the tattoo studio. The studio doesn't matter."

"What?"

"It's not about what color you paint the walls or those giant mirrors you have in the front—"

"You've seen my mirrors?"

"—or how your vines look or any of that other shit, okay? It's about you, Nova. And whether or not you're happy with what you're doing. The rest of it is just extra." His face twists as he thinks about it. "The . . . fertilizer on top of the soil. You've got good soil. Good dirt."

"I've got . . . good dirt?"

He nods.

I can sort of see the metaphor he's going for. "Okay, but—"

"The support I've given you doesn't come with a price tag. That's not how this works. I'm your brother and I love you. You don't have to hit a certain metric for that love to make sense. It's not going away and you don't have to earn it. It just . . . exists. It's there. I've already given it to you."

"But you've given me enough."

Beckett sighs and squeezes my hand hard enough to hurt. "I really want to put you in a headlock right now," he murmurs. "Is this why you won't let anyone help you with a goddamn thing?"

I shake my head, think about it, then nod. It's important that I do this by myself. I want to prove to myself that everything that's happened—all of my success and clients and the ability to turn my dream into a job—I want to prove that it won't disappear in a cloud of smoke. That I've taken every opportunity and sacrifice I've been given and turned it into something incredible. Nothing else will do.

Beckett grunts. "Well, cut that shit out. Asking for help doesn't make you less deserving of anything you've already achieved on your own." He leans back in the chair and lets go of my hand, dragging his palm across his jaw. "I wish I could put myself in a headlock. I can't believe I ever made you feel like you don't have the room to be anything other than perfect."

I let that sink in, aching to feel the relief I know those words should bring. Some of the knots loosen, but they're still tangled up. I blow out a breath and dig my knuckles into my cheek. I've got a feeling the uncertainty is going to be a work in progress.

And that's okay. For the first time in a long time, it feels like maybe it's okay that I'm a work in progress. Just like my studio. Just like the little plants breaking through the soil and reaching for the sunlight. I'm trying, and maybe trying is enough.

"Maybe . . . maybe you could come take a look at the studio," I say slowly. Beckett shifts in his chair. "You can tell me what you think. Honestly."

"If that's what you want."

I nod. I need to rip off the proverbial Band-Aid. I need to stop being so afraid I'm not going to measure up to someone else's expectations. Because Beckett's right. The details don't matter. The light I still haven't figured out how to hang in the back is not going to make or break my business.

I need to start giving myself more credit.

"Do you want to see the studio?" I ask.

Beckett rolls his eyes, then snatches the bottle of whiskey I brought over with our tea and honey. He tips some into his mug. "Of course I want to see it. I've been dying to see it. I know you have mirrors because I've been pressing my face up against the glass. Ms. Beatrice called Dane on me twice."

A laugh rolls out of me. I squeeze his hand one more time and then stand. Beckett stares at me with amused, irritated affection. A look only a sibling can perfect.

"All right, well. Grab your coat."

"We're going now?" he asks.

I nod. "Yeah. We're going now."

※ ‧ ⫷

BECKETT HAS BEEN standing at the back wall for sixteen minutes, squinting at the succulents in the vertical garden. It stretches from floor to ceiling, plants spilling out from between reclaimed wooden beams. My own private forest in the back.

I kick my feet back and forth on one of the tattoo chairs, watching him, the mug of tea he insisted we bring with us cupped in my hands.

"Your soil is too dry," he offers, his back still to me, fingertip tracing the edge of a leaf. "And these will need better sunlight if you want them to do well."

"The sunlight is fine."

"Says who?"

"Says Mabel, who installed all of those succulents."

He grunts and mutters something under his breath, squatting down to take a look at another section closer to the floor. I'm glad he's being critical. I'm glad he's taking it seriously. If he walked in and gave me a generic compliment, I'm not sure I would have believed him.

But I'd like it if he moved on from inspecting the plant wall.

"There's more greenery up here, if you want to take a look."

"In a second," he answers. He's too busy scooping some dirt out of my wall and peering at it in the palm of his hand. I take advantage of his distraction and slip my phone out of my pocket.

> NOVA: Did you make it off my roof alive?

His answer comes through immediately.

> CHARLIE: Ooh, what's this? You care about my
> well-being?

I smile.

NOVA: I care about my flower beds.

NOVA: Also, your legs.

CHARLIE: Well, my legs are fine. Can't say the same about your flower beds.

A picture appears on my phone of some squished hydrangeas. Then a selfie of Charlie, flower petals in his hair. Bare chest. Dirt on his cheek. Dear god, I hope he didn't run down the street like that.

I hesitate, then save the picture. Another message appears below the selfie.

CHARLIE: Everything okay with your brother?

I look at Beckett who has finally meandered away from the plant wall. He's looking at each tattoo station with his hands behind his back, his hat tucked under his arm. That knot in my chest unravels a little bit more, and I feel like I can finally take a breath.

NOVA: Yeah. Everything is good.

21

CHARLIE

"CHARLES!"

I stop halfway down the street and walk backward until I can peer around the corner toward Ink & Wild, Nessa hanging over the railing with a stack of papers shoved under her arm. It's not the Porter sibling I was hoping for, and I try not to let my disappointment show.

Have I been milling about downtown Inglewild for the better part of an hour hoping to see Nova? Maybe. I checked in with Mabel on floral arrangements for the harvest festival just so I had an alibi in case anyone bothered to ask, but I have no excuse for the aimless wandering I've been doing since then. I got a coffee from Ms. Beatrice's. I talked to Matty about his pasta sauce. I did three laps around the fountain in the town square. I fed some ducks.

I have things I should be doing, but I'm crossing the street toward Ink & Wild trying not to look through the windows like an asshole for a peek of blond hair and a sarcastic smile. I wave to Vanessa, but she's too busy trying to lock the door with a mountain of crap in her arms.

I pluck a stack of files out of her grip, and she blows out a sigh of relief. "Thank you."

"You're welcome." I glance at the papers and then at the top of Nessa's head. "Did I catch you breaking and entering?"

"Would I shout your name across the street if I was?"

"You know, Ness, you probably would." Of all the Porter siblings, she's the true wild card. The last time someone was stupid enough to leave us alone at a party together, we almost burned the entire place to the ground.

Coincidentally, we have not been invited back to the bingo hall.

She grins at me and pushes some hair out of her face. "You flatter me, Chuck. I need you to take those to Nova." She finishes locking up the door and tucks the keys in my breast pocket. "She asked that I stop by and grab them, but I've got somewhere I need to be."

I frown. "Why did she request files she can get herself?"

"I don't know."

"Where do you have to be?"

"None of your business."

Nessa pulls out another file she wedged into the top of her bag and shoves it in my hand. The top part is bent back. "Just do as you're told, Charlie." She pats me on the shoulder as she rushes past me, hip-checking me into the railing. "Oops, sorry!" she calls, hand raised above her head. "I'll owe you one!"

She's gone before I can so much as say, *You're welcome*, rushing around the corner of the studio with her gargantuan bag slipping off one shoulder. As I'm frowning at the place she used to be, I swear something moves in the window of the duckpin bowling alley. I study the empty window, the blinds rocking gently back and forth.

"Fucking phone tree," I mutter to myself. Everyone keeps playing dumb, but I know there's something going on. I haven't heard anything in weeks.

I've done enough meddling to know when I'm being meddled with. But joke's on the phone tree, or Nessa, or whoever orchestrated this particular scenario, because I want to see Nova. They could not have picked a more willing participant.

I make my way over to her house and hop up the front steps. I want some of the chocolate-covered peanut butter pretzels she's started to keep at the top of her pantry. She keeps telling me they're on sale when she goes to the grocery store, but I've been to the grocery store, and they have never once been on sale. She buys them for me, and it's adorable that she feels the need to lie about it.

I knock on the door. No one answers. I knock again.

"Nova," I call. "I've got the files you asked for."

My phone buzzes in my back pocket. I frown when I see her name.

NOVA: plch

That's it. Nothing else. I wait for a second to see if another message comes through, but it doesn't.

I entertain her preferred method of communication, even though I can see her boots stacked by the door and her keys on the table by the window. I know she's in there somewhere.

CHARLIE: What?

Her response is slow coming, the three dots at the bottom of my phone an exercise in patience I have never once possessed.

NOVA: Leve them onnnnn pfch.

CHARLIE: Are you drunk?

I rap my knuckles against the door again, harder this time. My phone stays silent and so does the house. Unease tugs at my shoulders and I stare at the tiny pot of lavender on the corner of the porch. The likelihood of Nova actually listening to me and moving the key after Beckett used it is slim to none. I tip up the planter with my foot and sigh at the glint of silver metal.

"Stubborn," I mutter to myself, slipping it into the lock and letting myself in. I'm going to melt this damn key down and make her a necklace with it. I'm going to toss it into the abyss.

I shut the door behind me.

"Nova?"

There's a heavy thump from somewhere upstairs. I hang my jacket next to hers on a hook shaped like a cat's ass and stack the files on the table. The stairs creak as I walk up, my heart somewhere in my throat. Nova's house is usually bursting with sound and light and color. It's too still in here. Too dark.

I push open her bedroom door with the palm of my hand. There's a lump in the middle of her bed, her blond hair on the pillow. She twists beneath her heavy comforter.

"Nova girl?"

She shifts beneath the blanket again. In the muted light I can see her face scrunched up in pain, tension in the lines by her eyes and her shoulders hunched up to her ears. She's curled in a tiny ball, like the smaller she makes herself, the easier it'll be.

"Charlie?" she rasps.

My heart squeezes like someone's got their fist wrapped around it.

I sit down on the edge of her bed and rub my hand up and down her thigh through the blanket. The little line between her eyebrows eases. "You got a migraine, baby?"

"Yeah," she whispers, eyes still shut tight. "Told Nessa to leave the files. What're you—" She makes a tiny, frustrated sound. "What're you doing here?"

I don't answer her question. "You didn't tell her you were hurting, did you?"

Nova blinks open her eyes, half lidded and heavy. Her lashes brush against the apples of her cheeks with every extended blink. She's not looking directly at me, but somewhere over my shoulder. "No," she whispers. "I didn't."

Of course she didn't. Because Nova is stubborn and doesn't do a damn thing she's told and would rather suffer alone than bother anyone for help. I blow out a breath and run my hand over the length of her thigh again. She shifts closer and all my frustration slips away when she carefully tips her forehead to my knee, like that tiny point of contact makes her feel better.

I stare at her hands fisted in the blanket. Her small form curled tight.

"What do you need?" I ask quietly.

"I'm okay."

"Nova."

"I'm fi—"

"If you say you're fine, I'm gonna lose my shit. And you know how dramatic I can be."

She huffs a laugh as I squeeze her thigh.

"My medicine," she finally manages after three heavy swallows. "I—"

I give her the space to let her try to find her words, but she doesn't finish her sentence.

"You, what?"

"I'm having trouble seeing," she tells me in a whisper. "I can't . . . I don't think I can do it by myself."

I know how hard it is for her to say those words and to trust me enough to hear them. I rub at the curve of her hip. "That's all right. I can help."

She mumbles the name of her prescription, and I go searching in her bathroom. It's already sitting out on the counter with two other orange bottles, like she couldn't tell which was the right one before she gave up and climbed into bed. I read the tiny instructions and shake a pill into the palm of my hand, then fill up a mug in the shape of a strawberry with water from the tap.

She's propped up against the pillows when I find my way back to her, hair tangled over one shoulder. I hand her the pill, but her hands are shaking too bad to manage the mug.

"Easy," I tell her, tucking my hands around hers. She scrunches her nose as she sips, bleary eyes blinking over the rim. Cute as all fucking hell, even when she's trying her best to be intimidating. A kitten without her claws.

Her pinky inches out to loop over mine.

"What else do you need?"

"M'okay," she mumbles, halfway to unconscious already, tugging the blankets until they're over her shoulders. She's so different like this, a dulled version of her usual bursting brightness. All of her edges soft and weary.

I sit on her bed and watch her as she falls into an uneasy sleep, her face still pinched and her shoulders hunched. I brush my fingertips over her forehead, and I rearrange her blankets until she's tucked just the way she likes, then stand and pick up the pieces of herself she must have unwrapped as she came into the room. I fold her chunky sweater and drape it over the back of a chair. I collect a black skirt and set it on the dresser. I find her thigh-high tight things sticking out from beneath her comforter and tug them free. I grab an extra blanket and tuck it around her curtains, something like satisfaction in my chest when she lets out a grateful sigh at the added darkness. I go to leave, but her voice holds me at the door.

"Do you think—" she whispers, slurred and slow. She releases a deep breath and her fingers twitch on top of the blankets. "Do you think you could stay?"

I trace her form in the middle of her bed, her hand in the place I just was. Resolve tightens my jaw. I've never had someone to take care of before. I'm not sure I'll be any good at it, but I'm going to do my best. For Nova.

"Yeah, of course." I watch her for another second, a lump in my throat. I try to swallow around it, but the feeling shoves deeper. That fist around my heart tug, tug, tugs. "I'll stay as long as you want me to, Nova girl."

SHE SLEEPS FOR hours, until the sun is burning orange through the window above her kitchen sink. I left briefly to grab my computer and some things from the grocery store—pocketing her not-so-secret planter key while I was at it—but for the most part, I've been here. Sitting in her kitchen, waiting.

I hear movement upstairs. The soft thud of feet moving across her bedroom and the whine of the squeaky hinges on her bathroom door. Her stairs creak as she makes her way down and then Nova appears in the doorway of her kitchen, the back of her hand trying to contain her yawn and a fluffy pink robe wrapped around her middle.

She looks comfortable. Cozy. I've never seen this robe before, three sizes too big and perpetually slipping down one shoulder. I wonder where she's been keeping it.

"How're you feeling?"

She answers with a shriek, her eyes snapping open and her back hitting the frame of the door. She reaches for the closest projectile, a small wooden figure of a cat that I'd bet my nonexistent Rolex Beckett whittled on his back porch. She whips it across the kitchen, and it smacks me in the middle of my forehead.

We stare at each other across the length of her kitchen, her palm pressed flat to her chest.

"You're still here," she breathes.

I frown and rub my fingertips against what I'm sure will be an impressive bruise. I guess I should be thankful she didn't hit my eye. "You asked me to stay."

"I did?"

I nod. "Yeah."

I mean, I left, but that was to get her some fruit and Gatorade. I don't know what she likes when she has a migraine. I wanted her to have options.

She keeps staring at me, like she's trying to piece together why I'm sitting at her kitchen table with my laptop and the rest of the peanut butter pretzels. She has lines from her pillow on her cheek and her hair is an absolute mess. She passes her hand over it like that'll do anything to help, and I have to duck my face behind my laptop screen to hide my grin. Fuck, she's adorable. Even as she shuffles her way to the sink, still silent, reaching for a glass and filling it from the tap, shooting glances at me out of the corner of her eye like I can't see exactly what she's doing.

"I thought that was a dream," she says after another extended beat of silence.

"Oh. I, uh—" Does she want me to leave? Have I overstepped, staying here in the kitchen? Stealing her key? I go to twist my wristwatch that isn't there. An old nervous habit. "I can leave," I offer.

She shakes her head. "No."

All right. "I cut up some fruit for you. It's in the fridge." I stare hard at the top of my computer. I don't know why, but I thought cantaloupe would be a good idea. She probably doesn't even like cantaloupe. Is this how you take care of someone? I have no idea. "Didn't know if you'd be hungry or not," I tack on lamely.

When I look up, she's studying me with her back pressed against the sink, one arm wrapped around her middle.

She still doesn't say anything.

"What?" I ask.

"You cut up fruit?"

It's a question that doesn't sound like a question. "Yes?"

I won't tell her that I also started a load of towels and rearranged her magazine collection. Or that I bought her a pumpkin and put it on her front step because it looked festive. I know she's been too busy to put up her decorations. I was about another hour away from carving the damn thing.

She takes a sip of her water. "What sort of fruit?"

"What?"

"What sort of fruit did you get me?"

"Strawberries," I answer. I saw them in her fridge two nights ago, only three left in the bottom of the carton. She wanders her way to the fridge and cracks it open, peering inside. "I got you some cantaloupe and grapes too."

She ducks farther into the fridge. "Did you cut the grapes?"

I did. I saw a video while I was scrolling endlessly on my phone about how to cut grapes into tiny hearts. I wish I could go ahead and take that back though.

"They came like that."

She glances at me over her shoulder. "Did they?"

"Mm-hmm."

"Interesting." She grabs the fruit tray from the bottom shelf and sets it on the table, then drops into the chair next to me and stretches out her legs with a groan. She picks up a piece of strawberry and bites into it.

I can't stop looking at her.

"How are you feeling?"

She shrugs and pokes at another piece of fruit. A piece of cantaloupe I cut into a star. "Okay. Fuzzy. It always takes some time for me to come back online after a migraine."

"Any pain?"

She pops the star into her mouth and chews slowly.

"Some," she says quietly. "But it'll pass."

She sits and eats her fruit, and I sit and watch her, a single beam of golden light traveling slowly across the hardwood floor of the kitchen. She seems to like the silence, her knee nudging mine beneath the table. After a few moments where she doesn't ask me to leave, I open my laptop again and scroll through my work email, answering the more obnoxious ones and putting together a list for the week.

It's quiet and still in a way I don't usually allow myself to be. She extends her leg so her ankle is crossed over mine beneath the table, and I try not to smile at an email about interest rates.

"Charlie," she says, after all the grapes are gone and half the strawberries. She's saving the cantaloupe for last, I notice. Mentally I'm doing a victory lap.

"Hmm?"

"Could you open that for me?" She nods her head toward the window above the sink. "I like the fresh air."

"'Course I can." I stride across the kitchen and open the window two inches, evening air that smells like dried leaves rolling into her kitchen. Her shoulders relax another half inch, and I reclaim the chair next to her.

"Thank you," she says when I sit.

"Careful there, Nova girl." I scoot my chair in and her legs tangle around mine again. "All this polite talk and I might start to think you like me."

She rolls her eyes, a smile ticking up the corner of her mouth. With her messy hair and that ridiculous robe, it's lacking its usual heat.

"I do like you," she says simply.

Warmth ping-pongs around in my chest. A bright, ferocious burst of it. It's a stupid reaction. We've been sleeping together for weeks. I should hope she likes me, at least a little. But here, like this, with the sunset painting her hair lavender and her socked feet tucked between mine, it feels more like a shared secret.

"I like you too."

She pops another piece of fruit into her mouth, watching me with her chin in her hand. "Do you like me enough to kiss me?"

"Are you . . . well enough for that?"

She snorts. "I don't have consumption, Charlie. I can manage a kiss."

"Consumption. Listen to you, Doc Holliday."

She rolls her eyes. "If you don't want to kiss me, you can just say so."

"I think I've proven that I like kissing you just fine." I stand from my chair, the legs making an obnoxious sound against the kitchen floor. She flinches and I want to pitch the damn thing out the window.

"See." It takes a monumental effort not to point in her face. "I'm not going to be kissing you if you're still hurting."

She pouts. Lips turned down at the corners, a jut to her bottom lip, Nova pouts at me.

I stop and look at her.

Sick Nova is soft in ways that Sarcastic Everyday Nova would be rolling her eyes at. Maybe it's how she normally is when she wakes up after a migraine or maybe it's . . . maybe this is how she is with me now. A version of herself that she doesn't get to be anywhere else. The idea of it makes me want to fucking glow, a warmth creeping into my chest the longer I look at her.

"I think a kiss would make me feel better," she says, still staring up at me.

"Well," I say, one hand on the back of her chair and the other cupped around the side of her face. I trace the line of her jaw with my thumb, back and forth. "I can't argue with that."

She tilts her face to mine and tugs at the front of my shirt. "I thought you'd agree."

"Shut up."

"You shut u—"

I cut her off with my mouth against hers. I hold myself there in the chaste beginnings of a kiss, and let myself breathe her in. Fresh autumn air and the barely there smell of her shampoo. The lavender dryer sheets she uses and . . . Nova. I'd know her taste anywhere. Blindfolded and in my sleep. Half standing in the middle of her kitchen. I kiss her again and again and again, light brushes of our mouths together until her fingers walk their way up my chest, palms cupped around either side of my neck. My hand on the back of her chair flexes as I move my mouth against hers, gentle and slow, groaning when her tongue swipes at my bottom lip. I open my mouth for her and let her set the pace, let her take what she needs, another sound from the base of my throat when our tongues slide together.

She tastes like sunshine. Like strawberries cut into tiny, ridiculous shapes and . . . toothpaste?

I lean back, our noses brushing. "Did you brush your teeth before you came down the stairs?"

She pinches at my chest, quick and sharp. "Were you going to kiss me with nap breath?"

I grin. "Were you planning for a kiss?"

Her cheeks pink.

"You said you didn't know I was here."

"I didn't know you were here," she mumbles.

"Were you hoping I was here, Nova girl?"

"Shut up, Charlie." She tugs my mouth back to hers.

"Yes, Nova," I mumble against her mouth, and I kiss her in the melting light of her kitchen, a half-empty bowl of fruit on the table in front of her.

22

CHARLIE

I CHECK THE tiny clock in the corner of my screen for the seventh time. "You've got me for three more minutes, Selene, and then I've got to go."

"You've kept me apprised of the countdown for the past fifteen minutes." She doesn't look up from her desk. "Are there chickens that are in need of rescuing, Farmer Charlie?"

"Look at you." I grin. "You remembered there are chickens."

She tilts her chin and squints into the camera. "Wait. The chickens exist? There are real chickens?"

"Eight of them, in a coop behind the bakehouse. You now have two minutes for any business-related questions."

She closes a file and rests her hands on top of it. "We've covered everything. This week is substantially slower. I guess your dad is occupied with something else."

Or maybe he's finally decided to listen. I'm trying a new approach where I hold my boundaries instead of willingly giving in to all of his demands. I emailed him after our last disaster of a phone call and told him I'd only be taking calls from him during work hours, organized and coordinated by Selene. It seems to be working out for me, despite the anxiety ulcer I'm giving myself in the process. No matter how much of a douche my dad is, I still struggle with the idea of disappointing someone. Him, in particular.

But it's difficult to care as much about it when I'm here. When I'm surrounded by people and projects and things to occupy my time. Especially when I'm in Nova's bed every other night. Or sitting next to her at her kitchen table, filling out expense reports while she flips through a magazine. Or on the back porch of the guest cottage, a fire in the metal drum and her hair shining, shimmering gold. I don't think it matters what we're doing, whenever I'm with her, everything else is pushed firmly to the edges.

"You're dressed up for an evening with the chickens."

I glance down at my shirt and smooth my hand over the buttons. I don't know how fancy I'm supposed to be for the soft launch of a tattoo studio, but I want to look nice, and Nova said she liked this shirt.

She said it while her hand was in my pants, but she said it nonetheless.

"No chickens. Nova's studio opens tonight."

"Nova." Selene leans back in her chair with a smug little smile. "I've been hearing that name an awful lot."

"Have you?"

"I keep a tally on the notepad on your desk. Would you like for me to calculate the results?"

"No, thank you." I don't need a reminder about how deeply I've slipped down this path. Blissful oblivion is the name of the game at this point. I'm not going to think about what comes next. I'm just going to enjoy what I have now. No expectations. "I can count them up when I get back to the office."

"I bet you're looking forward to that." She tidies up the rest of the desk. "Being back in your routine."

No. Not really.

I'm going to miss the way the sky comes alive at night, stars pressing in through the wide windows at the back of the little cottage. I'm going to miss the way morning smells, cold air and wet leaves and fresh apples and warm butter from the bakery. I'm going to miss Nova's hair across my chest and her knee pressed between both of mine while I cling to the edge of the bed because she barely allows me any room when I sleep with her. I'm going to miss being here in a million different ways.

But this isn't the place I belong. These are not things I can keep. I've been playing dress-up for weeks, and the cuffs are starting to get a little tight at the wrists.

"Yeah," I say instead, because it's better to start convincing myself now. "Yeah, I do well with routines."

BY THE TIME I get to the studio, there isn't a single parking spot left on Main Street.

I end up having to park in the short alleyway behind the bookshop, three blocks away. The hum of the party is a low buzz that grows in volume the closer I get, people spilling out from the open doorway to the sidewalk. There's music and lights of every color, crisscrossing back and forth from the awning of a taco truck to the entrance of the studio.

And standing by the door, lit up in shades of blue, is Nova.

My attention snags on her, just like it always does. She has her hair tucked neatly behind her ears, a drastically different look from when I left her at her house in her pink fluffy robe. Now, I can see the lines of her tattoos that dance up her neck to the hollow below her ear. I've traced that ink with my mouth. With my fingertips too. Her lips are painted bright red, and she's wearing some sort of strapless top that shows off the ink along her shoulders and down her arms.

There's a gnawing ache when I look at her, head tipped back in laughter at whatever the bozo in front of her is saying. I eye him critically. Black shirt with a hole near the collar. Black boots. Arms covered in ink. I check my cuffs and straighten my sleeves. I want to be the one making her laugh. I want to be the one by her side. I want to close the space between us, scoop her up until her legs are wrapped around my waist, and taste the edge of that smile.

But I've never had much luck with wanting things. The things I want almost always turn into the things I don't get to have, and Nova is not an exception to that rule. No matter how much I'm starting to wish she was.

The person in front of her moves, and she sucks in a bracing breath, taking in the crowd. Tonight represents months and months of hard work for her. I hope she's proud. I hope she's looking at all these people here for her and recognizing what a goddamn force of nature she is.

Jeremy pokes his head out of the front window of the taco truck and her lips lift in amusement. He calls something to her and she rolls her eyes. I'm smiling before I even realize, and that's when she finds me.

It's like stepping off the curb without realizing there's a curb. My heart trips over itself, seeing her face light up because of me. I glance over my shoulder just to be sure and when my eyes find her again, she's got that twist to her lips that tells me she knows exactly what I was doing and she thinks I'm ridiculous for it. *Of course I was looking at you*, I imagine in her voice. *Don't be stupid.*

I push through the crowd to meet her, her eyes on me the entire time. I don't stop until I'm close enough to press my boots to hers, about as much as I can get away with when all these people are around us.

I want to kiss her.

I want to hold her hand.

I want to throw her over my shoulder and go back to the guesthouse on the edge of the farm and lose myself in her.

"Hey," she says, and I want to kiss her so fucking bad my hands shake with it.

I curl them into fists in my coat. "Hey," I say back. "Quite the crowd."

She nods and looks around again. "The power of a taco truck."

"Nah." I rock back on my heels. "This is all you."

Her eyes snap back to mine. I've said too much or I haven't said enough. I don't know. I never really know with Nova. I clear my throat and nod toward her studio. "You managed to hang the light."

She glances over her shoulder at the neon light against the garden wall in the back. *Ink & Wild* glowing white. "Beckett figured it out," she says, turning back to me. "While providing a very colorful commentary on my soil quality."

"You worked it out, then?" I didn't want to ask when I was at her house the other day. I was more interested in feeding her fruit cut into various ridiculous shapes.

She nods. "Yeah, we figured it out. He saw the studio. He and Evelyn are going to swing by at some point tonight."

I'm glad. Maybe she'll start to realize she doesn't have to do everything by herself all the time. "I'll make sure I have my exit strategy planned."

She tips her head to the side. "Planning on being inappropriate? You need to hide from my big brother?"

No. I'm just afraid everything I'm starting to feel for her is painted across my face. For the first time, I wish we were in the sort of relationship where I could kiss her in front of all these people and not think twice about it. I'm so fucking proud of her and the only way I can show it is by standing a perfectly polite two feet away from her, smiling like an idiot. The constraints we've wrapped around this relationship are starting to chafe. I clear my throat. "When do you start tattooing?"

"In a little bit," she answers. "I wanted to mingle first. Say hi to some people."

Her fingers curl behind her ear again, tucking back another silky blond strand. My watch slips up her wrist. I grin and her eyes narrow. "What?"

"Nice watch."

"Oh, this old thing?" She twists it around. "I won it in a bet."

"Must have been some bet."

"The best kind," she says back, smile growing.

We stand there beneath the colored lights and stare at each other. It's hard to remember what we're talking about when she looks at me like that.

"Will you save a spot for me?" I ask. She arches an eyebrow and I clarify. "In the tattoo line. I want to get Oscar the Grouch above my belly button."

"Oh?" She sways closer. I feel the space left between us like a physical thing. I've gotten too used to tugging her closer when I want to. I'm having trouble holding myself in check now. "Have we moved on from the scorpion on your ass?"

"Maybe you can fit me in twice tonight."

"One per customer. You'll have to make a decision, Charlie."

I give in to temptation and tug my hand from my pocket. I let my knuckles graze the bottom edge of her top. It's silky smooth. Black and shiny. Her eyelashes flutter and I pull my hand away. "It's hard to decide," I manage.

She stares at me, everything and everyone moving around us in a vague impression of voices and colors. Someone laughs. Another person calls her name. She doesn't turn to look. She just keeps looking right at me.

Maybe I made a mistake when I told Nova I could keep it casual. Because not a single thing I'm feeling right now is casual.

"I'm glad you could make it tonight," she finally says.

A simple sentence, but it means more to me than I could ever possibly articulate. Most of the time I feel like I'm not wanted anywhere; I'm just the guy that keeps showing up with a bottle of tequila. I have to swallow three times around the thick feeling in my throat before I can manage a rough "Me too" in response.

She takes two steps backward toward the steps of the studio. I can't stop looking at how the colors from the lights dance along her skin. As per usual, I think I vastly underestimated my ability to play it cool with Nova Porter.

"I'll see you inside?"

I nod because she seems to be waiting for it. She could tell me to get in the taco truck with Jeremy and work on the carnitas and I'd probably do it.

"Yeah. Me and Oscar the Grouch."

"YOU'RE BEING WEIRD," Caleb mutters at my side, a tiny cookie in the shape of a succulent in the palm of his hand. He's eaten six of them in the span of ten minutes, and I'm really starting to think Nova should have handed out cookie tickets. For him specifically.

"I'm not being weird," I grumble. I'm being cautious. I spent the first twenty minutes of this party staring at Nova while she worked at her station, her head bent in concentration, tattoo pen in her gloved hand. I've never seen her work before. She's doodled on napkins and on the tops of pizza boxes. Flowers and vines and constellations that I can recognize now as part of her style. But I've never seen her like this. She's fully in tune with what she's doing, dedicated to the careful, delicate work of inking designs. She's moving to a soundtrack that only she can hear, loose lines and smooth, graceful movements. Her hair cascades over her shoulder, her face a mask of concentration.

I'm captivated.

She has a sign-up sheet for clients at the very front of the shop next to one of the giant mirrors. For all my teasing, I haven't put my name on it yet. I don't know if I can handle her hands on me in a room with this many people.

Also, I still haven't figured out what I want.

A common theme, I'm finding.

"I'm just taking it all in," I tell Caleb.

Specifically, the guy Nova has in her chair right now. It's the same guy from out front, the one she was talking to when I walked up. He's leaning into her space, dark blond hair combed back. They haven't stopped talking since he sat down, and I can't stop sneaking looks.

They look good together. Well suited. That's probably the kind of guy she usually goes for.

I bet he's absolute shit at doing his taxes.

"Who is that guy?" I ask Caleb, curling my hand tighter around my mocktail. Nova isn't serving alcohol at this event for obvious reasons, but god, I wish she were. "The one Nova is talking to."

What in the hell are they discussing? She has a line, for god's sake. A schedule to keep. One per customer. It says that clearly on the bottom of the sign-up sheet.

"I have no idea, but you might want to try looking somewhere else for a couple of minutes. You don't have a subtle bone in your body," Caleb answers, tossing the rest of the cookie in his mouth. "I didn't know you wanted a tattoo that bad," he mumbles to himself.

I blink away from the two of them. "And you lack restraint. Don't you get enough of Layla's cookies at home?"

He's already looking longingly at the table in the back where Layla has set up refreshments. "I never get enough of Layla's cookies."

I make a face. "Don't be gross."

A furious blush climbs his cheeks as he scowls at me. "I didn't mean it like that. I meant her actual cookies."

"Sure you did."

"As in her baked goods."

"I'm sure her baked goods are very nice."

Caleb gives me a long look. "I will punch you right in the face."

"You wouldn't dare," I reply, eyes tripping right back to Nova and the schmuck in her chair like a goddam magnet. She laughs at something he says, and I want to flip a table. I want to take the tattoo pen resting comfortably in her hand and scratch out whatever design she gave him. I don't want him walking around with a permanent mark from her while all of mine will eventually fade. It doesn't feel fair.

"You could put your name on her list, you know."

"Nah." I manage to tear my eyes away from Nova and glance at the place on my wrist that doesn't have a watch. Another mark left by

Nova. Her fingerprints are all over me. Frustration tears at me. I can't stand here anymore and watch all the things I want but can't have. It's a unique form of torture that I don't particularly want to indulge in anymore. "I think I'm going to head out. I have some stuff to catch up on."

Caleb frowns at me. "You're sure?"

"Yeah, I just wanted to stop by."

His frown deepens. "She'll wonder where you went."

Will she? I don't think so. She has a full house and plenty of things to hold her attention. I'll take the night to shove everything back into place and get myself in line. Nova was perfectly clear when she told me what she wanted. I'm not going to twist myself outside of those boundaries. It's not fair to either of us.

"I'll say bye on my way out," I concede. I can be a fucking gentleman despite the tight, anxious feeling swarming like bees in the middle of my chest. I blow out a deep breath. "Go get your cookies."

Caleb claps my shoulder and shakes me. "You sure you're all right?"

"Stop asking me that," I sigh. "I'm fine."

I'm fine, I'm fine, I'm fine . . . except I can't stop thinking about a woman I have no business thinking about and I'm pretty sure I'm having feelings that can no longer be categorized as business casual. And isn't that a fucking joke? To want another thing that is so far outside my reach it's laughable.

Caleb disappears to the back, and I drag my feet over to Nova's station, ignoring the constant peppering of thoughts that spin fast and faster. *You should stay. You promised. You're going to disappoint her. You can't handle what you said you could handle. You have no business thinking you deserve her time, her attention. She said casual and you agreed. You agreed.*

Stop acting like this. Be better.

I need fresh air. I need a drink. I need to not be watching Nova talk to someone else while it takes all of my willpower and then some not to touch her.

She glances up at me when I rap my knuckles against the top of the partition that separates her station from the rest of the shop. Her face brightens. It sends me sideways.

"Are you next on my list?"

I shake my head and her face falls. I hate that it makes me feel as good as it does.

I keep my gaze forcibly away from the man still sitting in the chair in front of her. His boot is almost touching hers, and it has frustration clawing at the inside of my chest. I don't want anyone else to touch her. I don't want anyone else to look at her. *Mine*, a voice in my head shouts, except she's never been mine at all.

"I'm heading out. I wanted to let you know because . . ." Because I'm a glutton for punishment, apparently. I clear my throat. "The studio looks great, Nova. I'm really proud of you."

"I thought you were staying for a tattoo," she says, and I want to. I want to give her whatever she wants, always, but I'm not good company right now.

I shake my head. "Another time, yeah?" I try for a smile and it falls flat. "Maybe I'll call and make an appointment. It'll be fun to give Jeremy the runaround."

Her mouth twists. "You don't need to make an appointment to get Road Runner on the small of your back."

"But I will if I want that full sleeve of tiny garden gnomes."

"That'll probably be several appointments."

"My point exactly."

She smiles at me and pushes back on her rolling stool. "I'll walk you out."

I laugh and shake my head. This whole place is full of people who want to see her. I can find the exit on my own. "You stay. I'll catch up with you later this week."

"You're sure?"

"Yup." I ruffle her hair because I'm at a loss for how else to say goodbye without pressing my mouth to hers. She slaps my hands away and something in me eases with the heavy slant of her eyebrows. See? I can do this. I can fall back into the roles we've made for ourselves. "Catch you later, Nova girl."

I push my way through the crowd of people toward the exit I know is in the back, relaxing as soon as I slip into the darkness of the hallway. Back here, I can slip off the mask. I'm exhausted but relieved, tipping against the side of the hallway and letting myself breathe for a second.

Until a body plows into me from behind and someone grabs at my arm, forcibly tugging me farther down the narrow space.

"What the fu—"

Nova drags me into her small office, shutting the door behind us and keeping the lights off. All I can make out of her is her silhouette and the flash of her hair. The smell of fresh ink and tart cherries.

She turns and closes the space between us, tipping her chin up so she can look at my face. "What's going on with you?" bursts out of her, a whispered accusation.

"Me?" I rub at my arm where she bulldozed into me. "I'm not the one bodily accosting people in dark hallways."

"No, you're just the one staring at me from across the room with a broody look on your face."

I frown. "It wasn't a broody look."

It was more of a what-the-fuck-am-I-doing-and-also-I-want-to-kiss-Nova look, if we have to categorize it.

"It was," she says, shifting closer. "And you were definitely staring."

Of course I was staring. I can't stop staring. I can't stop wanting either, and that's exactly the problem.

I sigh and try to find something to look at that isn't the disappointment on her face. I can't handle it. The light switch on the wall is an excellent choice. "What are you doing back here? This is your party."

"And I can cry if I want to," she says, hand reaching forward and squeezing mine. "Or follow you down dark hallways and ask why you're leaving after barely an hour. Is everything all right?"

"Yeah, of course." I swallow, and it sounds too loud, even with the muffled sounds of the party drifting through the closed door. "I've got—I've got some work stuff to handle."

"Right now?"

I nod. "Yes."

She sighs. "Charlie."

"Nova."

"What's going on with you?"

I grasp for the end of my control as a hot flare of frustration rolls up my spine. I've been trying to keep everything contained all evening, and I feel like I'm standing at the very edge of a bad decision. I've got no reason to be upset. No reason to care about who she does and doesn't talk to.

But I am upset, and I do care.

I'm jealous as fuck.

And I'm mad that I'm jealous as fuck.

I let go of her hand and scratch at my eyebrow, taking one step backward and putting more space between us. This room is too dark, and my thoughts are too quick, and Nova is too close. I never make good choices when I'm pushed in a corner.

"Nova, I'm—"

"What's wrong?"

"Nothing." My pulse thunders in my ears. I am terrified of saying something that I'll regret. "I'm going to go."

"No."

"Yes." Christ, this woman. She's always pushing me. I usually like it, but right now I need to leave. I reach for the door at my back. "I'll see you later this week. Harvest festival and . . . whatnot."

She closes the space between us and presses her palm to the door, snapping it shut again. Her chest presses against mine. I can feel every one of her exhales against my neck.

"Tell me," she says.

My heart is hammering. I'm a bottle, shaken up and ready to

explode. I'm thinking too many things, feeling too many things, the filter I struggle with on my best days flimsy and ready to collapse. "Tell you, what?"

"Why are you hiding from me?" She tips her face closer to mine, looking for all the world like she's trying to read the answers to her questions on my face. "What's going on?"

"It's no—"

"If you say, 'It's nothing,' one more time, I'm going to lock you in this room with me. I won't let you out until you decide to be honest."

It's not the punishment she thinks it is. And before I know it, I'm tumbling right over the edge. My restraint crumbles and frustration guides me forward.

"Fine." I give in to temptation and slip my hand under her hair, squeezing at the back of her neck. It feels like I haven't touched her in ages. Like I've been holding myself back from everything I want for an eternity. She collapses in a curve against me, her palm still flat against the door. "You want to know what's going on?"

"Yes," she breathes, pressing herself harder against me.

"When you said business casual, was that for me or for you?"

She blinks twice, her gaze and her breathing heavy. She likes the way I'm touching her. She likes that I'm being rough. "What?"

I lean closer so I can brush my lips over the shell of her ear. Her shoulders shake in a tiny shiver. Something dark and possessive uncurls in my chest.

"You said if you're fucking me, no one else is." I collar her ear with my teeth and nip, just once. "Do the same rules apply to you?"

"Charlie," she sighs, head lolling to the side. "I knew you were upset."

"I'm not upset."

"You seem upset."

"I'm not upset," I say again. I keep one hand at her neck and curl the other around her hip, walking us back from the door toward the desk shoved up against the window. I hold her there, tighter than I probably should. "I'm just trying to clarify."

"Clarify what?"

I drag my knuckles from her hip to her belly button and undo the top clasp of her jeans. My hands are shaking. I want her to forget anyone that isn't me. I want to overwhelm her the same way she overwhelms me. I want a bunch of things I absolutely should not want and yet I cannot stop myself from wanting them. I yank her zipper down, then slip my hand down the front of her pants. "Am I the only one allowed to touch you like this?"

Nova gasps as I trace her through her lacey underwear, then moans when I tug it to the side to tuck my hand beneath. She is bare skin and wet heat. I drag my fingers against her, and her hands clench tight in my shirt.

"Charlie."

"Spread your legs," I order. She does as I ask, resting more of her weight against the desk at her back. The thing in my chest that's in control roars in satisfaction. I love that I can request this of her with a crowded room full of people on the other side of this wall and she does it. I love that when I press harder against her, she fights to tip her legs wider, trying to feel more of me. I reward her with a rough stroke of my fingers and cup her jaw with my free hand, holding her still so I can touch her the way I want. I trace my thumb over the swell of her lips.

"Is it just me, Nova?"

She takes my thumb in her mouth and sucks. I clench my teeth and twist my hand so I can press two fingers into her. I grunt when she lets out a breathy moan. Fuck, I love that sound.

"Nova."

Her head drops back, and I trail my thumb that's wet from her mouth down the line of her neck to the hollow of her throat, farther still to the rise of her breasts through the tight material of her top. I hook one finger beneath the shiny material and tug it down until I can brush a kiss to my favorite rose, her tits straining against the hem. Another inch and I could have her half bare against this desk.

"What?" she breathes, circling her hips and pressing down harder. Chasing my touch.

"Am I the only one that gets to make you feel like this?"

I twist my hand, knuckles brushing against the lace of her underwear. I move my fingers faster, my forearm flexing. She gasps and then moans, hands scrambling from the desk to my shoulders. She pushes at my coat until it's half hanging on me and curls her fists into the back of my button-down. The one I picked out because she said she liked it.

"Am I the only one that gets these sounds? The only one that gets you this wet?" I ask. The only sounds in the room are our rough breathing and my hand working between her legs. "I am, aren't I? You don't get it like this with anyone else, do you? I know exactly what you need."

She nods. "You do."

"All you have to do is take it, isn't that right? You always let me do whatever I want to you."

She hums, hands clenching and releasing in my shirt. "Yes," she breathes.

"But I make it good for you too. Don't I?"

She blinks open her eyes and watches me. "Always," she says quietly. "You always make it good for me."

"Tell me." I move my hand harder in the constraint of her pants. She sucks in a breath through her teeth. "Say it."

I want it to be a demand but it tumbles from my mouth like a plea. Even when I'm the one controlling her pleasure, I'm on my knees for her.

I brush my mouth against hers. "Can you please say it?"

The fists in my shirt ease, and she slips her hands beneath, palms against my bare skin. She traces the lines of my back, drawing temporary tattoos that only she knows the design of. I gentle my hand between her legs and rub her clit in slow, wet circles. Exactly how she likes it.

"It's just you." She nudges me with her nose and buries her face against my neck, hands holding me tight. "You're the only one, Charlie."

The hand I still have at the back of her neck squeezes. "Good," I whisper, mouth against her ear.

She comes with a gasp and a whine, legs trying to shut around my hand. But I wedge my hips between her thighs and guide her the rest of the way through it, until her body is relaxed and her nails aren't digging half-moons into the skin of my back. I hope she's left marks. Maybe I'll have her tattoo those into my skin, so every time I glance at them in the mirror I can remember her exactly like this. Looking up at me in the moonlight from the window with her chin against my chest, some of her hair sticking to her neck, a satisfied smile on her color-smudged lips.

I pull my hand out of her pants and tug up her zipper. Redo the button. It's easier to focus on these tasks than the yawning, hollow feeling right in the middle of my chest. I shouldn't have done that. I shouldn't have pressed the issue. I shouldn't have—

"Charlie."

I curl my hands around her hips and drop my forehead to hers. I shut my eyes tight. "I'm sorry," I whisper.

She makes a low, amused sound. "I know you're not apologizing for that orgasm you just gave me."

"I shouldn't have—"

"—been honest with me? Given me a stunning orgasm? Which one do you regret more?"

I think about it for a second. "Neither," I finally sigh. I lean back and peer at her, trying to fix her lipstick with my fingers that aren't wet with her, but I only make it worse. She slaps my hand away and I let it fall to my side.

"That wasn't—I shouldn't have—" I pause and take in a deep breath through my nose. "Let's talk about this when you don't have a shop full of people waiting to see you."

She threads her fingers through mine. "Will you stay?"

"I don't know if I should."

The erection straining my pants, one reason. My foul mood, another.

"Stay, please." She squeezes my hand. "I want you to."

I study her face turned up toward mine.

Fuck.

I'd give this woman anything she asked for.

I take two steps back, still holding her hand. Her face falls, but I tug her with me. I extend my arm out with a stupid half bow, gesturing toward the door. I'm going to need to channel my inner showman if I hope to make it through the rest of the evening.

And I'm going to need ten minutes alone in this dark room.

"After you." I pat her ass once as she walks past me to the door, a cute little hop in her step that shouldn't make me smile but it does. I lean out of the doorway after her and whisper-yell, "But stop and fix your lipstick first."

23

NOVA

I FLIP THE sign on the door from OPEN to CLOSED, turning and resting my back against the frame.

Tonight was incredible. Beyond my wildest expectations. I think part of me was afraid that the people who RSVP'd wouldn't show, but they did. The studio was packed all night long. Evelyn showed me her phone right before she left. The feed of people who checked in to the Ink & Wild location was bursting with color. Pictures of tacos and tattoos and little cookies shaped like flowers.

I've been waiting for this feeling. Not quite *I made it*, but *I can fucking do it*. I've been chasing milestone after milestone since I decided I wanted to open a studio and for the first time I feel . . . good. Happy. Settled.

Like I can do it.

Some of it is the culmination of months and months of hard work and some of it is the look on my family's faces when they walked into the space tonight. Beckett's huff of a laugh when I made him sit in the chair for a tiny tattoo, right next to that maple leaf I gave him over a decade ago. His quiet *Proud of you, kiddo* when I wiped his new inked birch tree leaf down with a cold wipe.

But some of it is Charlie too. Charlie, who showed up at my house two days ago with some fresh fruit and a pumpkin and decided to rearrange half of my first floor. Charlie, who has chased away the buzzing, anxious feeling with his own brand of distraction. Charlie, who always makes it safe and easy for me to ask for what I need.

Charlie, who drove me to a ferocious, mind-numbing orgasm with his fingers in my office and is now at the back of the studio with a giant trash bag, collecting plastic cups with my logo printed on the side. He stayed because I asked him to, even though I know he didn't want to.

"You artist types are messy as hell," he comments from the back of the shop. He mumbles something under his breath about Caleb and cookies and dumps a plate in with the rest of the trash. "I think I got almost everything."

I circle around my station, collapsing on my stool. It rolls backward across the floor. "I didn't ask you to stay so you could play custodian, you know."

He drops the trash bag by the back hallway and walks closer. "Why did you ask me to stay?"

Because he was hurt earlier and trying to hide it. And I don't like it when Charlie is hurt.

I also have something I want to give him.

I pat the table in front of me.

He blinks at it. "You want me to clean the table?"

"No, Charlie. I want you to sit."

"On the table?"

"If you want, but you could also sit to the side of it. Whatever your preference."

"For what?"

I pull out a fresh pair of gloves and tug them on. "For your tattoo."

Both of his eyebrows shoot up. "You're finally giving in? You're gonna give me a scorpion on my ass?"

"If that's what you want, sure. But I had something else in mind."

He takes two steps closer. He's looking at me like I'm about to call his bluff and pull out a Big Bird stencil. "What did you have in mind?"

I pat the table again, then gesture to the stool that's tucked off to the side. "Take a seat and I'll tell you." I snap the gloves against my wrist. "Or show you, I guess."

Charlie drops himself in the stool across from me, staring hard at the table between us. His eyes drag up to mine and hold, their cobalt blue a brilliant sapphire in the soft glow of my studio. His hair is still messy from my hands and there's some scruff along his jaw. He looks weary. Exhausted.

Hesitant.

"It's okay if you don't want one," I say quietly. "If you've been joking, I understand."

He doesn't look away from me. "I haven't been joking. I just—" He drags his palm over the back of his neck. "I don't know what I want."

"I have an idea."

"Yeah?"

I nod. "I'd like to show you."

A smile kicks up the side of his mouth. "Is it the poop emoji?"

"Maybe. You'll just have to see, won't you?"

I grab a black ballpoint pen from the top of my station. I did stencils tonight because it's easier for quick turnover, but I usually hand draw with a ballpoint before I finalize with ink. I have more freedom that way. Every body is wonderfully unique, and I like to shape my lines accordingly.

I get out the rest of my supplies and place them in a neat line by my elbow, my body working on autopilot, this routine a familiar comfort. But I feel Charlie's gaze on me the entire time, his eyes soft and inquisitive, taking in each minute detail. He doesn't ask any of his questions, though I know he's probably bursting with them. He just sits, watching, unusually quiet.

I hold out my hand for his and he stares at it.

"What?" he asks.

I wiggle my fingers. "Your hand, please."

"Knuckle tats?"

I snort a laugh. "Now there's an idea."

He'd look good with tattoos over his big hands. I imagine dark lines decorating his fingers as his hands hold me in place, the way they might move when he squeezes my thighs. I have to take a second to compose myself.

He slips his hand into mine with a snicker. "I'd love to know what's going on in that mind of yours."

"I'm sure you would."

I rub my gloved thumb over his knuckles, cradling his hand in both of mine. He has a scar just beneath his pinky. A smattering of freckles over his wrist. So many details I still haven't noticed about him. So many things left to discover. I trace both and flip his hand over. I work on unbuttoning his cuff, then roll his sleeve. He's wearing a chambray shirt tonight, a blue so pale it almost looks gray.

"I was thinking right here," I say quietly, my index finger tracing a line over the inside of his wrist. His fingers flex up toward mine and then relax. "Something small. So your watch can cover it while you're at work."

His eyes drift toward the Rolex on my wrist. "Will I be getting my watch back?"

I twist it and make a show of checking the time. His legs shift beneath the table until both of his knees hug one of mine. "I thought you said you had other watches."

He laughs, his shoulders relaxing. "Yeah, you're right. I do."

I grin at him. "Does this spot work? Or do you want something different? You can be honest. You won't hurt my feelings."

I watch him swallow, the strong line of his throat working. He doesn't bother looking down at his wrist. "That spot is good."

"You're sure?"

"Yes."

"Tattoos are forever, you know."

"I'm aware, Nova." His fingers twitch up again, tracing the matching spot on my wrist right where my glove ends. "Do your worst."

I reach for the prep pad and tear it open. "My worst is still pretty damn good, Charlie."

His face melts into something appreciative, the most he's looked like himself since I saw him standing on the sidewalk outside the studio trying to decide if he wanted to talk to me or not.

"Ah," he says. "There she is."

"Who?"

"You," he says simply. "In full Technicolor. I like seeing you confident, Nova."

A blush warms my cheeks. "We're already sleeping together. You don't need to flirt," I deflect, trying to hide how proud that simple observation makes me. That I've managed to work through my anxieties and stress and confusion and shine just as bright as I've always wanted to. That he sees it. That he's been seeing it this whole time. "But thank you," I add quietly. "I like it too."

His smile settles into something softer. His knees hug mine beneath the table, and I wipe carefully at the place I plan to put his ink. His skin is so delicate here, his veins a web of blue beneath paper thin skin. I trace my thumb back and forth over the spot, even after I'm done with the wipe. Will my touch here carry all the way back to his heart? That spot between his shoulder and neck that always makes him sigh when I kiss it? I like to think so.

I clear my throat and try to scrape together my professionalism, but it's hard when my knee is tucked between his legs and he's staring at me like that.

"Are you afraid of needles?" I ask.

"No. Just clowns."

"Guess I'll have to change your tattoo design, then."

"Probably."

I pick up the razor and drag it over his skin. Tiny efficient movements. I toss it in the wastebasket and reach for my favorite cheap plastic ballpoint.

"You're going to draw?" he asks.

I nod and flick off the cap with my thumb. "I usually do it like this. Is that all right?"

"You don't have to keep asking me if it's okay. I trust you, Nova."

"Even if it's a poop emoji?"

"Even then. I'd probably deserve it."

I squeeze his hand. "You wouldn't deserve it."

I've known what I wanted to draw for Charlie for weeks now, since that night on his couch when he put Katharine Hepburn on and pressed his thigh to mine. I doodled it on the edge of the pizza box. Seven different variations, over and over again. I've been doodling them ever since.

I start in the middle of his wrist, right at that heavy blue line that goes all the way to his heart. I start there and draw outward. I keep my eyes on his skin and the tiny, incremental movements his body makes. The flex and flow of the ink from my pen to the canvas of his body. I inhale deeply through my nose. Spice. Cider. Evergreen and Charlie.

I release my breath and draw some more.

"Nova," Charlie says, voice low, a hitch in his breath.

I draw another line, my fingers flexing on where I hold his arm steady. "Hmm?"

"I'm sorry."

I don't look up, distracted by the tiny petal I'm trying to get right. "Thank you. You should apologize for thinking I'd ever tattoo a clown on anyone," I murmur.

"Not that. For . . . for the back room. Earlier. The way I acted."

"You already apologized for that," I tell him. I hate that he apologized before, and I hate that he's apologizing now. He has nothing to be sorry for. Because he gave me something without taking anything for himself?

Knowing Charlie, he probably thinks he took something. What did he tell me the other night? He thinks just the act of wanting something turns him into a selfish man. But that's not true. I followed him down that hallway because I knew he was upset, and I knew what was upsetting him.

But Charlie thinks he has to earn everything. Even the right to touch me, I guess.

It breaks my heart.

"I didn't like seeing you with him," he confesses quietly.

He's talking about Jake, a tattoo artist I worked with briefly at my old space. Jake has trouble with social interaction the same way Beckett does and tends to cling to people he knows when the room is crowded. He's kind and quiet, soft-spoken in a way that most men in this industry are not. He came to ask if I needed any help with overflow clients.

"You were jealous," I say, not a question.

"Yes," he agrees.

I lift my pen from his arm and look up. He's staring at me with a serious look on his handsome face, a furrow between his dark eyebrows. I drag my gloved thumb back and forth along the inside of his elbow where I'm gripping him to hold him steady.

"You have nothing to be jealous of," I whisper.

"I do."

"You don't, Charlie. I promise."

"I do," he says again, an uncharacteristic hardness to his voice. "Because I know what it feels like to be on the other side of that smile, Nova. That laugh. I know what it feels like to have all of your attention. And I wanted to drag him away from you by the back of that ridiculous TJ Maxx T-shirt for getting even a shred of it."

I blink at him, and his mouth settles into a firm line, a deep breath pushed out from his nose. His eyes trail along my face like he's trying to figure something out.

"I want all of your attention," he tells me. "Every last bit. And I feel like I should probably apologize for that too."

"I don't want you to," I hear myself say. I tilt my face back down to his wrist and pick up my pen. "I don't want you to apologize."

I like him jealous. I like him greedy. I like the wild, unrestrained version of him I got in the back office. It feels like he's finally possessed with the same sort of mindlessness I've been carrying around this entire time. I like him honest.

I think I just like him.

More than like him, actually.

I draw another line on his wrist and sit with that, waiting for the inevitable flare of panic. But there's nothing. There's only me and Charlie and the steady thrum of his pulse in the strong vein on the inside of his wrist, my heart skittering to match.

I finish with the design and toss my pen on the table between us, tilting my head to the side and taking a look. It's lovely. Thin, delicate lines that I'll have to be gentle with, but will be worth the extra care and attention.

I look up at him. "Do you want to see it before I get started with the ink?"

He doesn't even glance in the direction of his wrist. "No."

I frown. "Why not?"

"Because I said I trust you, Nova. And that doesn't have qualifications."

"But it's permanent."

He blinks once. "And I trust you," he says, the ghost of a grin brushing across his mouth.

It feels like we're arguing about something in two separate languages. I stare at him and wait for him to change his mind, to yank his wrist out of my hand and laugh at the design I've drawn for him, but he keeps his eyes on mine with a steady, calm look.

I reach for the tattoo pen and the tiny pod of black ink. I fill another disposable cup with deep blue and add a few drops of white until it's the color of the sky on a cold, cloudless day. Pale, pale blue.

Charlie arches an eyebrow at the color but doesn't say a word.

"If you're sure," I offer, one last opportunity for him to back out.

"I'm sure," he tells me.

I test the trigger of the pen so he can hear the sound. He doesn't so much as jump, his arm still extended on the table between us, palm up. Trusting.

"It'll be a pinch when I first start," I say. "It'll hurt, but once the blood starts moving in that direction it'll calm down. It's a small design. It shouldn't take me long."

"I can take it," he tells me with a cocky grin that falters somewhere in the middle. He's trying so hard tonight to be the person he usually is in front of everyone else. Good Time Charlie and all the shiny, sparkly things that are meant to distract. He said I'm in Technicolor, but tonight he's hiding in shades of gray, none of his usual colors shining through. He's watering himself down, for whatever reason.

I wish he'd stop.

I dip my pen into the pod of ink and let the needle fill, then settle over the design on his wrist. The hum of the pen vibrates from my fingers to my wrist, up my arm and over my shoulder until it feels like my entire being is alive with the rhythm. This is my favorite part. The anticipation right before I set my needle to skin.

I am the one in control. I am the one creating something beautiful on another person. Something permanent. Something lasting.

I tend to lose myself when I'm working, time turning into a fluid concept that slips right from my fingers as I dip my pen into ink over and over. I trace the lines on Charlie's wrist, my awareness of him reduced to the stretch of his arm across the padded table and his steady breathing. He doesn't flinch or twitch. His body relaxes into it, a curious, contemplative look on his face every time I flick my eyes up to check on him.

He's a natural.

"Do you remember when you asked me why I'm always down here?" he asks about ten minutes into my work. My body jolts at the scratch in his voice, bringing me back to the room where there is light and sound and something other than ink and skin and bone and vein.

I lift my pen from his wrist. I asked him about that weeks ago.

"Yeah, I remember. You told me you spend time here because you like the food."

"I do. Like the food. But that's not—" He swallows, and I know he's fighting to keep himself still. "That's not the only reason I visit."

I turn back to his wrist and trace another smooth line. "What's the other reason?"

I have my theories. Charlie might smile and laugh and joke when people are watching, but his shoulders curl in as soon as they turn away. He collapses in on himself in increments. It's like he's tired down to his bones from the strain of trying to pretend.

Charlie is always doing his best to make everyone around him happy. I used to think it was because it made him feel good, but I think it's deeper than that. I think he needs to be the loudest laugh in the room. He needs to entertain. He needs to feel like he's earned his spot.

His body collapses with a sigh, the hand not outstretched on the table scrubbing roughly at the back of his head.

"I'm lonely, Nova," he says, his voice cracking down the middle of my thoughts, sucking the air right out of my lungs. It's the simple honesty of the statement, I think, that hits me the hardest. He's not trying to hide at all.

I don't look up, offering him the privacy of my diverted attention. But there's a tremble in my hand that wasn't there before, and I have to take a second before I finish another two lines on his wrist.

Tell me more, my mind begs, even as my heart feels like it's going to thump right out of my chest onto the floor. *Tell me everything.*

His pinky flexes, grazing right below my glove again, and then relaxes. The trembling in my hands stops, my grip sure around the tattoo pen.

"I try to convince myself I'm not with all the ridiculous shit I do, but I'm lonely all the time. I go to work, and I keep myself busy with things I don't care about, and I come back to a fancy apartment with everything I could ever want, and I feel . . . nothing. Empty. I'm empty when I'm there, and my brain tries to fill the space with thoughts that go around and around, and I . . . I'm always halfway here before I realize it."

I don't say anything. I can't. I'm too busy picturing him in a gorgeous New York City apartment with floor-to-ceiling windows and a view of a glittering skyline. In a chair that probably costs more than anything I've ever owned, his suit jacket folded over the back of it and a half-empty glass of something at his elbow.

I think of him there, all alone, and I ink another line.

"I'm a disappointment to most people. My father in particular. He wants me to be something I'm not. I've tried my whole life to get there, but I don't think I'll ever reach the bar he's set for me. I'm not sure he wants me to." He drags his free hand through his hair until it sticks up in the back, the same way it does first thing in the morning. "I think I'm tired of trying."

I finish with the black and set the machine to the side, wiping a cold cloth over his skin. He releases another breath. "So, that's the answer. That's why I'm always here. Because I don't feel so empty when I'm spending time in Inglewild. I know it's not where I'm supposed to be, but I like to pretend it could be."

I refill my pen with the blue. "What do you mean it's not where you're supposed to be?"

"My whole life is in New York," he says gently. "This is temporary. I've . . . inserted myself. I don't fit here. Not really."

"You still think that? Even now?" I shade another petal. "Don't you have a standing lunch with Caleb and Alex's grandmother once a month?"

"I do, but—"

"And weren't you just sharing bean dip recipes on the street like a week ago?"

"I was, but—"

"Shut up for a second."

I finish with the last of the shading and flick the machine off, setting it behind me to clean later. I drag another cloth over the design and then glance up at Charlie, holding on to his wrist with both of my hands. He's staring at me with a smile in the lines by his eyes but nowhere else, a softness in his expression that he reserves for the dead of night when I've stolen his shirt to sleep in and I can't stop yawning in his face. When our legs are tangled beneath the blankets and his arm is heavy over my hip.

Stolen moments when he doesn't think I'm looking.

"No one feels bad for you, Charlie. No one is . . . entertaining you to make you feel better about yourself."

He cheeks pink, the slightest bit. I think it's the first time I've ever seen him blush. We stare at each other. His face is a mask. I can't tell what he's thinking. Despite the ease with which he supports others, I don't think Charlie has ever had someone do the same for him. I think he's been holding on to these secrets for a long time.

I never thought I'd want to be that person for anyone. But it's easy enough to twist my fingers through his and squeeze. He squeezes back.

I want to ask him if he feels like he fits with me. If he's comfortable in the spaces we occupy together. But I swallow the words back down.

I already know the answer to that question. Charlie has always made it very clear.

I peel off my gloves and toss them in the wastebasket, then grab some Aquaphor and start to slather it over his tattoo. He still hasn't looked at it. "Do you want to see what it is?" I ask gently.

"I'm working myself up to it."

"Do you want me to do a countdown? I can start at ten if you'd like."

"Maybe start at one hundred."

A laugh bursts out of me. His smile finally drops from his eyes to the rest of his face. It feels like a victory.

"You're really that nervous?" I ask.

"I don't know. It feels like a big deal."

"It is a big deal," I tell him simply. "I told you, tattoos are permanent." Not to mention I've been drawing exactly this for weeks on every piece of scrap paper I could get my hands on. Whenever my brain turned off and my hand started doodling, I'd find this tattoo scribbled along the edges. I finally realized what my brain has been trying to tell me. It's a gift for Charlie, sure, but it's a confession too. I swallow. "You can look when you're ready."

He breathes in deep through his nose and watches me, eyes trailing across my face like he's still waiting for me to tell him this is all one big joke. But it's not a joke, and I don't tattoo things I don't mean for the people I care about most. Charlie, despite my best intentions and probably his as well, is the person I care about most. And I'm not nearly as scared of that as I used to be.

Growth, maybe. Or maybe I'm learning to listen to myself a little bit better. I don't know.

Apprehension pricks between my shoulders as I wait for him to look. I don't think I've ever been this nervous for someone to see a final design. Not even Beckett, the very first time.

He flicks his gaze down to his wrist and the thin design I tattooed there.

"It's a flower," he says, bending his head closer to get a better look.

I nod and swivel back and forth on my stool. "Do you know what kind of flower it is?"

He shakes his head. "Frankly, I'm still trying to get over the fact that you had an opportunity to tattoo Colonel Sanders on me and you didn't."

I ignore him. "It's a forget-me-not. I think my brain sometimes thinks in flowers and plants. My dad talked about them so much when we were growing up, it was inevitable. He had this big botanical book on the edge of his desk in his workshop. Always in the same spot. I don't think he moved it once. I'd sit on the table while he worked and I'd flip through it. I liked to trace the stems and the flowers with my finger. Eventually I started tipping over flower pots to draw in the soil instead."

Charlie grins. "I bet your dad loved that."

"He didn't. By the fifth time I did it, he went out and got me a sketch book. I drew every flower and tree and root system in that book. And when I finished, I just started all over again."

"Ink and Wild," he says softly, still with that smile on his face. "The flowers in your logo. What are they?"

"You noticed."

His eyes are soft. Knowing. "I always notice you, Nova girl."

I smile back. Yeah. Yeah, he does.

"*Astrantia* 'Roma.' They're for courage. Strength. I wanted a reminder that I have both of those things. That I can do this."

Charlie's thumb nudges against mine when our hands lay flat on my table. "Fuck yeah, you can."

My smile tugs wider, something that always seems to happen when I'm talking to Charlie. I used to hate it but I think I love it now. I think I crave it. "I've always liked flowers best. They're pretty, but more resilient than people give them credit for." I trace my thumb along the bottom edge of the stem that curls along his wrist. The pale blue petal tucked carefully right next to that precious vein right under his skin. "Forget-me-nots, in particular. They're one of my favorites. They're almost constantly in bloom, always tilting toward the sun."

Charlie's eyes search my face. "And you picked this one for me?"

"Yes."

"Why?"

"Because—" I try to figure it out for myself, why I started drawing them on a pizza box while Charlie sat on the couch next to me, trying so damn hard to keep himself in bloom. "Probably because your eyes remind me of page seventy-three in the *Encyclopedia of Plants and Flowers*. Forget-me-not blue."

Charlie swallows and looks back down at the flower on his wrist.

"What does it symbolize?" He shifts in his seat like he's afraid of the answer. "This flower. What does it mean?"

"Fidelity," I explain. "Loyalty and respect."

Charlie keeps looking at the flower. "You respect me?"

"One of the most beautiful things about you is your big heart and your faithfulness to the people you care about. I know you think you're being selfish, taking affection for yourself, but you're not. It's generosity. The best sort of love. I know you feel like you need to earn your place, Charlie, but you don't. Not in this town and not"—*not with me*, I almost say—"not anywhere else."

I think of what Beckett said to me in my kitchen. The thing about love. "It's just yours," I whisper to Charlie. "Yours to have and yours to keep. You don't have to earn anything. You belong here. And I . . . I wanted to give you this flower because I want you to know that you don't have to be anything other than exactly who you are. I know you've been hiding, Charlie. But I see all of your colors. The bright ones and the dark ones too. I see how you're always tilting toward the sun. Forget-me-nots were always my favorite, and—well. You're kind of my favorite too."

That big knot in my chest untangles a little more. He keeps staring at the flower. He stares at it for so long without a single word that my tiny prick of apprehension turns into a fist pressing right in the center of my back.

He doesn't like it.

"It's small enough that you can cover it with your watch easily enough," I tell him quietly, trying not to let regret swallow me whole. He's too quiet. Too still. I assumed a lot and said too much. He probably hates the damn thing. "Or I could—"

"Nova," he says quietly, cutting me off. His voice is rougher than I've ever heard it.

I quiet. "Yes?"

He lifts his newly tattooed arm and wipes quickly under his eye.

He sniffs once and digs his knuckle into his cheek. His eyes drag up to meet mine, red rimmed but bright.

Forget-me-not blue.

"I've never been anyone's favorite," he whispers.

"Well," I say, feeling defensive. "You're mine."

He leans his body across the table and cups his hand around my face, hauling me to him. His kiss is slow and deep, a methodical undoing of every last hesitation I have.

I fall into it happily.

"Nova," he whispers, somewhere against my mouth. "I don't think my feelings are business casual."

I sigh into him. I hold on to him wherever I can reach. "I don't think mine are either."

24

CHARLIE

WHAT ARE YOU supposed to do after you've confessed to feelings you promised you wouldn't catch? What is the morning-after protocol for that? I'm familiar with the fun and the fucking, but not this part.

I think I was high on adrenaline or endorphins or maybe just the way it always feels to have all of Nova's attention on me. Like lying in a sunbeam or taking a shot of tequila. She finished the tattoo on my wrist, and everything came tumbling right out.

I have no idea what I'm supposed to do, so I'm making pancakes.

I'm making pancakes and staring at the batter sizzling in the pan like the crispness of the edges will determine the fate of the free world. Nova is somewhere behind me, lounging in an armchair I'm confident Stella stole from Luka's mom's house, peeling apart an orange and drumming her feet against the ottoman. I spin the spatula in my hand and watch her out of the corner of my eye, specifically the stretch of her bare legs where they peek out from beneath the hem of the shirt she confiscated, the crescent moon on her right thigh bracketed by an imprint of my teeth.

I took her home after the studio last night and backed her up against the floor-to-ceiling windows in the guesthouse, hands shaking, desperate to soothe the buzzing in my chest. I peeled her out of her clothes until it was just Nova in the moonlight, the flowers on her skin a match for the one she drew on mine. I wrapped her legs around my waist and fucked her against the window until I couldn't breathe, couldn't think, couldn't see anything but her. And then I carried her upstairs and tucked her in my bed, grabbing another blanket out of the closet because I knew she'd end up stealing all of mine.

And now I'm standing here wielding a spatula, wondering what the fuck I'm supposed to do.

Does she want to talk about it? Does she want to forget it ever happened? Did she say it because she meant it, or was she just trying to make the sad sack in front of her crying over a flower tattoo feel better about his emotional deterioration?

I've got no clue.

"Ready for the festival later?"

I startle so hard I almost send the pan flying from the edge of the stove. The batter goes tilting to the side, and the pancake I decided to make in the shape of Mickey Mouse loses an ear.

"What?" I yell the question, for some reason.

Her husky laugh drifts over my shoulders. I try to fix the ear with more batter, and the mess in the pan turns into a giant blob. The pancakes seemed like a reasonable way to channel my feelings, but they're starting to manifest whatever is bumping around inside of my rib cage instead.

One big, messy blob.

"The festival," she says. "The thing we've been planning. You're gonna go, right?"

"Of course I'm gonna go. Someone has to make sure the floral arrangements are symmetrical."

And that Gus and Montgomery don't murder each other, or a random citizen, when trying to erect their pumpkin sculpture.

I've seen the drawings. The odds aren't good.

Nova slips from her chair with a sigh. I hear the pad of her feet against hardwood and then a single finger traces up my bare spine. She commandeered my T-shirt as soon as she woke up this morning, muttering something about coffee and yanking the blankets over her head.

"What are you thinking about?" she asks. She curls her arm around my waist and rests her cheek against my bicep. A half hug. The palm of her hand rubs up and down my side. Right now, I'm thinking about how much I like her like this, soft and free with her affection. Wearing the shirt I'm supposed to be wearing, her warm skin pressed to mine. It feels like we're in a bubble—in this house, in Inglewild, in the terms of the relationship we set for ourselves—and I'm afraid of what might happen when we step outside of it.

"I'm thinking about using whipped cream to make a face on this pancake."

Her fingernails bite into my skin. I sigh and tilt my head, brushing a kiss against her messy hair.

"I'm thinking about how I have to leave in a couple of days," I say instead, deciding to be honest.

"That's better," she hums. "Is that what has you mumbling under your breath over here?"

I flick off the burner and slide the sad mouse pancake onto a plate. I drop a strawberry on top for his nose and hand it to her. "I've got no idea what I'm doing, Nova."

She stares at her plate. "I don't know. This is a pretty good bear."

I frown. "It's supposed to be a mouse."

A smile twitches at the corner of her mouth. "It's a very excellent mouse, Charlie."

I roll my eyes and grab the can of whipped cream, topping off my coffee with enough to send me into a sugar coma. I add sprinkles on top because I'm a grown adult man, then slap Nova on the ass, urging her over to the table.

She curls her legs beneath her in the chair and rests her chin in her hand, plucking the strawberry from the top of her pancake. "I don't know what I'm doing either, if that makes you feel better," she says quietly. She cuts off a square and pops it in her mouth. "Our business casual turned out to be not so casual, huh?"

I rub my hand over my jaw. I'm glad she brought it up. "I like you, Nova. I like what we're doing."

Her eyelashes flutter against the tops of her cheeks. She looks down at her pancake and then back up at me. "I like what we're doing too."

"But I'm heading out in a couple of days."

She shrugs. "That doesn't have to change anything."

"It probably changes some things."

She cuts off another perfect square, reaching forward and swiping it through some of the whipped cream on top of my coffee. I nudge my mug closer to her so she doesn't have to stretch for it.

"It doesn't have to." She takes another bite and drags the fork slowly out of her mouth, thinking. A bit of whipped cream clings to the corner of her bottom lip. I want to lick it off. "Who says we need to label this thing between us?"

Thing feels too small of a word for the overwhelming sense of panic and adoration that sweeps over me every time Nova so much as looks in my direction, but sure.

"Yeah," I agree slowly. "But this *thing* is going to change when I'm about three hundred miles up the coast."

I won't be able to drive over whenever I miss her. I won't be able to print miscellaneous tax forms and bring them to her just so I have an excuse to see her smile. I'll be caught up in my life, and she'll be caught up in hers, and I don't know how we'll fall together once I step foot out of this town. If once I stop coming around, she'll forget all the reasons she let me in to begin with.

She watches me from the other side of the table, her bare foot nudging at my knee. "Will you call me when you're in New York?"

"If you want me to call."

"I want you to call." She stabs another piece of pancake with her fork. "And will you text me? With all the ridiculous thoughts that are in your head?"

That was happening before we started sleeping together. I probably couldn't stop that if I wanted to.

"Of course I will." Especially if she keeps sending me those pictures I love so much. The ones of her in front of her mirror in ink and lace and the ones of her sitting in the studio by herself, cross-eyed and fish-faced, her sketchbook in the background.

She pushes her chair back and stands, rounding the corner of the table and climbing into my lap. I rest my hands on her hips and tip my head back against the chair, watching her face. Everything feels easier when she's touching me like this. Like the answer is simple enough.

Maybe it is.

"And when you come back to visit . . ." She drags her thumb along my jaw, scraping against my stubble. I swear I feel it in the pulse of my neck. In the healing tattoo on my wrist. In my half-hard cock. "Will you be in my bed?"

I curl my hand around the back of her neck and squeeze, angling her mouth to mine. "Good luck getting me out of it."

"Then that's what we'll do," she tells me.

"Just like that?"

"Just like that. You don't have to be lonely anymore. Not when you've got me."

I drag her mouth to mine and brush my lips to hers, sticky syrup and sweet strawberries and coffee with too much cream. I kiss her until I settle, until all the doubts buzzing around in my brain are erased with her hands in my hair and her mouth on mine.

She pulls away and cups my cheeks, her forehead against mine.

"I never felt like I was missing anything before," she says quietly, thumbs tracing the sides of my jaw, holding me close. "I never wanted to try with anyone, but I want to try with you."

"That's the thing, Nova." I kiss the tip of her nose, the slope of her cheek, my favorite freckle under her eye. "With me, you don't have to try at all."

THE PUMPKIN ART installation ends up looking okay.

Art is a loose word for it, and I'm pretty sure it's held together by good thoughts and the will of the produce gods, but it's . . . there. It's . . . something. Vaguely horrifying and moderately festive, it's a fine centerpiece to the rest of the harvest festival.

Cindy ends up serving her chili out of a stand like a reasonable human being, and someone was able to convince Beckett to sell pumpkins from Lovelight Farms in a makeshift pumpkin patch right next to the fountain. He lords over it like they're his children and glares at anyone who says anything disparaging about their size or shape, but Evelyn smooths his edges with her sunny smile and her photo booth props. Sunglasses that look like gourds and a top hat with acorns along the rim.

It's ridiculous and perfect and everything I love about this silly little town. I steal the acorn hat and wear it while sipping on cider out of a giant goblet shaped like a jack-o'-lantern. I flirt with Abuela while Caleb and Alex glare daggers at me, and I stuff my face with pecan pie and cider donuts and roasted pumpkin seeds. I try to soak up every bit of happiness this town gives me before I have to go back to my life in New York.

Which is how I end up dragging Nova into the same alley we kissed in before, slipping my hand under the back of her cropped sweater, splaying my fingers wide against her warm skin. I kiss her until we're panting into each other's mouths, my hand abandoning her sweater for the stretch of her thigh instead.

"Charlie," she breathes, tearing her mouth from mine. I drag kisses down the line of her throat and tug her closer. I've been intentionally avoiding her all morning for exactly this reason. I've lost all semblance of restraint. I can't keep my head on straight or my hands to myself when she's around. There's a ticking clock on our time together, and I want to hold her as much as I can for as long as I can.

We might have agreed to the tentative beginnings of a relationship, but I'm still leaving in a couple of days for New York.

"This alley is trouble for us." Nova laughs with her head tipped back. I trace a meandering path down her neck to the hollow of her throat. I nose there lightly, and her hips tuck into mine. "We should probably stop."

"Yeah, we probably should." I flex my fingers on her thigh and drag my hand up to the waist of her jeans. I hook my thumb there and rub at her bare hip beneath. "That would be the responsible thing to do."

"Mm-hmm," she hums. "And we are responsible people."

We stare at each other. A smirk tugs at her kiss-bitten mouth.

"One more," she mutters to herself. She presses up on her toes and catches my mouth again.

We decided before we left the house that we'd continue to keep this thing between us . . . between us. Nova has no interest in fielding small-town gossip, and I have no interest in bringing her to her senses. I'm still convinced that things might change for her once I'm gone. Not that I doubt what she's told me, I just—I want to enjoy this while it lasts.

She pulls her mouth from mine abruptly and turns toward the entrance of the alley. The narrow passageway is partially blocked by a giant inflatable pumpkin that I may or may not have placed intentionally.

"Did you hear that?" she asks.

"What?" I press a line of kisses down the column of her throat. "I didn't hear anything."

She pushes me away by my forehead. "I thought I heard someone calling your name."

"Was it you? Because you like saying my name when you—"

"Be quiet." She pinches my side. "I think someone is looking for you."

"Who would be looking for me?"

"I don't know, but—"

I hear it. It's faint through the music and the laughter and the buzzing of the six-foot inflatable grinning pumpkin, but I hear it. It sounds like someone is screeching my name, and it sounds like it's—

"Is that Stella?" Nova asks, slipping out of my arms and wandering to the edge of the alley. She crouches behind the pumpkin and peers around the edge of it.

"Stella isn't supposed to be back for another four days."

I follow her and search the crowd milling around the town square. Gus is making questionable adjustments to the sculpture in the fountain while Montgomery directs him from the top of a ladder. Alex is having what looks like a heated argument with Nova's sister, brandishing a historical romance like he's preaching on a street corner. And Beckett is cradling a pumpkin to his chest, shaking his head while Jeremy pleads his case about . . . something. I don't see Stella anywhere.

I inch my way out of the alley.

"Maybe we were just imagining—holy shit!"

Stella appears without warning in front of me, practically tackling me to the ground with her arms around my neck. She hugs me so tight she cuts off my air supply, Luka huffing and puffing as he comes jogging up behind her.

"Hey," he says, winded. Stella does not let go. "I tried to slow her down but she was determined to find you."

I pat between her shoulder blades and shoot a bewildered glance at Nova. Nova who is no longer standing in the alley but beelining her way toward the pumpkin patch. The little coward.

"That was the best honeymoon of my entire life," Stella says somewhere in the front of my sweater. I pat her head while simultaneously trying to push her away. "I had to tell you right away."

"You mean the honeymoon you're still supposed to be on?"

She finally releases me, swiping her fingers under her eyes. I suck in a much needed breath, spots at the edge of my vision.

"We had to come back early."

"Why?" I glance at Luka over her shoulder for an explanation, but he just shrugs. "Is everything okay?"

Stella gives me a watery smile. "I couldn't miss the harvest festival, could I?" She could have, but that's fine. Cindy's chili is good, but it's not better than the kind of pasta they make in Florence. Stella looks over my shoulder at the alley I just popped out of and frowns. "What were you doing down there anyway? Did I see you with Nova Porter?"

I put both of my hands on her shoulders and steer her toward the cider stand. In the opposite direction of where Nova went. "I was helping her find an earring."

"In the alley?"

"Yep."

"Does she wear earrings?"

I have to think about that for a second. I'm not even sure her ears are pierced.

I sigh. "It's really great to have you back, Stella."

25

CHARLIE

I SIT IN the chair on the opposite side of Stella's desk, my ankle resting on my knee and an entire box of cinnamon apple streusel cupcakes on my lap. Caleb brought them to me as a mood booster, though I'm not exactly sure why my mood needs boosting. I've been extremely pleasant to everyone this morning, starting with Nova when I woke her up with my head between her legs. I snuck over to her place after spending the rest of the festival with Stella and Luka, doing my best to seem happy that they came back early from their trip instead of slightly murderous and largely agitated.

I wanted more time.

I thought I had more time.

I shove another cupcake in my mouth and try not to feel salty about it.

Maybe I do need mood boosting.

Stella holds her hands out above her desk, hovering but not touching anything. "I'm afraid to move."

"Why?"

"I don't think it's ever been so organized."

"Not even when you bought the place?"

She shakes her head. "Luka almost wept when he dropped me off this morning."

I let some of the tension slip from my spine. It is nice to have her back. Luka too. I missed them both, even if I happily filled the space they left behind. It's not their fault I got used to sitting in the chair behind her desk, sipping my coffee from a mug shaped like a nutcracker. These things have always belonged to Stella. I knew that when I came here, and I knew that this morning when I woke up with Nova's legs tangled with mine. I've just been borrowing them.

Stella picks up a piece of paper and frowns at it. Shit. I was hoping she'd see that when I was gone and not sitting right in front of her, but I can't exactly reach across and rip it out of her hands. "What's this?" she asks.

"It looks like a piece of paper."

Her eyes narrow over the top of it. "Charlie. Did you"—she squints her eyes and tilts her head to the side—"map out an expansion? For the farm?"

"Possibly."

She picks up another piece of paper. My poorly doodled map and the sheet right beneath it. She holds them all fanned out in her hands, a bewildered look on her face. "Did you make budget sheets too? And list out possible partners?"

I shrug. "I needed something to keep me busy."

I thought I'd have more time to hide it before she got back. My plan was to tuck the paperwork under her recurring candy cane order invoice and play stupid when she brought it up. I think I organized everything a little too well.

She drops her hands on top of her clean desk. "Maintaining the farm and working your job in New York wasn't enough of an activity?"

"Apparently not."

"And hooking up with Nova Porter didn't add enough flavor? You needed to make me a business plan too?"

I freeze with another cupcake halfway to my mouth. "Um."

"Mm-hmm," she continues, not looking at me. She flips another page in her stack. "I am aware of what you were up to, Charles Abraham Milford."

"That's not my middle name."

"And that's not the most important takeaway from that sentence. The phone tree has been talking about it since we left. Luka kept a close eye on the situation while we were in Italy."

I drop my cupcake. "I knew it."

"And if that wasn't enough of an answer, I caught you slinking out of an alleyway with her lipstick on your neck."

I ignore that part. "So, the phone tree is still active, then."

"Again," Stella drawls, "not the most important takeaway from that sentence."

I wonder when they took me off. Was it at the wedding? Was it after that first harvest festival committee meeting? What have I missed? How do I get added back on? Is there an appeals process? Who makes these decisions?

I have so many questions.

"You know how invested I am in the phone tree."

"I'm aware." She reaches forward and plucks one of the cupcakes out of my box. "What's going on with Nova, Charlie?"

I hesitate. "What does the phone tree say?"

"Well," she takes a bite out of her cupcake and chews thoughtfully. "There was a video of you falling from her roof half naked. Luka watched it thirty-seven times. Between that and the alleyway, I can put the pieces together easily enough. But I'd like to hear it from you. Why didn't you say anything?"

"You've been back in town for twelve hours."

"And yet while I was away, you managed to share numerous selfies of yourself around the farm."

That's true. We texted frequently while she was in Italy. She asked how the farm was doing, and I decided to send her a photo diary in response. Me and the kittens. Me decorating a tree with mini pumpkins in the west fields. Me on top of Beckett's tractor. Me lying on the ground next to Beckett's tractor after he yanked me off it.

"Which one was your favorite? Mine was the one with me and Diego." I smooshed my face next to Beckett's cow while he had a mouthful of grass. I think we look adorable together. I might make it my Christmas card this year.

"Charlie," Stella sighs. "Enough deflecting. Why didn't you tell me about Nova? Why did you do all this extra work for the farm?"

"It wasn't extra work."

She looks down at the papers in exasperation. "You made an entire expansion plan. There's a . . . festive themed bar with a sample menu. You have leads for farmers market distributors. You somehow got Beckett to sign an agreement that he'll actually take part in a farmers market." Under the duress of half a bottle of tequila and the promise of an adopted pig, but whatever. "This is a business plan for the next five to seven years. It's not some little project you did when you were bored. This is a big deal."

"It's not a big deal."

Her cheeks flush pink. She's frustrated and picking up steam. She points at my face. "It is a big deal. Just like the trip to Italy was a big deal! There was a limo at the airport, Charlie! A limo!"

I blink at her. "There was supposed to be a limo. That's what I asked for."

"The whole trip was incredible! All of it! I ate so much pasta it's a wonder I didn't explode!"

I shrink back in my chair. "Why are you yelling at me?"

"Because you keep minimizing yourself and the things you do and I have no idea why!"

"That's not . . ." I frown. "That's not what I'm doing."

I like planning trips to Italy. I like thinking up ideas for the farm. It's a productive use of my time when my brain won't slow down and sleep won't come easy. It's also better than financial spreadsheets and never-ending emails and placating my father.

"You are," Stella seethes, one pale pink fingernail pointed in my direction. "And it stops now. No more of this"—she waves her hand in my face—"nonsense. I love you. I love you whether you send me to Italy or not. Whether you take over my job for a month or not. You don't need to prove anything to me."

I pick at the edge of a cupcake wrapper. This conversation is eerily similar to the one I had with Nova the night she inked my wrist. Too close to the battered pieces of my heart. "Fine," I mumble.

Stella cups her hand around her ear. "What was that?"

"I said fine."

"Fine, what?"

"Fine, I'll stop"—I make a face—"minimizing myself."

Stella relaxes. "Thank you. Was that so hard?"

"Kind of."

She ignores me and claps her hands together. "Now let's talk about Nova."

I groan and let my head drop back. "Who sent you the video? Did the whole phone tree see it?"

I'd like to know how many people saw me taking a nosedive into the hydrangeas and why no one decided to say anything about it.

"No. It was a very specific branch of the phone tree." Ah. That explains why no one asked me about it in the cheese aisle of the grocery store. The unofficial motto of the phone tree is Your Business Is Town Business. "This town isn't that reckless."

I stare at her over the stretch of her desk. "Do you remember during the Disney themed trivia night when someone tried to set off celebratory fireworks on the bar top? Or maybe the Easter egg hunt last year when Clint replaced all the plastic eggs with actual eggs for authenticity and the kids started pelting each other with them?"

"I forgot you were here for that."

"I got yolk on my Armani."

"All right," Stella agrees. "Fair point. This town is reckless."

I shift in my seat. It's not that I'm uncomfortable that people know;

I'm more concerned that one specific person knows. "Is Beckett on this branch of the phone tree?"

Stella shakes her head. "It was long ago decided that Beckett would not be added to any subthreads given he once launched his phone out of a moving vehicle when the phone tree called to tell him about ladies night at the bowling alley."

"Who decided this?"

"That is not for you to know, Charles Gareth Milford."

I drag my hand over my face. This conversation is officially off the rails. I have no idea how we got here.

Stella's face softens, and she leans forward, resting her elbows on top of her desk. "It's just me asking. No one else. We don't have to talk about it if you don't want to. But if you do need someone to confide in, I'd like to listen."

I scratch at a spot under my ear. Stella's gaze drifts over my wrist. A smile tugs at her mouth when she notices my new tattoo.

It would be nice to talk to someone about it. Maybe Stella can tell me what in the hell I'm supposed to do. I have no experience in lasting relationships. I have no experience in any relationships. I want this thing with Nova to work more than anything. Maybe Stella can offer some advice.

"Nova and I are . . ." I look for the right way to explain how all of this started. From a proposition on a dance floor to . . . pizza shared on a too-small couch in a too-small house. Me with my laptop and Nova with her sketch pad, her legs tucked underneath her at her kitchen table. A single beer passed back and forth in a chipped coffee mug. Nova in just her socks and one of my sweatshirts, the material down to her knees.

Laughing and talking and fucking and driving and kissing and sharing and stealing blankets in the dead of night.

A tattoo on my wrist and my heart in my throat.

The look on her face when she told me I was her favorite.

I've never been anyone's favorite.

"I think I'm in love with her" is what comes out of my mouth. I rub my hand against the middle of my chest. "And I'm terrified I'm going to fuck it up."

Stella drops her cupcake. It lands frosting first on top of a folder. "Holy shit."

I nod. That has more or less been the thought doing figure eights through the back of my mind since Nova told me she wanted to take me home. All those weeks ago.

"Mm-hmm."

"I mean. Holy *shit*," Stella says again. She keeps blinking at me. I think she needs a manual reset. Maybe I should call Luka.

I slouch down in my chair. "Yep."

"I thought you two were just messing around," she says, voice faint. "You were flirting at the wedding and with the video of the roof, I thought—Luka and I thought the two of you were just having fun."

"We were," I say. "We are. Nova, she's—" I'm having trouble finding the right words. "Being with her like this—it's the most fun I've ever had."

Stella smiles at me, eyes glassy. "Holy shit," she says again, voice hushed.

"Are you going to cry?"

She drags her knuckles under her eye. "I don't know. Probably." She releases a noisy breath. "This is all very unexpected."

"Tell me about it."

"Does she know?"

I cross my legs at the ankle and grab another cupcake.

"No, she doesn't." I don't plan on telling her either. Not before I leave. I want to see how everything settles first. It doesn't feel right to say it right at the edge of everything changing. No, I'll give her some time and then we'll see.

"Does Beckett know?"

I scratch once above my eyebrow. "He doesn't know anything

about what we've been doing," I answer quietly. I don't exactly feel good about that part, but I don't see an alternative. Beckett is notoriously protective of his sisters. At first, I didn't tell him because it wasn't serious, and now I'm not telling him because it is. I'm not sure what would break my heart more, Nova telling me she wants to end things between us, or Beckett telling me I'm not good enough for his sister. I guess I'm just trying to buy myself some more time. Across the board.

Stella's face does something complicated. "You've been keeping it a secret this whole time?"

"Didn't you get that impression from the roof video?"

"But if you love her—"

"I just figured that part out," I cut Stella off. "I've never been in love before. I didn't know."

This terrible, incredible feeling. Why I can't stop thinking about her, talking about her, looking for her whenever I'm in town. I want to tuck her in her blanket burritos, and I want to fuck her silly, and I want to hold her hand and tell her about tax forms. I want to open her window for her when she can't manage it for herself. I want to sit next to her at her kitchen table and do absolutely nothing.

That has to be love, doesn't it?

I really don't know.

I glance up at my sister. "What did it feel like? When you fell in love with Luka?"

Stella smiles at me and this time she's definitely crying. A tear falls from her lashes and lands on top of my neatly organized manila folders. "Like the most fun I've ever had."

I RAP MY knuckles against Nova's front door, not taking my usual care to park in the alley behind the bookstore and walk the couple of blocks over. Since the *very specific branch* of the phone tree knows about us, there's really no use army-crawling beneath the blackberry bushes in her backyard to surreptitiously knock at her door.

As fun as that is.

A light flicks on above my head. Nova's face appears in the window. She grins when she sees me, and my heart does something ridiculous.

Love, love, love loops around my mind in time with the beat of my heart.

"Hey." She leans against the frame with her arms crossed. She's wearing a tight black tank top and no bra. Baggy high-waisted sweatpants. Plain black socks. Her hair is loose around her shoulders and all of her ink is on display. Soft. Comfortable. I want to put her in my pocket. I want to bend her over my knee. "To what do I owe the pleasure?" she asks.

"Wanted to see you," I answer, the words bubbling out of me before I can think to contain them. I don't know how to temper myself when I'm with Nova. It's like the parts of me that I struggle to keep in check collapse every time she glances in my direction. I don't know what's too much and what's too little. I don't know how to do any of this.

But Nova smiles at me and those thoughts quiet, the strain in my neck easing. "And you're using the front door?"

"I am." I step over the threshold and pull her door shut behind me. I tip her chin up with my knuckles and brush a kiss over her lips. "I hope that's okay."

Her hands fist the front of my coat. "Of course it is."

"I'm heading out in the morning." I keep walking her backward until the small of her back hits the table she keeps tucked up against the wall in her hallway. Something rattles on it, and her breath releases with a sigh. "I wanted to spend tonight with you."

Her brows collapse with a cute little furrow. "Heading out?"

"Back to New York," I explain.

"Oh." Her whole face falls. "So soon?"

I shouldn't like it as much as I do, but it's nice to know I'm not the only one who will miss this. Kissing in the front hallway before I even take off my coat, her hands slipping beneath to press flat against my chest.

I trace my thumb over her bottom lip. "I've been here a month, Nova girl," I say as gently as I can, more for my own fragile feelings about it than hers. "Stella is back. There's no need for me to stay."

Her face collapses in a scowl. "No need, huh?"

A smile twitches at my lips. "Are you going to miss me?"

"Miss you destroying all of my landscaping? I don't think so." She pushes my heavy coat off my shoulders and it collapses at our feet. "I think you'll be missing me more than I'll be missing you."

"Another bet?" I drop my forehead to hers, our noses brushing. "I'm going to run out of watches."

"I'll take payment in the form of cufflinks too."

I laugh. "What are you going to do with my cufflinks?"

"Whatever I want," she breathes, her hands working at the buttons of my shirt.

"What do you think I'm going to miss the most?" I ask, my hand tracing a path from her cheek to her jaw to the strong line of her throat. I flex my fingers there, and she lets out a sigh, a whine vibrating under my palm. Desire coils tight. "What do you think I'll be thinking about, all alone in my apartment?"

"My peanut butter pretzels," she whispers with a rasp.

I laugh and bend so I can wrap both of my arms around her, hauling her up so her face is above mine. I want her closer. I want to feel all of her against all of me. Her legs curl around my hips and her hands frame my cheeks.

"Yeah, that's it," I whisper. "Your peanut butter pretzels."

Her thumbs make sweeping strokes from my temples to the curve of my jaw. I close my eyes and try to memorize the feel of her against me. Her ankles crossed at the small of my back and the weight of her in my arms. The steady thump of her heartbeat pressed tight to mine. The eager, unconscious rock of her hips.

It's not a goodbye, but it feels like one. Tomorrow I'll go to New York and she'll be here. No take-out coffee cups dropped off in the morning. No stolen kisses in the back hallway of her studio.

It makes me feel desperate. Itchy to have as much of her as possible as quickly as I can. I slide one hand up her back and fist it in her hair. "How do you need me tonight?"

She nudges her nose with mine, tipping my face up to hers where she's balanced above me. She kisses me carefully, then sinks her teeth into my bottom lip. I groan.

"You're always giving me what I want. How about you take what you want instead," she mutters against my mouth. Her kiss slips into something wet and deep. Slow and savoring. She pulls back with a hum and thumbs at the edge of my mouth. "For once."

"Yeah?" I'm usually content to follow wherever Nova leads, but there's a big part of me that desperately wants control. I want to make her remember me, stretch this time together a little more.

"Yeah," she whispers back. She bites at the slope of my jaw and then leans back, arms draped over my shoulders. She grins at me. "I want you to tell me what *you* want, Charlie boy."

I smile so wide my cheeks hurt. I untangle my hand from her hair and twist it in the butter-soft material of her tank top, tugging it over her head. I throw it in the direction of the living room, and she laughs, bright in the dark of her hallway. I bury my face between her tits, right against my favorite flower.

"I want your clothes off," I rumble into the deep, red petals.

"I can see that."

"And I want to take you upstairs."

I start moving, my hands holding her steady against me. Her nails scratch through my hair and her lips ghost across my forehead, my mouth busy licking the line of her flower stem. I trail a meandering path to her nipple and catch it with my teeth. Her back arches. I suck hard and she gasps my name.

"Do you want to fuck me on the staircase?" she asks, all breathy and sweet.

Promising, but . . . "No. I want the bed."

"That's fine. That's good," she babbles, and I reward her with another nip of my teeth as I carry her down the hallway. I'm tempted to press her against the wall, slip my hand into her pants and feel how much she needs me, but I want her bare skin against her blankets. I want to take my time.

I drop her in the middle of her unmade bed, hair half in her face as she laughs and rolls. She holds out her hands for me and that feeling in my chest spreads everywhere else. I still can't believe I get to have her like this, that she wants me like this.

I ignore her hands and slip my fingers beneath the waistband of her sweatpants. I tug them off with two quick jerks, surprised when I don't find a stitch of her fancy underwear beneath. No lace. No ribbons. Just Nova and all that pretty ink.

"You ripped three pairs last week," she explains with a grumble. "I'm going to need to go shopping."

I laugh and thumb at the flare of her hips. "You tell me this now? When I'm about to leave?" I drop down and press a quick kiss right above her belly button. "I want to go shopping with you."

She shrugs. "I can send pictures."

I slip my hand around the back of her neck and tug her to me. "You better."

I kiss her with everything that's pressing heavy at my lungs, twisting around and around in my chest. I hold her steady and lick into her mouth, tasting the edge of her moan. I plant one knee on the bed, and her palms find my chest, pressing me back with a laugh.

"Take off your pants," she orders, bossy even when she's handed me control. I thumb at her chin and drift it down the line of her throat to the flower between her tits. I cup her breast with a squeeze, and her eyes slip to half-mast.

"Charlie," she whines.

I drag my thumb over her nipple, back and forth. "What?"

"You're teasing," she says.

"Maybe. You said I could have whatever I want."

"That's not exactly what I said."

I pinch her nipple, and she drops her head to the side, blond hair cascading over her shoulder like a river of gold.

"Charlie," she says again, a gasp in her voice.

"What?"

Her hand slips between her thighs and my mouth goes dry. I watch her hand move, inked fingers playing over soft skin. I can hear how wet she is. How much she needs me where her fingers are.

"Okay, I was teasing you," I tell her, swallowing hard as her hand moves faster. "I don't want to tease anymore."

"Good," she breathes, eyes closed, hips chasing her touch. "Take off your pants."

I undo my belt buckle and shrug off my unbuttoned shirt. She slows the movement of her hand between her thighs and watches me with hungry eyes, her tongue at the corner of her mouth. She's so damn beautiful, hidden pockets of ink accentuating every curve. The flex and release of her arm as she makes herself feel good. I want to sink my teeth into her and make my own marks. Press bruises right next to the garden on her thigh and the galaxy at her hip.

I step out of my pants and kick them to a corner of her room, then curl my hands beneath her knees. I tug her flat to the very edge of the bed, a garbled squeak leaving her mouth when she goes tumbling backward.

I grab her wrist and suck her fingers into my mouth while I fumble through her nightstand for a condom. She tastes like smoke and sex and all my favorite things. My hands shake as I roll it on, thoroughly done with waiting.

"Tell me what you want," she says, shifting beneath me. "Tell me, Charlie."

"I want—" My cock nudges between her legs and all the air in my lungs rattles out of me. "I want you to feel me for days after I leave," I tell her, pressing her wrist over her head and holding her there. My body is trembling with the need to have her, hold her, possess her, keep her. I'm afraid I'll never get enough.

My other hand finds her throat, and I hold her still, fingers gentle against that fluttering, thrumming pulse. I trace up and down once with my thumb. "I want you to think about me every time you move."

Her eyes flash in the dark of her bedroom. "Yes," she breathes.

"I want you to take everything I give you."

"Yes," she says again, arching her back, hugging my sides with her knees. I press into her, and we both make deep sounds of agonized appreciation, her hips already moving against me, trying to ride me from below. My hand on her neck squeezes in warning. She stills her body and blinks up at me.

I pull from her slowly before I thrust back in hard.

The bedframe shakes beneath us.

"I want to watch you fall apart." I release her throat to put my face there instead, sucking a hard kiss where my thumb just was. I want this to never end. I want to stay in this bed with her forever. I want to press myself into her skin like one of her tattoos. I want so much and there's not enough time for all of it. "I want you, Nova girl. Over and over again."

Her hand curls around my jaw. She guides my mouth to hers.

"Take everything," she says with a smile. My favorite one. "It's already yours."

I WAKE UP to Nova perched on my lap, watching me like a little creep.

Everything is shadowed in blues and grays, Nova a brushstroke of golden sunlight spilling out overtop of me. She has all the blankets wrapped around her like a complicated wardrobe choice while I lie stark naked in the middle of the bed without a single sheet. I think it's the first time she's given me more than two inches at the very edge.

Progress.

I yawn and stretch my body beneath hers. Something in my ankle pops, and Nova shifts in her blankets, trying to accommodate the movement. But I don't want her to accommodate anything. I fist my hand in the front of her toga and tug, unhappy with the space between us. She collapses back on top of me with a snort, and I arrange her until her head is nestled under my chin. I curl one arm around her back and let my eyes slip shut again.

Better.

"What time is it?" I mumble.

"Your alarm went off ten minutes ago," she says into my neck. I drag my fingers through her messy hair, and her body relaxes on top of mine. "I was trying to figure out how to wake you up."

"Could have let my alarm go off again."

"Because that worked so well the first time."

I slide my hand over her bundle and pat in the approximate location of her ass. "It's okay, Nova girl. You can admit you were watching me sleep."

"Watching you snore," she corrects.

"I understand. It's hard to look away."

"From the drool, yes." She wiggles around on top of me until she can tip her face to mine. I trace my fingertips over her forehead and down the slope of her nose. I'll have to get on the road soon. I'm afraid if I wait any longer, I'll stay clinging to the edge of Nova's bed for the rest of forever, waiting for her to share some of her damn sheets.

"You keep doing that," she says quietly.

I trace the shell of her ear and the ink right beneath. "What?"

"Looking at me like I'm going to disappear."

I frown. "I'm not."

"You are."

I huff and shift beneath her. She goes rolling sideways until I tug her back. I didn't realize that some of my internal panic was bleeding through. "I don't want to leave," I confess.

A sad smile ghosts across her face. She leans up until she can rest her chin on my chest. "When will you be back?"

I lift one shoulder in a shrug. "I don't know yet. I've been away for a while. I'll have to get some stuff sorted in the city. Is that—" I drag my hand through my hair and then rest it beneath my head, trying to get a better look at her face in the shadowed light. "Is that all right?"

She mirrors my frown. "What?"

"Is it all right that I don't know when I'll be back?"

She searches my face carefully. "You'll text me right?"

I nod.

"And call?"

I nod again.

"Then, yeah. Everything will be fine." I accept the kiss she brushes against my mouth and will myself to settle, to believe her, to trust that I can be good at this. Mine to have and mine to keep. Isn't that what she said?

"We'll figure it out as we go," she says, yawning into my chin. Her hands pat at my sides. "Keep talking to me and we'll do it together."

She rolls out of the bed without another word, taking all the blankets with her. I watch her as she sleepily shuffles across her hardwood floor to her bathroom. The door clicks shut behind her, and I dig my thumb in the middle of my forehead.

"Together," I repeat.

Together is exactly where I want to be, but it feels a million miles away from where I'm going.

26

CHARLIE: This gas station has ketchup chips!!

CHARLIE: Chips that taste like ketchup!!

NOVA: Why don't you just buy ketchup?

CHARLIE: Ketchup in the car is not the move, Nova girl.

NOVA: How many gas stations are you going to stop at?

CHARLIE: It's only my sixth stop.

NOVA: In a three-hour drive.

CHARLIE: I am quite literally dragging my feet all the way back to New York.

NOVA: Did you order me a pizza?

CHARLIE: Depends. What's on the pizza?

NOVA: It is a heart shaped pizza with extra sauce.

CHARLIE: Then, yes. That was me.

CHARLIE: Who else would send a heart shaped pizza????

CHARLIE: Is some other bozo sending you heart shaped pizzas??????

CHARLIE: NOVA????

NOVA: Only one bozo.

CHARLIE: 👻

NOVA: And you ordered Jeremy a sauceless pizza with no cheese? In the shape of a . . . what is it supposed to be?

CHARLIE: I asked Matty to make a pair of eyes.

NOVA: . . . why?

CHARLIE: So Jeremy knows I'm watching him.

NOVA: Oh. They sort of look like boobs.

NOVA: He loves it. He keeps snickering and taking pictures of it.

CHARLIE: That's not what I was going for.

CHARLIE: Did I leave a sweatshirt at your place?

NOVA: No.

CHARLIE: . . . you're not even going to ask me what it looks like?

NOVA: If it's black with a badger on the front, I definitely haven't seen it.

CHARLIE: Nova.

CHARLIE: Nova girl.

CHARLIE: That's my favorite sweatshirt.

CHARLIE: It's an Inglewild High limited release.

CHARLIE: I had to push some PTA moms out of my way at the football game to get it.

NOVA: Then you can appreciate it's in very good hands.

NOVA: Healing update request.

CHARLIE: [picture.txt]

NOVA: Your wrist. Show me your wrist, Charlie.

CHARLIE: You're no fun.

NOVA: Which one do you like best?

CHARLIE: sdfjksldjfklsd

NOVA: That is not an answer.

CHARLIE:

CHARLIE: Nova.

NOVA: What?

NOVA: Pink or black? It's a simple question.

CHARLIE: Both. All of them. Use my card. Buy every set they have.

NOVA: This one too?

NOVA: [picture.txt]

CHARLIE: Fucking . . . fuck.

CHARLIE: Answer my video call right now.

NOVA: I'm in public.

CHARLIE: Then I suggest you figure out how to be quiet.

CHARLIE: Selene wants to know why I'm still in the conference room.

CHARLIE: I can't tell her I got a boner halfway through a budget meeting.

CHARLIE: I have to sit here until it goes away.

NOVA: I'm not sorry.

CHARLIE: Neither am I.

CHARLIE: But maybe no more pictures during business hours.

CHARLIE: I take it back.

CHARLIE: You can send me pictures.

CHARLIE: Please send me pictures.

NOVA: ☺

꙳· ꙳

NOVA: I asked Selene to block off some time for you on Wednesday afternoon.

CHARLIE: For something sexy?

CHARLIE: You wanna see me in my three-piece suit?

CHARLIE: I can wear suspenders if you want.

NOVA: No.

NOVA: I thought we could have lunch together. It's the only time we match up this week.

CHARLIE:

CHARLIE: Even better.

NOVA: But please feel free to wear your suspenders.

꙳· ꙳

CHARLIE: Are you awake?

CHARLIE: Nevermind. We'll talk tomorrow.

NOVA: I'm here. What's up?

CHARLIE: Did I wake you up?

NOVA: No.

CHARLIE: I did.

NOVA: Lucky for you, I like it when you wake me up.

NOVA: Feeling lonely?

CHARLIE: Feeling far away from you.

NOVA: I'm right here.

NOVA: Want to watch a movie?

꙳· ꙳

CHARLIE: I don't know how I feel about you and Selene being besties.

NOVA: You can feel however you want about it.

CHARLIE: She wants a tattoo.

CHARLIE: Coincidentally, she also told me I need to learn how to fight.

NOVA: I like her. I'm glad you have someone looking out for you.

CHARLIE: . . .

CHARLIE: But not more than me, right? You don't like her more than me?

NOVA: I like you the most.

NOVA: You're my favorite, remember?

NOVA: Sorry I missed you. I had a client.

CHARLIE: All good.

CHARLIE: Can I call you now? I've got five minutes before I need to head to another meeting.

NOVA: Now is great.

NOVA: Why does New York feel so far away?

CHARLIE: Because it is.

CHARLIE: Miss your peanut butter pretzels, Nova girl.

NOVA: So, weird thing happened today.

CHARLIE: What's up?

NOVA: I went to the grocery store and asked Sandy if she has any more of those heart shaped grapes.

NOVA: Apparently, they don't cut grapes into heart shapes.

CHARLIE: That's weird.

CHARLIE: Must have been a limited-time thing.

NOVA: It's cute that you're holding on to this.

CHARLIE: I have no idea what you're talking about.

CHARLIE: I'm going to have to cancel. My meeting is running late.

NOVA: That's all right. Call whenever you're free.

CHARLIE: It might be a while.

NOVA: I can wait.

[MISSED CALL FROM Charlie]

[MISSED CALL FROM Charlie]

CHARLIE: My calendar is a nightmare this week.

CHARLIE: I'll try you again later.

[MISSED CALL FROM Nova]

NOVA: I had a walk-in and squeezed them in between two other appointments. I'm sorry I missed you.

[MISSED CALL FROM Nova]

NOVA: You better not have left your phone at home again.

NOVA: This is harder than I thought.

NOVA: Wow. You must be busy if you
didn't immediately spin that into a joke.
NOVA: Call when you can.

[MISSED CALL FROM Charlie]
CHARLIE: I know it's late, but I wanted to try.

[MISSED CALL FROM Charlie]
CHARLIE: Fuck, I miss you.

27

NOVA

"IF YOU DON'T pass me the potatoes, I'm going to lose my fucking mind."

I blink up from where I've been studying my phone beneath the table, willing it to ring. Beckett is scowling at me. It would be more intimidating if he wasn't also wearing his pair of pink fluffy earmuffs. The ones he uses to muffle sound when he forgets his earplugs.

Or when Evie isn't here to remember them for him.

"That feels excessive."

"It's not excessive. I've asked you three times."

I grab the bowl of mashed potatoes and hold it out to him. He takes it with a grunt, and I go back to staring at the blank screen of my phone.

We usually have a strict no phone policy during family dinners, but I snuck it in. Charlie and I have been playing phone tag for three damn days, and if I miss another one of his calls, I might scream.

I miss him. I miss him standing shirtless in my kitchen inspecting the contents of my fridge, and I miss him lounging in the middle of my bed, asking me a million and one questions about nothing in particular. I miss his nose pressed against the back of my neck when he sleeps and the way his chin rests on the top of my head when he stands right behind me. I miss his smell and his taste and his smile when he thinks he's being funny and his eyes when he's trying not to be sad.

The way his knee jumps up and down when he's sitting for too long. The crumpled receipts he keeps in his pockets so he can write down notes when he thinks of them only to forget about them entirely and leave them shoved under the plants I keep on my windowsill.

He left one of his sweaters over the back of my chair in my living room, and his pale blue toothbrush is still in the cup next to mine in my bathroom. Some of his socks somehow ended up in my underwear drawer and his phone charger is plugged into the wall in my kitchen. I keep finding bits and pieces of him scattered throughout my house and my tattoo studio and the front seat of my car.

I didn't want a relationship because I was afraid of giving a part of myself to another person when it felt so important that I keep them all for myself. I like who I am and I like my independence. But I didn't lose anything to Charlie. It just feels like all the good things in my life got better. Amplified. I got someone to laugh with and someone to rub the knots in my neck and someone to remember to put oat milk on my grocery list because I always forget. I was so determined to not have a relationship with him that I missed the part where we were in one all along.

And I didn't lose a single thing.

Instead I got Charlie.

And now he's hundreds of miles away, and I haven't been able to talk to him in days. I feel like I missed out on all the good parts of a relationship before I even realized I was in one.

Beckett nudges me with his elbow, and I sigh, tucking my phone under my thigh. At least if it rings, I'll be able to feel it. I can make an excuse and disappear in the backyard.

I stab a piece of broccoli and move it around my plate.

"What's with the frown?" Beckett asks, an obscene amount of potatoes piled high on his plate. I don't think he left a single scoop in there for anyone else.

"Says the man who just yelled at me about potatoes."

"I have an excuse," he says calmly.

"What's that?"

"Evie's work trip." He reaches for the gravy boat that's shaped like a cat on a canoe. My mom is really out of control with the tchotchkes. "I won't see her for another week."

At least you know when you'll see her, I want to yell. I have no idea when I'll get to see Charlie again. Both of our schedules have been so booked we can barely find time to talk on the phone, let alone plan time to see each other in person.

"Doesn't mean you can be a jerk about spuds," I mumble, stabbing at my broccoli until it's smashed wreckage on my plate.

Beckett sighs and puts his fork down. "What's going on?"

"Nothing," I mutter. "Nothing is going on."

"Maybe she just needs to get laid," Vanessa supplies from the other side of the table. But the only place my sister has ever been delicate is on the dance floor, and it's more of a bellow than a quiet suggestion. My dad almost fumbles the platter of meatloaf. My mom pinches the bridge of her nose.

"What?" Vanessa asks, glancing around the table. "It's true. She's all wound up. Like a top."

"Vanessa," my mom sighs. "Don't embarrass your sister."

"Or traumatize your brother," Beckett grumbles. "Can we change the subject please?"

"Seconded," my dad adds. "Has anyone heard from Charlie lately?"

I narrow my eyes at my dad, still shoveling meatloaf onto his plate like it's the last time he'll have the opportunity. Everyone is acting like this is our last dinner before the end of days. "Why are you asking that?"

He shrugs. "I can't ask after Charlie?"

He can, but it feels targeted. It feels like he knows something I've been less and less careful to keep hidden. It doesn't seem as important as it did two weeks ago that no one knows about my feelings for Charlie. In fact, it's starting to feel worse keeping it all to myself.

"He hasn't been in the group chat much," Beckett offers. I glance away from my dad.

"There's a group chat?" I ask.

Beckett nods. "A group chat for the farm staff. Layla added him when he took over operations for the month. We never took him off."

"And he's been quieter than usual?"

Beckett blinks at me and then nods again, slower this time. "Yeah. Caleb even tossed a softball innuendo about planting seeds, and he didn't take the bait."

"Maybe he needs to get laid too," Vanessa yells across the table. Harper drops her forehead into her hand next to her. "I can set you up with someone, Nova, seriously. I have this friend who—"

Someone kicks her under the table. Everything rattles on top of my grandmother's hand-stitched tablecloth. Nessa and Harper exchange a brief, furious, whispered conversation.

"*. . . she needs to at least . . .*"

"*. . . you're being extra and . . .*"

"*. . . all I'm saying is . . .*"

Beckett clears his throat and tries to talk over them both. "I think work is probably keeping him busy. I'm sure he'll show up sooner or later. He always does."

My phone stays silent under my thigh. I use the edge of my broccoli piece to draw a forget-me-not in what's left of my gravy.

"I don't think Charlie likes his work," I say quietly. Every time we manage to talk, his voice is strained and distracted. He's hardly sent me any selfies now that he's in his glass-and-chrome office. He's a dimmer version of himself in New York. Smaller. "I actually don't think Charlie is very happy in New York."

Beckett keeps shoveling food into his face, half paying attention. He snorts. "Charlie is always happy. It's a core character trait."

"He's not though." I drop my fork against my plate with a clatter. Beckett stops eating and looks at me. So does the rest of the table. "He's not happy. He pretends to be, most of the time, because he thinks it's easier when he does. For him, maybe, or for everyone around him. I don't know. But he's not. He doesn't like his job and his dad is a piece of shit and he's—"

He's lonely. He's lonely, and I can't bear the thought of him sitting alone in his apartment thinking everyone has forgotten him.

That I've forgotten him.

"Nova—"

My heart pounds in my chest. "He's—he's funny and he's kind, and he's ridiculous most of the time, but he only does it so he can see other people laugh. And he pushes himself to the edges and shrinks himself down to make himself seem more tolerable. But he doesn't need to do that. He doesn't need to break himself down into pieces. But I think—I think I made him do that too. I'm just as bad as everyone else because I took from him. Didn't I? I asked for everything and what did I give him back? Not much. Not nearly enough."

I couldn't even give him the right words before he left. I couldn't tell him I wanted him. Instead, I put a flower on his wrist and hoped he understood what I was trying to say.

He's been so much braver than me this whole time.

"I'm not following—"

"I made him feel like he wasn't enough. We all did. He's been spending more and more time down here because he wants someone to ask him to stay. I think. And I sent him back to New York with a *let's hope for the best.*"

I put guardrails around my feelings for Charlie because I didn't want to want something I never thought I needed. And now he's there and I'm here, and he's not answering my calls, and we're both fucking miserable.

The table is silent. It's a freeze-frame of shock. I think this might be the most interesting family dinner we've ever had, including the time Beckett brought all the kittens and both the ducks and let them run free beneath the table. Beckett is rigid next to me. Vanessa is practically vibrating in her chair. Harper and my parents are watching me carefully like they're not sure if I'm going to collapse to the ground or flip the meatloaf tray.

I don't know either.

"I've been seeing Charlie since the first harvest festival committee meeting," I announce. Harper gasps like we're on a daytime soap opera. My heart clangs around in my chest, my throat tight. "I know this is out of nowhere, but that's it. Charlie and I were—I mean—we are together. Like a couple."

Everyone stares at me. The clock ticks in the hallway. The wind whistles at the windows. A log cracks in the fireplace, and my heart pounds in my throat.

"It's not," Beckett finally says. He collapses out of his stiff-as-a-board stance and reaches for the basket of bread rolls. He drops two on his plate.

"What?"

"It's not out of nowhere. We all knew you were seeing him." Beckett gestures around the table with his butter knife. "We've been waiting for you to say something." He gives me a bored look. "It took you forever."

"What?"

"Shit," he says. He drops the knife and digs in his back pocket for his phone. "I told Evie I'd call her for this."

"For what?"

Beckett taps at his screen and places his phone into the middle of the table while it rings. "For the moment you enter reality."

Evelyn answers on the second ring. "Is it happening?"

"Sure is!" Harper responds at the same time Beckett says, "Hey, honey."

I gape at the phone right next to the green bean casserole. At my family, arranged around the table. Not one of them looks surprised. Did someone spike the wine tonight? Are the potatoes laced with something?

"Why do you think I keep saying you need to get laid?" Vanessa asks. "I'm not actually trying to set you up with randos. I've been goading you, you tiny fool."

"What? I'm—what?"

"There was a picture on the phone tree text chain of him bringing you coffee," my dad offers. "You looked at him the same way you used to look at those expensive fine-point pens when you were a kid. You had little heart eyes."

"My favorite was the picture of Charlie and the goose," my mom adds. She snickers to herself. "I still have it saved as my wallpaper."

"I like the roof video best," Harper offers diplomatically. She threads her fingers together and rests her chin on top of them. "I hope your hydrangeas made a full recovery."

"Someone got a video of that?"

"Of course I did," Beckett says, still eating his dinner like I'm not having an out-of-body experience right next to him. What the actual hell is happening? "I heard your window open while I was waiting on the front porch. Voices carry."

"And you sent it to the phone tree?"

"To be fair," Evelyn's tinny voice echoes up from Beckett's phone, face up on the table. "I think he was trying to send it just to me."

Oh my god. *Oh my god.*

"You've been wearing his Rolex, Nova," Beckett says around a mouthful of meatloaf. "Honestly. I'm not an idiot."

"And you're okay with it?"

One of his eyebrows arches up. "Do I need to be okay with who you date?"

I don't know. I certainly don't think so, but he's always given the impression that he has an opinion on the matter. "He's your friend" is all I can think to say.

"So?" He shrugs. "That just means I know who he is. I love him. I love you. I don't see the downside." He pours gravy over everything on his plate. "That said, if he breaks your heart, I'll break his jaw. He doesn't get a pass on that detail. But if you break his heart"—Beckett points at me with his fork, cheek bulging with his dinner—"I'll have words for you too."

"I won't," I whisper faintly. "Break his heart."

I can't believe we're having this conversation at family dinner while he shovels mashed potatoes into his face.

"Good," Beckett says.

"I thought I was doing the right thing by keeping it hidden," I try to explain, even though I don't know why. "I thought it would be easier that way."

"Easier for who?"

And that's the thing, isn't it? This whole time, we've been doing things the way I've wanted to do them. Charlie let me set the terms, and he let me go at my own pace. He's given me everything I've asked for without requesting anything in return.

"It was just to blow off steam, at first. But then it turned into something, and I guess I thought if it didn't go anywhere else—if no one knew about it, we wouldn't have to talk about it. I didn't want to need anything from him," I say faintly. "I was afraid of it."

"What about now? Do you feel like you need Charlie?"

I shake my head. I can do just fine on my own, but I—

"I want him. I don't need him, but I want him all the time."

Charlie, who has made himself content with living at the very edges. Charlie, who thinks he's an imposition every time he visits. Charlie, who feels like he doesn't belong anywhere. Charlie, who wanted to hide our relationship just as much as I did but for another reason entirely. Because he didn't think he was good enough. Because he didn't think he was worth it.

Charlie, who has never been anyone's first choice. Who has never been wanted.

"I'm in love with him." I exhale, the truth of it cracking open inside of me, filling me with a delicate, boundless light. I thought I'd be afraid of this feeling, but I'm not. I feel exactly the same as I did before but lighter, like the weight of all the things I've been carrying around has somewhere else to go. Somewhere safe where it'll be looked after with careful hands.

Someone with an easy smile and a flower on his wrist.

"I should hope so," my dad says from the other side of the table. "The boy fell into a garden for you."

I stand up from my chair so quickly it screeches across the floor and slams into the wall. "I need to go to New York."

Evelyn whoops on the other end of the phone. Vanessa thrusts her fist into the air. Harper beams, and my mom reaches for my dad, clinging to his arm and shaking him once.

Beckett stands with me, digging around in his pocket. He's still wearing his hot-pink fluffy earmuffs. "I'll get the car."

"No!" comes a chorus from my sisters and Evelyn, still on the phone. Harper lobs a dinner roll right at his head.

"I think everyone has been as involved as they need to be in my relationship, thank you." I pat at my pockets for my keys. I check my phone again, just in case, but he hasn't called.

I'm going to do it. I'm going to drive to New York. I'm going to tell him all the things I was afraid to tell him before, and I'm—I'm going to be brave. I'm going to give him what he deserves.

"Let the girl make her grand gesture in peace!" Evelyn shouts, the phone bursting with static at her volume. Beckett drops back down in his chair.

"You know, when you get back"—he points at me with one finger—"we're going to have a long conversation about you hiding things from me."

"Sure." I edge around the table for the door. "When I get back."

Right now, I've got somewhere I need to be.

28

CHARLIE

"SELENE!"

Selene pokes her head through the door of my office, somehow managing to look both beleaguered and admonishing. I don't blame her. I've been an absolute terror this week and it's only Tuesday.

"You rang, boss?"

I hold up my phone charger that is somehow in two separate pieces. "Why does my charger look like this?"

"I have no idea what you do with your things when you're alone in this office, Charlie. Do you remember how many Nespresso machines we went through in the summer of 2018?"

At least four. Because I couldn't figure out how to get the pods out of the drawer and ended up destroying the machine in an effort to effectively and responsibly dispose of the minuscule coffee containers.

I frown at the cord in my hands and my dead phone. Nova called twice during my last meeting and then my screen blinked out, a bright red battery symbol flashing as the proverbial ship went down. I sigh and slip both in my pocket, standing and reaching for my coat.

"It's fine. I'm going to head out." I glance at the clock. Nova is probably still at dinner with her family, but I can catch her after. "Could you hold the rest of my calls and defer them to later this week? Or maybe just tell people I drowned in a horrible waterskiing incident and I'm no longer available?"

Selene winces. "While that sounds like fun, you can't."

"I know," I sigh. "I'm scary proficient on water skis."

Selene's lips tip up at the corners in a restrained smile. "You can't head out."

I pause halfway through pulling on my jacket. "Why?"

She bites her bottom lip.

"Why, Selene?" I'm whining and I'm not ashamed. "Why can't you hold my calls?"

She steps farther into the room, hands raised like she's trying to calm a deranged bear. It's me. I am the deranged bear. "I can hold your calls, but you have an appointment on your calendar for this evening."

"If it's not at the empanada truck on the corner of my street, I am not interested."

I want to go back to my house and call Nova. I want to hear the sound of her voice and convince myself everything that happened in Inglewild wasn't a fever dream. I want to turn on an old black-and-white movie and fall asleep with her voice in my ear, talking to me about tattoo designs and the croissant of the day at Layla's, and whatever the hell Jeremy is up to. I want to chase away this pressure in my chest with something good. I feel like she's slipping out of my hands. I feel like maybe I never had a grip on her to start with.

"You RSVP'd for a charity gala tonight at the New York Public Library," Selene says quickly. I drop my head back and groan at the ceiling. "Your tux is in the washroom."

"I was wondering what it was doing in there," I mumble, my eyes still closed.

"You only have to go for an hour." She hesitates. "Maybe two. Bid in the auction and show that pretty face and then you can have some empanadas."

"What is it a benefit for?"

"Seals, I think? Shit. Maybe a rainforest somewhere? I don't know why you rich people do what you do."

"Who is hosting?"

"Mr. Billings."

I drag my hand down my face. "Of course he is." Because the universe is hell-bent on punishing me for something this week.

I slip my coat off my shoulders and toss it back on my chair. I prop my hands on my hips and sigh at my desk. I'm so fucking tired. Tired of this place and this job and all the things I have to do to make everyone around me happy.

"Can you do me a favor?"

"That is literally my job description."

I pinch the bridge of my nose and try to find the well of patience and goodwill that usually isn't so difficult to summon. "Can you please call Nova in about an hour and let her know my phone died? Tell her I'll call her when I get back tonight."

"I can do that," Selene agrees. "I wanted to talk to her about my tattoo anyway. She said she'd design me something."

I frown at Selene. "When did you talk to her?"

"Yesterday." Selene wanders over to the other side of my office and turns on my coffee machine. She hits three buttons and espresso appears like magic in the mug I stole from Layla's bakehouse. "She called here looking for you while you were in that Q4 planning meeting with the Holsfields. We talked."

Great. Selene has officially talked to my girlfriend more this week than I have.

My brain skids to a stop.

Is Nova my girlfriend? I have no idea. We never discussed it. We said we felt more than business casual, but . . . we never discussed it.

Selene hands me my coffee. I stare at it.

"Thank you," I mutter.

"Two hours," Selene says in the most lackluster motivational speech I've ever heard. I have taught her absolutely nothing in the way of faking enthusiasm. "Two hours and you can go home."

❧ ⋅ ❦

I SPEND ONE hour and twenty-three minutes playing nice and then I find the bar, get a drink, and park myself in an archive of architectural photographs. Music from the string quartet down the hall echoes and spins, muffled voices and the clinking of glasses twisting with the melody. I imagine Nova in her silver dress, a glass of champagne in her hand. Tattoos down the strong line of her back and her hair tumbling over her shoulders. She'd like this room with the color and the quiet. And I'd like to press her up against the shelves and taste the edge of her smile.

But she's not here. It's just me and a half-empty glass of too-expensive whiskey. I loosen my tie with a sigh and take a sip, enjoying the bite of smoke. I stretch out my neck and try to organize my slippery thoughts.

I'll call her when I get back tonight. I'll grab some empanadas from the truck on the street and I'll call her. Maybe I can drive down this weekend if Selene rearranges some things. It'll be quick, but it'll be worth it. Nova is worth it.

We can talk. We can figure out what the hell we're doing. I'll tell her how I feel and maybe this thing between us won't feel so fragile.

"I thought I saw you slip out."

I turn toward the door and my father's voice, tearing my attention away from a stack of crimson volumes that match the color of the flower on Nova's chest. He strolls toward me in his tux, a matching glass of whiskey in his hand.

I wince but do my best to hide it. I feel like I'm always playing a part when I'm here, but with my dad it's the ultimate performance. I rub my thumb against the flower on the inside of my wrist and tip my chin up. "Here I am."

Of course he's here. He has a gift for appearing when my mood is at its worst, ready to sour it further with his commentary or critique. Dark hair combed back, a streak of gray at his temples, the blue eyes we share crinkled in amusement. I am a carbon copy of him down to the shiny shoes.

I've never hated it as much as I do right now.

His steps falter as he walks over to me, a burp tucked into his fist. I frown as I take him in.

Eyes glassy with too much drink. Sweat beading on his upper lip. He has a smudge of pale pink lipstick on the collar of his shirt and a cloud of perfume sticks to him like a film. He claps me on the shoulder and loses his balance, his shoulder nudging into mine.

Maybe we're not as alike as I thought.

"I didn't think you'd make it," he slurs. "Busy as you were with the farm life." He snickers like he's made a hilarious joke and waits for me to join him. I don't. "No one could believe it when I told them."

I pull myself out of his grip and put some space between us. I set my half-empty glass of liquor on the Returns desk. My craving for the numb relief of alcohol has disappeared.

"Told them what?"

"Where you were. What you were doing. You left New York for a tree farm," he says, laughing again. "All of this—" He gestures around him. At the ornate art, the music, the bottomless alcohol, and the sheer amount of wealth, accumulated just down the hall. "For a town that probably doesn't even have a dine-in restaurant—"

"They have several," I mutter.

"—to play out some farm fantasy for a sister that isn't even yours." He drains the rest of his glass with both eyebrows raised. "You sure do find new and interesting ways to color the family name, Charles."

"Well." I rock back on my heels, both of my hands shoved deep in my tux pockets. There's a fire in my chest that has nothing to do with alcohol that burns hotter the longer I look at him. This is who I've been craving approval from? "I've got you to keep up with, don't I?"

His eyebrows collapse in a heavy line, his face twisting in confusion. "What did you just say to me?"

I've always been the agreeable son, doing my best to meet the markers he's set out for me. It's like I said to Nova. I'm not sure he's ever wanted me to truly meet them. He'd rather lord his power over me in a cloud of disappointment and watch me struggle to catch up. I guess it's easier to feel better about your own shitshow life when you're constantly putting other people down.

And I'm fucking tired.

"Which part would you like me to repeat?" I ask.

His eyes flash, his knuckles dragging across his mouth. "Watch yourself, Charles. Everything you have is because of me."

"Everything I have is in spite of you," I spit back, losing the grip I have on my temper. I can't remember the last time I let myself get this angry. A match struck against all my rough edges. "The only things you've given me are an irrational desire to please people and a constant fucking headache. You don't give a shit about our family. If you did, you wouldn't have fucked your way through Lower Manhattan. You wouldn't have embarrassed your wife so thoroughly she felt the need to leave the country. You wouldn't have abandoned your daughter."

"She's not my daughter," he scoffs.

"DNA results say different."

I take another step closer to him, the flame in my chest catching and flaring bright. "You call me an embarrassment but you're the one who's been drinking yourself to incoherence at public functions. You're the one who was removed from his position because of his behavior. You've made selfish choice after selfish choice, while I've been the one who's been holding everything together."

He sputters, cheeks red with rage. "You think you can talk to me like that?"

"I can talk to you however I want." I cut him off. "I owe you nothing. The only thing you've given me worth a damn is my sister, and if you had it your way, I never would have known about her. But I'm grateful you were a deadbeat. I'm grateful you wanted nothing to do with her. She got to escape you, and she shines so bright because of it."

He blinks at me, eyes blown wide. I stare at him and wait for regret to tug at me, but it never shows. There's just the residual exhaustion from my anger. The taste of whiskey on the back of my tongue.

I stare at him and see nothing I need.

Not his approval and not his acceptance.

I study him from the top of his slicked-back hair to the tips of his scuffed shoes. All of it's for show, without a lick of substance beneath. A sad, lonely man who doesn't give a shit about anyone else.

Nova's right. I'm nothing like him at all.

I push past him toward the door.

"I'll expect an apology," my dad calls.

I don't bother looking over my shoulder. "You won't get one."

A breath gusts out of him. His laugh is disbelieving. "You walk out of this room without one and that's the end of it. I won't lift a finger to help you."

Thank fucking god for that.

I adjust my cufflinks and keep walking toward the door.

"I look forward to it."

I REWARD MYSELF with a soft pretzel from a street cart outside the venue, then two slices of pizza from the bodega on the corner of my street. I toss in a bag of gummy bears too, because I feel like celebrating.

I'm not disillusioned enough to think that one conversation will effectively change a lifetime of poor decision-making and narcissistic behavior, but I'm hopeful that what I said will have my father second-guessing the next time he attempts to yank on my strings. I'm tired of chasing after his acknowledgment. It's no longer something I care to have.

I've taught myself how to be content with scraps. I've portioned out the things that make me happy in manageable pieces so that I can savor them for longer. I've treated my trips to Inglewild as a reward for good behavior, a hit of dopamine to get me through the rest of an otherwise lonely existence. I've allowed myself doses of happiness while I cling to it with two hands, terrified if I indulge too much, if I give too much of myself, I'll be left standing without anything at all.

I've been doing that with Nova. I've allowed myself the sex and the teasing and the jokes while telling myself I can do without holding her hand in public. Kissing her on the cheek in the Inglewild grocery store checkout line. Telling her, out loud, how fucking proud I am of her and everything she's accomplished. I've held myself in check and settled for less because I didn't think I was worth more.

But now I'm cracked wide open, standing in the middle of my kitchen with my bow tie hanging loose around my neck, my hands on my hips, and all the things I've wanted to say but haven't thundering around in my chest. I stare hard at the still-black screen of my phone on the wireless charger, a half-crumpled napkin from Matty's right next to it, a delicate flower hand drawn at the edge. I've been carrying that stupid, slightly grease-stained napkin around with me everywhere like a goddamn talisman.

My phone blinks to life. Notifications cascade down the screen.

I ignore them.

I can be in Inglewild in four hours. Three if I'm liberal with traffic laws. I can sleep in Nova's bed tonight. Press my mouth to hers and watch the way her eyes dance when I tell her I love her. That I might fuck it up and I might make mistakes, but I'll always try my best to be exactly what she needs.

My hand is on my doorknob before I've thought about it, my keys in my fist and my bag of gummy bears shoved in the front pocket of my jacket. I'm buzzing with adrenaline, high on the confidence of a half-baked plan, powered by a street cart soft pretzel. I throw open my door and almost plow into the slim body on the other side of it.

I reach out and grab around the stranger's middle, fingers spread wide against the flare of her hips and the silky, soft material of her dress. I know these hips. I know this dress. I know her smell, like leaves beneath my boots and apple cider. Fresh-spilled ink and the pot of lavender she won't stop hiding her key under on her front porch.

Affection and disbelief tug at me from opposite ends as I stare down at Nova standing in my doorway, the same silver dress she wore to my sister's wedding poured over her curves and flaring around her ankles. The deep cut in the front. My favorite red rose.

Her cute fucking frown as she stares up at me. Her hands clench in the front of my jacket, gummy bears spilling all over the floor.

I blink three times. It's entirely possible I am hallucinating.

She tips her chin up at me and glares. "Where in the hell have you been?"

29

NOVA

"UM." HIS FINGERS flex at my waist before he pulls his hands back, touch lingering like he doesn't want to let me go. His eyes keep flickering between my face and the dress I'm wearing, confusion twisting the curve of his mouth. "I've been here?"

"You were supposed to be at the library."

It's where I just was, elbowing my way through designer dresses and a string quartet doing their best *Bridgerton* tribute. When Selene told me where he was, I thought I'd show up, find him, and confess my feelings while the violin reached a crescendo. I thought I could harness a lifetime of not caring about romantic moments into creating the kind of moment Charlie deserves. But he wasn't where he was supposed to be, and a woman wearing enough Chanel N°5 to take out a small army spilled her cocktail down the front of my dress. I'm annoyed and sort of hungry and—it feels like too much. Standing in front of him in a dress he probably doesn't remember while I yell at him.

So much for my movie moment.

But Charlie looks . . . well, he looks fucking delicious. He has one arm braced against the door, the other curled around my hip, the metal of his keys biting at me through the thin material of my dress. He takes two steps backward into his apartment, and I follow, watching him, backlit by the city lights, a million and one stars plucked from the sky and placed carefully along the towering buildings. He shoves his hands in his pockets and rocks back on his heels. His shirt stretches across his chest, the top two buttons undone. His tie hangs loose around his neck, and all I want to do is wrap my hands in it and tug him close. Press my mouth to his until I don't remember what it feels like to be apart.

"I was at the library, but I left," he explains, still looking at me like he's trying to figure out a puzzle. He tilts his head to the side and scratches at the back of his neck. "I'm sorry. I'm either unconscious on the street or having a very lucid dream. You're here?"

I nod. "Yes."

"In my apartment."

I look around at the bare walls, the shiny countertops, the luxury finishes without a single hint of personalization. He has a postcard from Lovelight Farms taped to the front of his fridge. One of the flyers from the tattoo studio soft launch is there too. "I assume it's yours, yes."

"You're here, in my apartment, in New York."

"Yes," I say, tighter than I mean to. I had hoped that standing in front of him would inspire me to say something beautiful and poetic, but all I feel is slightly off-balance and distracted by the sight of him.

"And you wore the dress," he says, a grin breaking out on his face, so sudden and bright I almost tumble backward through the door and back into the hallway. I nod, mute, and watch the little crinkles by his eyes deepen.

He sighs, still smiling. "C'mere," he breathes.

I narrow my eyes. "Why?"

A chuckle rumbles out of him. "Because I want to hug you, Nova girl, and you're too far away."

That's easy enough. I close the space between us and collapse into his arms, feeling myself settle and center for the first time in weeks. I've been missing this—the way he holds me just shy of too tight. His nose in my hair and his thumb inching down the line of my spine.

"You were supposed to be at the gala," I grumble into this shirt.

His palm settles at the small of my back, fingertips toying with the edge of my silver dress. "Is that why you wore this?"

I nod. "I had a plan."

"Not a very good one, apparently."

I pinch his chest and another rough laugh rolls out of him. He grabs my hand with his and squeezes once, our palms slipping together. He presses our tangled hands against his heart. It's beating slightly too fast. Mine skips to match.

"Can you tell me about it?" he asks, a plea in every word.

I tuck my smile into his shoulder. I haven't given Charlie nearly enough of what he deserves. I want to change that.

"I was going to show up at your fancy gala in my fancy dress and find you across the room. Maybe the crowd would have parted just right or maybe I would have bribed the DJ to play a slow song, I don't know. But I would have found you. And I would have asked you to dance."

"You probably would have bellowed my name until I folded, huh?"

I laugh and rub my nose back and forth against his neck. "Yeah, I would have."

"That sounds like something you'd do."

I lean back until I can see his face, greedy for the sight of him after being without him these last couple of weeks. I missed him so much, this man I was never supposed to miss at all.

"In my plan"—my voice wobbles, and Charlie's face softens—"we were going to dance, and we were going to talk, and I was going to tell you all the things I've figured out since you left."

"Like what?"

"Like you were right about the phone tree," I tell him with a grin. "They've been plotting and planning. Apparently we've been the topic of conversation."

"I knew it," he says. His hand inches lower, over the curve of my ass. His smile tugs wider. "Will they add me back on?"

I nod. "You should be getting messages as we speak. We're old news. They've moved on to the Halloween costume contest. They're scheming to get Dane in a couples costume with Matty. The front runners are Batman and Robin or Bert and Ernie."

"I'm sure that will go well."

"They're making good progress." I wedge myself closer to him. "But that's not the only thing I would have wanted to tell you in the middle of a library, at a gala I definitely did not sneak into."

He huffs a laugh. "What else?"

"I probably would have tried to kiss you."

"That wouldn't have been talking, would it?" He smiles, slow and quiet. A fraction of his usual grin. "But, yeah, I would have let you," he says quietly. "I would have kissed you back."

I smile and keep going. "And then after I kissed you, I would have told you how much I've missed you. That I thought it would be easy, but it hasn't been easy at all." I blow out a deep breath and make sure to keep my eyes on his. "I've always wanted to be independent. I thought being strong meant I had to be alone, that I could only have one thing at a time, but then I fell for you without even trying and . . . I think you might be my very best friend, Charlie. It's nothing like I thought."

"What is?"

"Falling in love," I tell him, a tremble in my voice. "Being in love with you. I was going to tell you all of that and then ask you to come home with me. That was my plan."

He stares at me for a long time. So long, I begin to get nervous that I've said the wrong thing. But his shy smile slowly creeps into a grin, his eyes shining bright in the glow of the city beyond the window.

"For snacks?" he asks, his voice rough.

I laugh and tip my forehead against his chest. He cups the back of my head and tucks a kiss against my crown, then lets his hand slip to my neck with a gentle squeeze.

"Can I tell you my plan now?" he asks.

I laugh into his shirt, weightless. Once upon a time I thought a relationship meant having shackles on my wrists, binding me to the needs of another person. I thought I'd have to sacrifice the things I've wanted most to be half of a whole. But now I know it just means I've got a safety net. Someone to lift me up and hold me steady. Someone to nag me about the spare key under my potted plant and someone to cut my grapes into tiny hearts.

A partner.

A friend.

"I was coming to you," he says. "I was standing in that library thinking of you and how much I miss you. How fucking stupid I was for not telling you the truth before I left." He leans back and brushes a kiss across my forehead. He holds himself there, just breathing, and I slip my hands beneath his jacket to press tight to his ribs, feeling every deep inhale and exhale. "I've taught myself how to be okay with fragments of feeling, but I don't want that with you. I want more than what you've given me. I want to give you more of me too. I love you, Nova girl. I tried my very best not to, but you wiggled your way right in there with no respect for my opinion on the matter."

"That sounds about right."

He hums and I feel the curve of his smile. A half-moon against my forehead. "There's plenty to figure out, but I know I don't want to be anywhere you aren't. I'm tired of letting myself be happy in incre- ments. I want to feel all of it, and I want to feel all of it with you."

I loop my arms around his waist and squeeze. "So, what do you think?" My voice is thick and my nose is burning and there's a pres- sure behind my eyes, but I can't stop smiling. "Do you want to come home with me?"

"Yeah," he laughs. "I really do."

WE DECIDE TO drive back to Inglewild together, Charlie in the driver's seat of my truck with his hand on my thigh. We drive until the city is a pinprick of light in the rearview mirror and the interstate rolls out in front of us, streetlights guiding us home.

He tosses me a bag of gummy bears, and I kick off my shoes, slipping my bare feet under me on the leather seat, the skirt of my silver dress pooled around my knees and Charlie's jacket around my shoulders. We slip in and out of conversation as Charlie debates the best flavor of gummy bear and wonders after the history of interstate rest stops, and I close my eyes and listen to the rhythm of his voice. The rush of the wind at the windows and the low sound of the radio. It's nothing special and everything wonderful at exactly the same time. Charlie and his thumb tracking back and forth over the top of my knee. Tip-tapping up until he can trace over the bottom of edge of my crescent moon. My hand finds his and he squeezes, my thumb tracing over his flower on the inside of his wrist.

By the time we make it back, the streets are quiet and dark. The pumpkin sculpture looms tall and proud in the fountain in the middle of the town.

"Still there, huh?" Charlie muses.

"I have no idea what they used on that thing."

Charlie turns the wheel with a yawn, and I echo it with one of mine.

"Sleep?" I ask, stretching my legs with a groan.

"Sure." Charlie stares at my exposed thigh with interest, a heated, heavy look in those blue eyes. "Right after I fuck you on that cute little table in your entryway."

I blink at him, a flip low in my belly. "My table?"

"Mm-hmm, I've been thinking about it."

Now I'm thinking about it too. The way he gets when he *wants*. Rough hands and biting kisses. His teeth against my shoulder. My name panted in syllables against the hollow of my throat. Clothes still half on, my legs looped high around his waist.

He turns onto my street. "I haven't seen you in three weeks, Nova. You really think I'm going to take you to bed and go to sleep?"

I blink some more and shift my legs against my seat. Charlie notices and chuckles, a low, rumbling sound from somewhere deep in his chest. I want to feel that sound with my body pressed to his. I want to feel it between my legs.

We pull into my driveway and I frown. It's full of cars that don't belong to me and all the lights are on in my living room. A halo of golden light spills out from the front windows, making my front garden glow.

"That might have to wait," I say slowly. Charlie puts the truck into Park and my front door opens. Beckett steps out onto my porch, his hands on my hips. "Yeah. It's definitely going to have to wait."

Charlie swallows hard. "Is he going to kill me?"

"I don't think so."

Beckett takes off his hat and drags his fingers through his hair, then tosses the hat to the side and cracks his knuckles. He points directly at the windshield, then at the pavement in front of him.

"Hmm," I amend. "Maybe a little bit."

Charlie blows out a breath and looks at me out of the corner of his eye. "What does killing me a *little bit* look like?"

I shrug and unbuckle my seat belt. "I guess we'll find out."

"Awesome."

I hop out of the truck and Charlie reluctantly follows, grabbing for my hand as soon as I'm close enough. Beckett stares at our hands clasped tightly together, an unreadable look on his face.

"What are you doing on my front porch at two in the morning?" I call out.

He ignores me. He keeps his gaze steady on Charlie, his eyes narrowing.

"You love her?" he yells from the steps of my porch, a challenge in his gruff voice. Charlie's hand tightens around mine.

"Yeah," he calls back.

Beckett shifts on his feet. "Is there a reason you didn't feel the need to tell me you have feelings for my baby sister?"

Charlie shrugs. "Didn't think I was good enough to."

Beckett scowls. "Well, that was fucking stupid of you."

I snicker. He turns his attention to me. "What are you laughing about? You weren't exactly forthcoming either."

The smile slips off my face. "That feels vaguely hypocritical, Mr. Elope-in-the-Middle-of-the-Day."

"This isn't about me." He tips his chin in Charlie's direction. "Do you love him?"

"You know I do."

I literally shouted about it at family dinner. But Charlie releases a breath, and I know why Beckett asked the question. He wanted Charlie to hear it too.

Affection for my big brother warms my chest.

"Good," he says. "Don't fuck it up."

And with that, he turns and disappears back into my house, slamming the door behind him. Charlie and I stand in my front yard holding hands, staring at the wreath made of dried mums on my front door as it swings back and forth.

"Was he talking to me or you?" Charlie asks.

"Both of us, I think."

"Are we supposed to follow him, or—"

"I really don't know. It's my house."

Charlie scratches at his jaw and glances at the rest of the cars in my driveway. "That looks like Caleb's car."

I nod. "And Stella's."

He grunts. "I guess this is what we get for hiding it as long as we did." Charlie sighs, weary, and leans over to smack a kiss against my cheek. "Shall we?"

"I guess." I tighten my grip on his hand and together we step onto my front porch. "I don't think we have much of a choice."

It quickly becomes apparent there is absolutely no choice, because Luka, Stella, Caleb, Layla, Beckett, and Evelyn are all in my living room.

I stare at Evelyn, standing with her back to my kitchen with one of my sweaters draped over her shoulders. "Aren't you supposed to be in Houston?"

"Flew back early," she explains. "Didn't want to miss this."

"Miss what?" I frown and look at the coffee table, currently covered with various plates and bowls. "Are those my pizza rolls?"

Caleb kicks out his legs in front of him, arms stretched over the back of my sofa. "They were your pizza rolls."

Layla pats his knee with a warning look and then gives us her full attention. "I'm so glad you both could join us."

"This is my house," I point out. Again. It looks like they rearranged my furniture to make a large open space in the middle. There's a stack of laminated, bound packets on one of my end tables. A large white poster board set on an easel next to the hallway. "Is that a presentation board?"

"It is." Stella stands up from the armchair that's been shoved in the corner, grabbing on to Charlie's elbow and dragging him across the room. He clings to me and I'm forced to follow. She pushes him down in the chair and then pushes me onto his lap.

"All right." Stella claps her hands together. "Places everyone. Just as we practiced it."

There's a flurry of movement. Luka and Caleb drag the coffee table into the kitchen and Layla rushes to grab the packets. Stella flips the poster board around on the easel.

Lovelight Farms Business Plan!!

It's written with what I assume is glitter glue. There are big, silvery sparkles over the entire thing. Wobbly candy canes drawn around the border.

Evie brings us both a packet with the same title on the front page. There are little hearts for the *i*'s. I'm assuming that was Stella.

"What is going on?" Charlie whispers in my ear. He shifts beneath me and curls an arm around my waist, tugging me further into him like a security blanket. Beckett clears his throat on the other side of the room.

I roll my eyes and settle, lifting the top page of the packet in my lap.

"No flipping ahead, please. There's a flow to this presentation." Stella clears her throat and knits her fingers together in front of her. "We would like to present, for your consideration, our five-year plan."

Charlie's arm tightens around my waist. "Stella, it's two in the morning."

"It's two thirty, actually," Luka offers from his spot on the floor, one arm thrown over his eyes.

"This couldn't wait. Now please, hold your comments until the end. We would like to present, for your consideration—"

"For whose consideration?" Charlie asks, frowning.

My god. We're going to be here forever.

Stella sighs and props her hands on her hips. "For your consideration, Charlie. It is for your specific consideration."

"Why?"

She throws her hands up in the air. "Listen to the presentation!"

"Okay, okay. Fine. Please proceed."

"Thank you," she sighs. She points at the poster board to her left and then holds up the stack of paper in her hand. "If you flip to the first page, you'll see a rough outline of what we'll be talking about this evening."

"Morning," Luka corrects from his starfished position on the floor. He's using one of my scarves as a blanket. "It is morning."

"We've incorporated a lot of your ideas, Charlie, and we're excited about what the future holds."

"Why do you sound like an infomercial?"

"Please shut up."

Stella then proceeds to walk through an incredibly detailed outline of the future of Lovelight Farms. There are spreadsheets and bar graphs and figures with little holly berries as status points. She hands it over to Layla to talk about bakery expansion and initiatives, and Beckett grumbles his way through his commitment to sustainable farmers markets. Luka rattles off some financial figures with a yawn, and Evie jumps in with some notes about the social media potential and organic growth. It's fine—interesting from a business perspective, I guess—but we're not even halfway through this document and I still don't understand why all these people are in my living room giving a business pitch. This is not *Shark Tank*.

Charlie shares my confusion, frowning down at the paperwork in his hands. "This is all really great, Stella, but I don't understand why you're telling me." He blinks up at her and fixes a half smile on his face. "I'm really proud of you. You know that. Are you—" He glances at Beckett, at Layla, at Caleb, and at Evelyn. Luka has managed to fall asleep halfway beneath my coffee table. "Are you applying for some sort of grant? Is this your practice run?"

Beckett drags his hand over his face. Caleb grins. And Stella keeps staring at her brother like she wants to hug him and throttle him in the exact same breath.

And that's when I realize what's happening.

I straighten in Charlie's lap, the nicely laminated document sliding from my legs to the floor. "Oh!"

Charlie glances at me. "Oh, what?"

It's a presentation. For his consideration.

They're giving the full picture of where the business is and where it's going. They're trying to entice Charlie. With a job offer.

I think, anyway. They're certainly taking the long way around.

And Charlie—Charlie who has always met the needs of the people around him without waiting for them to ask, Charlie who has given so much of himself over and over, Charlie who is used to being selected last or not at all—he has no idea.

"If you flip to the next page," Caleb offers, a laugh in his voice, "you'll see that Abuela would like to sweeten the deal with twice-monthly deliveries of tres leches. I promise not to take bites before it gets to you."

"And Gus said you can pick the trivia team of your choice," Layla adds. "You don't have to wait for the new season to register."

"Family dinners are on Tuesdays," Beckett barks. "Your attendance is mandatory."

They don't just want him to join the business but the town, I realize. This family and these friends and—according to page thirty-eight, appendix twelve—the phone tree. The back half of this document is a list of all the things he'd receive if he decided to move here full time. A standing booth at Matty's on deep-dish pizza night. Hazelnut lattes from the café with no hassle from Beatrice.

Charlie flips through the next couple of pages, his knuckles brushing against my thigh through the slit in my silver dress. I grin at the top of his head and try not to let it burst out of me, wanting him to come to the realization on his own. And I think maybe this might be it, the best part of loving Charlie. This bright, incandescent joy that's spilling over in the middle of my chest that's a little for me but mostly for him. Getting to hold on to his happiness like it's my own. Getting to share it.

"I don't—" Charlie's sentence stutters to a stop, his gaze caught on a page that has a series of four stacked photos. Black-and-white and grainy, *Peters, Stella* in the top right corner. Luka sits up on his elbows and grins.

Not asleep, I guess.

"I want it to be a family business. Our family. You were right when you said we missed too much time together," Stella explains. She sets her palm low against her belly. "And this little one is going to need Uncle Charlie around, don't you think?"

Charlie stares at the presentation in his hands. His thumb traces the edge of the picture with his little niece or nephew, and he heaves a deep, rattling sigh. I rub the place between his shoulder blades and his other hand squeezes my leg tight. He looks at Stella. "I knew you were crying too much."

She's crying now. Fat, silent tears sliding down her cheeks. To be fair, she's not the only one. Caleb sniffles but tries to hide it. Layla hands him a tissue from her pocket.

"We figured if Nova couldn't close the deal on her own, we'd give it a shot," Beckett says. Evelyn leans against his chest, and he wraps both of his arms around her with a rare grin. "Take it or leave it. The offer is on the table."

Charlie swallows hard and looks up at me, faint disbelief in the blue of his eyes.

"Is this—" He has to pause to clear his throat. "Is this too much?" His voice cracks on the question. I hear what he doesn't say, still staring up at me like he's not quite sure he's in the place he's supposed to be. *Am I too much? Are you going to want me for longer than this? Can I stay here with you?*

I scratch my nails through his hair and tip my forehead to his. I circle his wrist with my fingers and trace my thumb over the flower I gave him when I wasn't brave enough to find the right words.

But I have them now.

I kiss the bridge of his nose. The corner of his mouth. His hands tighten on me, and he tugs me closer, tipping my mouth to his.

I smile into his kiss.

"I think it's just enough, actually." I press another lingering kiss against his lips.

Beckett is grumbling somewhere behind me about public displays of affection. Stella is still sniffling. Caleb is back to rummaging through my fridge for snacks, and Luka is snoring on the floor. I hold Charlie's face to mine and hope he sees it. The friends and the family and the home. The love that's offered without strings or conditions.

"What do you want?" he asks, searching my face.

"I want you to stay," I tell him. His eyes light up like clouds clearing after a storm. A smile lifts the corners of his mouth. I want to be the cause of this exact look every single day. I want to be the reason he believes he deserves this sort of love. I trace my thumb over his clean-shaven jaw. "What do you want?"

"I've been telling you, Nova. I want to give you whatever you want," he says quietly. "For a long fucking time."

I laugh. "That's a good answer."

"I thought you'd think so."

I tip my head closer to his. "Do you think you could be happy here, Charlie?" I whisper.

"I am happy here." His eyes dart over my shoulder at the buffoons in my living room. There's a conversation happening about Hot Pockets or taquitos. I don't know and I don't care. Especially when Charlie slips his gaze back to me, his eyes tracing my face like I'm something precious. Like I'm something he can't believe he gets to keep. "I don't think I've ever been this happy in my life, Nova girl."

He says it in a whisper. Like a secret.

I drop my mouth to his and make it a promise.

"Me too."

EPILOGUE

NOVA

Three Years Later

"YOU HAVE A walk-in."

I glance up from the weathered binder open in the middle of my desk, Jeremy standing with his head and shoulders hanging in my office, his hand gripping the frame of the door. I don't think I'll ever get used to this version of Jeremy, his hair neatly combed back, his faded badger sweatshirt swapped for a button-down tucked into a pressed pair of navy-blue slacks. Charlie organized a whole *Princess Diaries* makeover intervention the last time Jeremy came home for spring break wearing Birkenstocks and white tube socks. The two of them have been swapping pattern recommendations and tailor information ever since.

"Can you schedule them for later in the week? Whatever open slot there is."

Jeremy shakes his head.

"You can't schedule them?" I ask.

"No."

I blink. "Why not? Did you forget how to use a pen and paper at NYU?"

He only works at the tattoo shop sparingly, whenever he's in town to visit his parents. I don't need the help with the rotating receptionists we have on staff and the other artists in the shop, but he says he likes spending time here when he can, and I like the company.

He's also still angling for that free tattoo. Apparently, there's a girl in his Italian language class he's been trying to impress.

"They said they need to be seen tonight."

"That's nice, but they don't make the rules." I'm supposed to meet Charlie at Matty's in twenty minutes. If I'm late, he starts making complicated maps of the town using parmesan shakers and toothpicks.

And I hate making him wait. He's done enough of that.

"They said it was an emergency."

"Who did?"

"Your walk-in."

I narrow my eyes. "A tattoo emergency?"

Jeremy rolls his lips against his smile and taps his palm against the edge of the door. He might have tidied himself up over the years, but he still shows flashes of that impertinent teenager. The little shit that used to put his pet gecko in my hair when I babysat him. "That's what they said, yeah. I'm going to put them in room two."

"Jeremy, no—" But he's already gone, disappearing down the narrow hall that leads to the front. I hear the low murmur of conversation and then a door opening. Fuck. He's put them in a private studio. A private studio means it's either an extensive piece or they want it on their ass. I'm not in the mood for either of those things tonight.

I snap the binder closed and push back from the desk, sliding my phone out from my back pocket.

NOVA: I just got a walk-in. I'm going to be a few minutes late.

CHARLIE: ☹ ☹ ☹

NOVA: I know. But I'll make it up to you.

CHARLIE: I'm listening.

I snort and tap my thumb to the photo gallery icon at the bottom of my phone. I scroll until I find the picture I want, then send it over.

> **CHARLIE:** Fuuuuuuuck.
>
> **CHARLIE:** We've talked about you sending indecent photos, Nova girl.
>
> **NOVA:** It's a slice of chocolate cake.
>
> **CHARLIE:** It's the last slice of chocolate cake that you've hidden like a tiny gremlin. Where is it? Is it at Beckett's? Layla's? Buried in a secret bunker in the middle of the south field? Tell me.

It's actually behind the milk in our garage fridge, but I know Charlie thinks I'm more devious than that, so he hasn't bothered to check. Layla made me a double-fudge brownie cake for the third anniversary of the studio opening, and Charlie was a man possessed from his first bite. I thought he and Caleb might get in a fistfight over the frosting.

> **NOVA:** It's yours. An apology for being late.
>
> **CHARLIE:** Apology not needed but passionately accepted.

I sigh. Charlie and I have been on opposite schedules for the past week. The harvest festival has finally achieved the level of notoriety the town wanted for it all those years ago, thanks in large part to a pumpkin sculpture contest and the enthusiasm of the new mayor. But as a result, I've been slammed with walk-ins in town for the festivities, and Charlie's been occupied with the committee he demanded a permanent place on. I'm tired of only seeing his face when we're both dead on our feet, his cheek smooshed in the pillow next to mine, his arm thrown over my hip.

I have another picture on my phone that Charlie hasn't seen yet, the second part of my apology. Pale pink lace and colorful embroidered flowers that curl up around the edges. I snapped a picture in front of the mirror when I was getting dressed this morning and promptly forgot to send it.

I send it now, just as I slip into room two, tucking my phone back in my pocket with a smile. I hate missing Charlie, but I like the games we play until we find each other again, tension spooling out between us until I yank on it, tugging him back to me.

There's a muffled groan from the person waiting propped up against the tattoo chair, a familiar gruff, grumbling sound that rolls low in his chest. I stop just inside the entryway watching Charlie blink down at his phone.

"Well, that's more in line with the indecent photos you usually send," he mutters, palm scratching roughly at the back of his head. "Fuck, Nova. When did you get this one?"

"Last weekend." I fold my hands behind my back and stare at him. It feels like I dreamed him right up and dropped him in room two. "When I went shopping."

"You told me you bought flowers."

"Don't those look like flowers?"

He swipes with his thumb at the screen and tilts his head to the side, his tongue at the corner of his mouth as he studies the picture. "I suppose you're right."

"Of course I am."

He keeps staring at his phone and I keep staring at him. He's wearing the suit I watched him shrug into this morning, navy blue with a crisp white shirt beneath. Long legs crossed at the ankles and hair messy from dragging his hands through it too many times today. He rubs his knuckles over the scruff on his jaw, and I get a glimpse of the ink on his wrist. I smile.

"Are you going to keep staring at that picture or are you going to kiss me?"

"To be honest, Nova, I still haven't decided." He clicks off his phone with a tap of his thumb and tosses it over his shoulder on the padded chair. "Just kidding. Come over here and plant one on me."

I roll my eyes but close the space between us with three quick steps, sliding into his open arms and pressing up on my toes to catch his mouth with mine. He sighs as soon as my mouth is on his, relief and wanting and comfort in the press of his palm at the base of my spine, urging me closer.

"Hey, Nova girl," he whispers with a nudge of his nose against mine. His knuckles press under my chin, and he drops another quick kiss to my mouth. "Missed you."

"Hey, Mr. Mayor." I smile at the sound he makes under his breath. He loves when I call him that, even if he blushes furiously about it every damn time. I thumb at the lapel of his suit jacket. "Thank you for making time for your constituents."

A half smile hitches the corner of his mouth, blue eyes soft as they take in my face, tipped to his. "You're my favorite constituent," he mumbles.

"Don't let Ms. Beatrice hear you say that."

"Christ, you're right. I just got back on the hazelnut latte list."

"Don't you two live together?" Jeremy calls from somewhere in the depths of the shop. I snicker and press my face into the front of Charlie's shirt.

"One day, young Jeremy, this will all make sense to you," Charlie sighs wistfully, one hand cupping the back of my neck and the other inching up my sweater. I wrap both of my arms around him and squeeze.

I denied myself this comfort for so long. I did have my heart bubble-wrapped, but not because I was afraid of getting hurt. Precious things should be protected, and I did a damn good job of flourishing beneath my own light. I thought being half of a whole meant

I'd have parts of myself tugged away by another person. That I'd be distracted, compromised, diminished. But everything I've given Charlie I've handed over willingly. I want him to have all of it—my friendship, my trust. The good moments when I laugh so hard my stomach aches and the hard moments when the voice in the back of my head is louder than I'd like. He lifts me up when I need it and holds me steady when I need that too. I haven't lost a single thing with Charlie.

"What are you doing here?"

"Been missing you," he answers with a quick kiss to my hair. "Thought I'd make an appointment to see you."

"You don't have an appointment," I point out, not moving my face from the hollow of his throat. I brush a kiss against the dip between his collarbones and his arms squeeze me tighter. "This is a walk-in."

"Semantics," he says, relaxing his arms so I can lean back. He curls a strand of my hair around his finger, tugs once, and then tucks it behind my ear. "Do you have time for a session before I take you home?"

I raise both eyebrows. "For a tattoo?"

"That is what you do here, yes?" He releases me from his hug and slips his suit jacket from his shoulders. He folds it carefully and drapes it over the table, then works at his cufflinks. "It's about time I got that scorpion on my ass, don't you think?"

Jeremy drops something behind us, and I turn to see a stack of sketches fluttering to the ground, folders still in his hands and the gold tray they were balanced on top of turned on its side.

"On that note," Jeremey says, bending to collect the pieces of paper with a pained expression twisting his face. "I'm out of here."

"You don't have to leave," Charlie calls. "I'm fine with you seeing my ass."

"I'm not fine with it," Jeremy replies quickly. His lips flatten in a line, and he tosses everything back on the desk. "I have no desire for a repeat of August second."

August second. Charlie came in for the tattoo on his hip. We barely made it through my pen on his skin before we were reaching for each other, his mouth on my neck and both of my hands on the curve of his bare ass.

"What happened—oh, yeah." A grin blossoms across Charlie's face. My cheeks flush pink. We weren't exactly quiet, and we definitely left a dent in the wall of room three. But to be fair, I didn't know Jeremy was still lurking around. Charlie tips his chin. "Good call, man. See you later."

"Bye, I'll see you guys—"

Charlie shuts the door in Jeremy's face, flicks the lock, and takes my hand, guiding me over to the tattoo station I have set up against the wall. He urges me down on the stool and then starts to work on the buttons of his shirt, fingers dancing nimbly down the neat line.

"Oh, wow. Okay. You're serious."

Charlie frowns at me. "Am I not always serious?"

I shake my head. "No, you most certainly are not."

"Well," he tugs his shirt off his arms and tosses it on top of his jacket. I'm distracted by the stretch of his biceps, the smooth lines of his torso. "You should know by now I'm usually serious about a few things."

Car snacks. Classic movies. Themed festivals and how I color code my budget sheets. My lingerie shopping trips.

Charlie drags his palm over his chest, and my eyes trip down his torso, lingering on the tattoo I can barely see the top of, peeking out from the waist of his pants. A burst of blue and purple at his hip, dotted with stars. The supernova tattoo starts on his thigh and climbs up over his hip bone, reaching toward his stomach. It took three sessions and a stern warning to Charlie to stay perfectly still, though he was liberal with that instruction. You can see the wobble in some of the lines at his hip. Every time I glanced up and found him watching me, or when his fingers traced gently over the back of my neck as I bent over him.

He says the imperfections are his favorite part. That it makes it his and his alone.

I'm inclined to agree.

Charlie stretches his arms wide with a yawn, finally free from the constriction of his clothes, and I get a good look at the pinup girl across his ribs. She has blond hair tumbling over her shoulder and a coy smile, one hand tucked under her chin, a bouquet of tiny flowers on the back of her hand. Something in my chest turns over the way it always does when I see my work on Charlie's skin. His ink is just for me, in places only I get to see it, hidden beneath his fancy suits and designer shirts. *Mine*, those marks say. *Mine* and *mine* and *mine*.

Possession and affection.

I let my gaze touch the flower on his wrist.

An acknowledgment and a promise too.

Charlie rubs his palm over his ribs with a content rumble, then plops down on the table in front of me.

"I want a new tattoo."

I grin at him. "I gathered that." I reach for my gloves and the rest of my supplies. "You're addicted, aren't you?"

"I like your hands on me."

"You don't need a tattoo for that." I drop a quick kiss in the middle of his bare chest. "What were you thinking?"

"Your name," he says seriously. "Across my forehead."

I give him a look. "Don't joke about tattoo design, Charlie."

"Maybe here instead." He traces his pointer finger over his heart.

I stare at the blank spot on his chest where I just kissed and then tip my face to his. His eyes are serious, his lips twisted down at the corners. He opens his mouth only to snap his jaw shut half a second later, a huff of frustration pushed out from his nose.

I drop the supplies I've been messing with and press my palms to his knees instead, creeping closer on my stool. He makes room for me like he always does, his legs inching wider, both of my arms draped loosely over his lap.

"What's this about?" I ask.

He shrugs and grips the edge of the table, hands flexing and releasing. "I just want your name somewhere," he mumbles, reluctant, a tilt to his voice like he's embarrassed about it. He scratches once behind his ear, his tell for when he's feeling anxious or uncomfortable. "I want it to be permanent."

"You have my face on your ribs, Charlie."

"I want it to be extra permanent."

My confusion melts into affection, warm and easy. "It is permanent," I tell him, looping my hands around his wrists and tugging until our fingers are twined together, palms pressed tight. I squeeze. "You don't need my name on your skin for you to belong to me. Or for me to belong to you."

"I know," he sighs. "I know that. But sometimes . . . sometimes I want it."

Charlie has come a long way with how he talks about the things he wants, but he still holds himself back when he thinks he's being selfish. When he thinks he's reaching for more than what he's earned.

I squeeze his hands again. "I have a better idea."

He perks up, interested. "Is it across my collarbones? You like to bite me there."

I shift in my seat. I do like to bite him there. He makes the prettiest sounds when I do. "No, it's not across your collarbones."

"Beneath Pinup Nova?"

I glance at the tattoo across his ribs and feel a smile tug at the corners of my mouth. "No. Not Pinup Nova."

"Then where?"

I drag my thumbs back and forth over his knuckles, looking at our hands. He has some blue smudged on the side of his palm, likely from whatever notes he was taking during his meetings today. I trace it gently and then move my touch to his knuckles. The space right above. I tap at the smooth, pale skin of his ring finger and look back up at him.

He thinks he's been sneaky about it, but Charlie doesn't possess an ounce of discretion. He's been looking at engagement rings for over a year now. I know it's something he wants—something he's been wanting—and I also know if he thinks it's something I don't want, he won't ever ask.

"Charlie."

He's gone still, his broad shoulders inching up toward his ears. "Yes?"

I scoot closer on my tiny wheeled stool. Five years ago, if you would have told me I was planning on proposing to a man in the back room of the tattoo studio I own in the town I grew up in, I would have laughed in your face. I never thought a committed relationship was something I could want, but Charlie has shown me every day that wanting and needing and loving and living are all strings on a braid twisted together. I tug on one of those ribbons and everything pulls tighter. Stronger.

I rub at his finger. "What about a tattoo right here?"

He glances down at our hands, then drags his gaze to my face. He stares at me for a long time. "Right there?"

"Mm-hmm."

"That specific finger?"

"Yup."

"What would you—" He takes a deep breath and then releases it, a tremble in his hands where mine grip his. "What would you want to put there?" he asks.

"A simple black band, I think," I answer. It's a monumental effort not to grin. "Not too thick. You could wear a ring over it, if you wanted. Maybe silver to match that new watch I got you last—"

Charlie grabs me under my arms and hauls me up his body, not waiting for me to finish my sentence. One hand cups the back of my neck and the other sinks into my hair, my body perched above his. He drags my face to his and kisses me, wild and wonderful, tongue and teeth and messy, delicious delight. He kisses me like he's been dying to do exactly that since he walked into the studio.

Since we danced on a bunch of mismatched rugs.

"To be clear," he whispers against my mouth. "You're asking me to marry you, right?"

I laugh. It feels right to do it like this. In the back room of my studio with Charlie shirtless beneath me, his hands tight on my body and my knees hugging his hips. All of my marks on his body. Some of his on mine. We've always been a mess, the two of us. Impulsive and fumbling our way through. But there's no one I'd rather make mistakes with than Charlie.

"Yes." I drag my fingers through his hair and curl both of my arms around his shoulders. "I'm asking you to marry me. What do you think?"

He sighs, low and slow. His fingers spread across the small of my back, holding me tight. Holding me steady.

"Yes," he says quietly. He drops a quick kiss to my shoulder, voice thick. "I'd love to marry you."

We stand there like that for a long time, just the two of us, my cheek pressed to his heart, the steady thump of it in my ear. I drag my nails up and down his spine until he shivers. Then I do it again.

"Could I—" He stops abruptly, swallowing down the rest of his question. His bare arms tense and then relax against me, fingers twitching against my sides.

I tip my chin against his chest and stare up at him. "Could you what?"

He shakes his head and drops a kiss on my nose. "It doesn't matter. We'll figure it out later."

"Figure what out later?"

"It's not important."

I sigh. "Charlie."

"Nova."

"Tell me."

He watches me carefully, and I wait as he struggles to find his words.

"Could I take your name?" he finally asks. His Adam's apple bobs in his throat with a heavy swallow. "When we get married, I mean. Could I—could I be a Porter?"

I have to take a second to breathe through the pinch in my chest. "Is that something you want?"

He nods.

I feel myself smile. "I'm pretty sure you've been an honorary Porter for a couple of years now."

"Yeah." He tucks some of my hair behind my ears, hands framing my cheeks. The look on his face is so tender, it makes me want to cry. His thumb rubs right beneath my eye and I think maybe I might be. "It's a good thing no one else in your family has an encyclopedic knowledge of nineties R&B groups. I've really made myself valuable at trivia."

"More than that," I tell him, voice cracking.

He nods. "Yeah. More than that. You're right." He traces his thumbs beneath my eyes again and lets out a breath. "But I don't want it to be honorary. I'd like to be a Porter. I want to be your family. Your biggest cheerleader and best friend. The guy who you keep peanut butter pretzels stocked for." His eyes search mine, honest and true. "I want to be your husband. Full formal. Tuxes and everything."

"Okay," I answer.

His whole face lights up. "Yeah?"

I nod and press my forehead to his chest. Hold him tight.

"Yeah," I say, smiling so hard my cheeks hurt. "Full formal sounds nice."

ACKNOWLEDGMENTS

I started writing *Lovelight Farms* during a time in my life when I was deeply craving community. I had just had a baby, my husband was working long hours as a physician during the pandemic, we were away from family and friends, and I spent a lot of time feeling lonely, sad, and overwhelmed. Lovelight became the place I could escape to. Someplace warm and kind, with butter croissants and fresh Christmas trees.

It has been one of the greatest joys of my life that this fictional community has turned into a real-life community. So many of you have found comfort in these pages, and there is truly nothing better than that. Lovelight and the tiny town of Inglewild represent so many of the things I hope for: kindness, generosity, inclusivity, diversity, belonging, and above all things—love. I hope whenever you need a place to disappear to, you come back to Lovelight Farms.

I dragged my feet through writing *Business Casual* because I didn't want to say goodbye, but then a very good friend reminded me I don't have to, so I won't. Instead, I'll say thank you. Thank you to the readers who picked up a book about a Christmas tree farm and gave it a chance. You have changed my life is so many wonderful ways. I hope to keep telling stories for a long time, and I hope to keep sharing them with you.

Thank you to my agent, Kim Lionetti, for championing these stories and making all of my dreams come true while I was sitting on a bus at Disney listening to unhinged banjo music. Thank you to the incredible team at Berkley—Kristine, Mary, Kristin, Chelsea, Anika—for all their hard work getting these stories into the hands of new readers. Cheers to the immaculate team at Pan Macmillan—Kinza, Chloe, Ana—for their unbridled and everlasting enthusiasm. And a big, huge, gigantic thank-you to queen of cover art, Sam Palencia of Ink and Laurel. Sam, your work has done so much for my stories, and I am entirely and forever grateful. You sure do make the bookshelves prettier.

This weird, wonderful job of mine can sometimes feel pretty lonely, and I'm forever grateful to my fellow authors, who are the best coworkers a gal could ask for. Thank you to Sarah (my little acorn), Chloe, Chip, Elena, and Hannah for being my own personal cheer squad. And for listening to the absolutely unhinged voice memos. And thank you to Adri, for your boundless enthusiasm and delight.

And to my dear friend Annie, whom I owe a lot of this weird and wonderful to. When I said I wanted to write a book, you said, "Of course you will," and you haven't stopped believing in me since. I'm putting it down in writing. Charlie is entirely yours. He wouldn't have happened without you or that late-night text where you said, "Wouldn't it be funny if . . ." I am forever grateful we get to travel this wacky road together. Cheers to more trips with wine and laughs and dreams and stories. I never want to stop doing this with you.

And my biggest thank-you, as always, goes to my husband. My biggest promoter and proudest partner. Getting to live our love story is better than any romance I could ever write.

This is the final chapter of the Lovelight series as I intended it, but I won't be permanently closing the door. Who knows, we might get a trip back to Inglewild sometime down the road. But for now, I'm saying a quiet and sincere goodbye.

The gates to Lovelight will always be open. I'll meet you at Layla's for some coffee and we'll hunt down the perfect tree.

If only in my dreams . . .

Keep reading for an excerpt from Stella and
Luka's love story,

LOVELIGHT FARMS

Available now!

"LUKA, LISTEN." I lean backward in my chair and fumble for the stack of papers on the file cabinet behind me, cursing under my breath when my fingertips barely glance the corner edge and it goes cascading to the floor in a flurry of white. "Listen, I need you to stop talking about pizza for a second."

There's a pause on the other end of the line. "I was just getting to the good part."

What he means is he was just getting to the part where he talks at length about homemade cheese, and I don't think I can handle him talking about mozzarella with that level of detail right now. As a data analyst, Luka is ridiculously thorough in all things. Especially cheese. I rub at the ache between my eyebrows. "I know you were, I'm sorry, but I've got something else to talk to you about."

"Everything okay?" There's a honk in the background, Luka's muffled curse, and the steady click of his turn signal as he merges into another lane.

"Everything is . . . fine." I peek down at the budget spreadsheets littering my floor and wince. "It's good. Okay, I mean. I just—" The fleeting confidence I entered this conversation with leaves me, and I slouch down in my chair. Every time I've called Luka this week or Luka has called me, I've chickened out. I don't think this time is going to be any different.

"I actually have to go. One of my vendors is calling." I frown at myself in the reflection of my computer screen. I have bags under my eyes, my full bottom lip is bright red from nervous chewing, and my mass of dark hair is twisted up into a bun that looks better suited to a haunted Victorian doll.

I look every bit as rough as the farm's budget sheets.

"One of your vendors is not calling you, but I'll play for now." Luka sounds amused. "Call me when you're done working, okay? We can talk about whatever you've been running circles around all week."

Reflection me frowns deeper. "Maybe."

He laughs. "Talk soon."

I hang up my phone and resist the urge to toss it clear across the room. Luka has a knack for cracking me right open, and I don't want that right now. I don't want it ever, to be honest, afraid of what he'll find when he starts connecting all of his data points.

My phone buzzes in my palm with an incoming text, and I flip it face down on top of a stack of invoices. It buzzes again, and I pinch the bridge of my nose.

With the farm's finances the way they are, I'm quickly running out of options. I had thought—I guess I thought owning a Christmas tree farm would be romantic.

I had big dreams of a holiday season filled with magic. Kids weaving their way through the trees. Parents stealing kisses over hot chocolate. The stuff Christmas songs are written about. Young couples getting caught beneath the mistletoe. Low-hanging lights and oversized stockings. Wood railings painted red and white. Gingerbread cookies. Peppermint sticks.

And at first, it was great. Our opening season was as magical as it gets.

But since then, it's been one thing after another.

I'm eyeballs deep in debt with a fertilizer supplier who conveniently forgets my shipment every other month. I have an entire pasture of trees that look like something out of a Tim Burton movie, and there is a family of raccoons orchestrating a hostile takeover of my Santa barn. It is, in short, not a magical winter fairyland.

It is a frigid hellscape from which no one can escape, topped with a pretty red bow.

I feel lied to. Not only by every Hallmark movie I've ever seen but also by the previous owner of this land. Hank failed to mention he stopped paying his bills months ago, and as the new owner, I'd inherited his debt. At the time, I thought I had gotten a steal. The land was at a good price, and I had exciting ideas for expansion and marketing. With a little love, this little farm could make a big impact. Now though, I just feel stupid. I feel like I ignored several red flags in my desire to create something special.

I was blinded by the Douglas fir.

But I do have a solution. I'm just not sure the email sitting at the top of my inbox is something I'm willing to explore.

Honestly, at this point, harvesting my own organs sounds less scary.

"Stella."

I jump when Beckett elbows his way into my office, my arm knocking over my coffee, a halfway-dead fern, and a stack of pine tree–scented air fresheners. It all tumbles to the ground on top of my destroyed filing system. I frown at my lead farmer over the mess.

"Beckett." I sigh, and the headache pressing behind my eyes spreads, curls at the base of my skull. The man is physically incapable of entering a room in a normal, understated way. His knees are caked in mud and my frown deepens. He must have been in the south pasture. "What is it now?"

He steps over the pile of plant and cardboard and coffee and folds his large frame into the chair opposite my desk—a horrible, too-small leather thing I found on the side of the road. I had wanted to re-upholster it a rich velvet evergreen, but then the raccoons happened. And then the fencing by the road randomly collapsed twice.

And so there it sits. Horrible cracking brown leather with bits of stuffing spilling out onto the floor. It feels like a metaphor.

Beckett peers at the faded trees decorating the carpet, the cardboard curling up at the edges. One eyebrow shoots straight up his forehead. "Care to explain why you have seventy-five gas station air fresheners in your office?"

Leave it to Beckett to forget an apology and start digging into something personal instead. My phone buzzes again. Three staccato bursts in rapid fire. It's either Luka's dissertation on pizza crust consistency or another vendor looking for their late payment.

Beckett's eyebrow creeps higher. "Or perhaps door number two. Care to explain why you're ignoring Luka?"

I hate when Beckett is feeling clever. It almost always ends poorly for me. He's too astute for his own good, despite the dumb farmer act he plays a majority of the time. I bend down and pick up an air freshener, tossing it in the bottom drawer of my desk with all of the rest. A big ol' mess of tangled strings, stale pine, and unrequited feelings. A single pine tree for every time Luka has been home, starting back when we were twenty-one and stupid. I typically find them a week or two after he's left—tucked away in some hidden spot. Beneath my snow globe, under my keyboard.

Wedged in my coffee filter.

"I'm not and I don't," I mumble. Hard pass on both those options, thank you. "Care to explain what you found out there this morning?"

Beckett slips off his hat and runs his fingers through his dark blond hair, working a smudge or two of dirt in there. His skin is tanned by the sun and from spending his days in the fields, the flannel rolled up to his elbows displaying the color and ink on his forearms. All the women in town are crazy about him, which is probably why he doesn't go into town.

Also probably why he frowned at me when I suggested a Hot Farmer calendar to boost profits.

I swear, I'd have no financial concerns if he let me take that one to market.

"I don't understand," he mutters, thumb rubbing at his jaw. If

Cindy Croswell were here right now, she'd drop dead on the spot. She works at the pharmacy and sometimes pretends she's hard of hearing when Beck comes in, just so he has to lean into her space and yell straight into her ear. I even saw that old bat pretend to stumble into a shelf so Beckett would help her back up. Hopeless.

"These trees are probably the lowest maintenance crop I've ever had to support." There's a joke in there somewhere, but I frankly don't have the energy. My lips tilt down until my frown mirrors his. Two sad clowns. "I can't think of a single reason why the trees in the south pasture look like—like—"

I think of the way the trees growing at the base of the hills curve and bend, the brittle texture of the bark. The limp, sad needles. "Like a darker version of the Charlie Brown Christmas tree?"

"That's it, yeah."

Strangely enough, there's a market for lonely looking Christmas trees. But these don't fall into that category. These are unsalvageable. I went out the other day, and I swear one of them crumbled when I looked at it. I can't imagine one of these things sitting in anyone's home—ironically or not. I pluck at my bottom lip with my thumb and do some quick calculations in my head. There are dozens of trees in that lot.

"Will we be all right without them?" Beckett looks worried and he has every reason to be. It's another hit we can't afford to take. He's the head of farming operations. I know I owe him the truth. That we're hanging on by the skin of our teeth. But I can't make the words come out. He took a leap of faith when he left his job at the produce farm to work here with me. I know he's counting on this being a success. For all of the promises I made him to hold true.

And so far they have, thanks to my savings. I've had to scrimp and save and eat ramen more nights than not, but no one who works here has seen a dip in their pay. I'm not willing to sacrifice that.

But that won't last forever. Something has to give soon.

I glance back at my computer screen, the email at the top of my inbox. "Well," I say, chewing on my bottom lip. In for a penny, in for a pound, and all that. If Beckett wants us to make it through this next season with the farm in one piece, there is something he can do. I breathe deep and summon the scraps of courage that didn't abandon me during my call with Luka. "Want to be my boyfriend?"

I'd laugh at the look on his face if I weren't so serious. He looks like I asked him to go out into the orchards and bury a dead body.

"Is that—" He shifts in his chair, the leather squeaking under his legs. "Stella, I'm not—I don't really see you—you're like my—"

When was the last time I heard this man stutter? I honestly can't think of it. Maybe when Betsy Johnson tried to cop a feel in front of a group of schoolkids during his Arbor Day presentation at the middle school.

"Relax." I press the toe of my boot into another air freshener and drag it toward me. "I don't mean a real boyfriend."

I'm struggling with dragging the piece of cardboard toward me, so I don't see the way Beckett's body goes ramrod straight in the chair. All I see is his leg jumping up and down a mile a minute. I snort. When I look up, his eyes are wide, and he looks like I've put a gun to his head. It's the same thinly veiled apprehension and mortification he wears on his face every time he steps foot in town.

"Stella," he swallows. "Is this—are you propositioning me?"

"What? Oh my god, Beck—" I can't help the full-body shudder. I love Beckett, but—*god*. "No! Jesus, is that what you think of me?"

"What do I think? What do *you* think?" His voice has hit a register I have never heard from him before. He gestures wildly with his hand, clearly not knowing what to do with himself. "This is all a little out of left field, Stella!"

"I meant like a fake boyfriend thing!" I shriek, like that was obvious. Like this is a normal thing people request from their very platonic friends. Like my overactive imagination and half a bottle of sauvignon blanc didn't get me into this mess to begin with. I click to open the email and stare at it mournfully, ignoring the animated confetti that explodes across my screen. I watch it three times in a row and pretend Beckett's eyes are not currently drilling a hole into the side of my head.

"I did a thing," I supply, and leave it at that.

"A thing," he parrots.

I hum in response.

"Do you want to share what that thing is?"

No.

"I—"

As if summoned by sheer force of will, Layla tiptoes her way into my office, a tray of something preceding her around the edge of my door. I smell cinnamon, dried cranberries, and a hint of vanilla.

Zucchini bread.

Like an angel descending from the heavens, she brought zucchini bread. The one thing that always, *always* distracts Beckett.

Beckett makes a noise that is borderline obscene, and I vaguely consider recording it and putting it on OnlyFans. That might bring in some dollars: *Hot Farmer Eats Zucchini.* I chuckle to myself. He reaches for the tray with grabby hands, but Layla smacks his knuckles with a wooden spoon she pulls out of her . . . back pocket, I think? She balances the tray neatly on the edge of my desk. I peer into it and almost weep. She added chocolate chips.

"Made you something, boss lady."

She nudges it forward with the edge of her spoon and rests her chin prettily in one hand.

While Beckett embodies rugged recluse with all the charm of a paper bag, Layla Dupree brightens any room she walks into with her sweet Southern hospitality and no-nonsense wit. She is striking with her crystal clear hazel eyes and cropped dark hair. She's kind to a fault and makes the best hot chocolate in the tristate area. I snatched her up to manage the dining options at my little tree farm as soon as I tasted one of her chocolate chip cookies at the firehouse bake sale. She's the third member of our humble little trio, and if she's bringing me sweets, she wants something.

Something I probably can't afford.

I shove a slice of bread into my mouth before she can ask, bound and determined to enjoy at least one thing before I have to tell her no.

My phone takes advantage too, buzzing merrily across my desk. Layla blinks at it, exchanges a glance with Beckett, and then looks at me.

"Why are you ignoring Luka?"

"I'm not—" A spray of golden, flaky, delicious crumbs accompanies my denial. "I'm not ignoring Luka."

It sounds more like *M'snot snore ukeah.*

Layla hums and pivots. "So, I was thinking," she starts. Bingo. "If I add another stove in the back corner of the kitchen, we could almost double our output. Maybe even start some prepackaged things if people want to take a little basket out into the fields with them."

Beckett crosses his arms as I continue chewing my massive bite. I ignore Layla for now and stare him dead in the eye.

"It's still warm," I tell him.

He groans.

Layla relents and rolls her eyes, plucking a slice off the top and offering it to him.

"If people start leaving trash in the pastures, I'm going to have a problem with that," Beckett grouches. He shoves the whole slice of bread into his mouth and then collapses against the back of the chair in rapture, the leather once again releasing an ominous squeak of defeat. Just like I'm about to.

"I love the idea, but we might need to put a hold on any big purchases right now." I think about the sad little number in my savings account. How I was barely able to cover operational expenses this past quarter.

Layla's face falls, her hand reaching out to mine. She touches my knuckles once. It's a kindness I don't deserve, given that I haven't been completely honest about how bad things are right now. "Are we doing okay?"

"We're doing"—I search for a word to categorize *hanging on by my fingernails*—"all right."

Beckett finally swallows his ridiculous bite of food and kicks out a leg. "We were just talking about that, actually. Stella propositioned me."

"Oh? That's interesting. Don't understand how it plays into our operational status though."

"Yeah, me too. But that's what I got when I asked her the same question."

"Do I get to be propositioned too?"

I roll my eyes and choose not to dignify that with a response. Instead, I turn my computer screen around so they both can see the animated confetti in all its glory. Beckett doesn't so much as blink, but Layla throws both arms up in the air with a high-pitched screech that has me wincing.

"Is that for real?" She grabs the sides of my desktop and leans closer, nose practically pressed up against the screen. "You're a finalist for that Evelyn St. James thing?"

Beckett eyeballs the zucchini bread as it balances precariously on the edge of my desk, eyes glazed like he's been drugged. "Aspirin Saint what?"

Layla slaps his hand again without even looking at him. "She's an influencer."

Beckett makes a face. "Is that like a political thing?"

"How do you exist in this century? She's a big deal on social media. She does destination features. Sort of like a mini Travel Channel thing."

I feel a small burst of pride. She is *the* influencer for destination hospitality. Snagging a feature on her account is equivalent to thousands in ad spend—thousands we have never had the budget for. It would turn our farm into a place people want to visit, not just a stopping point for locals. And the $100,000 cash prize for the winner of her small business sweepstakes would keep us afloat for another year, if not more.

Too bad I lied on my application.

"Where does the propositioning come in?"

"I didn't—I didn't proposition Beckett." I swing my computer screen back around and minimize the email. I drum my fingers against my lips and remember the night that got me into this mess. I had been on the phone with Luka, a little bit dizzy off white wine and the way his eyes crinkled at the corners. He had been making some stupid joke about ham sandwiches and couldn't stop laughing long enough to get the full thing out. I still don't know the punch line.

"I said in the application that I own the farm with my boyfriend," I mumble. Color heats my cheeks. I bet I look as red as one of my barn doors. "I thought it would be more romantic than *Sad, lonely woman who hasn't been on a date in seventeen months*."

"I hope to god you're having meaningless sex with someone."

"Why do you need a boyfriend to be successful?"

Layla and Beckett speak over each other, though to be fair, Layla makes a much more aggressive effort as she propels herself forward in the chair and yells her statement about my sex life. She collapses back, jaw hinged open, hand pressed dramatically against her chest.

"Holy cannoli, no wonder you are—" She gestures at me with her spoon-wielding hand, and I fight not to blush a deeper shade of red. We're probably hitting crimson territory by now. "The way you are."

I fidget in my chair and press on. I don't have to tell Layla that dating in a small town has its complications, let alone starting a no-strings-attached situation. "She's coming for five days for an in-person interview, and she'll feature us on her social accounts. The boyfriend thing, I don't know. I guess I thought having a boyfriend would make this place seem more romantic. She loves romance stuff."

Beckett sneaks another piece of zucchini bread. He's taking advantage of Layla's continued shock and awe at my celibacy. "Well, that's fucking stupid."

I give him a look. "Thank you, Beckett. Your input is helpful."

"Seriously though"—he breaks his zucchini bread slice in two—"you've made this place amazing. You. On your own. You should be proud of that. Adding a boyfriend doesn't make your story any more or less important."

I blink at him. "Sometimes I forget you have three sisters."

He shrugs. "Just my two cents."

"You sure you don't want to pretend you find me irresistible for a week?"

Layla shakes her head, finally emerging from her trancelike state. "Bad idea. Have you seen him try to lie to anyone? It's horrible. He turns into a monosyllabic fool every time he has to go into town for groceries."

It's true. I've had to pick up his order from the butcher more than once. I'm convinced he became a produce farmer purely so he'd have to make fewer stops at the Save More. Beckett doesn't enjoy people, and he especially doesn't enjoy the overt flirtations from half the town whenever he stops in. Sometimes I feel like Layla and I are the only ones immune to his good looks, probably due to his considerable lack of charm, but I suppose that's what happens when you've seen a man muttering obscenities to trees half the day every day.

And when your heart has been hopelessly occupied with pining over another person for close to a decade. It's hard to notice the charm of anyone who isn't Luka.

I grab another slice of zucchini bread and begin to nibble, considering my options. My non-Luka-shaped options. I could ask Jesse, the owner of our town's only bar. But he'd likely think it's more than it is, and I don't have the time or energy for a fake breakup for my fake relationship. I could look into escort services, maybe. That's a thing, right? Like, that's why escort services exist? For people to—I don't know, escort others?

I press my fingers under my eyes, forgetting that one hand is still clutching a piece of zucchini bread. There's an obvious answer here. It just—it scares me to death.

"There it is," Beckett mutters, and it takes every fiber of my being not to hurl this bread at his face. "It just hit her."

"I don't know why you're freaking out. It's a simple solution. He'd do it in a heartbeat," says Layla.

I peek through my fingers at Layla. She's smiling a smug little grin. She looks like she should be wearing a monocle and stroking a hairless cat Bond-style. Why I ever thought she was all sweetness is beyond me. She's a spicy little thing.

"Ask Luka."

Photo by Marlayna Demond

B.K. BORISON is the author of cozy contemporary romances featuring emotionally vulnerable characters and swoonworthy settings. When she's not daydreaming about fictional characters doing fictional things, she's at home with her family, more than likely buying books she doesn't have room for.

VISIT B.K. BORISON ONLINE

BKBorison.com
AuthorBKBorison
AuthorBKBorison

Ready to find
your next great read?

Let us help.

Visit prh.com/nextread

Penguin
Random
House